A darkness at dawn . . .

Intent on fulfilling her destiny and revenging herself upon the Guardian of Mirrodin, the elf Glissa must once again dare to cross the forbidding lands that surround her. Accompanied by her loyal companions Bruenna, the human mage, and Slobad, the goblin tinkerer, she must plunge into the depths of the world.

There the party will come face to face with Memnarch and his minions, followers who will stop at nothing in their pursuit of Glissa and her power. There they will see the world of Mirrodin itself fulfill its long-delayed destiny.

Cory Herndon completes the story of magic and madness that embraces a world of metal.

EXPERIENCE THE MAGIC™

MIRRODIN CYCLE · BOOK III

THE FIFTH DAWN

Cory Herndon

THE FIFTH DAWN

©2004 Wizards of the Coast, Inc.

Distributed in the United States by Holtzbrinck Publishing. Distributed in Canada by Fenn Ltd.

Distributed to the hobby, toy, and comic trade in the United States and Canada by regional distributors.

Distributed worldwide by Wizards of the Coast, Inc. and regional distributors.

Printed in the U.S.A.

Cover art by Jim Murray
First Printing: May 2004
Library of Congress Catalog Card Number: 2003116418

9 8 7 6 5 4 3 2 1

US ISBN: 0-7869-3205-8
UK ISBN: 0-7869-3206-6
620-96542-001-EN

U.S., CANADA,
ASIA, PACIFIC, & LATIN AMERICA
Wizards of the Coast, Inc.
P.O. Box 707
Renton, WA 98057-0707
+1-800-324-6496

EUROPEAN HEADQUARTERS
Wizards of the Coast, Belgium
T Hofveld 6d
1702 Groot-Bijgaarden
Belgium
+322 467 3360

Visit our web site at **www.wizards.com**

Acknowledgments

Many thanks to:
My collaborators and co-plotters Will McDermott and Jess
Lebow, authors of the first two parts of this story—*The Moons of
Mirrodin* and *The Darksteel Eye*, respectively; Peter Archer, who
offered me the chance to run my third elf heroine in a row through
the wringer and was patient enough to edit every single final version of the manuscript; Andrea Howe, the mightiest error-hunter
in the Tangle, who pointed out someone can't climb out of the hole
and still be at the bottom of the hole; Brady Dommermuth, *Magic*
Creative Director, who kept me honest; Scott McGough, who
knows what sounds right in a surprising variety of circumstances;
Bayliss, Remo, and Ripley, my advisors on leonin behavior; the
guardians of the *Magic: the Gathering* storyline past and present;
the designers and creators; and everyone that makes sure those
cards and these books get out the door.

Extra-special thanks and love to Stephanie Poage Miskowski, who
provided support, advice, reality checks, and reminded me to eat
when I locked myself in the office for weeks at a time.

Dedication
For Richard Herndon, artificer-in-training.

Wake up.

The voice slithered through the tangled mess that was his mind.

Mind. Yes, that was the word. A mind that seconds before has been cold, dark, and dead. A mind that was somewhat shocked to be aware of itself once more.

Wake up, now.

The voice became a little more insistent. Urgency played around the soggy depths of his brain. The hissed words coaxed a little more clarity into his mind.

Yert's mind.

He was Yert. What was a "Yert?"

It was . . . his name. He was a man. A . . . Moriok. A Moriok man called Yert. A controller of nim. A controller of a mighty reaper that was, like him, dead. Though Yert's death apparently hadn't taken hold.

Visions flashed behind Yert's eyes as optic nerves sparked inside his brain. He saw images of a strange world, an organic world of soft earth and flesh creatures, horrible and horribly unprotected from the elements. A white stone city filled with humans—tanned and leathery in gleaming silver armor—appeared, then was gone in a sudden burst of white light. Now open seas of some thin, translucent liquid covered the strange landscape, and verdant stands of trees exploded in clusters amid rolling green and gold fields. A flash. Yert saw a grim-faced man with no hint of metal on his skin, a flesh-and-bone warrior swinging a savage chain in a grimy pit. A third burst of white light, and he stood on the command deck of a massive living vessel, cutting through miles and miles of the translucent liquid he'd seen before. He knew somehow that it was as corrosive as acid, and the experience of touching it, even in his vision, made Yert's skin tingle.

This physical sensation was lost in yet another flash. The mental scene shifted to show him another fleshy human, this one a magician with a strange hat, call forth nightmarish things made of skin, hair, muscle and tendons. Monsters pulled from thin air without a scrap of metal to protect their hides, yet as savage as a nim zombie, plated with some kind of grayish white mineral.

The magician in the odd chapeau disappeared, and Yert's vision filled with a perfect silver sphere floating in swirling blackness.

Another flash.

Now Yert hovered over a gargantuan globe that he knew was Mirrodin, even though it was a Mirrodin he had never seen. Everything on this world was pure, glittering metal, a thousand shapes of silver, gold, and copper. Not a hint of corrosion was apparent. Fractal shapes hovered in the sky, casting mathematically complex shadows across the perfect surface. Soon, those shadows began to stretch and distort, disrupting the beauty of the world and spreading across the surface like living things. These shadow-shapes began to take on colors and strange forms, as all over the plane of Mirrodin an imperfect, organic life took hold. Tiny flashes like a million stars winked into existence on the surface, and suddenly the plane crawled with sentient beings that had not been there seconds before.

Seconds. Second. That was a unit of time, Yert's brain managed for him. And time . . . well, time was time. At the moment, he had plenty of it.

Yert's inner eye still soared over a much-changed Mirrodin. He took in the blackened swamps of the Mephidross and the glittering, snarled, verdigris vegetation of the Tangle. He mind leaped into open space, and Yert soared over the glittering red spires of the iron-and-copper Oxidda mountains; the dazzling and fluid surface of the Quicksilver Sea punctured by the blue spires of the Lumengrid; and the blindingly bright razor grass plains of the Glimmervoid. Yert saw it all at once.

The Mephidross was his home, the swamps. Instead of letting the vision-ride pull him along, Yert focused his inner eye on the Mephidross.

Why did the thought of home fill Yert with such panic? The swampland of Mirrodin, with its snarl of rusty, tangled, wiry branches, thick black water, and smoldering smoke-spire chimneys that spewed charged green mist into the fog—all of these things were familiar, should have felt comforting, but Yert could not contain the fear they drove into his gut. He instinctively sensed that he belonged in that swamp, but could not imagine going back. Something in there hated him, and the feeling was mutual.

Had he gone completely mad?

Yert, the voiced slithered in his awakening consciousness. *Yert, wake up. Wake up NOW.*

Yes, Yert thought. Excellent idea.

CHAPTER 1

TANGLED

Glissa and Slobad lay on their backs in the melted wreckage of the Tangle, exhausted, battered, and drained. Neither the elf girl nor her goblin companion said a word, relishing the simple pleasure of breathing, the smoldering calm left in the wake of Memnarch's storm.

Or maybe it was fear. Talking about it meant it had happened.

She thought about the friends she'd lost and felt warm tears begin to form in her eyes, and decided silence was golden.

The new green moon cast an emerald glow over the blasted forest, darkening the copper trunks of shattered trees and dulling the normally glittering verdigris leaves to gray. Glissa rolled her head lazily over to look at Slobad. The diminutive artificer, a resourceful goblin who had been her constant ally ever since the death of her family, had one hand draped over his eyes. His vision was remarkable in the dark and sensitive to the light, but the glow of the green moon was anything but glaring to the elf girl.

"Slobad?" Glissa asked. "What's wrong with your eyes?"

"It's bright!" the goblin said. "You go blind, you keep staring at that, huh?"

"It's not that bright," Glissa observed with a grin. Good old Slobad. He would grieve when there was time. She wiped her own eyes and let her head loll back to gaze up at Mirrodin's newest satellite. "In fact, I'm staring right at right now."

"Slobad take your word for it," the goblin replied groggily. "Right now, Slobad just need a little shut-eye, huh?" After a few moments, he added, "Besides, in sleep, Slobad don't have to think."

Glissa tried to do the same, shut her eyes for just a moment and try to relax. She failed utterly. Instead, she stared at the new moon until her eyes started to play tricks on her, making the glowing green globe appear to pulse like a beating heart.

This was no good. She painfully called on stiffening muscles to prop herself up on one elbow, and poked Slobad gently with the back of one clawed finger. "Hey, Slobad. Are you asleep yet?"

"Uh-huh," the goblin grunted without moving. "Elf eyes not getting any better, huh?"

"We have to go. We have to check."

"Check what?"

"We have to check out the lacuna," Glissa said. "That blast might not have been enough—"

"Memnarch? You crazy?" Slobad replied, apparently forgetting how often he'd answered that question already. "Big ugly has to be dead, huh? That tower was right between moon and the core." Slobad traced a lazy line in the air with one rusty claw. "You saw what that thing did to Kaldra? You saw that, huh?"

"Of course," Glissa said, "I just wanted to make sure. Memnarch is so…ancient. We hardly know anything about him, really. We don't know what it might take to kill him."

"If ol' crab-legs still kicking, would have sent levelers, huh?" Slobad insisted, obviously settling the issue, at least for himself. Glissa was too tired to argue the point. Even if Memnarch had survived the blast somehow, he couldn't be in any shape to attack her. And with the new moon in the sky, Mirrodin's self-proclaimed Guardian had lost his chance, she hoped, to capture Glissa's "spark."

She thought she felt a tiny flare of warmth in her breast, but had to be imagining it. It wasn't every day you learned you possessed the rare, innate ability to become a planeswalker. But one crisis at a time.

Glissa flopped back onto the blasted ground and stared up at the green moon. "Okay, compromise. We rest now, check on Memnarch later. But it has to be a *sooner* later, huh?" Her vision was filled with the green orb. "It's going to need a name," she said.

"What needs name? That hole? All right, we call it green lacuna," Slobad mumbled. "That tree? Let's call him Leaf-face." He made a show of covering his eyes. "Now just let Slobad sleep, huh?"

"The moon," she said softly, gazing up again at the radiant emerald light. The green glow invigorated her, she could already feel her sore muscles becoming relaxed and her skin began to warm pleasantly from the inside. "There's the Doom Bringer, there's Ingle . . ."

"Right," Slobad replied. "Oh, right!" Squinting and keeping his eyes averted from the green glow and, he sat up and hugged his knees. "We first to see, huh? No one else around, that for sure! What about—?"

Glissa saw Slobad's eyes widen with shock despite the glare, and the goblin let out a small gasp of exclamation. The little artificer's eyes slowly tracked upward from a point just behind Glissa's ear.

The elf girl froze for a heartbeat and raced through her options. Lying propped on one elbow on her side gave her lousy leverage, and she didn't even know what kind of enemy she might be facing. If it was four-legged Memnarch, a swift kick to the ankles wouldn't help at all. Even if he fell, he might land on Glissa or Slobad. But she had to do something.

Okay then, not a kick.

Glissa shoved off the ground with her elbow and rolled hard in the direction Slobad was staring. With luck, she might be able to slam into her foe's ankles and knock his feet out from under him, maybe even give Slobad an opening to try a more effective attack. Like a fire tube to the groin.

She slammed into a pair of muscular, armored legs covered in reddish-green wool with the consistency of tangled wire. It took Glissa a few seconds to comprehend what she was seeing. Vorracs were common throughout the Tangle, and Glissa had dispatched her fair share on the hunt. But she'd never laid eyes on a vorrac with a head as big as her family's house.

"What that, hu-hu-huh?" Slobad stammered.

The vorrac turned its shaggy head to the green moon and let loose a screaming howl. Glissa had heard that sound countless times, but as a high-pitched squeal at the end of an arrow or hunting knife.

Glissa slowly raised one claw tip to her lips. The enormous vorrac finished its eardrum-piercing cry and shook its neck like a soggy khalybdog, clanking large misshapen plates of armor together and knocking loose scattered chunks of debris and filth that rained down on the prone elf girl. Glissa carefully began to scoot back to Slobad, her eyes locked on the vorrac's jaws. The creatures were omnivorous, though the only animals they were fast enough to catch were small arboreal rodents or fat insects like copper beetles.

The vorrac didn't look like it was hunting to Glissa. The creature was ignoring her, and seemed much more interested in gazing around at its surroundings, drooling, and breathing with heavy chuffs that reminded Glissa of the Great Furnace in the Oxidda Mountains.

"That doesn't sound healthy," Glissa whispered when she

reached Slobad. "Something's wrong with that vorrac."

"No kidding," Slobad hissed, gaping at the massive creature. "Vorracs usually big enough to eat, huh? Not big enough to eat goblins?"

Glissa jumped as the enormous creature shifted its weight on thick legs, causing the ground to jolt with each step. The vorrac turned around with a heavy shuffling dance that looked as painful for the creature as it was slow. "But I also mean that's not a healthy animal, big or not. Did you hear that breathing?"

"Elf magic," Slobad said, "Make stuff big, that's elf trick, huh? How that vorrac pull it off?"

"I don't know, but whoever it was *didn't* pull it off. The job's only half done. Flare, that poor animal," Glissa sighed, relaxing her grip on her sword hilt.

"What? I'd give an ear tip to be that big," Slobad said. "Then they'd all answer to Slobad."

"The spell wasn't done right. It can't take in enough air, and its skeleton is giving under the weight. See the way its legs are bowing under the pressure? No one with the skill to perform a growth spell of that magnitude could possibly botch it that badly. It's…it's obscene." Glissa shuddered.

"Weird," Slobad said, relaxing enough to lean up against a nearby iron boulder. His eyes remained trained on the slow-moving creature receding into a shattered tree fall. "Some elves crazier than most, huh?"

"What makes you think it's an elf?"

"Couldn't be a goblin."

"No, but—trolls, it could be trolls."

"Doubt it," Slobad said. "Kaldra took care of them, huh?"

"Oh. Right." Glissa had tried not to dwell on the toll of their latest costly victory, which saw the destruction of the legendary artifact creature that Slobad and Glissa had reactivated to fight

Memnarch. As soon as they'd tried to use Kaldra against Memnarch, their enemy seized control of the enormous construct, which had finally been destroyed by the erupting lacuna in the center of the Tangle. Before that, the trolls had held off Kaldra long enough for Glissa and Slobad to reach the Radix and help trigger the explosion of the new green moon into the sky.

The mighty trolls had lasted but a few minutes. Glissa and Slobad had to assume their strongest allies were dead. Surely if any had survived, they would have seen one by now. Trolls were hard to miss.

"We were pretty lucky, huh?" Slobad asked.

"Lucky," Glissa said. "And I think we still have the edge over Memnarch when it comes to sanity. He was just begging for a moon in the face, if you ask me."

"Hey, Glissa?" Slobad asked.

"Yes?" Glissa replied, still tracking the monstrous, snuffling vorrac.

"Just me, or this boulder feel . . . warm?"

As he spoke, the heavy rock supporting Slobad moved of its own accord and growled. The goblin jumped directly into the air and landed in a roll, coming up on two feet and facing directly away from Glissa and the giant glimmer rat he just realized he'd been using as a pillow. Glissa drew her sword as the fat, muscular creature's snout turned to face them. The glimmer rat's rusted fangs dripped corrosive acid that sizzled in smoky droplets in the underbrush, while the thick, spiky hairs that covered its back flared and bristled. A tail as thick as woven cable slashed noisily in the underbrush.

"Glissa, look out!" Slobad shouted. Glissa whirled and came eye-to-compound-eye with a half dozen gold and iron wasps, hovering just off the ground. Like the rat and the vorrac, the magically enlarged insects seemed to be having a little trouble operating as they should. The insects' wings flapped mightily and blasted Glissa's face with a dusty breeze, but their venomous stingers only just cleared the ground. Glissa muttered a quick oath promising vengeance on the fool that was torturing the creatures of the Tangle with inadequate magic, and her sword appeared in her hand.

"Slobad . . . I think it's almost . . ." One step back. The wasps didn't move. The glimmer rat crept closer, snarling and slavering. "Time for us to . . ." Another step.

"RUN!" the goblin cried then whirled and dashed into the dark woods.

Glissa ducked her head and charged after Slobad, wondering what else in the Tangle might have suddenly grown to an impossible size. "Slobad, wait! You can't just—ow—run *anywhere* in the Tangle! We have to find a trail!"

"There are trails?" Slobad hollered back, but didn't slow down.

The elf girl heard a shriek, and felt the heavy footsteps of the giant glimmer rat charging into the thicket behind her. A low drone almost out of the range of even Glissa's sharp ears told her the wasps were following closely behind. She risked a look back over her shoulder.

One of the wasps was buzzing and dive-bombing the rat, which swatted at the mammoth insect with its cable-tail. The hulking rodent couldn't seem to score a hit, but kept the insect at bay without slowing its own charge into the brush. The other wasps were heading straight for Glissa, but the thick undergrowth was slowing them down. Their thin wings, already straining to keep their heavy bodies in the air, were too wide to slip easily through the thick undergrowth.

Glissa couldn't risk her own growth spell in the middle of the thicket; she could end up impaled on a tree. But she didn't need magic. She knew this forest better than anyone. She could make it through. But where would they end up?

When she turned back, Slobad was gone.

"Slobad?" the elf girl hissed into the darkened woods. "Slobad, this isn't fu—hey, back off!" One wasp had gotten close enough that Glissa had to swat at it with her sword, but the creature sluggishly avoided the blade. "Slobad, where *are you*?"

Another wasp moved in too close and Glissa whirled, slashing backward furiously and feeling the sword tip connect with a thin metal exoskeleton. The wasp shrieked—Glissa was surprised to hear the voice of an insect, she hadn't realized they had them—and turned in mid-air, crashing back the way it had come like a drunken goblin. Half of a translucent silver wing fluttered to the forest floor. There, it joined a severed stinger six inches long that twitched as it pumped wasp venom into the ground.

The other wasps swarmed on their fleeing cousin, stinging the defenseless insect repeatedly. The savaged creature dropped onto its back, kicking spasmodically as its kin tore it to pieces with powerful mandibles. One of the wasps, the smallest, couldn't get to the cannibal feast—twice, the other wasps batted the runt away with legs and wings—so it turned and continued to chase Glissa, followed closely by the rat, which gave the insect feeding frenzy a wide berth.

"Up here!" came Slobad's voice up ahead, about twenty feet in the air if her ears weren't lying. Glissa kept running and craned her neck to see where Slobad had found refuge.

He stood upside down on the bottom of a tree branch, his arms crossed and the worn satchel hanging awkwardly from his armpit.

"How—?"

"Just run up that tree! Trust me! Straight up! Meet you there, huh?" And with that, Slobad turned—still upside down—and ran toward a wide Tangle tree trunk directly in Glissa's path. The tree was ancient, and had no low-hanging spikes for leverage. Her claws would be useless in the bark of a tree that age, hardened and weathered by centuries of moonlight.

But she trusted Slobad and her eyes. Claws would not be needed.

Glissa reached the tree in seconds, swatting blindly with her sword but never feeling contact with the giant beasts she knew were right on her tail. She kicked out with a flying leap, extended one foot parallel to the tree trunk, and hoped she hadn't been hallucinating.

Her foot found solid purchase and gave no resistance as she pulled it loose, brought up her other foot, made firm contact with the tree trunk, lifted that foot . . .

If she hadn't been running for her life, Glissa would have slapped her own forehead. She was using a climbing spell. Or rather, one was affecting both of them. Glissa looked over her shoulder and saw the ground like a wall receding in the distance. Her horizontal had gone vertical.

The wasps finished off their cousin's corpse, and now four of them buzzed lazily around the base of the tree, but their wings couldn't lift them clear of the ground. One still dive-bombed the rat, which had been forced to slow its pace and fight back.

All giant creatures. All obviously subjected to growth magic. Glissa had seen no mage, and the creatures had materialized seemingly out of nowhere. And now she was running easily along narrow, spiky limbs and boughs that should never have supported her weight. Stranger still, so was Slobad. Suddenly, it all clicked.

"Slobad, wait up! I think I know what's happening!"

The goblin skidded to a halt when he saw Glissa had lost their pursuers. "Yeah?" he asked as Glissa bounced off a springy tree spike, somersaulted, and landed in a crouch on a small, flat terrace. "Slobad thinks it's all that elf-magic floating around back there."

"It's all the magic floating around after the—" Glissa stopped. "What did you just say?"

"Elf-magic. So thick back there Slobad could smell it, huh?" the goblin continued. "Was going to tell you, but didn't want to slow down."

"Right," Glissa nodded, casting her eyes about the forest canopy lest a giant beetle or wall of spiky thorns pop up out of nowhere and take them by surprise. "You can, uh, smell magic, Slobad? I didn't think you and magic got along."

"Know how elf magic smells, huh?" Slobad said, wrinkling his nose with distaste.

"How does it smell?" Glissa asked.

"Like rotten moss mixed with rat dung," he said. "Sorry, but true."

"Huh," Glissa said. "Never noticed that. Do you know anything about mana? The elemental forces that give magic its energy?"

"Like blast powder and a fire tube?" Slobad asked, arching a spiky eyebrow.

"Sort of. Mana's more like the ingredients for a good stew. You can make a stew out of almost anything, but to make something good, you've got to use the right vegetables and meat."

"So different magic needs different meat, huh?" Slobad said. He began to turn his foot on one toe like a nervous student.

"And I'm attuned to Tangle magic because this is my home. And that moon, it's made of pure green mana."

"So why don't all the monsters go there?" Slobad asked, jerking a thumb upward in the general direction of the dazzling emerald orb.

"The lacuna," Glissa said. "The moon had to burn right through the surface to get out." She gazed back down through the thick trees and saw the slow-moving wasps and the shambling rat buzzing around below them, unable to resist their instincts but equally unable to actually reach their prey.

"So the magic burned into the ground, huh?" Slobad said.

"To put it simply. That much energy floating loose, it's trying to coalesce. To take shape before it dissipates." Glissa began pacing, and took two steps up the side of the tree, deep in thought. "But there's no intelligence behind it, so the spells aren't entirely taking sha—oooOOF!" Glissa's feet slipped as though on ice, and she dropped three feet back to the terrace, landing on her rear. She shook her head to clear the ringing.

"See what I mean?" Glissa muttered. She hung her head between her knees and rubbed either side of her temple. "Its centered on that big hole in the ground."

No one answered.

"Slobad?" Glissa asked, head still between her knees. "What do you think? Does that make sense?"

"Oh yes," a gruff voice said calmly, "That makes perfect sense. You'll have to tell us all about it."

That wasn't Slobad.

Glissa placed one hand on her sword hilt and drew her blade as she leaped to her feet, ready to strike in the direction of the voice. At least, that was the plan, but her attack was over before it started. Glissa only made it into a crouch, and her sword never cleared its sheath. The elf girl was eye-to-blade-tip with three swords, all pointed at her throat. Glissa followed one silver blade up its three-foot length, where it ended in a familiar golden-filigreed hilt. The hilt was in the hand of a tall elf. Slobad was scooting backward, apparently hoping the warriors had not yet seen him, which the elf girl could already tell was pointless. Glissa couldn't hold back a smile as she raised her hands.

"Where have you been?" Glissa asked.

* * * * *

"Thought these guys on our si—*ow*!" Slobad whispered, then yelped as a the point of a sword poked him between the shoulder blades. The goblin risked a look back over one shoulder and said irritably, "Cut it out, huh? Know who this is?" he asked, cocking his head in Glissa's direction. "Huh? Greatest warrior in the Tangle, here! You not know. Asking for trouble. Crazier than she is."

"Quiet!" the gruff voice behind him barked. "She's a criminal, and if you're with her, you are too. But I only have orders to bring one of you in alive. Guess which one, goblin?"

"Banryk, this is ridiculous," Glissa managed as she narrowly missed tripping over a newly exposed tree root that had melted around the edges. "I'm not a criminal, and neither is he. This is foolish. Something amazing had happened. I have to talk to the elders."

"I said, quiet!" the growling elf hissed in return and gave Glissa a shove that nearly sent her sprawling face-first into the thick, wiry undergrowth. She managed to keep her balance, no thanks to the enchanted leather straps that the Tel-Jilad warriors had used to tie her hands behind her back. The bindings blocked the natural currents of mana that should have been at the tips of her claws here in her home range. Even though she'd tried to convince the trio of Chosen that Slobad couldn't even use magic, they'd tied him up the same way.

The Tel-Jilad warriors had easily subdued the exhausted pair. Glissa cursed her luck. She still hadn't been able to rest, and now she had neither the emotional or physical strength to fight her own people. Even if that included fighting an ambitious blockhead like Banryk.

The other two were unfamiliar—they'd probably been inducted into the Chosen after Glissa's family had been killed and she left the Tangle. Neither had said a word since the capture.

Despite the situation—arrested on her home turf after helping stop a madman from destroying the world—she couldn't fight back a stab of melancholy at seeing the distinctive, rune-inscribed armor the Tel-Jilad Chosen wore proudly on their chests. It reminded her of Kane. For all she knew, one of the newcomers was his replacement.

The vedalken murdered Kane only a few weeks ago, but they were weeks that felt like a lifetime. A few weeks ago, she would have given anything just to have her old life back the way it was. A few weeks ago, she was an idealistic hunter with no conception of the wider world or her place in it. Now, knowing the things she knew, the Tangle suddenly felt very . . . small. She wondered if the pang of sadness was truly over the loss of Kane, or her own loss of innocence.

The three guards poked and prodded their prisoners down a narrow game path that cut through the foliage. Glissa recognized it as one that led directly back to her village.

Banryk had never been the most enlightened of the Tel-Jilad Chosen. She'd been forced to repel his clumsy romantic advances on numerous occasions. Glissa got the disturbing feeling that Banryk was taking more than the usual pleasure in his duties as one of the Chosen, and silently promised he would regret his thuggish behavior when she got out of this.

After a three-hour hike through the Tangle, the forest finally began to thin out a little and the guards prodded their captives off the game trail and onto the wide forest thoroughfare that led to Viridia. Through the glittering leaves, Glissa finally saw the distant glow of hanging gelfruit and open terraces in her home village. The green moon cast a dim jade light that gave the warm hearth glow a sickly pallor. Here and there, a sickly looking corrosion grew on the spiky limbs. The rough, rusty spots consumed the green.

As they drew closer, Glissa began to wonder where the people were. Even in early evening, even after an event like the ascension of a new moon, there should have been dozens of elves going about their business in the village. From her vantage point, Glissa could only see two more Tel-Jilad who stepped silently onto the road ahead, near the old Tangle tree stump inscribed with the village's name and protective runes that served as a marker for this entrance to Viridia. The warrior on the left had a familiar stance Glissa couldn't quite place, and a hand resting on his sword hilt. The other's face was obscured by a drawn bow and an arrow pointed at Glissa's heart.

"Halt!" Called the familiar-looking elf. His companion kept an arrow trained on Glissa. "Approach slowly, and no one will get hurt."

"Yulyn, we've got the situation under control," Banryk objected. "She's not going to get away so easily again."

Yulyn. That was a name she knew well, but hadn't expected to hear. Before Glissa came along, Yulyn had been the greatest hunter in the Tangle, but he'd disappeared several months ago while tracking a pack of migratory ferroclaws. Viridians, Glissa included, had assumed the predatory creatures had finally beat Yulyn at his own game. Despite his long absence, the old warrior didn't look any worse for his experience, whatever had happened to him.

But Yulyn had never worn the armor of the Chosen. What was going on?

"Banryk, you idiot, I sent you to fetch one prisoner. You've got one and a half," Yulyn said. Glissa could tell from his tone that the older elf held Banryk in a much lower regard than the "half prisoner."

"Half!" Slobad exploded.

"Slobad, not now," Glissa whispered.

"Listen to your confederate, goblin," Banryk said. The thuggish guard gave Slobad a shove, and the little man pitched forward onto the road face first.

That did it. Nobody shoved Slobad while Glissa had anything to say about it. The goblin continued to scream and curse about stupid elves as he rolled on the ground like an overturned insect, creating the perfect distraction. She hoped Yulyn's friend with the bow would be unwilling to fire into a group that included three of his own allies.

Glissa bent her knees slightly and hunched forward then flung her head backward with all her might and let out an invigorating yell. She felt her skull connect with the face of one of her unknown captors, and warmth flowed over the back of her head—whether the blood was her own or the guard's, she didn't know and didn't care. The important thing was that her move caused the guard to release her in surprise.

With her foe still off-balance, Glissa had to act fast, and without the use of her bound hands. She bent at the waist and spun around, leading with one shoulder and trying to knock her captor over. In the process, she hoped to dodge the arrow she knew would be coming. But the guard was ready for her move, and danced back out of the way—then stumbled backward over a twisting, rolling goblin shouting a stream of epithets that could melt tree bark. One down. Glissa turned again and charged head-first at Banryk, whose jaw was still hanging open in shock.

Her head slammed into the loud-mouthed Tel-Jilad's gut and

Glissa heard a satisfying whoosh of expelled air as she made solid contact with Banryk's solar plexus. He doubled over and collapsed on all fours, gasping.

Glissa heard an expletive-ridden goblin battle cry. Slobad had regained his footing, clutching a small, broken blade of Tangle-adapted razor grass in one bleeding hand. The goblin's bindings lay in tatters on the ground. Slobad launched himself at their last standing captor, who let out a yelp of surprise as the goblin landed on his chest and began slashing at him with the sharp but flimsy plant. The stumbling guard, blinded by ninety pounds of goblin, accidentally kneed Banryk in the side and then went over backwards, struggling to keep Slobad from inflicting a mortal wound. Still fighting her own bonds, Glissa turned to face Yulyn and his bow-happy friend. They were nowhere in sight.

Glissa turned around very slowly. The gleaming silver tip of the arrow rested an inch from her right eye.

"I said, 'Halt,' " Yulyn, whose sword had not left his belt, remarked calmly. With lightning speed, one strong arm flashed down and picked up Slobad by the scruff of the neck, heaving Glissa's friend in the air with surprising strength. Slobad flailed in the air pitifully. "Both of you. You've been accused of crimes against Viridia. You will answer these charges, or attempt to flee again. I promise if you choose the latter, things will go very badly for you. Choose the former, and face those who accuse you of murder."

"Murder?" Glissa spat incredulously. "What are you talking about? Look up! You see that thing in the sky? Did you see the giant wasps? The rat as big as a ferroclaw? You *do* know that the world almost ended this morning?"

"Don't know anything about that," Yulyn replied. "That's something for mages to worry about. My job is enforcing the laws. What I know is, your parents are dead, and the elders think you had something to do with it."

"Big elf crazier than Glissa!" Slobad bellowed, still wriggling a foot and a half in the air. "Barely escaped with her life, huh? Want murderers, head back down the big hole, huh?"

Slobad looked to Glissa, eyes pleading. Glissa didn't see him. She hadn't moved since she'd caught sight of the lithe figure standing on the terrace before her. The losses of the recent past suddenly didn't seem to matter. Every bizarre accusation fell by the wayside.

Glissa leaned slightly on Yulyn, her knees weak. Finally, something had gone right for her. She opened her mouth to speak, but the figure above beat her to it.

"Hello, Glissa," her sister said. "I'm going to enjoy watching you hang."

"I was there, Yulyn," Lyese called, her voice strong and cold. "She did it. She called the levelers, and killed our . . . my . . . mother, and my father." Her little sister, not so little anymore, trained her one remaining eye on her older sibling, and Glissa saw hatred reflecting back. "She's a danger to us all."

Glissa was dumbfounded. She could see the pain of death etched on Lyese's youthful face, marred by a silver eyepatch, the choppy golden hair now cut short and lying flat on her head, the graven Tel-Jilad armor on her breast and the wicked-looking spear she clutched in one hand telling the elf how the joyful girl she'd known and loved had changed in just a few short, painful weeks. Weeks Lyese had spent hating her.

Glissa fainted.

CHAPTER 2

UP A TREE

Glissa dreamed she was walking through the strange, soft, brown forests she had seen in her flares. A world without metal, even the people. A tree tapped her on the shoulder. Twice.

No, not a tree. A small, clawed, goblin hand, tapping her on the shoulder. "Hey. Hey, elf. Craaazy elf. Wake up, huh? Making Slobad nervous." Another shove, and the goblin's voice grew more anxious. "Glissa? Glissa, come on, huh?"

She opened her eyes and the flare, or dream—it felt like a little of both—vanished in a flash of reality. Glissa blinked and called her surroundings into focus. The flare had made everything blurry, and she could make out only colors and shapes. One large round shape directly in front of her face was unmistakable and had breath that smelled slightly of sulphur and glimmer rat.

"Slobad? Is that you?"

"Who else, huh?" The goblin's face split into a wide smile. "What, those eyes, they getting worse?"

She blinked, clearing her vision, and with it her real problems returned to sharp focus. She looked around the interior of the Prison Tree. "I can't remember the last time someone was locked in here. If we are where I think we are."

"Slobad know where we are. Goblins don't faint," Slobad said. "Big, wide tree. No spikes, no terraces. Prison, huh?"

"Nothing gets past you, Slobad." Glissa patted herself down and found her scabbard and travel pouches empty. Only her mother's ring remained. "Did you see where they took our things?"

"Nope, stuff's gone," Slobad said. "Had that firetube since Slobad was a goblet, too."

"This isn't good. You only end up in the Tree if you're accused of a capital crime," Glissa said.

"Oh, good," Slobad said. "*What*!" He leaped to his feet. "That mean execution, huh? Huh?" The goblin started to pace, growing agitated.

"Slobad," she said, but didn't seem to catch the goblin's attention. He was now hopping up and down in front of the cell's sole window, trying to get a look outside and muttering something about building a pair of wings.

"Slobad!" Glissa shouted.

"What?" the goblin cried, unable to hide the panic in his voice. "Stupid elves gonna kill Slobad's only friend!"

"No, they're not. And thanks, I think."

"Yeah, how come, huh?" Slobad said.

"For one thing, I'm innocent. I didn't kill my fam—my parents," Glissa replied haltingly. "No matter what Lyese says."

"But this always happen to Slobad!" the goblin exploded, stamping his foot on the tanglewood floor. The sound rang through the floor and reverberated off of the walls in every direction. "Always Slobad get a friend, or someone nice to Slobad, or Slobad find a pet, and they always die! The curse, huh? Remember?" The goblin fell to the floor on his knees, pounding at the wall with one rusty, iron-plated fist.

Glissa crawled over to her friend and put one arm around his shoulder. Slobad leaned close and whispered, "Hey, look what I just found, huh?"

In his palm, Slobad held three thin pieces of jagged metal, no thicker than a leonin hair. The inside of the tree had splintered under the goblin's persistent wall pounding, and now he had a set of crude lock picks. Glissa saw Slobad's hand fuss near the belt around his waist as he tucked the tools out of sight.

"Course, door's got no lock Slobad can see," he said.

"It's enchanted with heavy countermagic," Glissa said. "This is the Prison Tree."

Slobad patted his belt. "But they take us out in shackles, huh?"

"Good thinking," she grinned.

"So, Prison Tree, huh? Nice name," Slobad said.

"Elves can be pretty literal sometimes," Glissa said. "The Tree of Tales? It's a tree with tales inscribed on it. Anyway, there are other safeguards to prevent someone from using magic in the tribunal court, so you might be our only chance if things go bad."

"Elves too complicated," Slobad said. "Goblins never do trials. Someone does wrong, toss 'em in the furnace and move on."

"Doesn't sound very pleasant," Glissa said.

"That why Slobad left," the goblin said.

* * * * *

The next few days passed in with alternating periods of dullness and boredom broken by conversation; on the third day the conversations quickly became arguments. In an effort to reign in the irritation, they taught each other simple games to pass the time. No one had given them a clue when to expect a trial.

The elf girl did her best to keep her uncertainty and the darkness from driving her into depression, but it wasn't easy. She'd thought her homecoming would be a cause for celebration, or at least a few friendly greetings. Yet Glissa hadn't seen any others of her kind since she and Slobad had been locked up. A loaf of nanyan bread and a pitcher of water materialized twice a day, providing enough nourishment to keep them alive. The other amenities were simple and changed regularly via remote spells, though there was no way for either of them to bathe. Glissa didn't envy the noses of the Chosen when the time did come for her to stand trial.

The Chosen. That reminded her again of Lyese. Her sister had changed so much in such a short time. She could only imagine what Lyese's life had been like since she left, since the night the younger elf girl had dressed up in her finest clothes to impress Kane at dinner. The night their parents had been slaughtered by Memnarch's levelers. The night Lyese believed Glissa had betrayed them.

Something about it all was a little too convenient.

* * * * *

"Lyese," Glissa said aloud one morning, the dawn of their seventh day in captivity. "She's the key."

"Wha—?" Slobad yelped, waking with a start. Glissa had learned over the last week that Slobad was a very light sleeper, something he claimed was one of the main reasons he was still alive.

"My . . . my sister. I think she might be under someone's control," Glissa said. "What she said, it just doesn't make sense. She can't think I . . . I killed them."

"Yeah? Why not?" Slobad asked. He still sounded groggy from sleep. Glissa felt her way across the floor, and sat beside him. "Seem to remember crazy elf saying something like that, once."

"It was still fresh. That was guilt. But I know who kept me from saving them, and I know now who sent the levelers. It wasn't me. I didn't kill my parents, I know that," she whispered. Glissa didn't think there were any scrying spells on them at the moment, but better safe than sorry. "It must be the trolls. Strang is dead, but he must have had an ally in Tel-Jilad."

"No trolls left, huh?" Slobad was right. Kaldra had seen to that. But maybe one or two bad eggs had stayed behind in the nest when Drooge had led his people to fight at Glissa's side.

"No trolls we liked," Glissa said. "I'm telling you, someone's controlling her, or feeding her lies."

"Maybe, maybe not, huh? Look, sister elf home when levelers attack, huh? Glissa, not. Now Glissa alive, parents dead. Sister elf's young, huh? Of course she's blaming you." Slobad said bluntly.

Glissa felt like she'd been socked in the gut by a golem. Could it really be that simple? Had she gotten so used to every single event or problem in her life relating to some sinister secret that she'd missed the obvious, seeing conspiracies where there was just her own neglect?

"But she's my sister. How could she think that?" Glissa asked.

"Elves still people, huh? Just like goblins, leonin, even humans. And when people get hurt, want explanation, huh? Want someone to blame," Slobad said.

"She holds me responsible because I couldn't stop the levelers from killing mother and father," Glissa whispered. "For being alive while they're not."

"Or she's blaming herself, huh? Taking it out on you?" Slobad asked. "Might run in family, huh?"

"Maybe," Glissa said. She was beginning to feel a little sick. She'd lived the last few weeks with one goal: to make

Memnarch pay for her family's deaths. If Glissa had believed in gods anymore, she would have prayed for a chance to speak to her sister alone before the trial. She wondered if it would do any good.

"Sometimes," Slobad said gently and placed a hand on Glissa's shoulder, "People take so much time figuring out tricky answers, forget to look for simple ones, huh?"

"Where'd you hear that?" Glissa asked.

"Bosh. And experience," Slobad said and sighed. "I miss Bosh. No offense. Bosh always have something wise to say, huh? Once he started talking."

"I miss him too," Glissa said. The towering metal man, ancient beyond Glissa's imagination, had sacrificed his newfound life as a flesh and blood creature to give his friends a slim chance of survival. "I miss them all."

* * * * *

Bruenna took one last walk around the courtyard before turning in, a habit she'd fallen into over the last week. The overtures from the vedalken had been welcomed by the elders of her people, weary after weeks of fighting the vedalken artifact creatures. Representative Orland claimed that the vedalken wanted to free the humans, live alongside them—and so far, some surprising changes had been made in Lumengrid. The humans were paid for their work in vedalken coinage, and technically the word *slave* had been abolished. Humans still didn't have many rights, but they were theoretically on the road to more freedom.

So why couldn't Bruenna bring herself to trust Orland and the vedalken?

The problem, she decided while gazing out over the

Quicksilver Sea in the dim green light of the new moon, was that even if the vedalken claimed they were embracing freedom and some kind of self-rule they were still at heart religious fanatics. They still served Memnarch. Pontifex was dead, maybe Memnarch too. The green moon had come, yet here Bruenna was, alive. Surely if Glissa had failed the Neurok mage would have seen evidence of Memnarch's ascension by now. Yet she couldn't bring herself to believe the god of the vedalken was truly gone.

Even if Memnarch was dead, and Bruenna's world faced a future free of the ancient creature's "guardianship," how long before another Pontifex rose to power? What would her people do if their vedalken "friends" called on the Neurok to help hunt down Glissa? What would Bruenna do?

She didn't think she had it in her to turn on her Viridian friend. But Bruenna hoped she'd never have to make that choice.

The mage danced back from the viscous silver of the sea, which had been restless of late. The new moon had thrown the tide patterns into an uproar. She hadn't been around when the first four moons erupted from the surface, but she imagined that each time a new satellite had come forth, the same thing had happened—the sea went crazy. At the moment, the new green moon hung low behind Lumengrid, the only light in the night sky. The scattered light of the city cast strange shadows on the quicksilver water and gave the illusion of monstrous swimming creatures.

They were almost upon her before Bruenna realized that she wasn't looking at any illusion. Dark shapes moved just below the surface, creating shallow wakes that belied their location. The lights of the city were still there, but now they camouflaged…what?

Bruenna backed away from the waves to get a better look at the mysterious sea creatures just as the shoreline erupted in a spray of silver foam. She found herself staring back at hundreds of red, glowing eyes.

Bruenna stumbled on a piece of driftmetal as she turned and ran back to her village, shouting at the top of her lungs.

"To arms! To arms! Levelers on the beach!"

CHAPTER 3

IN THE COURT OF THE BLIND . . .

They received no warning before the day of the trial. Slobad had just torn open the day's nayan loaf and was about to hand half of it to Glissa when they both simply stopped being inside the cell.

They stood in shackles on a large, broad platform that offered a view of the whole of Viridia, dominated by the massive shadow of Tel-Jilad, the Tree of Tales. Glissa was struck again by how empty the village looked, but still there was a small crowd.

"Okay, this might be bad," the elf girl whispered.

"Why's that, huh?" Slobad hissed, his eyes bugging.

"Because the trial is going to be public." Glissa formed her clawed hands into fists. "And I've never, ever, seen that happen before. In fact, I can't remember the last time *anyone* stood trial under threat of execution."

"So? That good, huh? Means elves don't like to kill each other, right?" Slobad asked hopefully.

"No, it just means that they're really serious this time. They really expect me to hang, and they want everyone in the village to watch."

"I don't like your home very much, Glissa."

"It feels less and less like home all the time."

"Hey, cheer up. Manacles," Slobad said, waggling his eyebrows with the exact opposite of subtlety. Slobad could pick the locks on a set of manacles. Glissa had no doubt about that at all. But how were they going to escape standing on an open terrace in the middle of the village? Still, she silently wished him luck.

Glissa felt she had run out of options. She had to prove her innocence, for Lyese's sake if not her own. The crash of a gong signaled that the judges had assembled, and they called the trial to order.

"Okay," Glissa said, "judges. Silver-hair's got to be Lendano. He's one of the oldest elves in the Tangle. I don't think he'll fall for any tricks. You know Yulyn, and . . . I'm not sure. I don't recognize her. She's no elf. That looks like one of the Sylvok druids."

"Sylvok?" Slobad asked. "Looks pretty elfy to Slobad."

"They're human. But Viridia hasn't had high-level contact with the Sylvok in years. They keep to their part of the Tangle, and so do we." She grimaced. "They've always given me the creeps."

The gong sounded a second time, followed by a familiar, gravelly voice that reverberated in the natural amphitheater. Glissa brightened a bit at the faint sound of metal scraping metal. Slobad was wasting no time working on his bindings. She hoped he could be subtle enough to do them some good.

"Who accuses this Viridian elf?" Yulyn bellowed. "Step forward, and face the accused."

Yulyn referred to a piece of parchment and called Banryk to testify. Glissa heard heavy footsteps approaching her from behind, and a needle-sharp spear tip pressed into her shoulder, right behind her heart. She smelled sour, fermented gelfruit oil—a simple, abundant intoxicant the Viridians brewed called *nush*—as he leaned in close to her ear.

"Quiet," Banryk whispered. "Or I skewer you, then cut up the goblin while you're bleeding out."

Glissa seethed. At least they hadn't seen Slobad fumbling with his manacles. She was sure that would have created a little stir.

"We will have order," Yulyn said. "Who accuses this woman?"

"I do," Lyese said, stepping to the witness platform.

"Of what crime do you accuse this Viridian elf?" asked the Sylvok judge. Her voice was soft, almost elven, but her humanity was unmistakable. Her green robes glittered like sheets of jade.

The human's presence was baffling. How bad had things gotten in the last few weeks, Glissa wondered, if the Viridians had to rely on human elders to judge her? Had her people and the Sylvok formed some kind of hasty alliance in the face of the leveler threat?

"Murder. This Viridian killed my parents," Lyese continued.

"Did you see this act?" Yulyn asked. "How was the crime committed?"

"I had gone for a walk," Lyese said, her voice strong, clear and tinged with bitterness. "To pick moon's breath flowers. I was only gone for an hour." Lyese's voice trembled slightly, but she held her composure.

"And when you returned?" Yulyn asked.

"There was blood everywhere," Lyese continued without faltering. "The levelers—"

Glissa heard a gasps from the crowd at the mention of the hated constructs.

"The levelers had my mother and father, and were cutting them to pieces."

"Where was the accused?" the Sylvok asked, "Surely she, too, was . . . attacking them?"

"I didn't see her at first. I tried to fight the levelers, but there were too many. And," Lyese added, "I was too weak then. They took my eye, but I escaped with my life."

"I'm confused," the Sylvok woman continued. "When did you see the accused attack your parents? It sounds to me like she was lucky the levelers didn't find her." Glissa could hardly believe her pointed ears. This human was defending her against her own people.

"I saw her when she came back to my home, and led them away!" Lyese shouted, her composure breaking at last.

"Lyese, I wasn't leading them," Glissa said, "I didn't know—"

"The accused will have the opportunity to speak in her defense when she is called," Yulyn interrupted. "There will be no further outbursts, or this tribunal will immediately find the accused guilty. Is that understood?"

Glissa nodded. She wanted to scream.

"Very well," Yulyn said. "The witness may continue."

"I got out of the house, but I couldn't just leave. I didn't know what else to do," Lyese said. "I saw Glissa head in, and when she came out the levelers were following her. And she had my mother's ring."

The ring. Glissa's last piece of her mother, which she'd recovered at the grisly scene. And it was still on her finger, a damning piece of evidence.

"Does the accused still have this ring? Do you see it?"

"Not from here. Her hands are tied," Lyese said.

"Banryk," Yulyn ordered, "Bring the accused to the witness platform and unlock her manacles."

"What?" the thuggish guard blurted.

"We must see her hand, Banryk," Yulyn said. "We can't do that if it's tied behind her back. Don't make me ask you again."

Banryk seized Glissa's bound wrists in one meaty hand. He yanked upward roughly, wrenching the elf girl's shoulders and sending her half-stumbling forward. Banryk jerked back on her wrist before she could fall, but though this helped her keep her footing it sent more pain through her hyperextended shoulders. "Forward, prisoner," he growled.

She felt a key slip into the locks on her manacles, and the metal bands slipped off. Banryk still held one wrist in his hand, and he leaned in again for another nush-scented whisper. "Try something. Please."

"Present your hand for inspection," Yulyn called. Glissa raised her free hand, the one on which she wore her dead mother's ring.

"Yes, that's it," Lyese said, and Glissa could hear one last, faint hope die in her sister's heart. "That's my mother's ring. How could you, Glissa? It's just a ring! Why?"

"The witness will not address the accused!" Yulyn bellowed, raising his voice for the first time. "We will keep order in—"

"Yulyn," said Lendano, his gentle, musical voice sounding out of place in this grim court. "This is ridiculous. Such a trial, in such a time of trials. Our numbers are now few. We have had to strike alliances with the humans just to protect ourselves. It is obvious to me that this girl did not command the levelers. No one commands the levelers. They are a force of nature." Glissa felt an unexpected surge of hope. "Glissa?" Lendano asked, turning to her. "What do you have to say for yourself?"

Glissa hardly knew where to begin. So much had happened since the night the levelers came and turned her world upside down, but soon her story came spilling out in a torrent. She told the tribunal and the assembled elves—and, now that she was looking for them, a few Sylvok as well—everything that had happened to her in the past few weeks, from coming home to find her house in shambles and her family dead, to her first encounter with Slobad in the leveler cave, all the way up to the destruction of Kaldra and the creation of the new green moon. She told them of the strange lands she'd visited outside the Tangle, lands most

Viridians had never seen: the Glimmervoid and the noble leonin that lived there; the cancerous Mephidross, filled with creatures undead and worse; the Quicksilver Sea, where dwelt four-armed vedalken who enslaved the local human population; and the Oxidda Mountains, where the goblins of Slobad's tribe dwelled in tunnels surrounding the Great Furnace.

She did leave out some details, especially concerning serum. She also skipped over some things she just wasn't ready to talk about yet—Bosh's connections to Memnarch, her own vengeance-driven slaughter of the vedalken mage Janus, and her repeated mercy toward Geth, the master of the Mephidross. Some things were better left until after the trial.

When she was finished, Slobad whistled. "Wow, we sure did a lot, huh?" he whispered.

Lendano was the first judge to speak. "A very interesting tale, Glissa. Tell me, these soul traps you spoke of...you said they were scattered throughout the inside of the world?" Glissa heard Yulyn snort when the elder elf made reference to Mirrodin being hollow.

"Yes, elder," Glissa replied. "I think they . . . keep us here. In this world. All of us. We don't belong here. I've had visions—"

"Don't belong here? What is that supposed to mean?" Yulyn interrupted. "We are the Viridian elves, we live in peace with the Tangle. Where do you suggest 'we' belong?"

"No, everyone. Every person on this world," Glissa said. She raised one hand and pinched her own forearm. "You see me as you see yourselves. Flesh and metal. Metal and flesh. But the metal came later."

"How do you know this?" asked the Sylvok judge.

Glissa muttered something unintelligible.

"Please repeat that?" the judge prodded.

"I said, a troll told me."

"That would be this 'Bosh' you spoke of?" the judge replied.

"No, Bosh was a golem. A very old golem. I'm talking about Chunth," Glissa said. She placed special emphasis on that name of the troll. He was a legend among his own people, and a folk story among elf children. Most elves didn't believe the so-called "First One" even existed. She didn't know about the Sylvok.

But Chunth was dead, betrayed by a fellow troll who was working for Memnarch. She would have given anything to have the wise old shaman at her side right now, explaining everything to this silly tribunal.

"I have heard enough," Lendano said. "And I do not believe we will be learning any more about the night in question. I am ready to vote, and as is my right, I urge you both to vote with common sense."

"Are you passing judgment already, Lendano?" Yulyn asked, still calm but more threatening than ever in his ice-cold way. "Have you given up all pretense of observing our laws? This trial is—"

"This trial is a needless distraction, Yulyn. Did you not listen to a word Glissa has said?" Lendano interrupted, sternness creeping into his mellifluous voice. "We have assembled a capital tribunal for the first time in hundreds of years, at a time when our people are disappearing. And this Memnarch may still be a threat. We are wasting valuable time. It is also my opinion that we will be less safe, perhaps even enslaved like the humans, if we do not take Glissa's words of warning to heart."

"Disappearing? Is that why the place is so empty?" Glissa asked, procedure be damned.

"The accused—"

"Shut up, Yulyn," Lendano interjected. "We do not know why, but we believe it is tied to the new moon. Most of the disappearances took place at that exact time."

"Most?" Glissa asked, the urgency of the trial fading as her curiosity grew. "How long have people been disappearing?"

"Since you left," Lendano replied. "Glissa, Lyese, I have known you and your family for centuries. I know that your sister is not capable of what you accuse, Lyese."

"But the goblin—"

"I have allowed this to go on long enough," Lendano said.

"You allowed? The law allowed!" Yulyn objected.

"No!" Lyese screamed. Without a word, she hauled off and slapped Glissa in the face. The older elf girl was so surprised that she stumbled over backwards and landed on her rump. Glissa placed one hand where Lyese had struck her. Without warning, Lyese leaped on Glissa again, hands now balled into fists that pounded Glissa's chest. The accused felt herself starting to lose consciousness, but she couldn't strike Lyese.

"Get off her!" Slobad wailed. Lyese's weight left Glissa's chest as the goblin caught Glissa's sister in a flying tackle. Slobad had gotten free on his own and blown the element of surprise. But Glissa wasn't complaining.

She looked for an opening, some way off the terrace. Then a rolling ball of elf and goblin slammed into her legs, sending all three of them tumbling to the forest floor.

* * * * *

Glissa sat up, rubbing her temple. A knot of scrub brush had broken their fall. Above, she could still hear confusion reigning at the disrupted trial.

"Slobad, where's Lyese? Is she okay?" She crawled over to where the goblin was hunched over her sister's unmoving form.

"Breathing okay. Not dead," Slobad assured her. "But we're gonna be if we stay here, huh?"

"You're not going anywhere," said a familiar voice, and Glissa felt a pair of meaty hands clamp onto her arms.

"Banryk?" Glissa said.

"Going to beg me for your life? Make it worth my while," Banryk growled.

Glissa snapped her head back and heard a sickening crunch followed by the sound of Banryk crumpling to the ground, unconscious.

"Wish I could do that," Slobad said.

"I wish I could stop," Glissa said, clutching the back of her aching skull. "He'll be all right."

"Gonna need a new nose though, huh?"

"I hope he does," Glissa said. She returned to Lyese.

Glissa saw the outlines of a youth she knew, and the eyepatch and cropped haircut of an adult she'd just met. Her sister was breathing softly, and was probably safer than Glissa was for now.

"Okay, Slobad. Let's get out of here before the rest of them make it down the tree."

"I would, but there's one problem, huh?"

"What? Is it Yulyn? I don't see anyth—" Glissa stopped when she heard the sound of hundreds of flapping metal wings, buzzing like giant flies and growing louder by the second. The last time she'd heard that sound had been on the ramparts of Taj Nar.

"Nope. We got company. Not just elves, huh?" Slobad said. "Have to talk to sister elf later. Ol' crab-legs not want to stay dead."

CHAPTER 4

FRIENDS LIKE THESE

Bruenna spared a glance over one shoulder. The aerophins were gaining on her, in seconds they'd be close enough not to miss. She pulled hard on the steering controls of her stolen vedalken combat flyer and forced the limber, lightweight vehicle into a steep dive as another bolt of blue fire lanced overhead.

She couldn't keep this up. Eventually, the aerophins would land a shot, and she wasn't sure if she could still summon the energy for flying magic. That's why she'd taken this craft in the first place. She had to reach the Tangle soon, or she was doomed. If the 'phins didn't get her, the fall would.

Or the crash, if she didn't pull out of this dive. Bruenna's golden tresses whipped back into her face as she leaned hard on the stick, turning the dive into a roll and leveling off much closer to the ground. She was at the edge of the Tangle. If she could get below the tree canopy she'd have cover from the energy blasts, but sacrifice speed. With luck, any aerophins that followed would have the same difficulty. Bruenna poured on as much power as she dared and entered the forest.

Even with the wind whipping past her ears, she heard the swarm of aerophins enter the Tangle behind her. It sounded like all of them had given chase. "Very well," Bruenna muttered. "Have it your way."

The magical energies of the Tangle felt strange and wild to the mage from the Quicksilver Sea, and she had trouble shaping the power to her purposes, to say nothing of the fact that she had to control the flyer at the same time.

The flyer had not been easy to come by. The levelers that attacked her village had been only the first wave. The vedalkens personally led the second, riding flyers like this one and, at the rear, this fleet of damnable aerophins.

Bruenna hadn't even had time to mourn the dead. She had to survive long enough to find Glissa and warn her of the vedalken resurgence. She decided to risk slowing down a bit, and concentrated on her home, feeling the distant lines of power sending her what she needed. The familiar mana let her tame the wild magic of the forest.

Directly behind Bruenna, the ground erupted. Jagged silver spires packed tightly together like predator's teeth shot upward through the forest floor, rising to a height that rivaled the tallest Tangle tree.

The results were better than the Neurok leader had hoped. She heard a series of tinny explosions reverberate through her temporary magical wall as several waves of flying constructs found the sudden appearance of a silver wall too much information to take in at once. Bruenna risked another look back.

The aerophins were still coming. Her trick, while impressive, had not appreciably decreased their numbers.

The wall had been the last major spell she had in her. Bruenna was running out of options. She also realized with some dismay that she had no idea where specifically in this vast forest she had to go. All she had to go on was a name: "Viridia."

Bruenna broke through the thick woods and emerged on a narrow trail that was just open enough to give her room to maneuver and concentrate on magic at the same time. Behind her, the buzz of 'phin wings grew to a roar, and again she was forced to waste time and energy dodging a barrage of energistic flame that shattered the copper tree trunks and tore up the soft metallic duff that covered the trail floor.

Viridia. Bruenna might still have enough for a magical trace. Glissa was in Viridia—that much she knew from the scrying spell she'd invoked before everything went to hell. Now Bruenna didn't know where else to turn.

Centering herself on the trail and praying no 'phin would get off an accurate shot before she finished, Bruenna cast her mind out to the Tangle, sensing every living thing in the forest.

Okay, too much. Focus.

A blast from a closing aerophin clipped Bruenna's robe. A tree took the second shot and exploded in a hail of jagged copper shards just in front of her. Splitting her concentration, she dodged most of the shrapnel, but felt a few tiny knife-like blades pepper her face, arms, and chest.

The spell was done. It wasn't flashy. Bruenna simply became aware of where the elf girl currently was, as if it was the road to her own home.

Not that Bruenna had a home anymore.

Bruenna wrenched on the flight controls and tore off through the Tangle in search of her last hope. She saw the clearing in the trees that had to be Glissa's village, and angled in for what she hoped would be a soft landing.

Bruenna shouldn't have bothered—a pair of aerophins scored direct hits on her tail. The control crystals exploded, temporarily blinding her with sparks and oily smoke. She pulled mightily on the steering yoke, but shouldn't have bothered. As soon as she did, the magical engine that drove the flyer sputtered and died. Bruenna's stomach lurched as the sky dropped out from under her, and the flyer's nose dipped toward Mirrodin.

* * * * *

Glissa had hoped she'd seen the last of the vedalken aerophins. The sound of the winged artifacts was unmistakeable.

But Pontifex was dead. If the vedalken artifacts were attacking now, someone else was behind it. It had to be Memnarch.

"Why you stand there, huh?" Slobad said, grabbing her wrist and pulling her away from Viridia.

Glissa watched the sky, but also listened with sharp ears. The flapping wings were drawing closer, and amid the hum Glissa could also hear elves descending the Trial Terrace. Below it all, something strange, but also familiar, coming in ahead of the aerophins. Then she heard a small explosive popping noise and the familiar sound cut out.

"Slobad, did you hear that?"

"I see it! Duck!" Slobad slammed into Glissa's side, knocking the elf girl flat as a sleek silver object moving impossibly fast narrowly missed a perfect opportunity to deprive Glissa of her head. The whoosh of displaced air was followed by the grating screech as the speeding, smoking thing collided with a tree.

"What was that?" the elf girl gasped.

"Don't know, but the 'phins were chasing it," Slobad observed. "And here they come!"

"Wait!" Glissa cried. "Lyese! Slobad, I can't leave her lying here." The elf heaved her sister over her shoulders. "Okay, lead the way. I'll keep up."

Slobad jogged ahead of her and away from the encroaching roar of flying constructs. A barrage of sliver-blue fire struck a few feet away, shattering the ground. Glissa stumbled after Slobad as best she could with the weight on her shoulders, for once thankful that goblins had such short legs.

Another volley of crackling firebolts exploded in the canopy above them. Glissa yelped as bits of shattered copper peppered her hind quarters, sending her stumbling over an exposed root. Glissa tumbled face-first to the ground. Lyese fell limp and rolled a ways ahead. Slobad stopped, scooped up Lyese on his own back, and kept running.

"Slobad! Run! I'll catch up," Glissa said, turning to face the 'phins. She'd had enough.

"Are you cra—never mind, stupid question," Slobad shouted back.

"I can handle them. You have to get Lyese out of here. Please," Glissa said.

"Don't get killed, huh?" Slobad said.

" 'Course not. Just get to whatever crashed up there. If it's the vedalken who's behind this, and it's still alive, try to keep it there until I'm finished. And don't drop my sister," Glissa said. "Go, they're almost here."

Slobad nodded and charged ahead as best he could. The elf girl returned to the problem at hand.

"Great," Glissa muttered. "No weapon, no goblin. No problem." Despite their bizarre vedalken design and deadly energy blasts, the accursed things were still just constructs, after all. Glissa had a way with such constructs. She felt a familiar tingle in her spine as they drew closer.

Looking inward, she called forth the jade fire. Glissa's copper skin began to crackle with energy, and her eyes glowed with eerie light. Glissa pulled her hands toward her chest then flung them outward. A wave of green fire slammed into the forefront of the aerophin formation then split in a fractal pattern that resembled a pane of shattered crystal in the sky.

Glissa poured death into the killing machines, and they died in droves. Tendrils of swirling, smoky energy snaked around each individual artifact. Glissa felt each one as the energy slammed into their magical power sources, causing some to shut down immediately, making others attack allies, but causing most to simply explode like a goblin cannon.

Glissa felt quite peaceful, and very strong. Was this what it felt like to be a planeswalker, to touch that power?

The aerophins' formation crumbled. With the mental equivalent of a snapping lute string, Glissa felt the last aerophin die, and the spark energy dissipated as rapidly as it had coalesced. She opened her eyes, which she realized she had held clenched shut the entire time. She'd somehow seen the aerophins anyway.

The aerophins were dead, but their corpses hadn't simply vanished. They'd built up considerable momentum, and now thousands of burning, twisted hunks of jagged metal rained down. Glissa raised her hands again, hoping to stop the tumbling wreckage somehow, but the power had either been spent or left her entirely. She tried to run, but her legs refused to move, and her vision began to blur.

Heavy, booted footsteps crashed through the foliage behind, and Glissa slowly tried to turn. Whoever approached was running into their doom. "Slobad? Stay back!" Glissa called, "They're going to hit any second!"

"I've lost enough family recently," a distinctly ungoblinish voice replied, scooping Glissa up and slinging her over steady, armored shoulders.

"Lyese!" Glissa coughed as the rough movement knocked the wind out of her.

"Just shut up," her younger sister replied. "Before I change my mind." Without another word, Lyese bolted away from the hail of burning wreckage.

CHAPTER 5

CRASH AND BURN

"Ha!" Slobad said, trying to clap Glissa and the new arrival on the shoulders but succeeding only in smacking both on the small of the back. "Told you you could do it, huh? Slobad have faith! Strength in numbers, huh? Ha!"

Bruenna had survived the crash of her stolen flyer with only a few scratches and bruises marring her bluish skin. Glissa had been relieved to see the mage, about whose fate she'd feared the worst. The small group was now gathered amid the smoking aerophin wreckage.

Glissa stood on unsteady legs and gazed at the new hell she'd brought to the Tangle. Slobad offered her an arm, but she waved him away.

The rain of burning constructs had crashed with thousands of fiery impacts into the Tangle, knocking some trees down and causing them to burst into oily flame, turning others to glowing slag in explosive collisions. The ground was covered in twisted hunks of vedalken artifacts and a viscous, sticky substance that leaked from the wrecked artifact creatures and burned with thick black smoke.

Of Yulyn or any of the other Viridian elves, there was no sign. "I hope those all cleared the village," Glissa said softly when her jaw would work again. "The Tangle can't take much more of this."

"What happened, huh?" Slobad asked.

"Memnarch's not dead," Bruenna said.

"Tell me something I don't know," Glissa replied.

"All right, something you don't know. My people are," Bruenna said. "My village, at least. I can only guess what might have happened to the workers in Lumengrid."

"Your people are what?" Glissa asked.

"Dead."

"Oh, Bruenna," Glissa whispered, raising her claws to her lips. "I'm . . ."

"Sorry?" Bruenna shot back. "Don't be. They died fighting. Fighting those." The mage waved a hand at the mess of wreckage and shattered forest. "Too bad I didn't ask you to come back with me. You could have stopped them at any time, couldn't you? You could have stopped them all with that green fire."

"I don't—I don't know," Glissa said. "I don't understand this power I've got, Bruenna, and I don't know where it comes from." Not the entire truth, but it was as much as Glissa wanted to share right now.

"You see, lady," Lyese said, "She doesn't understand anything. Death just follows wherever she goes, and the rest of us have to follow or get out of the way."

"Seven hells, Lyese!" Glissa exploded "I didn't ask for this!"

"Yeah?" Lyese barked back, stepping close enough to get into her sister's face. "No one did. No one ever expects anything, and no one's at fault, right? You're just a hunter. You don't want to defend our home, you just wanted to run through the woods playing games with Kane."

Glissa drew a sharp intake of breath at the mention of her dead friend.

"Oh, sorry, he's dead too, isn't he?" Lyese asked innocuously. "Well, I didn't ask to lose an eye, Glissa. I didn't ask to see half the village disappear *into thin air* when you called up that damned moon. And I didn't ask to find pieces of Mother and Father in the garden. But at least you're alive. So why don't you crawl back inside the world and stop bringing death down on everyone around you?"

Glissa opened her mouth to speak, but she'd forgotten how.

"Child, shut up," Bruenna interrupted. "You're not the only one who's suffering. And she's right. She's not the cause of this, she's the focal—"

Lyese's sword was in her hand and within an inch of Bruenna's windpipe in the blink of an eye. "Call me a child again, human. You're not much better than Glissa. I never saw you before today. How do I know you're not as guilty as she is?"

"EVERYBODY QUIET!" Slobad screamed at the top of his lungs. The three women froze, staring at the furious goblin. "You," he said, pointing at Lyese, "Don't know what Glissa's been through, huh? Glissa, sister was scared. Now she suspicious. Got every right to be, huh? But sister will learn she's wrong." Slobad's eyes narrowed. "You both family. Slobad got no family, huh? Get over it, elves are both alive. That's family. Be happy for that, huh?"

"Goblin, I couldn't have said it better—"

"And you!" Slobad said, cutting Bruenna off and jabbing a stubby claw up at her chin. "Uh . . . actually, you okay," The goblin said once Bruenna's words had made the perilous journey through his ears and into his brain. "Uh, thanks. For support, huh? Sorry about your tribe. That's rotten, huh?"

"That's a good word for it," Bruenna agreed. She turned to the one-eyed elf girl and bowed slightly. "You are Glissa's sister? It's an honor to meet you."

Lyese, surprised, took the Neurok woman's offered hand.

"Bruenna, meet my sister Lyese. Lyese, meet Bruenna of the Neurok," Glissa said.

Bruenna appraised Lyese. "The family resemblance is uncanny."

"I'll pretend you didn't say that," Lyese said with a scowl.

"We're—uh, it's a long story," Glissa said. "Lyese, Bruenna is not your enemy. Any more than I am. If you'd really earned that armor, you'd speak with more respect."

"Don't tell me what I earned, Glissa!" Lyese snapped, "I'll make my own judgments."

"Bruenna, what happened?" Glissa asked with a sigh. "I need details."

"They attacked us, intentionally," the Neurok woman replied. "Hunted down every last one of us."

"Except you, huh?" Slobad said.

"It started with levelers," Bruenna said.

"Levelers?" Glissa, Slobad, and Lyese asked at once.

"They came ashore from Lumengrid. The vedalken said they wanted peace, but . . . We fought back, but it was late. Most of the villagers were cut down in their beds." Bruenna coughed awkwardly, and Glissa could tell she was on the verge of breaking down. "I fought them, with everything I had. But then the 'phin swarm came across the sea from that cursed vedalken city, and they hit a tower I was using for cover. It toppled and pinned me underneath."

"Lucky," Lyese remarked. Her good eye was still examining the human with suspicion.

"Yes," Bruenna nodded. "Very lucky. I was standing over an underground food storage area. The tower fell and knocked out the roof of the warehouse cave the same time it came down on me."

"You fall through ground and land in a cave, huh?" Slobad said. "That happens to Slobad all the time."

"We'll have to swap cave-in survival tips sometime, goblin," Bruenna said. "When I came to, everyone was . . . it was a slaughter. I can only imagine what happened to the poor folk that lived in Lumengrid itself. So I borrowed a flyer from a vedalken."

"Didn't see you coming, huh?" Slobad asked.

"No, he didn't," Bruenna said with a grim smile. "Bastard was picking through the bodies, checking for wounded, I guess, but wasn't finding any. Caught him with a bolt of lightning right in the fishbowl. Then I hopped on the flyer, which must have woken up the 'phins and levelers, because took off after me." Bruenna shrugged wearily.

"What's a fishbowl?" Slobad asked.

"Later," Glissa interrupted, and swung Bruenna around by the shoulders. "There are levelers coming too?" Even as she asked the question, Glissa's sharp ears picked up the clacking of the leveler hordes, still many miles away but closing. And between the elf girl and the sounds of metallic death was her home.

"Flare," Glissa swore. "This is not good."

"Can you stop them?" Lyese demanded. "Can you do to them what you did to these?" She waved an arm to indicate the shattered aerophins.

"I've got to try," Glissa said. "Otherwise, Viridia's going to be destroyed." Privately, she didn't think she had it in her, but she was Viridia's only chance.

"Let me help," Bruenna said, brushing flecks of copper and oil from her robes. "Together, maybe we can—"

"No, I've got to do this myself," Glissa insisted. "You three need to get someplace safe. Someplace where there might be an army big enough to take on Memnarch." She turned to the goblin. "Slobad, you've go to lead them to Taj Nar. Raksha might be able to help. At the very least, he deserves to know what's happening. And I can't think of any safer place on Mirrodin right now."

Slobad shook his head. "Oh, no. Where you go, Slobad goes."

"Viridia's my home, too, Glissa," Lyese interrupted. "If you're going back there to fight them, I am too."

"Both of you are being foolish," Bruenna said softly. "Glissa is right—she must go alone. I've seen how many there are, and we wouldn't last five minutes. But if Glissa's magic can do it all at once . . ."

Lyese looked from Bruenna to Glissa then back the way they had come. She placed her hands on her hips and stared a dagger at her older sister. "Okay, go. But if I find out you're just going back to help them finish the job, I'll kill you."

Glissa grimaced, but nodded. "If I don't succeed, you probably won't get the chance. But I'll try and save you a piece. Now please, go with Bruenna and Slobad. You can trust them, even if you still don't trust me."

"Glissa," Lyese said, "just go."

Glissa turned from her sister to Bruenna and spread her arms wide. "So, think you can get me airborne?"

Bruenna grinned. "I can do better than that, now that my feet are back on solid metal." The Neurok woman closed her eyes and began summoning the magical power of flight.

* * * * *

Glissa caught up to the levelers a few hundred yards before they would have swarmed over Viridia. They were well over a thousand strong, each one bristling with blades, claws, teeth, and armor, gleaming green in the moonglow. The constructs flattened most of the smaller trees in their path, skirting the larger trunks that even levelers would be hard pressed to bring down. But Glissa wasn't concerned with the plant life, destructive as Memnarch's creatures were. The unsuspecting people of Viridia were hers to protect now, for better or worse.

Bruenna's flight magic gave her complete control over her movement in the air, meaning she could hover as she concentrated on calling forth the destructive energy that had wiped out the aerophins. It had worked before against levelers, though she'd never faced this many at once. She closed her eyes, willing the destructive green fire to rain down on her foes.

Nothing happened. With renewed urgency, she cast about deep inside herself, picturing the levelers bursting apart. Nothing. The power had been exhausted defeating the aerophins. Either that, or it was gone altogether. Glissa didn't want to consider what that might mean.

If she couldn't stop them, maybe she could warn the Viridians in time. Maybe that Sylvok could use some kind of druidic magic on the things. Glissa opened her eyes to check on the levelers' progress.

The levelers were no longer advancing on the village. They weren't advancing at all, not horizontally. As she watched in horror, the clattering silver beasts clambered over each other, slowly creating a mountain of levelers directly underneath her.

"They weren't coming after Bruenna," Glissa muttered. "They're after *me*."

To test her hypothesis, she flew back and forth in a straight line over the levelers. The crude pyramid of constructs attempted to shift direction as she moved, always tracking her.

And that meant she could still save the village, power or no.

Glissa shouted taunts at the levelers below, daring them to follow her as she started to circle, slowly widening her arc and moving away from Viridia. The swarm of machines moved like a giant living shadow, trying to keep up with their prey and snapping futilely at the flying elf girl. The role of bait wasn't her favorite, but at least she was dangerous bait. If this worked, Viridia should survive. She hoped. The only problem was where she would lead them and whether her borrowed flight magic would last long enough to get there. But an idea was beginning to form.

However this situation worked out, Glissa had lied about meeting the others at Taj Nar. She wouldn't be coming back until she had Memnarch's misshapen head on the end of a sword.

Glissa tucked her chin to cut back on drag and gained just a little more speed. The army of levelers faithfully gave chase, still not comprehending they couldn't catch Glissa as long as she flew above them. She wondered if, like the mindless nim zombies of the Mephidross, the levelers simply followed an order until given a new one.

Or maybe, Glissa mused, they know I can't do this forever, and they're waiting for me to drop. It didn't strike her as likely that Memnarch would use constructs that weren't at least smarter than the average walking corpse.

By following a wide slagwurm trail that led in the general direction she wanted to go, Glissa was able to keep the constructs from leveling too much of the forest in their wake. Even so, a cacophony of hoots, cries, and howls arose on either side of the army as wildlife fled in terror. For a second, Glissa's heart jumped when she thought she saw a wolf, but it might have just been a shadow or her imagination.

Of all her lost friends, the death of Al-Hayat, the giant wolf, had been especially brutal. The ancient forest creature had joined her cause simply because it was right. Memnarch's forces had cut him down, and the wolf's heroic death had saved Glissa's life. Bosh had been a marvel, and a good friend, but in many ways the golem had been like a child. Al-Hayat had been more like a surrogate father who had come along to protect Glissa just when she'd lost her own. Sometimes she missed the big wolf almost as much as her mother and father.

The elf girl returned her attention to her flight path, the construct army still clacking and rumbling along after her. The slagwurm trail had grown fresher over the last few minutes, and Glissa realized that this might work even better than she'd planned. A slagwurm could inflict some real damage on the leveler army. The mammoth, legless monsters spent most of their lives underground—well, underground depending on your point of view, she supposed, remembering the dazzling interior of the world—and only ventured onto the surface when hunger drove them to it. If this slagwurm was still above ground, it could prove a potent, if unwilling, ally. She didn't see it on the trail ahead, but it could easily be concealed under the thick Tangle canopy. She hoped it was. With her spark-driven power apparently drained, she needed every advantage she could get.

Glissa glanced down. The levelers were still keeping pace, scattering stunned fauna and flattening inconvenient flora. Slobad passed languidly by and rolled so he faced upward. "So where we goin' huh?"

"Slobad!" Glissa blinked. "How long have you been following me? I told you to go to Taj Nar!"

"What?" Slobad replied. "Hard to hear up here, huh? Where we goin'?"

"You—I said you should—"

"Yeah, thinking you want excuse to go back down that lacuna, huh?" Slobad continued. "Need someone who knows what's going on, huh? Who knows better than Slobad?"

"Slobad, you might get killed," Glissa said bluntly. "Especially if you don't fly a little higher." She nodded, indicating a wobbling tower of stacked levelers that snapped at the goblin's feet. "Please, go back," she said, gripping Slobad's shoulder as he rose. "I'm not losing you, too. And they can't find the den without you."

Slobad just stared, and folded his stubby, clawed arms across his chest. "Got far enough to give directions. Wasn't easy to convince sister elf, but Bruenna helped."

"Look," Glissa said. "This might not kill me. It's dangerous, but I'm not suicidal. And I need you to look after Lyese. Slobad, you're the only one I trust. Don't you know that?"

"What about Bruenna? She big-time mage, huh?"

"Right," Glissa agreed. "She also worked for the vedalken for a long time, and she's just lost all of her people. She seems fine, but I'm not sure she's stable. Please, Slobad."

"Only if you say you come back, huh? Not going to let Slobad be a ball of string for Kha?"

"Okay, I'm coming back," Glissa said. "Now go, will you? This enchantment won't last all day."

"But—okay," the goblin sighed. "See you soon, huh?" Slobad added, veering off toward Taj Nar. Glissa watched him go for a precious pair of seconds, then continued on course. She glanced down to check on the levelers.

The constructs had completely stopped. Glissa was alarmed to see that many of them seemed to be watching a tiny, flying speck of goblin soar overhead. Once Slobad had passed the chittering levelers, something even stranger happened.

Half of the levelers followed Slobad. The other half continued to chase Glissa.

"Flare," Glissa swore as she headed back after Slobad, half-expecting to drop out of the sky at any second. "What do you want with him?" Her voice raised to a shout as she closed in on the goblin. "Slobad! Wait! Come back!"

Slobad came to an immediate halt, turned, and headed back toward her.

"Hey, what they want with Slobad?" he asked when he got within earshot.

"That's what I want to know. But we don't have time to find out," Glissa said. "You're just going to have to come with me. You were right. I'm going back inside."

"Slobad knew it!" the goblin barked.

"But first, we're going to get that to help us," she said, pointing at a large shape that had burst through the treetops just ahead.

CHAPTER 6

WURM'S TURN

"A slagwurm!" Slobad shouted at Glissa as the wind whistled past the elf's pointed ears. "How you gonna talk to a slagwurm, huh? They're monsters."

"I know," Glissa said, getting a good look at the thick, legless reptilian wurm as it whipped its toothy maw in the air, letting loose a keening screech that rang inside her head even at this distance. "But this one's hungry. Hear that? It's calling for its kin."

"That's how it says 'soup's on,' huh?" Slobad asked, natural curiosity overcoming fear. Glissa knew that Slobad was fascinated with big things, though usually he reserved his adoration for large machinery. Like golems.

"Yes," Glissa said and pointed at the swarm of levelers tracking them on the ground. "But it's not getting another wurm for dinner this time. Look past the wurm," Glissa said. "What do you see?"

"Trees, sky, a big . . . round . . . clearing. The lacuna!" Slobad exclaimed. "Wait, that full of monsters too, huh? Giant rats? Big bugs? Ring a bell?"

"You're the one who said I was crazy," Glissa said. "Now stay with me—we're going to get close." She explained what she had in mind then peeled off toward the writhing slagwurm.

Slagwurms were probably the largest creatures on Mirrodin, by simple virtue of the fact that they never stopped growing.

Glissa had learned about their life cycle as a youth. They were not truly reptiles, despite their thick scales and plates of metallic armor. Slagwurms actually began life as foot-long grubs that hatched from egg clusters laid by the hermaphrodite parent.

They were also cannibals. The strongest, or sometimes simply the first, slaggrub would wait for the others to hatch then consume its kin ruthlessly as their writhing mouths broke through the rubbery shells. Each egg cluster generally produced a single wurm that reached maturity in under a week, though fortunately slagwurms laid them only once a year.

Slagwurms never lost the taste for the flesh of their sibling, and that was the only reason their populations hadn't taken over all of Mirrodin. For the most part, the only thing that could kill a slagwurm was a bigger slagwurm.

This one had the rusty coloring of a mountain variety. It must have burrowed into the ground under the Tangle, and surfaced only recently. Glissa was sure she would have noticed the monster's path on their recent walk from the lacuna to Viridia. As they drew closer, she could make out the patterns that covered the wurm's armor plates, and smell the sulphurous odor of the enormous annelid.

"You remember what to do?" Glissa asked.

"Yep!" Slobad nodded.

"Go!" Glissa shouted, and the pair dived straight for the writhing torso of the towering slagwurm. Please, Glissa thought, stay in the air. Keep screeching. Keep your head up, you big ugly wurm. Don't drop just yet. . . .

Just before the elf and the goblin would have collided with the wurm's armored hide, they split, peeling off in opposite directions, missing the wurm by inches. Glissa reached out with one hand and caught the lip of one armored plate, then swung herself around and grabbed hold with the second, which left her half-hanging, half-floating two hundred feet in the air. She heard Slobad squeal as he did the same.

"Here they come!" Glissa shouted. "Wait for it!"

The single-minded levelers treated the slagwurm as if it was just another part of the landscape, something to be overcome on the way to their prey. The levelers began to climb the mammoth annelid, jamming their sharp claws into the wurm's side. So far, the creature was paying the levelers no more heed than it had Glissa and Slobad, but the elf knew it would have to notice the extra weight soon. Just then, the slagwurm screeched and started to wave more vigorously against the sky.

"That's it, Slobad! It feels them! Let's get out of here!"

"Don't need to tell Slobad twice, huh?" the goblin shouted from the other side of the slagwurm. The pair continued on at top speed to the still-smoldering hole in the ground that would lead them to their enemy—and would hopefully lead their enemy's minions to their doom.

Behind them, the wurm screeched again, a sound now filled with pain. The creature's death scream was soon followed by a tremendous crash as its massive bulk flopped back to the ground like a heavy chain. Glissa checked back over her shoulder. The wurm was thrashing in the midst of the swarm, tossing silver bits of levelers and a growing spray of its own ochre blood all over the forest. She felt a pang of regret that the majestic wurm was going to die—she had held out a faint hope that the creature might be able to take on all the constructs, at first—but in its death throes the slagwurm had cut the number of levelers by a third.

She silently thanked the wurm and pressed on. Pitting the monster against the levelers had been a trick of opportunity. Her real goal was just ahead.

The lacuna looked even bigger from above. Surrounded by

trees and foliage knocked flat by the shockwave of mana that had launched the new moon into orbit, the hole that led to the center of Mirrodin resemble an enormous pressed bladeflower.

Glissa was gratified to see—and feel—that the residue left by the passing of the moon still pulsed with magic. Giant vorracs snuffled around the lacuna's edge, baffled at what from their perspective must have been a suddenly shrunken world. Massive porcine djeeruks scampered over the wrecked trees, shattering any semblance of calm with the thunderous crash of cracking metal. Here and there, patches of debris had woven themselves together into shambling parodies of magical walls, covered in thousands of skittering stinger monkeys picking for tasty needlebugs. The average pack of stingers numbered around a dozen.

Slobad pulled up alongside Glissa and looked down. "Huh," he commented. "Why can't Slobad see all the way to the center?"

"That little point of light—I think that's the end," Glissa said. "We'll be there soon enough. You ready?"

"Ready," Slobad replied. Glissa checked on the levelers, which had left the twitching wurm behind, its corpse oozing ichor into the forest floor. But many had been destroyed, and with luck, the lacuna would take care of the rest.

"Okay. Try not to lose sight of me."

"You sure this work, huh?"

"Of course not. I just couldn't think of anything else."

As if on cue, Bruenna's flight spell finally gave out, and the pair dropped like stones into the lacuna.

* * * * *

"Good plan!" Slobad shouted as they plummeted into the lacuna's maw.

"In the plan, I was—ow!" Glissa yelped as a wiry, melted

treeroot hanging from the inside wall of the lacuna smacked her in the shoulder. "I was alone, and I had time—oof—to call on the energy here!" She flailed, trying without much luck to get a grip on the lacuna wall. The walls were smooth and freshly polished by the heat of an erupting moon, but her claws did come back with a few splinters.

Glissa could make out screams and howls from above as the levelers reached the clearing and cut into the many hapless creatures that had been drawn to the magical energies. The animals reacted as any animals would—by fleeing or fighting back. The result was that many of them were tumbling down the lacuna as well, along with wrecked or unbalanced levelers.

"So? We're still here, huh?" Slobad shouted. "Give a try!"

The goblin had a point, Glissa realized. She was in the heart of the magical field, which was just where she wanted to be. She kicked at the nearby wall, pushed herself closer to the center point of the lacuna, and closed her eyes. This time, instead of imagining the end result of her attack, she focused inward. She visualized the power flow from the spark into her bones, down her arms, to the tips of her claws, the raw energy of the lacuna . . .

Glissa felt flickers of energy crackle down her arm, and opened her eyes in time to see green-white flame erupt from her hands and shoot straight upward. The destructive blast richocheted off the smooth walls of the lacuna, crashing back into itself and creating a maelstrom so bright that anything on the other side was lost. Glissa held her arms upward, ignoring the effect the massive output of magic was having on her rate of speed, rocketing her downward.

The energy was going to carry her past Slobad, but she managed to hook the toe of her boot in his tunic as she blasted downward. The goblin grabbed onto Glissa's shin for dear life as they shot toward the center of the world on a rising plume of fire.

Glissa felt the levelers dying above her, both in the circular tunnel and on the rapidly receding surface. Surrounded by the greenish glow of intense mana residue, the experience made her feel more like a conduit than a destroyer. She felt as if all the magic in the Tangle flowed through a central point in her chest, filtering through her willpower to become ribbons of light that cut into wriggling segmented torsos and slashing, scythe-like blades. She struggled to maintain control.

Half a minute later, the last of the levelers burned out under Glissa's withering assault. As the realization came, she felt the well of energy go dry, and she was once again just an elf falling to her doom. Only now she could expect to find herself under several tons of twisted metal, when she landed.

Wait. Where *would* they land?

"Hey!" Slobad cried through the storm, still clinging to her leg. "We slowing down, huh?"

"What?" Glissa shouted in reply, but realized the goblin was right. The downward pull of gravity wasn't as strong, and their descent was slowing by the second. Fortunately, the ruined leveler army over their heads didn't get any closer. "It must be something affecting everything in here," Glissa said. "Look, the levelers are slowing down too."

"Glissa?"

"Yeah?

"Why we slowing down when I still barely see end of tunnel, huh?"

Glissa craned her neck to look down to the other end of the lacuna, where they would emerge among the towering mycosynth spires in the light of the burning mana core. It was bigger than the pinpoint she'd seen before, but they were still easily as far from the center as they were from the surface.

"That's it!" Glissa shouted. Though the wind whistling in her ears was no longer as loud, the clatter of construct parts tumbling down from above had become almost deafening. "We're reaching the center!"

"No, that down there," Slobad bellowed. "Big ball, remember?"

"I mean the center of the lacuna. It's magic."

"You think?" Slobad asked.

"I mean a big, big enchantment. Something that covers the whole world. Makes it so you can stand on the inside and fall 'down' toward the surface, or—"

"Stand on surface and fall just plain down, huh?" Slobad said. They were drifting like feathers now, almost floating. The wreckage above them had become a slow-moving chaotic swirl, like a handful of sand released underwater. But these grains of sand were jagged, twisted, and occasionally burning. Even if everything dropping down the lacuna came to a stop in midair, which was looking inevitable, it would still leave them floating in a deadly mess of metal with very sharp edges.

"Slobad, we have to get to the wall."

"How?" Slobad asked. "Can't swim through air, huh?"

"If we get there, we can stand. Remember the last lacuna?"

"Right, we run down inside. Been trying to forget that," Slobad said.

"Well, if we can't outrun that falling metal, you're going to forget everything you ever knew, and so am I." Glissa flapped her arms and kicked her legs, trying to get closer to the side of the tube. Slobad yelped and finally let go of her leg. Flare, why had she kicked out to the center in the first place?

Glissa's efforts didn't help much. She got a few inches closer, but it was slow going. She needed a push, but the far side of the lacuna had to be half a mile away.

"Hey, have idea, huh?" Slobad said, floating alongside.

"Watch." He reached up at the nearest hunk of shattered leveler, and pulled himself closer to the wall. Then he caught another piece, carefully, and pushed himself closer, repeating the process. Glissa thought he looked like a bottom-feeding scavenger fish pulling itself along a silvery river bottom. Glissa reached up and grabbed her own hunk of leveler, careful to avoid the sharpest parts, and pushed off, floating after her goblin friend.

"Slobad, your gift for finding obvious solutions is vastly underrated," she said.

As soon as she made contact with the lacuna wall, Glissa felt gravity shift again, this time becoming stronger and pulling her upright—with her feet flat on the wall. A chunk of construct smacked her in the back of the head. "Ow!"

"Duck," Slobad said, a little too late.

"Thanks."

Slobad extended his hands. The left contained a small, sharp piece of metal that looked like a leveler mandible yanked out at the root. In his right he held, point down, a blade that Glissa knew had recently been attached to the forearm of one of the deadly constructs. "Which one you want?" Slobad asked, though Glissa could see his right arm was drooping under the weight of the severed scythe blade.

"The big one, I think." Glissa said diplomatically, and took the proffered weapon. It was a little off balance, but felt surprisingly good in her hand. The blade had not broken off, but had been severed—by what, Glissa couldn't say, but she suspected it had been a piece of fellow leveler—just below the joint of where it had been affixed to the construct's limb, leaving just enough metal to form a hilt. Not perfect by any means, but better than nothing. It would go through Memnarch's chest, and that was the important thing.

"Better do this if we're gonna do it, huh?" Slobad said,

tucking his improvised dagger into his belt and marching off toward the far end of the tunnel. The goblin was going to waste no time getting clear of the remaining leveler wreckage. Glissa set off after him before another of her fallen enemies could get posthumous revenge.

They made good time down the long, cavernous lacuna, though the walk was long. Unlike the older tunnel under Lumen-grid, this one was fresh and free of moisture and muck. Glissa was surprised to see wiry mosses and flaky copper lichens grow-ing bountifully on the lacuna walls, and patches of soft Tangle grass sprang up every few feet.

"Glissa?"

"Yeah?"

"How you going to kill Memnarch, huh?"

Such a simple question, and one she was going to have to answer soon. For now, she replied, "The way I'd kill anyone else that was trying to wipe out everything I know and love."

"That not an answer," Slobad said.

"All right. I don't know. Is that what you want to hear?" Glissa said. "I can try magic, or this 'sword.' Maybe I'll just talk him into taking a flying leap into the Great Furnace. But we've got to do something. I don't know what doing that—" she jerked her thumb in the direction of the clattering wreckage that still unhung suspended in midair behind them—"takes out of me."

"Slobad can see," Slobad said. "You still on fire, huh?"

Glissa looked down at her clothes. A few wisps of persistent greenish smoke still clung to them, and she batted at it with one hand.

Glissa suddenly felt very weary. "I can't keep doing this. I feel so drained," she confessed. Her voice echoed down the tunnel, rebounding around the tube and coming back to her strange and altered. *Drained. Drained. Drained . . .*

That wasn't her voice. The slippery tones rang ominously in her head, a stranger who hadn't been invited. The words slithered through her consciousness, whispering, pleading, threatening and inviting. *Drained* . . .

Glissa shook her head, and the sound faded. Odd. She rubbed her ear with one thumb and jogged to catch up with the goblin.

"Did you hear something?" She asked.

"No, but echo crazy in here," Slobad replied. "Hey, something making no sense, huh?"

"What's that?"

"The levelers, the aerophins, all of it," Slobad explained. "Why attack you on the surface, when this tunnel is wide open? Why not send levelers up the other way, too? Slobad no general, but even I can see that just bad strategy. No need to attack from so far away when good tunnel right here."

"Flare, that hadn't even occurred to me," the elf said. She wished she had an answer.

"Hold up," Glissa said, eyeing the distant end of the lacuna. She could see the swirling anti-color of the mana core crackling at the center of Mirrodin, but nothing else. She had no way of knowing what might be on the other side. The lacuna appeared empty, but Glissa was a hunter. Appearances could deceive.

"What you think, huh?" Slobad asked.

"Flare!" Glissa swore and clenched her fists in frustration. "That's it. So, so stupid." She slapped a hand to her forehead. "They weren't chasing us. They were herding us. He wants me to find him."

"Why? You wanna kill him, huh?" Slobad said. "Why he want you to find him?"

"Because I think it's a trap, and we dropped right into it."

"So why chase Slobad, huh?"

"I don't know," Glissa confessed. "Maybe because you're important to me."

Slobad blushed, blood flushing his greenish face a rusty crimson.

"But he played with us either way," Glissa continued. "He couldn't lose. The levelers—and the aerophins—were sent to either chase me back here, or kill me. Damn Yulyn! If he hadn't taken us in, we could have made sure Memnarch was dead. This might all be over now. We gave Memnarch time to regroup, and he took it."

"But crab-legs blew it, huh?" Slobad said in a transparent attempt to brighten her spirits that failed miserably. "No way to get the spark. The moon was the only way, right? Right?"

"Yeah, sure," Glissa replied, but she wasn't. "Now he just wants me dead. I hope." She slapped a hand on Slobad's shoulder. "Well, what do you say? Should we go check out this track, or try to get back up through that floating deathtrap?"

Slobad cinched up his belt, puffed his chest, and grimaced. "One second," he said, then reared back and released a long, lingering belch that echoed through the lacuna. "Sorry. Ate too much elf food," he said when he saw Glissa's incredulous look. "Onward, huh? Don't want to stick around here."

"Slobad, I can't imagine why you lived alone when I met you."

"That nothing, huh? You stop by the Feast of Krark sometime—you see the real talent."

* * * * *

The lower half of the lacuna took a while longer to traverse than the upper half, but then again, Glissa and Slobad were no longer plummeting. The elf girl was surprised to see small animals dashing and hiding amongst the brill moss and razor grass. She wondered if they'd been spontaneously summoned by the magic that still hung thick in the air, or if the little creatures had overcome fear of the unknown to colonize this strange new home. Some she recognized immediately, but a few were peculiar. Denizens of the interior, perhaps.

Odd to think of the ground she had walked and hunted for so many years was only a silver eggshell surrounding a very large yolk, and she was reminded of the flare-vision that had struck her when they first arrived at Viridia.

"You know," Glissa said, "I think we might be paranoid after all. We're almost through. If he doesn't try something soon, we won't be cornered anymore."

"What, you trying to get us killed?" Slobad hissed just ahead of her. "Don't crazy elves know anything about bad luck, huh? Jinxes?"

"Sorry," Glissa said. "Just thinking out—"

She froze in mid-sentence when a tall, humanoid figure materialized from thin air at the edge of the lacuna, maybe twenty feet in front of them. The glare from the mana core—what Slobad's people, especially his friends in the Krark cult, referred to as "Mother's Heart"—obscured the figure's features and face, but a corona of silver outlined the shape. Slobad skidded to a halt and had his mandible-dagger drawn before Glissa could say a word.

"It's him, Glissa!" Slobad hissed.

Glissa brandished her makeshift scimitar. "What do you want, Malil? You're in my way, and you don't want to be, trust me." She hoped the stolen leveler's scythe blade looked menacing as she added, "I'm here for Memnarch."

The metal man's response was unexpected as it was perplexing. He tossed his head back and laughed. The sound was tinny, and betrayed something that bordered on mania.

"Oh, you're 'here for Memnarch,' is it?" Malil sneered, and stepped a few feet into the lacuna toward Glissa and Slobad. "You are right. Just not the way you think." Memnarch's lieutenant raised his right arm with a clenched fist, and flicked his silver hand at the wrist. In less than a second, a blade that rivaled Glissa's stolen weapon slid into place, extending from the metal man's forearm. The quicksilver blade glowed faintly in the dim light of the lacuna.

It seemed like ages since someone had challenged her to a fair fight, and Glissa was sick of battling armies, judges, and mindless machines. She twirled her weapon and grinned. "Well, why don't you correct me, then?" With her empty hand she threw a subtle wave to Slobad, hoping he would get the message: Stand clear.

Artificial being though he might have been, Malil was easily goaded. With a metallic roar, he charged, the blade that his right arm had become raised high.

Glissa once again focused on the spark. Malil was as much an artifact as the levelers. He didn't know what he was getting into. Glissa's inner eye saw the spark, saw magic dancing around it in her heart, and willed destruction at Memnarch's charging lackey.

Nothing happened. Again.

Malil's sword arm whistled through the air at Glissa's skull, and she was able to raise her own weapon in time to deflect most of the blow, though the metal man drew first blood when his blade clipped Glissa's shoulder on its way past her head. The powerful strike threw Glissa off-balance, but she recovered quickly and danced back, tossing her blade back and forth in her hands, taunting her foe. She hadn't wanted to destroy this one quickly, anyway. And it would be good practice for fighting her true enemy.

Glissa waited for Malil to relax slightly then swung in with an uppercut that her enemy blocked easily. She slashed back with the not-quite-balanced ersatz scimitar. She could handle it well enough by instinct, but her specialty was the longsword.

Malil's unreal speed caught her off guard. The elf girl couldn't believe how fast Memnarch's servant was on his feet and with the blade. Malil moved in again, but Glissa caught his sword-arm with her curved blade, spun her arm to envelop the blade, then snapped it back in a disarm move. With an ordinary foe, she might have won then and there, but her attempt only snapped off that end of the quicksliver sword. The rest was still attached to Malil.

"You are here for Memnarch," Malil said as new quicksilver flowed into place in a heartbeat. "You are here for *his* reasons, and to suit *his* purposes. You are here for him. And so are you, goblin."

"Yeah, wanted to ask someone about that. . . ." Slobad began.

"I thought *I* was Daddy's favorite," Glissa said. "He doesn't need the goblin."

Malil and Glissa's duel continued for several minutes with neither gaining a clear advantage. Glissa tried to press the metal man to the lip of the tunnel, hoping to knock Malil off balance long enough for a fatal strike. But Malil turned her attack at the last second and drove Glissa back. Malil matched her strike for strike, parry for parry, and didn't even seem to be breaking a sweat. Not that he would, Glissa supposed.

"How long can you keep this up, elf girl?" Malil taunted as their blades locked and the pair grappled for advantage. "You will tire. I will not."

"You might be surprised," Glissa said. "I get a lot of exercise." She let loose a yell and swung the leveler weapon with all her might at the metal man's abdomen. The blade slid through Malil easily, like a knife through a quicksilverfish, and came out the other side with a slurping sound.

The slash hadn't even left a mark on Malil. One second, he'd been solid, the next he'd been liquid, and it was as if she'd tried to slice the sea in half with an oar. The metal man's chest swirled and solidified before her eyes, and her foe chuckled.

"Oh, I enjoy surprises," Malil said. "Did you like that one?"

"Not so much," Glissa replied, dodging Malil's sudden lunge. How was she going to fight this creature?

That, Glissa thought, was the problem. She was relying too much on this single blade, but she had other weapons: imagination, creativity, her own limbs…and, if she could concentrate for a few seconds, magic. Unfortunately, Malil wasn't going to give her the opportunity to concentrate if he could help it.

Okay then, the limbs. Glissa danced back out of Malil's reach, blocking a strike only if she couldn't dodge it. The metal man pressed what he thought was his advantage, and Glissa soon had to block as many thrusts and slashes as she dodged. She had to try something soon, she thought as the tip of Malil's blade sliced neatly through her cheek. Glissa ignored the sting on the side of her face and made ready. The metal man was definitely close enough now.

Glissa caught Malil off guard as he followed through with an especially ferocious strike, and brought a knee up into his groin. The metal man doubled over and staggered back, stunned, then dropped to all fours, coughing. Guess you're not *all* metal, Glissa mused. She followed up with a boot to Malil's face that knocked him onto his back.

"Surprise," Glissa said.

On a good day, at full strength, she would have followed through and taken Malil's head. But she wasn't sure the blade would work any better on the artificial man's head than it did on his ribs, and she was emotionally and physically exhausted. It was time to make a break for it. If they could get into the interior, they might have a chance. She realized now, though, that facing Memnarch might be suicidal. She was having enough trouble with the Guardian's henchman.

Glissa spared a quick glance at the spot she thought she'd left Slobad—the shape of the lacuna and lack of landmarks outside made it tricky to be sure she was looking at the right place—but the goblin was gone. With one eye on Malil, who was clutching his abdomen with one hand and struggling to get back to his feet, she scanned the inside of the lacuna, trying to find some trace of her goblin friend. Nothing.

"Lose something?" Malil asked.

"Where is he?"

"I told you. He was here for Memnarch. Memnarch has taken him."

"No!" Glissa cried, and rushed the smug, grinning, mockery that had taken her last friend. The ferocity of her attack caught Malil by surprise, and he steadily gave up ground, backing slowly toward the end of the lacuna. Sparks flew as their blades clashed. Still Glissa pressed on, driven by fury. Malil reached the lip of the tunnel and teetered on the edge.

With a yell, Glissa swung the heavy scythe-arm like a hammer, causing Malil to jerk sideways to avoid the blade. The elf girl's leveler scimitar came down on Malil's wrist, and she felt the blade connect with flesh and bone. Yes, definitely not all metal.

The makeshift sword cut clean through her foe's wrist. Malil's sword-hand clanged against the floor, and the blade melted into a puddle of silver. Scarlet blood sprayed from the stump of Malil's wrist, and the metal man gaped in shock. He obviously hadn't expected this, yet he didn't scream. Didn't make a sound, in fact.

"Well, what do you know," Glissa said with a smirk. "Like father, like son."

Malil slowly clamped his remaining hand over the bleeding end of his right forearm, and squeezed. The flow of blood slowed to a trickle. The metal man winced.

Glissa couldn't ask for a better opening than that. She took three steps toward her stunned enemy and drew the scimitar back for a clean cut through Malil's neck. The metal man simply looked up from his stump, smiled, and twitched his intact hand in an imperceptible movement. The elf girl heard a sound like a knife scraping a whetstone, and a second sword-length blade popped into existence, this one extending directly from the stump of Malil's wrist.

Unfortunately for Glissa, by the time the weapon had fully extended, the business end was sticking out of her lower back.

CHAPTER 7

DIVIDED

Since he'd met Glissa, Slobad had been in danger on count-less occasions. The goblin had been shot at, stabbed, cut, singed; gained and lost more friends than he wanted to think about; endured leonin threats and shamanic torture; found himself imprisoned by crazy elves and put on trial for a crime he hadn't even seen, let alone committed; and was once briefly buried under a stump by a giant beetle that had mistaken Slobad for baby food.

The goblin would have rather have gone through all of those experiences, one after another, all over again, than be where he was right now. He wriggled in the iron grip of three strong hands, each big enough to cover the goblin's head. As if to confirm his assessment, a fourth hand clamped over his mouth, forcing him to take deep breaths through his pointed nose. Held fast, Slobad assessed his predicament as best he could.

The goblin had expected some changes, but was stunned to see what had happened to the interior in the short time since the explosion that created the green lacuna. Things had changed, all right, but not for the better. The interior of Mirrodin had gotten noisy. That was the only word for it, Slobad decided. The clanking and clacking of millions of sets of silver legs reverberated weirdly in the atmosphere, scattered by the spires that grew like stalagmites toward Mother's Heart—the seething mana core at the world's center described in the holy Book of Krark. Everywhere Slobad looked, he saw movement, and spotted at least a dozen different varieties of constructs of all shapes and sizes. Millions of living machines climbed up and down the crystalline towers, filling every crack and crevice of the inner surface. It looked to Slobad for all the world like a bug's nest turned inside out, except the smallest of these bugs was still big enough to swallow the average goblin's head in one gulp.

Most were built on the arachnoid model Slobad had grown intimately familiar with in the form of levelers, harvesters, and worse. But the variety and specificity he saw in the design of each one was fascinating. The goblin would have given a bag of fire tubes and might even have thrown in a toe for good measure if he could just get his hands on some tools, break into one of the bizarre creatures, and see how it worked.

Or maybe not. Slobad got a good look at one chittering insect-toid that dashed in along the edge of the lacuna in front of him, and saw it was not entirely metal. Patches on its back and legs showed where pink flesh had replaced cold metal. Just like Bosh, Slobad thought.

The death of his golem friend had almost shaken Slobad's faith in his own peculiar luck, which despite his oft-repeated claim to being cursed always seemed to come through. But Slobad had more immediate concerns than his faltering fortunes. He wasn't in the clutches of a machine—something he might have been able to deal with—but a vedalken warrior. Hundreds of them ringed the edge of the mile-wide hole, standing with what felt to Slobad like palpable anticipation.

There was something very different about the globe-headed villains. For one thing, they had gotten bigger—judging from the one that was holding him aloft in vise-like hands, most were at least fifteen feet tall.

Their increase in size was no more bizarre than their change in appearance. The silvery glass "feesh-boals" the vedalken wore over their natural heads were no longer spheres, but had been replaced by fierce-looking translucent battle helmets topped by a fin-shaped crest. The helmets topped a full suit of armor similarly adorned with sharp fin-blades and unfamiliar runes. The familiar vedalken robes were gone.

They also weren't saying anything, which in his experience with the vedalken was downright inexplicable. The masters of Lumengrid loved the sounds of their own voices. Yet not one of these vedalken had said a word to him. They stood there, clutching wicked-looking hooked spears, breastplates glittering under Mother's Heart.

Were these a different kind of vedalken, some warrior caste he hadn't seen before? Or were these the vedalken he knew, transformed by Memnarch?

And where *was* Memnarch?

Slobad heard a strange, garbled sound like a goblin maiden singing her wedding vows in a tar pit. The giant vedalken holding Slobad in a visegrip tilted the goblin's head upward. Huh, so you're reading minds now, too? the goblin mused.

Of course. Now look, a cold voice sounded inside his skull. Slobad looked. And blinked. He'd been so caught up in the wild variety of machine life he'd missed the enormous, gray-black structure that towered over his head. The Panopticon had seen better days, and looked like it had been welded together by a goblin apprentice—and not a particularly talented one. From his vantage point below, Slobad could really only see the underside of the structure. Four enormous struts, each as tall as the lacuna was wide, supported a ring shape that might have been a platform, but for all the goblin could tell might just be the underside of a huge cylindrical tower. The gaping hole in the center of the ring lined up right over the green lacuna, which had given Slobad and Glissa an unobstructed view of the mana core from inside the tunnel.

Well, not quite unobstructed. Half a mile over his head, the goblin saw a tiny diamond shape, improbably suspended in the exact center of the ring. No struts or lines supported it; it was just there, and almost impossible to make out against the light of Mother's Heart.

"Oh, *there's* Memnarch," Slobad muttered.

* * * * *

Glissa's eyes goggled in surprise as she stared incredulously at the blade that neatly skewered her through the gut. The pain hit, and her makeshift weapon clattered to the floor as she doubled over the blade, flailing at Malil's twisted, bloody stump.

The metal man slid the blade out of Glissa's belly as easily as he had inserted it, and the sword disappeared into his wristbone. The elf girl dropped to her knees, coppery green blood pouring from her wound. It felt like he'd definitely hit an organ. She grasped vainly at Malil, but dizziness soon won out, and the elf girl fell over sideways.

"Do not fear, elf," Malil said calmly. "My master will not allow your death, but you really must stop breaking his playthings." He picked up his severed hand, which lay inches from Glissa's face. She struggled to keep drawing breath, and thrust a fist into her gut to staunch the bleeding as she watched the metal man.

Malil pressed the severed end of his hand into his wrist and whisper a few strange phrases that reminded her of the lilting tongue she'd heard among the spires of Lumengrid. Then a bluish-green glow wrapped around his wrist like a bandage for a few seconds, and dissipated just as quickly. When the spell was done, Malil's hand appeared as good as new.

Glissa knew she was on the verge of passing out, and as soon as she lost enough blood, she would never wake up again. She dragged herself with one hand to Malil's feet. She tried to raise a hand to grab his shin, but the metal man simply stepped back, depriving her of even that last defiant act.

"She is fading, Orland," Malil called over his shoulder. "Be a good minion and bandage her up, won't you?"

Glissa blinked, trying to stay awake. She pushed her fist hard into her gut, amplifying her pain but also her determination to be ready for this Orland when he came for her. She wasn't going down without a fight, and she wasn't going to be Memnarch's tool. It would be better to die here than see the so-called "Guardian" take her spark and use it to spread his madness at will.

Glissa gasped as Orland rose into view at the lip of the lacuna. First, she saw the toe of a black, shiny boot. Then the vedalken swung his bulk over the edge, not unlike a door on a hinge, and he stood towering in front of her. "Vision going fast," she muttered. "No vedalken's that big."

The only answer Glissa got was two vise-like hands that clamped around her shoulders. She couldn't hold back an anguished scream as the giant vedalken jerked her to her feet. She felt warmth spread over her belly as her fist slipped from her open wound and blood began flowing freely again.

Orland didn't say a word, but held Glissa firmly in his upper set of hands. She felt the vedalken's second, lower set of palms press firmly against the entry and exit wounds. Without warning, something flat slithered around her abdomen, binding her wound but not so tightly that the pain made her pass out. She gazed down at her belly and saw wide, silvery cloth encasing her torso. A few spots of blood peppered the cloth, but the bandages seemed to have slowed considerably, if not stopped, the hemorrhaging. The cloth glowed with a faint blue corona.

Glissa's head rolled back, and she stared up at Orland. The helmet that encased the vedalken's head looked more martial than before, and a lot bigger. Slobad would have been able to tuck himself completely inside one of the helmets with ease. As her head bobbed like a child's toy, she mumbled, "Don't you get dizzy up there?"

The helmet cocked to one side.

No.

What the—? Unlike the voice that had taunted her while they were in the Tangle, this one was cold, mechanical, but without a hint of deception to it. Had the word come from the vedalken?

Yes.

You can hear my thoughts, Glissa projected, still fighting the haze in her brain that threatened to consume her.

Obviously. With that, Orland released his grip on her shoulder, and Glissa dropped to the floor like a rag doll, sending new lances of pain jabbing through her gut. The towering vedalken was already heading back out of the lacuna and into the interior.

"Better?" Malil asked innocuously, and kicked her in the side. Glissa moaned pitiably and rolled onto her stomach, hacking up clots of blood. She needed real medical attention soon, or she really was going to die. Now that she'd seen the giant vedalken, the prospect no longer seemed such a favorable option. What good would it be to stop Memnarch's ascension through her own death, if it meant everyone on Mirrodin faced enslavement at the hands of magically mutated vedalken?

"Yes, I thought so," Malil said, and reached down to grab Glissa's ankle.

The elf girl put everything she had left into the kick. Her boot caught Malil squarely in the jaw. The metal man was thrown backward and tumbled over the edge of the lacuna, and disappeared.

Glissa winced and coughed as she struggled to her feet and gave chase. She tripped over her own feet when she reached the edge, and felt a fresh wave of nausea as gravity turned sideways again.

The silent vedalken assembly stood waiting. One who she thought was Orland—she hadn't gotten a good look at him, and frankly they all looked alike to her—broke from the ring of menacing four-armed beings and lunged at Glissa. The elf girl dropped to a crouch when the vedalken was on top of her then came up leading with one shoulder and caught her attacker where his abdomen should be, using Orland's increased weight against him. The vedalken still didn't make a sound as he tumbled into the open lacuna.

"It's a little pointy about halfway down!" she shouted over her shoulder. She didn't know if it was the healing properties of the bandages, or simple adrenaline, but Glissa felt reinvigorated. She clenched one hand into a fist and extended the other palm upward in invitation. "Anyone else?"

She was met with silence, both inside and outside her head. The milky fluid that filled the helmet of the nearest warrior obscured any hint of emotion or intent. If she had to read anything in their behavior, it would have been confusion. They seemed uncertain.

"Glissaaaaaaa!" a familiar voice screamed from directly above. "Heeeelp!"

Glissa searched the dazzling sky above and spotted Slobad and his captor, another huge vedalken. The pair were lazily floating upward toward the center of what looked like a patched-together Panopticon.

"Flare," she swore, and turned back to the looming vedalken, several of which were closing in slowly, obviously wary of being tossed into the pit behind Glissa. "Sorry boys, no time to play."

Hoping they were as slow as they looked, Glissa charged between two of the towering beings.

Malil finally emerged from the lacuna behind her, and bellowed, "After her!"

Glissa wasn't sure exactly where she was going. She couldn't fly—not without help—and even if she could somehow bring Slobad down safely, the goblin would be in even more danger once he hit the ground. She hopped and danced around dozens of small, skittering artifact creatures that had not been here the last time. Why did Memnarch need millions of diminutive constructs? Why now?

The elf girl ducked as a heavy, three-fingered hand swiped overhead. The vedalken were right on her tail. She skidded around the wide base of a mycosynth spire and almost collided head-on with a wall of iron.

No, not a wall . . . a leg. Her eyes ran up the length of the flat black tower, one of four holding up the massive black ring overhead.

"Oof!" Glissa grunted as a fist connected with the small of her back, where Malil's blade had skewered her, and she slammed face first into the massive support strut holding up one quarter of the rebuilt Panopticon. Despite the blinding pain, it was exactly where she wanted to be. She dug into the iron surface with the claws at the end of each hand, gaining solid purchase, then kicked back like an angry pack animal. She felt a satisfying crash as one foot shattered a vedalken faceplate. She scrambled hand over hand up the side of the mammoth black support strut.

Every time Glissa pulled herself up another few feet, agony pierced her abdomen, but she kept going, ignoring it. She ignored the warm blood that once again flowed from her wounds, and the greenish copper stains that seeped into her bandages. She ignored the ominous hum of vedalken machinery kicking into gear far below, and growing closer by the second.

She craned her neck and caught sight of Slobad and his vedalken captor once again. They were hard to make out against the dazzling energy output of the core, but they were the only things moving up there. She involuntarily groaned and dug in her claws to continue her ascent when a wide shadow fell over Glissa. Keeping one set of talons firmly embedded in the metal, she slowly turned out, one hand in a fist, to see what she could see.

Malil stood before her astride one of the many varieties of vedalken hovercraft with which Glissa had grown far too familiar over the last few weeks. His arms were crossed, and his cold metal features twisted into a smile. The effort to show amusement looked ridiculously awkward on the metal man, but maybe he just hadn't had much practice, Glissa thought deliriously. She was fading fast, again. What little blood she'd had left drained into the soaked bandages around her torso. Her grip was slipping.

"Tell Memnarch . . . he can find his spark somewhere else," she said, and squinted up at the tiny dot that even now moved through the ring above and disappeared against the bright light of Mother's Heart. "Sorry, Slobad," she whispered and let go.

CHAPTER 8

THE CONSCIENCE OF THE KHA

"Please, my Kha, you must hold still," the healer insisted, "I cannot set the bandages if you keep moving. Now please, just breath as steadily as you can, and be patient. Be *my* patient, and behave."

"Only a healer would speak with such impudence," Raksha Golden Cub snarled with a deep growl, and involuntarily sneezed. Glittering green flies buzzed about the tent, causing metallic dust to swirl in the candlelight. The sounds of battle on the plains, no more than half a mile distant, failed to penetrate the enchantments that helped maintained a calm, quiet atmosphere. Though a fighter born and bred, the leonin Kha of Taj Nar was glad for the brief respite from the howling din of war.

Of course, at the moment that respite made him Shonahn's only patient, and his childhood nursemaid felt free to speak her mind—at least, now that the two of them were alone. Shonahn's unusual familiarity would be a gross breach of custom, and a disrespect technically worthy of execution according to ancient law.

Still, he could no more blame Shonahn than he could ever bring himself to punish her for being honest with him. He had almost gotten himself killed.

"If we—ow—if I could . . . breathe steadi . . . ly, I wouldn't be—" Raksha wheezed.

"Hush." The older female placed a paw over the end of the

Golden Cub's mouth. "Only a Kha would give his healer such grief. How long have I looked after his every cut and scrape? Some thirty years?"

"Yes," Raksha managed. "Could you just—?"

"Haven't I always managed to put you back together after these adventures? Remember that time you tried to grow night-blooming razor grass under your bed?" Shonahn's light brown muzzle split into a grin that exposed only the tips of her eyeteeth. "I must have been pulling blades from your haunches for a day and a half," she said, wrapping the last length of silver gauze around the bound wounds that cut across Raksha's chest. The healer closed her golden eyes and purred a soft incantation, and the leonin Kha felt the bandages fixing firmly around his torso. The sharpest of the pain began to ebb away, leeching into the enchanted wrappings. He drew a breath and felt only a tingling where before the pain had been like a thousand razor cuts. The material didn't just help with the pain, it also expanded with his diaphragm as he breathed, and remained fast against his hide, even as he slipped off the side of the bed and straightened to his full imposing height.

"The nim's claws have proven to be quite resistant to our healing magic, my Kha," Shonahn said, flashing teeth in an expression of frustration, "That's why I had to rely on those stitches, by the way, and the bandages. They're of Lumengrid manufacture, I found them on my travels. I ordered several lots for distribution to the healer's corps while I was there. Come to think about it, they're late. But what do you think? They work, do they not?"

"We did not need stitches . . . or vedalken trickery . . . to heal—"

"Yes, you did," the healer interrupted, "And you must listen for a change, my Kha, to your elder. Grant me that courtesy."

Raksha nodded.

"You were unconscious when they brought you in from the battlefield. Every binding spell I attempted simply flashed into nothing. You were bleeding to death. The nim have some enchantment—something—that I can't counter." She turned and busied herself with putting away her medicines. "The bandages are a stopgap measure, and will let your body heal the wound on its own. I despised turning to the slavemongers for aid, but our losses . . . many more warriors will die without this 'vedalken trickery.' " She bowed her head. "My Kha, I must be blunt."

"You usually are."

Shonahn nodded in respect. "You must let Yshkar take command of the troops. You know he desires command, even if he won't tell you directly." Shonahn left her medical kit and placed a hand gently on Raksha's shoulder. "And our people cannot afford to lose you. The bandages can only do so much."

He thanked the gods once more that the old nurse had survived so many campaigns at his side. Her counsel, even when he didn't agree with it, always prompted him to find a better solution on his own. The Kha doubted he'd be the leader he was if not for Shonahn, and her recent return from journeys abroad had been welcome. Though ostensibly a sabbatical, the wise old leonin had acted as an ambassador with some scattered tribes, forming trade pacts with other humans, goblins, and others that had never met a leonin before.

Still, some of her more outlandish claims were best taken with a grain of salt. In her later years, Shonahn had developed a habit of embellishing her stories for effect. Or maybe he'd just started noticing. She claimed to have seen, for example, a pit in the Oxidda Mountains that went all the way to the center of the world.

Whatever her proclivity for fanciful stories, her advice had never steered him wrong. Raksha placed his paw over Shonahn's. "I have already considered it," he said. "But I cannot return to Taj Nar. They drove me back there once."

"But they had help, did they not? These artifact creatures? Please, Kashi," Shonahn pleaded, "Think of your wounds, and your recovery—and the omen."

Raksha bristled slightly at the childhood nickname. "You were right, Shono," he growled, responding in kind and lapsing into less formal speech, "Our people can't afford to lose me. That means I can no more return home than leave this world. Our survival will be decided on these plains, under my watch, though I give immediate control of the troops to Yshkar. Nothing else is acceptable." He added, "As for the omen, you said yourself the seers hadn't been able to determine whether it's even an evil one."

"My Kha," Shonahn insisted, "how could a new sun be a good omen? The very world we stand upon is coming apart!"

"I don't think so," Raksha said, shaking his head. "I can't explain why, but the presence of that green sun—it feels right. The world feels right. Like a great weight has shifted in the sky, bringing everything into balance. I can sense it in my bones. It can only be an omen of victory. It is no disaster."

"Really, that's what you 'feel in your bones,' is it? With all due respect, my Kha, I think it's tied to that Viridian elf girl. The sun did emerge from the Tangle, the elves' homeland." Shonahn made a noise halfway between a growl and a snort. "Has it occurred to you that Ushanti may have been right about her? That this new sun is just the beginning of the end?"

"If it is tied to Glissa, whom I remind you we have called friend," Raksha shot back, "then it can only be a good omen. And Ushanti no longer has my confidence. You know this. We allow you to speak freely, Shon, but we are the Kha. We guard the temple of light and the secrets of the Great Deep. We will fight, and we will survive. If anything, the green sun is a sign that should bring us renewed hope."

The healer sighed. "So should Yshkar begin writing his coronation speech? I can only do so much against this nim necromancy, my Kha," Shonahn said, sidling to the closed tent flap. "You will not heal if you do not rest for at least a week. If you do not heal, you will die. It is that simple. Need I remind you that you have not produced an heir? Your cousin is a noble leonin but proud. He is not ready to rule, but he is ready to lead." The healer crossed her arms across her chest, straightened as best her age-racked body would allow, and locked eyes with Raksha.

The Kha was silent, lost in contemplation. Shonahn stood her ground, cocking her ears curiously. "Very well, Shon," Raksha finally said, "We shall stay off the field. You are right. Yshkar is ready to command them." There, he'd said it. He felt curiously exhilarated and more relaxed, which might just have been the vedalken bandages working their magic.

"He's been ready for months."

"Maybe so. And he's desired command for even longer. But unless our warriors trust his command, it doesn't matter how ready anyone thinks he is," Raksha said calmly as the soothing curative magic diffused through his body. "His performance in this campaign has earned that trust, and that is why he is ready for field command. But this must be taken slowly. If the Kha retreats to Taj Nar and leaves Yshkar in command, morale suffers. You know how soldiers are. The rumors about the 'horrible wounds the Golden Cub suffered at the hands of the fearsome nim' will be back to Taj Nar before we are. And the nim will have won."

"What do you propose?" Shonahn asked expectantly. Raksha could tell that she was beginning to think along the same lines as he was.

"The nim press forward every day. Every hour, the damned Mephidross swallows another few acres of the Glimmervoid. Every minute, another blade of razor grass rusts away into that rot."

"The corrosive properties of the Mephidross aren't exactly something you can change through sheer will," Shonahn said pragmatically. "Nor is Geth. We were mistaken to think he wouldn't raise another army sooner or later. He was only cowed for a time by the elf girl. You have enemies, my Kha, and he's more mercenary than necromancer. He could be working for anyone."

"Unless he's finally acting independently," Raksha said. "The new moon, the leveler attacks, these damned vedalken . . . they've thrown everything up in the air. But it is no matter. If it is him, we shall take his head personally. The more immediate concern is how to stop the things that are spreading the Dross. We've slowed them down, but it's still been one long retreat, ever since the resurgence."

"You don't think Geth is in charge anymore, do you?" Shonahn asked.

"Something's different about them now. They're more organized, they're—they're smarter. A tangled mob of zombies is one thing, an organized army is another matter. This isn't Geth's style." Raksha began to pace slowly in front of the healer, oblivious to the way Shonahn winced with every step he took.

"That still leaves you with a war to fight. This new leader, if he is someone new, will reveal himself in time," Shonahn said. "But if it is the one who sent the machines against you, a change of command may not be enough."

"Shon, we may need you to pull ambassadorial duty again. See if you can get help from any of the human tribes, starting with the Caravaners. If you can find them."

"Yes, my Kha," Shonahn replied. "By your leave, I shall assign my finest apprentice to tend to your health. But what shall you do?"

"The men need to see we're fighting back with our brains as well as our blades. Starting tonight, we stop retreating. We are establishing a field command post. A den away from home where we can plan strategy and house troops, as well as stockpile supplies, weapons, and armor."

"Can you really spare the resources? The men?" Shonahn looked doubtful.

"We don't have a choice. It's either draw the line here, or lose the Glimmervoid to the nim. Taj Nar will never fall," he added with a toothy grin, "but we'll be damned if we going to lose any more of the ancestral plains." Raksha walked gingerly to the tent flap and drew it back slightly, allowing the clamor of battle to suddenly burst into the tent. The Kha's ears twitched, listening to the night. His whiskers detected nothing moving in the blackness. Greenish-silver mist, a foul blend of the dust of the plains and the necrogen atmosphere of the Dross, obscured the distant fighting, but the howling nim and roaring leonin fighters sounded just a little closer than when he had gone into the tent. He twitched his ears and focused his sharp hearing on a particularly violent fight that he should have been leading.

Raksha's ears snapped forward. For a moment, he could have sworn he'd heard a human voice chanting. He vainly scanned the night with feline ears, but the voice, if it had been there at all, was lost in the din of clashing blades and dying warriors.

Despite his promise to Shonahn, he instinctively rested a hand on his sword hilt and waved in one of the guards at the door, a young leonin named Jethrar. The inexperienced warrior somehow simultaneously straightened to attention and ducked awkwardly into the tent, careful not to jab the Kha with the silver battle-scythe clutched in his hand. The warrior was new to the Raksha's guard detail, and was painfully and obviously anxious at being called into an audience with his lord and master.

"Y-yes, my Kha?" Jethrar stuttered.

"We need to speak with Yshkar. Fetch him immediately."

"My Kha, sir, Commander Yshkar is on the front line."

"We know that, Jethrar, we sent him there." Raksha grinned. "We have every confidence in you, warrior." The Kha slipped a slim dagger from his belt and offered the hilt to the youthful guard. The small dagger had been a gift from Yshkar, and carried a moderate morale-boosting enchantment. It would help the young guard's confidence, he knew. "Show him this, and he'll understand the urgency. But do not give him the dagger. That would be an insult. Do you know why?"

"Presenting a weapon to a field commander in the field, even if his life is threatened, symbolizes a lack of confidence. A commander must rely on what he brings with him, for he leads alone," Jethrar said crisply, falling into the military discipline of the well-trained leonin warrior.

"Correct, Jethrar," Raksha said. "But remember also that only a fool refuses an ally. You want to know a secret?"

"Er, of course, my Kha," Jethrar stammered.

"The prohibition against giving weapons to field commanders arose long ago, before Great Dakan united the tribes of leonin," Raksha said.

"Yes, my Kha."

"Be quiet and listen. It started as a competition among the strongest fighters of tribes at war, who led those tribes. Our people knew the futility of waging all-out war against their own kind even before Dakan, and these leaders, champions, settled disputes between tribes one-on-one. It saved a lot of lives."

"Yes, I imagine so, my Kha."

"Any leonin champion who accepted help from anyone in such a contest was disgraced. The fight would end immediately, and the rulebreaker would forfeit. But not only did he lose the fight, he dishonored his tribe. The only way to redeem themselves was to tear their own champion apart with their bared claws," Raksha said. "It was a fine system. Do you understand why we tell you all this, Jethrar?"

"To, er . . . educate me, my Kha?"

"Yes . . ."

"In the history of our people?"

"Not exactly," the Kha said, smiling. "We tell you this for two reasons: First, you must realize that some of our proud traditions have a reason very different from what you have been taught."

"And the second, my Kha?" Jethrar asked nervously.

"Traditions are made to be broken," Raksha said. "Yshkar adheres rigidly to our traditions, but if you ever see him surrounded by nim without a weapon in sight, toss him a scimitar."

"Thank you, my Kha," Jethrar said. "What should I do after delivering your message, my Kha?"

"Well, sticking that dagger into the nearest nim would be a good start," Raksha replied. "Point the sharp end away from you."

"Yes sir!" Jethrar said, eyes flashing, and he turned to leave. He opened the tent flap and promptly collided with a blonde human female clad in silver and aquamarine robes. Her skin bore a metallic tinge of cerulean, and she carried an air of authority. The strange human stepped calmly into the tent as if it were her own.

Raksha, stunned by the intrusion but not yet feeling threatened, placed a hand on his sword hilt. "Who dares enter the our presence? How did you gain entry to our camp? Are you a friend, or an enemy?" he asked.

"A friend of a friend," the human woman said. "I am Bruenna, I have traveled here by magical means. Glissa needs your help."

Raksha had not expected to hear that name again soon. Glissa had left Taj Nar a friend of the leonin, but he could not help but blame her in part for Rishan's death. Still, the elf was courageous, and the Kha did not give his friendship lightly or retract it without an honorable reason.

"First, tell us how you got here," Raksha said. "Then we shall hear what you have to say."

"Magic. I used a teleportation spell," the woman explained. "Your perimeter is secure, I assure you. I regret I don't have time to greet you with the protocol due a regent of your stature, Raksha Golden Cub, Kha of Taj Nar. But my business is of the utmost—"

With a roar, Jethrar leaped to his feet and stepped between Raksha and the newcomers, battle-scythe at the ready. "You will leave at once!" the guard bellowed. "The Kha's presence is invio—"

The robed woman raised a hand and traced an ornate pattern in the air. Jethrar froze in mid-sentence. Raksha opened his mouth to ask what the mage had done to his guard, when he saw that Shonahn, too, was completely still. In fact, neither she nor Jethrar appeared to be breathing. Only the human moved as she calmly advanced on the Kha.

Raksha's sword was in his hand in a flash, causing the robed woman to stop short. "What did you do?" he demanded.

"Stopped time, briefly," the mage explained. "Forgive me, but I must speak to you without interruptions."

"You claim to know Glissa? Why should we believe you, wizard? Why should we not cut you down where you stand?" Raksha snarled, brandishing his sword menacingly.

The human woman stood her ground. "Bring her in," she

called over her shoulder, and the tent flap parted to reveal a young elf girl wearing a patch over one eye and an ornate slagwurm breastplate carved with intricate runes. In her arms she held a still, familiar form. The girl's resemblance to the unconscious woman she held was unmistakeable. Sisters, Raksha guessed.

"Glissa," the Kha whispered. "What happened to your eye?"

"This is Lyese, Tel-Jilad Chosen and Glissa's sister," Bruenna said, and raised her hands, palms upward. "The unconscious one is Glissa. I was able to magically retrieve her from . . . a perilous situation. But I am no healer. I got her out, but I don't know if I can keep her alive."

Raksha sighed, and sheathed his weapon. "Very well. But you shall have to let time commence, human. The finest healer in the Glimmervoid is standing right over there, but she can't hear a word you're saying."

CHAPTER 9

FAMILY MATTERS

"Slobad!" Glissa cried, sitting bolt upright on the cot. She couldn't see a thing, and for a moment she thought she was back in the Prison Tree. Then sensation returned in a rush, and the elf girl gasped. Someone was pressing a cool, damp cloth against her forehead, which was why she couldn't see.

"There, there," a soft, purring voice whispered in her ear. The accent and dialect were leonin, and probably female, though it was difficult to be sure. Glissa felt a warm feeling of safety wash over her being as the voice began a soothing chant, and the elf girl relaxed a bit.

"Where am I?" she asked.

"The private quarters of the Kha," a deep, familiar voice rumbled. The chanting leonin lifted the cool cloth from her eyes. Glissa sat on a cot made of soft djeeruk leather inside a cavernous room—no, a tent, she corrected herself when she saw one "wall" wafting in the wind. Four small firetubes lit the room, dimly illuminating three figures that jumped from their seats at a table not far away and dashed to her side. Raksha Golden Cub, wearing fresh bandages like the one around Glissa's own wound, moved slowest of the trio, or perhaps that was his regal demeanor in action—a king. A king does not arrive anywhere first.

Bruenna wore a look of relief, and Lyese, Glissa was

somewhat relieved to see, had a grin a mile wide. Her sister's attitude seemed to have improved since she last saw her.

"How did I get here?" Glissa asked.

"The connection between siblings allows many forms of magic to work over long dista—" Bruenna began but was cut off by Lyese.

"Glissa!" gasped her sister, and she launched into a rapidfire recount of the events that had brought them all back together. "It was me! We were almost here—we had to walk after a while, Bruenna needed to regain her strength, I guess. When you were in trouble, I heard you, or felt you, or something. It's hard to explain. Then Bruenna used *me* finding *you* to find where to focus her magic, and then she cast this teleportation thing that made all my hair stand up on end, and there you were!"

Lyese sounded very much like the excitable youth Glissa had left behind only weeks ago. She a hand tentatively on Glissa's shoulder. "Glissa, I'm so glad you're okay. I'm sorry I blamed you for—I'm just sorry. It wasn't your fault. None of it is." Glissa gaped. Lyese hadn't just had a change of heart, she'd had some kind of magical epiphany.

"Among the Neurok, close family can often feel each other's strong emotions over long distances," Bruenna offered. "Perhaps you experienced something similar, Lyese."

The chanting leonin healer standing nearby had obviously not gotten to her abdominal wound yet. Glissa held her sister's hand for a few seconds then gently pushed her away.

"Lyese," Glissa said, clutching her temple in one clawed hand and unable to disguise the irritation she suddenly felt welling up. A brand new headache that had set up shop in her temple didn't help matters. "You were supposed to come straight here. What were you thinking?"

Lyese looked as if she'd been slapped in the face.

"I can't believe you. All right, next time, I'll just let you die," Lyese said. "Follow your example. Won't even try to help somebody who's *shouting in my brain*."

Okay, maybe Glissa had misplayed this. She clenched her fists and rose from the cot, feeling her own temper rising as her health returned. "Do you really want to do this now?" Glissa asked, taking a slow step toward her sister, and before her brain thought better of it, added, "I thought we were past this. Just grow up, will you?"

"Way ahead of you," Lyese said bitterly. She flipped up her eyepatch, revealing an empty red pit. Glissa involuntarily gasped. "Take a good long look, sister. I grew up fast."

"The healer—maybe she can help," Glissa said.

"She tried," Lyese said. "Nothing works. Magic cauterization or something."

"I spoke out of line. I'm sorry," Glissa began. "Sorry for everything. Everything that's happened, and my part in it. If that makes you hate me even more, fine. And I'm grateful you saved me. That was…incredibly brave. I *was* scared, and I had given up hope. Thank you."

Lyese eyed Glissa incredulously. "I—you're welcome," she said at last.

"It was still dangerous," Glissa added.

"That didn't scare me," Lyese said.

"No, but it should," Glissa said. "We're all we've got left, Lyese. You and me. And our friends," she added, indicating the others in the tent. "But please, just promise me something."

"What?"

"Don't play games with your life again. Even to save me," Glissa said.

"I can't do that, Glissa," Lyese said. "And I don't . . . I don't hate you."

"I know," Glissa said. "And I know you're probably not going to listen to me. But I had to ask."

Lyese's look flashed to concern. "Slobad! What happened to him?"

"Slobad? What has become of our old friend?" Raksha interrupted, his ears pinned against his skull in a display of alarm that surprised Glissa, who had been under the impression the Kha thought of Slobad as little more than an ex-slave with keen mechanical talents. The leonin spun Lyese around by the shoulders none too gently. "Speak, elfling!"

"Easy, your Kha-ness," Glissa said, placing a hand on the leonin's chest and shoving him back. Raksha was so surprised he only looked from her hand to his chest and back. "Haven't you been listening? Don't jump to conclusions."

"Strange things are indeed afoot, my Kha," Bruenna said. "We must all remain more open-minded."

"You shoved me," Raksha said.

"She doesn't know what happened to Slobad," Glissa said, "So back down."

"You *shoved* me," the Kha repeated.

"Raksha, you can execute me later. When this is all over, you can bring me up in front of Great Dakan himself and have my entrails read for prophecies. But right now, just . . . lay off my sister. You're asking the wrong elf."

Raksha's ears twitched, but he muttered, "Certainly."

"Okay. One of the vedalken took Slobad," Glissa said.

"Took him? Why not just kill him?" Raksha asked.

"Because as it turns out, I'm not the only one Memnarch was after," Glissa said.

* * * * *

Battered, cut, and bruised, Glissa stalked the floor in the dim candlelight that glittered around the silver tent. She reminded Raksha of a skyhunter. Indeed, she'd taken to the pterons readily enough when he first met the Viridian elf, though she still needed work on landings. Perhaps there would be a place for her at Taj Nar, if what she wanted him to believe was true.

It didn't take long for Glissa to get through the rest of her tale—how she and Slobad had fared after leaving Taj Nar. Raksha was stunned. An entire world beneath his feet; a madman at the center of it all. The Kha had always considered himself well-traveled. Indeed, the historians assured him he had ranged wider and farther in his conquests and exploration than any Kha for a thousand years. Yet it seemed there was much about Mirrodin that he had never reckoned. He wondered bitterly how much of this truth Glissa now related to him had been kept back by Ushanti over the years. He and his seer would be having a long talk when he returned to Taj Nar.

If he returned to Taj Nar. Glissa's story of her travails with Memnarch, from the Guardian's plan to ascend to godhood to the knowledge that nothing on Mirrodin was native to the metallic plane had dashed most of the beliefs Raksha had ever held sacred. For the first time in decades, the Golden Cub began to doubt that the nim were the worst things fate had to throw at him.

They were the only two still awake—the Kha had dispatched a battered but still confident Jethrar to retrieve Yshkar from the front lines and left Shonahn to treat another wave of wounded. Bruenna and Lyese were both asleep on the far side of his spacious quarters. The pair needed the rest, and with a full company of Raksha's personal guard standing watch outside, they finally felt safe to do so. The Kha could still clearly hear fighting far off on the razor plains.

"Shonahn knows far more than we do on the subject," Raksha

said, "But my people also have legends of a world inside the world. Dakan called it Tav Rakshan."

"Tav Rakshan?" Glissa asked, arching one slim green eyebrow.

"Rakshan means Hall of the Eternal Sun."

"So your name is really 'Eternal Sun Golden Cub?' " Glissa asked.

"Raksha is a family name. It's literally 'Lord of the Eternal Sun Golden Cub,' if you must know. That is beside the point, however."

"I wonder what elves would remember if we could?" Glissa thought out loud.

"The generational memory cleansing. You told us of this. It strikes us as rather unwise," Raksha said. "But these troll-creatures had actual written records?"

"No, I said they used to. Chunth erased them so I—so we, the elves, wouldn't know the truth," Glissa said.

"You described this Chunth as an ally who fell bravely in battle," Raksha protested. "Why did he hide the truth from you?"

"I guess he never thought someone like me would come along," Glissa said. "By the time Chunth figured out the role Memnarch wanted me to play in his scenario, all he had time to do was save me."

They sat silently for a moment. Glissa idly twirled a strand of rope of her black-emerald hair at the end of a claw, and seemed to become intimately intrigued with the fine decorative patterns that ringed the lightweight folding table. Raksha smoothed his whiskers with one paw and coughed.

"This lacuna…it is still there? In the Tangle?" Raksha asked and rose from his chair.

"It's there all right." Glissa nodded.

"That explains the new sun—"

"Moon."

"—the new sun," Raksha continued with mild irritation, "It's not an omen, or a sign."

"No," Glissa said, "It was an eruption. I suppose you could call it part of the natural process of things. The core just couldn't stay out of balance like that." Her eyes flashed with anger. "The lacuna, and the new moon—"

"Sun."

"—the big green ball in the sky are just raw energy, like the core. It's pure mana, and it doesn't have a conscience. But that power, in the hands of Memnarch—that could have been the end, right there. That's your bad omen . . . or a warning."

Raksha returned with two mugs of steaming oil that smelled somewhat like well-aged *nush* and offered one to Glissa. "Thanks," she said, and took the heavy iron container in both hands, balancing it on her knees.

Raksha remained on his feet as habit took over and he paced the interior of his tent. "Why didn't the explosion kill this Memnarch as well?"

"I don't know," Glissa said. "Protective magic? A big mirror? Dumb luck? My *bad* luck? How isn't important right now, but we'll find out. Still, at the time Slobad and I thought it *had* killed him. The blast flattened a few square miles of the Tangle. It killed hundreds, maybe thousands of creatures from what I could see. It did *this* to my hair. And the elves..." She took a deep breath, and her voice became cold. "Yulyn mentioned that dozens of elves disappeared when it happened. No elves have ever lived close to the Radix, but anyone who was in the Tangle when the lacuna blew open must be dead. It's the only explanation."

"But also dead are those armies of artifacts," Raksha said. "You destroyed them. Had we not already witnessed this power of yours firsthand, we would doubt your claim."

"The inside was crawling with them, though. Some kinds I'd never seen. Some looked like normal animals, but entirely metal. I don't know how he's making them, or even *if* he's making them, but it looked like he had plenty of company down there. And yes, I do seem to have some kind of ability, but it doesn't always work. It drains me."

"What do you think might have happened to the goblin?" Raksha asked.

"Isn't it obvious?" Glissa said, settling into a soft folding chair in Raksha's tent. "He's going to use Slobad to manipulate me. The little guy's a hostage. And damn it, it's working. I'm feeling pretty manipulated, but I'm still going to save him, Raksha."

"We do not doubt it, Glissa," Raksha replied.

The Kha was glad for this time to speak alone with Glissa. Among all these strange visitors who of late kept turning his well-ordered, albeit violent, world upside down, he trusted her the most. What's more, he liked her, for an elf. The two of them were bound by a common enemy that had singled out each of them for death—he too had been attacked by Memnarch's machines the night Glissa's family was killed, though he'd heretofore thought the vedalkens were behind the plot. Yet for some reason, Memnarch and his vedalken minions had sent no more cursed artifact beasts to attack Taj Nar once the elf girl had departed. Glissa claimed it was her special power, this "spark" that Memnarch desired, that made all the difference.

Raksha didn't like being attacked by mysterious forces he didn't understand. But to be attacked, and somehow found not worthy of the fight, made him hate this Memnarch even more.

Glissa drew on the mug of leonin nush and stared into the sparkiron coals burning in a small pit in the center of the tent. The flammable metal, a common enough substance all over Mirrodin, crackled as a bit of oil dripped off the small game animal Raksha was preparing on a spit. The leonin Kha followed Glissa's eyes as she watched a tiny orange spark flutter up the column of heat, through a vent, and into the night sky. In moments the cinder had joined the thousands upon thousands that filled the heavens.

"Forgive me," Raksha's baritone rumbled. As the drink soothed his nerves, he slipped again into a more informal tone. "The last few weeks have been hectic. Violent. I've lost too many men, and the leonin need to make a stand soon, before we're fighting the nim at our front door again. I do not like being cornered. I do not like to lose warriors or friends."

"Rishan." Glissa spoke the name that Raksha could still not bring to his lips without breaking his composure. "Sorry, I'd—I'd forgotten. Slobad used to tell me how he thought he'd been jinxed. Thought he was a jinx. But I guess I'm the one who's really bad luck, huh?"

Raksha turned, wincing as the bandages moved with him and made his chest feel like a pincushion again. "You are not responsible for Rishan's death," he whispered, choking slightly on the name of his lost beloved, the seer Ushanti's daughter. "And despite what you say, I doubt you caused Slobad's either." He raised his iron mug. "To the lost. And the missing."

Glissa lifted her mug in two hands. "The lost. And those who will be found." They drank, and passed the next half-minute in silence.

The moment shattered with the clamor of scattered skirmishes that still rang in the distance. Jethrar appeared at the entrance to Raksha's tent. Behind him stood Raksha's cousin Yshkar, an imposing figure in burnished silver armor plate that like the rest of him was spattered with alternating patterns of green and red blood. The green came from the nim—it was too light to be Viridian. Fortunately.

"My Kha, sir! Reporting as ordered, with Commander—" Jethrar began. Yshkar unceremoniously pushed his way past the young guard and came muzzle-to-muzzle with Raksha.

"What is it, Kashi? I'm needed on the front!" Raksha's cousin roared.

Raksha's reaction was immediate and painful for his impertinent cousin. The backhand caught the commander across the right jaw and knocked him back into the hapless Jethrar, who fell backward out of the tent. Yshkar stayed light on his feet and kept his balance, hissing, but the younger leonin turned his ears forward and bowed his head slightly—body language that told Raksha he'd made his point clear to his cousin. Such language from a subordinate was intolerable.

"You, Kyshka, are required where and when your Kha says you are required," Raksha growled, the menace rising in his voice. "You're also blood, and that means we trust you, even if we don't particularly like you. We trust your nature, which is as honorable as ours. You are impulsive. You are headstrong. You are not yet the finest commander in the field, but you will be."

"My Kha!" Yshkar snarled, and dropped to one knee, head still bowed. "My blood is still hot with battle. Forgive you humble kin. I serve Taj Nar and the Golden Cub. What is it you will of me?"

Raksha grinned. "Don't overdo it, Kysh."

Yshkar looked up and noticed Glissa, who watched the scene over her mug with an arched eyebrow. The commander's fur bristled along the back of his neck, and his inner ears blushed a rusty red. He shoved off one knee and returned to his feet. "All right, we're even, my Kha. Yet still I stand ready to serve."

"Good," Raksha said and indicated Glissa, who set her glass on the floor and made to rise. "No, please, stay where you are. You are a guest in the Kha's home. Yshkar, meet Glissa of the

Tangle. The human is her ally, the younger elf her sister. Glissa brings news that makes what we're about to tell you even more important than it was when we sent for you."

"My cousin, always direct and to the point." Yshkar smirked. Raksha raised a lip and exposed a few teeth, and the smirk disappeared.

"You're fortunate we value your independent spirit as much as our blood kinship, commander. That as much as anything is why you've earned a promotion to general." Yshkar's jaw dropped.

"My Kha, the leonin armies have but one general," Raksha's cousin said. "You. Are you—?" The meaning of the bandages wrapped around the Kha's golden torso finally sank in.

"We have been ordered by the royal physician to leave active duty for at least a week. But just because the Kha cannot fight on the field does not mean he is not fighting. We're going to hew a line in the grass, and establish a permanent field command that will be our den home fortress until we beat these foul things back into their nests. But you will have to be the Kha's adjunct on the battlefield."

"My Kha, I am ready to serve," Yshkar said.

"Excuse me, your Kha," Glissa said, "but there are a few things you need to know before you begin planning your defenses."

"Of course," Raksha said. "Yshkar, we'll explain all of this later. For now, you're free to return to the front. Spread word among the field commanders that we will soon be moving out, but do not make it sound like a retreat." Then, in a casual move that belied the act's importance, he drew his sword and offered it blade-first to Yshkar. The younger leonin removed his gauntlets and clutched the blade with his naked paws, squeezing until blood welled up. With a snarl, he pulled the sword smoothly from Raksha's paws, still holding it by the blade, which was now dripping silvery scarlet onto the tent floor. Without wiping either the blade or his own paws clean, Yshkar slid the sword into his own belt and replaced his gauntlets.

"The blood drives us. The blood of the Kha unites us," Yshkar said. The bloodstained blade would leave no doubt about his cousin's promotion to general.

Raksha felt naked. But he hid it well.

"So tell me about this fortification," Yshkar said, flashing a toothy, conspiratorial grin.

"Not yet," Raksha said, showing his teeth in return. "Remain in contact with the runners, and await word from your Kha." He cocked his head, thinking, and added, "It will not be long. Fight well, General."

"Yes, my Kha," Yshkar nodded, then whirled on one padded foot and strode purposefully outside, casting a glance over his shoulder at Glissa as he slipped through the tent flap.

"Charm runs in the family, I see," Glissa said.

"He is impertinent, and you are lucky you're an elf and not one of our subjects."

"Raksha, I know I promised I wouldn't return until it was safe to do so. But I didn't know where else to go." Glissa bowed her head respectfully. "I really thought I was a goner, but they got me out. And now you're giving us a chance. Thank you for your help."

"It is good to speak with you again, Glissa of the Tangle. No more apologies. The past is the past. The only part of that past that concerns us is your story, and what we're going to do next," Raksha assured her. "One thing is certain, my forces must soon fall back to a more defensible, permanent position."

"They've really been giving you the sharp end, haven't they?" Glissa asked. "The Mephidross, I saw it from above. Is it bigger? Mind you, I never knew how big it was in the first place, but—"

"You are observant," Raksha said. "The Mephidross had

consumed our ancestral plains at a pace unheard of since the days of Great Dakan. It hasn't just gotten bigger—it's the nim. They're a disease, spreading the Dross like a plague on this land. They're not fighting like the nim we know, they're smarter. Faster. Do you have any idea why that might be?"

Glissa appeared to bristle. "No," she said, "I don't." She gazed upward, remembering. "I thought we'd beaten them back before I left for the interior. But believe me, Golden Cub, we've got bigger problems than just the nim."

"We believe you. Yet they are still a problem," Raksha said. "Our problem."

"Look," Glissa said, getting back to her feet, "I thought the four of—the three of us might get some help here. Maybe the goblins. Or humans. There have got to be some around here—"

"Please," Raksha laughed. "We get your point. Arguing which threat is greater is fruitless. We must deal with them both. We have been quick of temper these last days, and regret implying in any way that you had something to do with the nim's resurgence." He ran a hand through his wiry mane, and growled deep in his throat. "We've been on the retreat for weeks. After beating them back only to have them come back so soon, and so strong—this is unprecedented."

Glissa smiled sympathetically. "Your nerves are shot."

"Our courage has been tested. Our nerves are steel." He grinned, fangs glistening in the dim light.

"Right," Glissa said, and took a pull of the oily not-nush. She held up her mug and examined the bottom. "What's this stuff made out of, anyway?" she asked.

"Razor grass and thresher oil, we think," Raksha said with a grimace. "The soldiers brew it when they're away from Taj Nar. It isn't practical to travel with a lot of heavy fluids."

"Not bad," Glissa said, and coughed. "Don't know if I want to make a habit of it." She shifted her position forward and rested the mug on the woven metal fibers of the tent floor. "Raksha, I know my last visit didn't end . . . well."

"That is the past, Viridian. You must let the matter rest, as we have. Rishan is with the gods, and her mother has fallen out of our favor. Perhaps you did not understand the significance of our friendship. The friendship of the leonin Kha is the friendship of the leonin people. Rishan's death is not on your hands, nor is it on mine. Nor," Raksha added with conviction, "is Slobad's capture your fault."

"I let him out of my sight. I should never have done that. He's so—he was so—is so—small . . ."

"We have known that goblin much longer than you have, Glissa. He is no weakling, and his size is no indication of his ability. Over the years, I have counted him lost several times, and he has always returned to Taj Nar, looking for more work, eager to share tales of his latest misadventure."

"What's that supposed to mean?"

"It means," Raksha growled through a toothy grin, "that you shouldn't count him out just yet. From what you have told me, that lacuna is very deep. And Slobad, though he is many things, is a survivor above all." He stood and bowed his head to the elf girl. "Now please. Sleep. You shall have the royal cot," Raksha said, "and we shall curl up on the rug and sleep in front of the fire."

"Really?" Glissa said, and Raksha could tell she was forming a mental image of the Kha rolled into a ball and purring like a domesticated tanglecat.

Raksha winked. "No, not really. Spare bedroll. Just wanted to see if you were paying attention. Good night, Glissa of the Tangle. Tomorrow, we will make plans. You shall help us, and we shall help you. But for now, sleep."

CHAPTER 10

GOBLIN IN THE MACHINE

Every bone in Slobad's body ached. It was a mixed blessing that he was in too much agony to care much about something as minor as aches.

He didn't know what was worse—being captured by Memnarch, or watching helplessly as Glissa plummeted to her doom. At least she was getting some peace. Slobad wished he'd been able to follow her on that last adventure, and while he mourned his only friend, he also envied her. Death would be preferable to his current predicament. But the goblin's fierce survival instinct was still keeping him alive in spite of himself. Instinct, and Memnarch's twisted form of "mercy."

Now he was on his own again. No one for Slobad to rely on but Slobad. And this time that probably wouldn't be enough.

The goblin hung spread-eagled in an iron torture rack of some kind mounted on one inner wall of what had once been the Panopticon. The rack had obviously been designed with larger victims in mind. The thing was big enough to hold a vedalken— one of the new, augmented vedalken big enough to go toe-to-toe with a golem. Short chains shackled Slobad's wrists to the top of the rack, while his feet were bound to either corner. He was left swinging lazily in the chains like a fly in a spider's web. He'd been stripped of possessions and clothing.

Before him, the Guardian of Mirrodin paced, displaying great agitation. The bulbous serum tanks strapped to his carapace sloshed noisily, only half full. Slobad noted with bitter pleasure that Memnarch limped and still wore silver bandages over patches of new flesh. Two of his eyes looked milky and half formed.

"It thinks it can resist us, my Creator," Memnarch said to the sky. "It has much to learn. Malil will show it the error of resistance to the inevitable." The Guardian's six eyes—including the two fresh ones—flashed with hatred, and instantly a second metal man stepped into the chamber from the shadows. Slobad recognized this one, too. Memnarch clackety-clacked away, giving his lieutenant room to work. Slobad saw that the smaller of the pair also bore scars of new flesh.

"Goblin," Malil said, "you will tell me what I wish to know. The whereabouts of Glissa, please." Without warning, he slammed a cruel backhand across Slobad's face.

Slobad couldn't understand what they hoped to achieve, let alone why Memnarch seemed to be having a conversation with an invisible 'creator,' but the goblin wasn't about to dishonor Glissa's memory with betrayal. He spat warm blood and a rusty tooth at Malil's feet, and raised his head to meet the metal man eye-to-eye. "You outh of your mind," he groaned. "Glitha'th dead. You looth. No big thpark for you, huh?" Slobad chuckled, and winced. He had two fat lips, and at least one broken rib. Stupid vedalken, with their stupid gigantic hands. No finesse at all. Finesse was important. If not for finesse with machines, Slobad would have been dead long ago.

"Yes, we should have increased the safeguards, kept this goblin filth clear of the perfect world, my Creator," Memnarch said, continuing his apparently one-sided conversation. "They are rather disgusting, and obviously only capable of imitating sentience. Mountain vermin." The Guardian laughed at something only he could hear.

"The elf girl," Malil snapped again.

"I know tho many, huh?" Slobad said through his battered mouth. "Those elfth girlth lovfe goblinth, huh? Whith one ya want?" He closed his eyes and awaited the next blow.

The blow never came. Instead, Malil turned the crank attached to the rack one full revolution.

Slobad screamed as he felt the sickening snaps of his right, then his left shoulder forcibly separating from the sockets. He felt something pop in each knee, and his lower legs went mercifully numb. If they were still attached, he thought. Through the blinding agony, the gears of Slobad's unusually analytical mind—unusual for a goblin—continued to turn. It dawned on him with sickening certainty that the only thing holding him in one piece was his skin and muscles, stretched almost to the breaking point themselves.

His cries reverberated inside the indestructible Eye, ringing back into Slobad's bleeding ears.

After what felt like hours but was probably only a few seconds, Malil released the cranks, which let a little slack return to the chains that suspended the goblin. Slobad whimpered. "Wathtin'…time," he coughed. "You can't get her. You only got Thlobad, huh? Believfe me. Glitha outh ofth your reaf now."

"I assure you she is alive," Malil said simply. "Do you doubt the Guardian?" The metal man followed the question with a punch to the belly, which made Slobad lose what was left of his last meal in a green spray that spattered Malil's gleaming exterior.

"That'th what—urp—I thinkth of the Thaurdian, thuh?" Slobad said, and passed out.

* * * * *

"Strange little vermin," Malil said. "But highly resistant to torture."

"This one is different, my Creator," Memnarch said. "You have sent him to us, as you sent the elf girl. We shall make good use of him. Once Malil has his fun."

"Fun? I merely—"

"It denies, denies, denies the cruel streak," Memnarch said. "But not matter, my Creator. As you say, we do not really need any information from the mountain vermin."

"His perceptions are ours to control?" Malil asked. It was difficult trying to speak to the master sometimes. More accurately, all the time.

"The device is truly wondrous in design, Karn," Memnarch said. "The goblin will serve its purpose perfectly."

"But master, I do not understand the purpose," Malil confessed.

Memnarch locked the goblin into the device, sending thousands of tiny needles tipped with a quicksilver anesthetic solution into Slobad's skin. Perhaps it was overkill, Malil supposed, but his master was not about to let this prisoner escape. The Guardian then stepped into a teleportation circle recessed into a far corner of the chamber and disappeared.

Malil took another long look at the goblin. The repulsive creature drew slow, shallow breaths, but was stable. He felt a brief twinge of something his analytical mind identified as jealousy. This ridiculous thing, no more than an animal, really, was more crucial to his master's plan than Malil himself. Memnarch had made it plain that Malil was expendable, beneath notice, yet had taken extraordinary measures to ensure he possessed this goblin, alive. The Guardian had even deigned to personally seal the creature in the torture device.

Malil could not understand it. Nor could he understand why he adjusted the restrictive, hypodermic-lined braces that held the goblin fast, pressing the needles another half-inch into its rusty green hide. Slobad moaned in pain, even in his comatose state.

Malil smiled. He felt better. Curious. There had to be a word for such a feeling of cruel joy at the suffering of one he despised, but he couldn't think of it.

The metal man stepped into the circle and recited the exact incantation Memnarch had used with mechanical precision.

Malil felt a brief hiccup of nonexistence and reappeared on the edge of the green lacuna, beneath the rebuilt Panopticon. The dark-steel frame of the structure had protected them both when the green lacuna was bored out, but he doubted the Panopticon could ever again be the mathematically perfect creation it had once been.

Memnarch stood a few feet away, staring into the long, dark tunnel that led to the forests the elf girl called home. Malil noted that his master locked two of his eyes on his lieutenant as soon as the latter appeared.

"It must learn part of your grand plan, my Creator," the Guardian said, beckoning Malil but still looking down the lacuna. This was as close as Memnarch would get to telling his lieutenant to listen. "Malil has a destiny to fulfill, as do I. Malil will make my destiny possible. And Malil will die, along with everything on this world. When the time is right."

Malil looked at Memnarch impassively. "I have never expected to die anywhere but in your service."

"Will it miss its life, do you suppose?" Memnarch asked the absent Karn. Malil was a bit taken aback at the question.

"My life? My life is yours to do with as you please, master. How could it be anything else?" Malil dodged. He had not taken a vial of serum with him, and now that his supply was a mile in the air over his head, he found he was unable to concentrate on anything else. Of course I'll miss my life, Memnarch, he thought. You can't drink the serum when you're dead. He felt the patches of skin on his face and arms begin to sweat.

"As it should be." Memnarch scuttled sideways and finally gave Malil his full attention. "Life should not be on this world, I am convinced of this now, Karn. You left this world pure, and despite my efforts, it became tainted with the flesh. As have I. I shall make this right when I ascend. And the removal of life from this sphere shall be a glorious cleansing." Memnarch rocked his head slowly right and then left, and shivered as serum pulsed into his system from the massive tanks on his back. The Guardian's gaze lifted to the mana core. "Malil shall lead the armies that I have created as you instructed, Karn, and take control of the surface world."

"Master? I do not understand. The elf girl has devastated the leveler ranks, and—"

"The magic! I have bathed in its power, as you surely intended, my Creator," Memnarch said. "Behold."

The Guardian spread his silver, humanoid arms wide, and all six of his eyes took on an emerald sheen. A glossy silver field enveloped Memnarch, who clenched both hands into fists. The Guardian's veins bulged along his forearms and temple, and Malil saw spots or reddish blood seeping onto his master's bandages.

"The army shall rise!" Memnarch cried, and swept his arms to the sky. The silver glow grew into a translucent sphere then rapidly grew, dissipating into the surrounding interior of the plane like ripples on a quicksilver pond. Malil's sharp eyes—mercifully as yet untouched by the spore—followed the edge of the shockwave until it completely disappeared over a mile away.

The ground swirled like quicksilver seen through fogged glass, then burst to life. Thousands of small, segmented creatures that hadn't been there before simply grew from the metallic ground.

Malil saw myr, some as small as a goblin, others that would tower over the heads of the cursed golem that had fought at the elf girl's side. Wicked levelers of cruel design, their whirling rotary chopping blades sending an eerie buzz echoing through the interior, grew to mammoth size within seconds. Arachnoid constructs armed with spiked clubs and scythe blades clanged noisily against the ground, the mycosynth spires, and each other. Sleek, predatory ebony shapes that vaguely resembled the beetle-like nim shambled among them, taking wide swipes with hooked talons at the air and filling the interior with a chorus of low, metallic growls that echoed weirdly off the inside of the great sphere. Lupine creations with tusks sharpened to a molecule's width were covered in metal fur lined with barbs. A sterling airborn serpent with iridescent platinum scales swooped low over the growing crowd of bizarre constructs, hissing like shattered glass. Mycosynth dust swirled up in clouds as the artificial reptile flapped lustrous wings of membranous silver and joined its brethren.

"Your orders are simple, my Creator, simple enough for Malil to understand. There will be more of my children. Armies born of a single thought."

"Orders, master?" Malil asked, more than a little awestruck by the forces that the Guardian had handed to him.

"Yes, great Karn, simple is best. He has not yet touched the faces of gods." The master began to mumble and hum, then whirled on Malil. "Malil shall find the elf girl and return her to me. Surely this is simple enough for the first order."

"She will be yours," Malil finally replied. "And what else do you—does the Creator ask of the Guardian's army?"

The master laughed like a cawraptor about to make a kill. "Malil is going to retrieve all of the soul traps and return them to me. Then he shall take the surface world in the name of Memnarch."

CHAPTER 11

FLARE UP

Bruenna, Glissa, and Lyese rode golden zauks over the glittering fields of razorgrass. The leonin domesticated the large flightless birds as mounts. After years of breeding the creatures were incredibly tough, agile, fast, and most of all versatile. They could outpace a flying pteron over open ground, climb vertical cliffs with their foot-long, hooked claws, and swim a mile underwater without taking a breath. Odd, Glissa thought, that with all that, these birds still couldn't fly.

Still, the three of them needed fast transportation that wouldn't waste magical energy or give them away to anyone watching the skies. The zauks had been one of Raksha's gifts. Considering the jobs he was asking them to perform for him, it was the least the Kha could do, in Glissa's opinion.

Fortunately, Raksha Golden Cub was not the sort to do the least of anything. Though far from Taj Nar, he allowed them to choose armor, weapons, and other gear from his personal supplies. The trio had found complete sets of fine pteron-bone armor, enchanted to improve the wearer's swordsmanship, prompting Lyese to cast her Tel-Jilad armor aside, adding she wasn't working for Yulyn anymore. The armor was accompanied by polished helms that carried no magical enhancements, but were remarkable lightweight and exceedingly durable.

Naturally, Glissa found herself most impressed by the

weapons. Silver longbows now hung from the saddles of each elf, while Bruenna had passed over the unfamiliar bow for a bandolier full of knives. Raksha had told her they had been blessed by Great Dakan himself, and could not miss their target. Lyese had been awestruck that the Kha had let her take a short sword engraved with an image of the Golden Cub and encrusted with protective crystals. Glissa reminded herself that for all her protestations, her sister was still a youth in many ways. Glissa also suspected her sister was beginning to develop a bit of a crush on the leonin Kha.

Glissa was stunned to find a flawlessly preserved elven long-sword among the weaponry on hand, and Raksha had insisted she take it. He claimed it had been a gift to Great Dakan from the elves of old. Glissa didn't bother to point out that a lot of the elves of old were still in the Tangle, they just forgot everything once in a while. The sword was perfectly balanced. Glissa even used it to disarm Raksha during a brief sparring match.

A wave of vertigo made Glissa list in her saddle, and she let out an involuntary groan as flashing lights and stabbing pain erupted in her temple. She saw shadowy shapes, Bruenna and Lyese, whirl on their mounts in alarm, but could not make out what they were saying. Her ears felt filled with quicksilver, and a dull roar was increasing in pitch somewhere in the back of her head.

Then Mirrodin was gone, and Glissa floated in a cold, empty, utterly silent void. She realized she was moving through the inky black when a tiny pinprick of light appeared up ahead. Glissa felt herself moving more quickly, and the light steadily grew, gradually gaining definition. The light became a sphere, the sphere a world, familiar features became clearer. Glissa flew through the shadows toward Mirrodin.

There were the glittering hexagonal plates that covered the

Glimmervoid and provided purchase for dozens of different species of razor grass, running to the edge of jagged, rusty scabs that could only be the Oxidda mountain range, whence came Slobad and his goblin kin. The Tangle she felt in her bones before she saw it, the forests pulsing with the magical energies to which she was most closely attuned. From this distance, it looked like an especially large hunk of moss clinging to a tarnished silver ball. The Quicksilver Sea shone like a glittering mirror, reflecting the light of the moons, while the dark stain of the Mephidross seemed to devour the glow of four satellites—the green moon was absent—spewing a huge cloud of brownish-green ochre into the atmosphere. From her godlike point of view, Glissa could see that those fumes spread much farther than anyone below suspected, dissipating across the plane in a thin haze.

And they were moons, not suns. She saw that now, there could be no doubt. Four glowing balls of energy, each spinning around the hollow world that spawned them, twirling in a complicated, unpredictable dance. Mirrodin reflected and absorbed the energy the orbs projected.

She wondered if this was what it really looked like when one flew through the heavens, or if this was the best her imagination could muster. She was beginning to suspect this was more vivid hallucination than flare, for this was not a vision of the past. There were simply too many moons.

Glissa felt an unbidden urge to swoop down close to the Tangle. The forests of home rapidly grew before her into a rich carpet of green, then crystallized into the familiar verdigris foliage she'd hunted for decades. There was something there she needed to find, but she couldn't put her finger on it. Something she'd lost, or maybe something that had lost her. Or someone. She pulled her focus down and watched the world move by below her, scanning the ground. She became a moon of Mirrodin herself, soaring around and around the great metallic sphere in an expanding orbit, taking in the entire surface. And everywhere she went, everywhere she looked, whether skimming the Quicksilver Sea or knifing through the thickets of the Tangle, she noticed one thing was absent from this living metal world.

There were no people. Every settlement, from Taj Nar to the Vault of Whispers, from Lumengrid to Viridia, was completely devoid of anything walking on two feet.

No, there was one thing. A small silver dot that ambled over the dream-Mirrodin on four legs, like a crab. Memnarch walked the surface of the metal world, and he was utterly alone.

Glissa felt a pang of sympathy, then quickly buried it. Served the twisted monster right. Alone on an empty world, with no one to worship him as a god, not even his favored vedalken. The metal monster's face turned up to stare at her with six glittering eyes, and he opened his mouth as if screaming, yet Glissa could not hear.

The globe below her began to visibly shake, vibrating impossibly fast as Memnarch's wail reached into the heavens, eventually striking Glissa's keen ears. What appeared to be simple vibration from her vantage point became massive tectonic quakes on the surface as the hollow sphere began to crack. And still Memnarch screamed, as white light sliced through the widening crevices in Mirrodin's skin, raw magic that erupted violently now.

The latticework of cracks finally gave way. The globe of Mirrodin collapsed inward in a colossal implosion, then the mana core exploded. In a conflagration of energy and power never before seen by mortal eyes that lasted no longer than a heartbeat, Mirrodin suddenly ceased to be.

"Glissa?" Lyese said, "What happened? Can you stand?"

Glissa blinked. The flare was over. She shook her head and allowed Lyese to pull her to her feet. "I'm fine."

"Was this a 'flare'?" Bruenna asked as she pressed a silver

cloth against Glissa's forehead. The stabbing pain that had preceded the flare disappeared instantly.

"Either that, or I'm losing my mind," Glissa said. "But this one was strange. I'd seen other worlds before, this seemed—almost like someone was trying to give me advice."

"Is it good advice?" Bruenna asked.

"I think so," Glissa said. "Something along the lines of 'keep doing what you're doing.' So right now, that means we help the Kha with his immediate problems, which are also our problems, and somehow we all might come out of this—whatever 'this' turns out to be—alive."

"Makes sense," Bruenna replied in a tone that indicated the matter was anything but settled, but she wasn't going to push the point. She eyed the sky and saw the small group of skyhunters who were heading out to meet the mage at the edge of the Mephidross. "It's time we split up if I'm going to keep my appointment."

"You're right," Glissa said. "Good luck with Geth. Don't trust him. Not even a little bit. And protect your neck at all times."

"I can take care of myself," Bruenna said. "And what I can't take care of, the leonin will," she added, nodding at the approaching riders.

"I'm sure of it," Glissa said, though she was anything but. The flare had shaken her, but she still wasn't sure why. The Mirrodin she had watched die had no green moon. The Mirrodin she lived on did and so far hadn't imploded. What kind of message was that? 'Stay the course' had been her best guess for the others' sake but Glissa knew that was an evasion.

Fortunately, she would have plenty of time to mull the matter over on the long ride out to the leveler cave, where they would hopefully find the Krark. "Okay, Lyese, you're with me. Let's go find some goblins. And remind me not to stare straight into the green moon."

* * * * *

Glissa bit off a strip of dried djeeruk meat and handed the rest to Lyese. She wasn't that hungry, and the thought of coming to Dwugget as a leonin ambassador—to say nothing of the residual effects of the powerful flare—already had blinkmoths fluttering chaotically in her abdomen. It wasn't unlike the way she used to feel those rare times she and Kane been free of duties and studies long enough to enjoy each other's company. Except Kane had never put her off her food.

Maybe that's why I wanted Bruenna to do this, she thought. She's a leader. Leaders negotiated. Negotiation was not Glissa's style. Glissa liked problems that could be solved with a sword, or in exceptional cases, a construct-flattening explosion of magic. Still, they needed information to stop Memnarch, and the Krark seemed to know more about the inner world than anyone else on the surface, except perhaps the trolls and the vedalken. That the leonin might receive aid from the goblin cultists against the nim was secondary to Glissa, though ostensibly the main reason the Kha had sent them on this mission.

They had reined their zauks to a trot so they could eat while moving, giving the elf girl a chance to really take in the landscape of the Oxidda foothills. Their surefooted mounts easily navigated a collision of rocky outcroppings, flat, ferrous mesas, and corroded iron boulders. Here and there, magnetic energy held similar boulders floating above the ground, adding an air of unreality to the landscape.

The tall, rustling razor grass of the plains was gradually giving way to hardier varieties, and clusters of silvery scrub became thicker, rustier, and more frequent the farther they went. Corroded gullies cracked the dusky ochre ground, but the zauks easily cleared them with one step even at this pace. Glissa patted the bird on the neck, and it cawed affectionately. Or hungrily. Or angrily. The elf girl really wasn't sure.

Glissa slipped the seeksphere from a pouch on her belt and held it up to inspect the fine markings. The silver ball was no bigger than a goblin's eye and bore tiny notches and symbols that remained fixed in position no matter which way she turned the object. Shonahn had shown her how to enchant the seeksphere to home in on a single individual, but Glissa had been called on to perform the spell herself, which consisted of simply saying the name of the person you were searching for three times while holding the ball close to one's lips. The trick was that only someone who had seen that person could activate the device. Bruenna had one too, also enchanted by Glissa, to find Geth.

Despite Shonahn's assurances that the seeksphere was such a simple artifact that it was virtually impossible to fool, Glissa was beginning to suspect the gadget was broken. At first, they'd seemed to be going in the right direction, but they'd veered off into the rocky foothills and now it seemed as if they were headed straight into the mountain caves ruled by the despotic goblin shaman and his fanatic followers.

"Lyese, this can't be right," Glissa said, waving her sister to a halt. She shook the seeksphere with frustration, but it still pointed straight into the iron peaks. "The Krark were not this far into the mountains. And the goblins that *do* live in the mountains aren't friendly with the Krark or anyone else."

"You've been through a lot," Lyese said with a game attempt at maturity. "Okay, maybe that's an understatement. But is it possible your memory might be, I don't know, a little knocked out of alignment?"

"Don't be—" Glissa began, but the suggestion gave her pause. Who knew what toll the last few weeks had taken on her mind? What had the flares done to her sense of self? For that matter, what had the frequent loss of blood done to her brain? "You could be right, I guess. Or maybe they just left. Or maybe . . . damn."

"What?" Lyese asked.

"Or maybe I'm overlooking the obvious answer—they've been taken by the shaman's followers. The mountain goblins might have attacked Dwugget's people just out of spite."

"You think they're captured?"

"It's the most logical conclusion," Glissa replied. She cast her eyes back over the foothills to the open plains. "Those leonin had better show up soon."

"Why?" Lyese asked.

"Because this just turned into a rescue." She patted her saddle to reassure herself that her bow and quicksliver arrows were close at hand. "I'll go without the leonin if I have to. You can stay here and let them know where I've gone."

"No way!" Lyese objected. "I can fight just as well—okay, maybe not just as well as you, but I am Tel-Jilad Chosen, you know."

Glissa turned her mount around to look her sister in the eye, and came face-to-face once more with the mutilation and injury Lyese had suffered. She was young, yes, but no younger than Glissa had been when she bagged her first djeeruk. And she was fairly certain that Lyese, young as she was to Glissa's eyes, was much older than Slobad or Bruenna in actual years. What right did she have to keep her sister away from a fight? None, she knew. It was entirely selfish. She just couldn't stand to put her sister in danger again. It wasn't fair, but it was true.

With effort, she buried the impulse.

"Okay," Glissa said grudgingly, "but don't get out of my sight."

"Touching," a gravelly voice said. "We'll make sure to lock you up in the same cell." Glissa whirled and scanned the area, trying to pinpoint where the sound was coming from. She needn't have bothered. In a flurry of movement, over a dozen armored, thuggish-looking goblins rose from the scattered scrub brush. Most had shortbows trained on the elves, while some brandished wicked hooked spears that Glissa knew were as deadly at a distance as they were in close combat.

"Lyese . . . don't move." Glissa said softly.

"Way ahead of you," Lyese whispered.

"Stop this at once!" the gravelly voice bellowed, and Glissa saw a hulking human step from behind a large boulder. Glissa had never seen a human like him before. She hadn't even know humans lived in these mountains. The man's huge frame was clad in the robes of the priests, which covered jagged spiked armor that looked like the wearer had attached raw pieces of the mountain to his body. He wore black, irregularly shaped gauntlets covered in rough edges and what looked like dried goblin blood. Wiry scarlet hair topped his unprotected head, and the human's eyes glittered with red fire. "Much as I would enjoy it, there is technically no need for violence. My lord wishes to speak with you, and would appreciate it if you were unarmed."

"Your lord?" Glissa said. "New shaman in town, I suppose? What's a human doing working for a goblin fanatic, anyway?"

"I am no mere 'human.' I am a Vulshok high priest, elf. And the old goblin shaman is dead," the human replied. "These creatures have been called to serve a far nobler cause. Now, if you would be so kind to step down from those remarkable birds and follow me—keep them covered, my friends—everything will be made clear to you."

The elf girl shot her younger sister a look, and saw Lyese return a faint nod. She was thinking the same thing. This was *not* a friendly invitation, and if the elves were going to act, it had to be now.

"Go!" Glissa shouted, and kicked her zauk firmly in the flanks. The bird reacted as expected, and bolted toward the nearest goblin warriors. She heard a squawk as Lyese did the same, and then cries from another group of surprised goblins. Those who had held drawn arrows released them at targets that suddenly weren't there, and ducked as projectiles from their fellows opposite clattered to the ground around them.

Two goblins went down under Glissa's charging zauk, and she was free. Arrows whizzed past her head and one ricocheted off her helmet, but the goblins, as it turned out, were not particularly good shots. "Come on, Lyese!" she cried. She received no reply except the sound of clashing blades behind her. As Glissa's sleek mount bird charged toward the looming mountains, the elf girl looked back over her shoulder to see what the big human was doing. This Vulshok was an unknown quantity.

The Vulshok hadn't taken a single step, though Lyese was fighting his goblin warriors right in front of him. Lyese hadn't gotten through the line as Glissa had, though she'd certainly put up a fight. Her sister's sword rang as she batted back goblin spears. The human reached into his robes and produced what looked like some kind of silver mesh fabric. Before Glissa could shout a warning, the Vukshok had tossed the net over Lyese and her zauk. The bird and the elf girl quickly became entangled and fell over sideways, the panicked mount kicking wildly.

"Flare!" Glissa cursed and yanked hard on her zauk's reins, trying to turn around. The bird's muscular neck didn't give an inch. "Come on, you stupid—" Glissa snarled, pulling vainly with all her might. "Stop!"

Maybe I kicked it a little too hard, Glissa thought as she fought the panicked creature. She looked back again at Lyese, who was kicking in the air as four goblin warriors dragged her out of the net. Her zauk was now motionless except for quick, shallow breaths and blood that poured from several spear wounds. So the prohibition on violence didn't apply to their mounts.

"Halt! Whoah! Slow down, bird brain!" Glissa was almost raving now, and started pounding the zauk's necks with her fists. This only seemed to make the bird run faster.

When she again checked on Lyese, her sister and the goblin ambush team were specks in the distance, almost lost among the rusty, rocky spires of the Oxidda Mountains. She had to do something, or she really would lose Lyese again. She didn't even want to think what this Vulshok and his goblins would do to her little sister, especially if the "new lord" the human had mentioned was who Glissa suspected it was.

There was really only one solution, and it was going to hurt. Clutching the strap that held the longsword to her back, she let her feet slip from the stirrups and rolled backward off of the zauk's rump.

She landed hard, but was able to flatten out and keep the sword on her back from flapping around and doing her more harm than good. She came painfully to rest against a jagged black boulder, shattering her pteron-bone helm, which saved her skull from the same fate.

Dazed and bruised all over again, Glissa sprang to her feet. Still dizzy, the elf girl drew her blade with an unsteady hand and stumbled as fast as she could back to the fight. It took her a full minute to cover the same distance that had taken the zauk seconds, a full minute Glissa had to plan what she was going to do to that Vulshok. Size wasn't everything, and Glissa had taken down foes that large before. But by the time she reached the enclosed area where the goblins had ambushed them, there was nothing left but an dead zauk and Lyese's helm, which still wobbled back and forth on its side. She'd missed them by moments.

The elf girl scanned her immediate surroundings looking

for some sign of the goblins or her sister. It didn't take her long to spot the band of diminutive figures surrounding the towering Vulshok as the group moved over a narrow path that cut into the mountains. They had a good head start, but they gave no indication—no quickened pace, no shout of alarm—that they had spotted her yet.

Glissa, on the other hand, had good aim. She pounced behind the dead zauk and heaved it over into its belly. She fumbled with the saddle until she freed Lyese's longbow and arrows.

Staying low, the elf girl dashed from hiding place to hiding place, slowly gaining on the surprisingly fast-moving goblin pack. Glissa almost lost them a few times when they rounded ferrous outcroppings or passed under natural bridge formations, of which there were many. After twenty minutes she had closed within bow range. Glissa stalked the goblins and their Vulshok leader, carefully selecting a target—a fat, slow moving goblin that was conveniently bringing up the rear. Far enough from Lyese to ensure she wouldn't accidentally be hit, close enough to Glissa for a successful shot. With a quick inhalation of held breath, the elf nocked an arrow, took aim, and let fly.

The arrow whistled in the air, and the elf saw the fat goblin look up in surprise just before the shaft skewered him through the leg. Fatty went down, howling in pain. The remaining goblins scattered and took cover behind massive natural growth of copper ore and scatter, scraggly trees and bushes. Glissa charged, ducking the goblins' wild return shots and a few wobbly spears with ease.

The Vulshok, however, remained perfectly still, and so did Lyese. The human had a wicked-looking dagger pressed against her sister's throat. "Stop!" the human bellowed. "Come any closer and you're an only child again."

Taken by surprise, Glissa blurted, "How do you know—?"

"You'd be surprised what I know, Glissa," the human said. "How about this one? I know what you've been seeing in your dreams. A world without metal. A world of flesh, and wood, and rock, and earth and bone and skin. A world where life, as they say, goes on. Something like that?"

Glissa was baffled, but tried not to let on. "No need to do anything rash," she said. "Yes, you're right. We can talk about it. Just let her go. If you hurt her, the next shot goes through your eye. I don't care how big you are, you've got to have a brain in there somewhere."

"No deal," the human laughed. "I thought you were smarter than that, Glissa. You want to deal? Drop the bow and come quietly, or she dies."

Glissa slowly released the bowstring and slipped the arrow back into the quiver. Her eyes never leaving the human's steely gaze, she crouched slowly and set the bow on the ground.

"The sword too," the man barked.

"You're too far away for me too—"

"The sword. If it helps, you'll get it back. You just can't take it where we're going," the human said conversationally, though he didn't loosen his grip on Lyese for a second. In fact, he pressed down a little on the blade, making Lyese yelp. Her feet kicked uselessly in the air.

"Okay," Glissa said. "No problem, just relax." The elf girl reached slowly over one shoulder to draw her sword then cautiously set it next to the bow.

She hoped the goblins would attack her now. If they thought Glissa was helpless just because she didn't have a sword or a bow, she'd love the chance to correct them with her bare claws.

The human feinted lowering his knife a few times, probably to make sure Glissa wouldn't jump him as soon as he did. Apparently the Vulshok knew exactly how dangerous she could be.

Finally, the massive human released Lyese and gave her a shove that sent her stumbling into Glissa, who barely managed to catch her. By the time Glissa had propped her sister up with her shoulder, the goblins again had them surrounded, arrows trained on the elves' chests. The fat goblin wore a crude brown bandage around his leg and looked like he might fire an arrow no matter what kind of deal the Vulshok struck.

"Now ladies, please," the human said, "It appears we have gotten off to a bad start. I had hoped we could be friends. My lord wishes it. And so I wish it."

"You ambushed us, 'friend.' Who's this lord of yours, anyway? Wouldn't be a really ugly son of a vorrac with four legs and six eyes, would it?" Glissa was in no mood for small talk.

"I'll be sure to put your lord's head and your own on the same stick," Lyese said darkly. The younger girl rubbed her throat gingerly and stared daggers at the short man.

"You are bitter. Understandable. Forgive me, I'm operating under a different set of rules these days, but sometimes I still slip. Now, come with me, won't you?" He turned and started to walk away. Two of the spear-toting goblins ran forward and collected the elves' weapons.

The other goblins hadn't moved, apparently waiting to see if the elf girls were going to try anything. Glissa remained still and noted with pride that her sister didn't move either.

"Why should we do that?" the older elf girl called after the strange human that dressed like a goblin. "Who are you supposed to be?"

"My girl, you do not know my name, but I had thought my . . . position would be apparent," the man said, turning to favor them with a toothy smile. "I am call Alderok Vektro. I am the Vulshok high priest of Krark's Prophet. My other titles include master-at-arms of the revolution, commander of the Prophet's commandos—" he waved an arm, indicating the goblins holding them at arrowpoint—"and I believe I've been made chief of Oxid-dagg village. Don't worry. I'm assured it's an entirely honorary position. The real work is done by the elders."

"Krark's what?" Glissa asked.

"Prophet," Alderok Vektro replied. "Do try to keep up. Do not be alarmed. My lord tells me you are an old friend. I believe you know him as 'Dwugget.' "

CHAPTER 12

TURNABOUT

"Why does it resist, my Creator?" Memnarch asked the empty air. "Does it not know how fragile life truly is? Has this creature not yet seen enough pain?" The Guardian paused, listening to a voice that Slobad couldn't hear. "Oh, very well. More pain, then." He lumbered over to where the goblin hung in the rack and pressed a blue jewel mounted on the base with one pointed clawtip.

Flaming agony shot through Slobad, making his tortured muscles spasm chaotically. But a tiny part of his mind ignored all of this. A tiny part of Slobad had walled itself off within his brain, like the goblin himself had done so many times to escape danger. And that part of his mind refused to give up.

Glissa was alive. When Memnarch had given Malil his orders, Slobad could hardly believe it. Now that slim thread of hope—Glissa, alive, and still causing trouble for Memnarch, no doubt needing Slobad's help—was all that kept the goblin from dropping into an open pit of despair. So while Slobad screamed as every nerve in his body burned, his hidden self still held out hope of rescue.

Finally, the Guardian stepped forward and depressed the blue gemstone a second time, and the fire dissipated.

Slobad sniffed gingerly—his nose was already broken in at least three places—and detected the distinctive aroma of cooked goblin. It was a lot like normal goblin, but with many of the more noxious surface odors burned away. He spat blood and bile.

"Hey . . . uh . . . ugly," the goblin wheezed. "Call that . . . torture? Should try to eat . . . my cooking. Huh?" He laughed, which came out sounding more like a dry, persistent hack, then descended into a half-minute coughing fit. When that had run its course, Slobad added, "Oh yeah . . . where Glissa. Huh? Can't find crazy elf . . . some god."

"It tests me, my Creator," Memnarch said. "It actually think it can taunt me. Me." The Guardian chuckled, and reached out with a silver claw. He gently stroked the side of Slobad's face, and the goblin found the energy to jerk back as if burned. Which he was, now that he thought about it. "Such a curious creature. Does it know it's here by accident? Rusty, dusty, *aggravating* goblins crawling over this world like vermin. They *all* crawl, my Creator. Elves. The cat folk. The thrice-damned humans. Even my vedalken are truly nothing but infections, like this spore. I know that now." Memnarch chuckled again, which disturbed Slobad a great deal more than the Guardian's more predictable maniacal laughter. That laugh was maniacal, but something about that low chuckle was *insane*.

"Look who talking, bug," Slobad managed.

The Guardian waved a claw, and Slobad felt an invisible hand slap him hard across the face, leaving three thin lines of ochre blood welling up on Slobad's cheeks.

"Does it appreciate the honor?" Memnarch's claws curled into a fist, and the goblin flinched, but the Guardian just rapped lightly on Slobad's forehead, like a nervous suitor knocking on a lady's door. "The instrument by which I ascend. It is in this puny insect brain. Waiting to be realized."

"What?" Slobad managed. "I got spark now too . . . huh?"

"The vermin attempts another joke, my Creator. Yet this little ovoid atop its shoulders has displayed a remarkable affinity for building. It is an artificer. A designer and builder of things."

Slobad couldn't imagine what Memnarch was getting at. Or how he knew about Slobad's abilities, for that matter. Then again, the Guardian had thousands of years to study the denizens of "his" world. Maybe it wasn't such a surprise. "Been over this, crabby. You built a world, huh? So build your own stuff—Slobad's busy. All tied up, huh?" Slobad giggled a little too madly.

Memnarch smiled, a look Slobad had grown to fear ever since his capture. He scuttled over to the goblin and pressed the flat side of a clawed finger into Slobad's esophagus—not hard enough to break the skin, but Slobad preferred his windpipe open.

"Its torture is about to end."

"Great," Slobad rasped, his voice reduced to little more than a squeak by the claw tip now pressing against his throat. "How about now?"

Memnarch released his pressure on Slobad's throat and crab-walked over to a small, radiant scrying pool. "Its body is alive, and it will stay that way. The machine will see to that." He muttered a few soft words Slobad didn't understand and the pool flashed brightly for a moment then went dark. "The vermin-with-a-mind is about to touch greatness. And then we shall reassess the timetable, yes, Karn?"

Memnarch held out a fist, which shimmered briefly, then opened his hand palm-upward. A pair of flat, pearly shapes, each no bigger than a goblin's ear, undulated rhythmically in the Guardian's open hand. Something about the way they wriggled reminded Slobad of the slagwurm he and Glissa had faced in the Tangle.

"Think I skip dinner, huh?" the goblin rasped. "Slobad ate maggots for breakfast. Roughage."

In a flash, Memnarch lashed out with the spiny end of one

crab-leg and with delicate precision stabbed it into Slobad's tongue. The goblin squealed like a stuck djeeruk. The Guardian slapped the hand holding the two writhing silver worms over Slobad's open mouth.

The goblin had to stop screaming—he could no longer draw any air. Slobad started to shake, choking, when the wriggling creatures in his mouth slid down his throat, turned upward to enter his sinuses, and finally settled on either side of his head in his inner ears. Slobad feared the worms were entirely too close to his brains.

He was right.

* * * * *

Glissa and Lyese, their hands bound behind their backs with wiry rope, marched up the long, dusty path that Alderok Vektro promised would soon lead to some answers. He had steadfastly refused to answer any other question Glissa asked, least of all her pointed, specific questions about Dwugget.

They had left the razor fields far behind and climbed the steadily rising trail for over an hour. The path wound round, under, and over bizarre gold and iron mineral formations. At the moment one side of the path was open to the sky, affording a clear view of the shining lands now far below. Most of the moons had set, leaving only the emerald newcomer to cast its ethereal pall over the landscape. Soon, that moon too would set, and they would be in darkness. And when that happened, Glissa hoped to be heading back down the mountain.

The only trick was how. Try as she might, she couldn't loosen the hard, fibrous bindings, and she had no weapons or even any way to warn Lyese what she had in mind. She wasn't going to take off and just leave her sister to face Dwugget.

As far as the "Prophet" Dwugget was concerned, Glissa was still baffled. First, the Krark cultists hadn't been where they were supposed to be. Now Dwugget was this Vulshok's lord? It didn't make any sense, and she wished again that she hadn't lost the seeksphere in the fight. The wise old goblin that Slobad had introduced her to was gentle and intelligent. He'd been a valuable source of information when she had first set out with Slobad to find out if the world really was hollow. These thugs weren't acting under the auspices of the Dwugget she knew.

But how well did she know the old goblin? Slobad had vouched for him, and Dwugget had even given Glissa a copy of the Book of Krark, an ancient tome that convinced her she was on the right track. But Slobad, cunning and bright as he was, could also be too trusting. It was possible that the wizened elder her friend knew was but one face of a despot. Or worse, Dwugget had taken on the mantle of the shaman that had once cast the Krark out of the mountains.

As she turned back from the razor plains, the elf girl thought she saw movement out of the corner of her eye, but when she looked again there was nothing. Great, she thought, something's hunting us on top of everything else. Or I'm going crazy.

Or maybe, she thought as she spotted a glimmer of silver and a pair of flashing golden eyes, just *maybe,* this is going to work out.

As casually as she could, Glissa sidled ahead until she was side by side with her sister. The goblin guards didn't seem to take notice. They were herding the pair of elves and expected a little movement as the loose formation trudged onward.

"Hey," Glissa whispered softly, hoping the ringing footsteps of the armored goblins on the hard bronze path would mask her voice. None of the goblins looked up, and Alderok Vektro continued his slow, heavy strides.

Lyese cocked her head slightly.

"Something's following us," Glissa continued. "Stalking us."

"I know," Lyese replied, "Leonin?"

"I hope so. Get ready to run."

"Way ahead of you."

"Silence!" the fat goblin snarled, and smacked Glissa on the back with the flat end of his spear. "No talk!"

"We'll be good," the elf girl replied. She glanced sideways at Lyese, who winked. Or blinked. It was hard to tell.

The attack came as they entered a narrow draw between jagged, natural iron walls that rose hundreds of feet on either side. A half dozen furious roars exploded in the dusky night, and six feline shapes descended on the goblin brigade from above. Curved silver blades flashed, cutting down several of Glissa's captors before the first one had a chance to scream.

"Good timing!" Glissa shouted to the leonin. She let out a battle cry, ducked her head, and charged the fat goblin. She caught the little brute full in the chest with a savage kick, and he flopped onto his back, unmoving. She whirled on one foot and swung the toe of her boot into the groin of another goblin, whose spear clattered to the rocky ground as he doubled over in pain.

The rest of the guard was either engaged by the leonin commandos, or trying to close on Lyese, who had a kick for any goblin that got too close. This was Glissa's chance to get out of her bonds. She dropped onto the ground and scooted over to the spear the fat guard had dropped and sawed her bindings against the sharp edge of the tip. After a few second, she felt the last fiber of the painful cable snap, and she was free. Glissa grabbed the spear and scrambled back into the fray.

Before she could get her bearings, a fleeing goblin barreled into the elf girl from the side. Glissa snapped the blunt end of the spear into his gut and vaulted the diminutive soldier into the air.

She heard the goblin smack into a towering iron ore spire with the clang of a bell clapper.

Scanning the melee, she finally spotted the big Vulshok. Alderok Vektro was standing clear of the fray, furiously summoning magical aide for the goblins. A flash of red from Vektro's gauntleted hands, and the diminutive warriors were encased in thick bronze armor that fused to their rusty red hides, making them look like miniature golems. The goblins' weapons burned with unnatural red flames and sparked as they clashed with leonin longkives. None of them had been able to reach the Vulshok priest yet. Glissa noted the leonin were all wearing the helmets and lightweight armor of the Taj Nar Sky Guard, and wondered why they hadn't attacked from pteronback. Had the pterons been lost? It would explain why they'd been late to the party.

With his footsoldiers holding the leonin at bay—even the leader, who faced three of the magically augmented guards—Vektro had turned on Lyese. Glissa charged into the fight, kicking goblins aside and plowing a path to her sister. She saw a ball of orange-red flame forming in the Vulshok mage's upturned palms. The glow cast deforming shadows that made Vektro look like a monstrous goblin-human hybrid, and he cackled as power surged into existence at his command.

Lyese didn't see her peril or Vektro. Glissa's sister was doing her best to help the leonin fight off the triple-team of goblins with another stolen spear, but was having trouble finding an opening.

"Lyese! *Watch out!*" Glissa shouted, and launched herself at Vektro.

The next few seconds passed at a crawl. As her sister spun toward Vektro, one of the goblins slammed a fist into the small of Lyese's back. The human raised the fireball over his head, apparently willing to fry his own troops to get at the others. Glissa heaved her stolen spear.

Lyese arched her back and screamed as the goblin followed his punch with a sweeping kick to the younger elf's ankles that sent her sprawling backward.

"Guluhr immohl!" Vektro bellowed, and released the fireball just as Glissa's spear skewered the human's unprotected shoulder. The priest's spell went wide and slammed into the canyon wall over the heads of a pair of goblins slugging it out with two leonin commandos, sending the combatants bolting for cover as chunks of slag and white-hot ore rained down.

Glissa slammed into Alderok Vektro with the speed of a charging zauk, her momentum helping her drive the big man down hard on his back. But Vektro was faster than he looked, and surprised the elf girl by tucking his legs as Glissa came down. He kicked out hard at the elf girl's gut as he rolled over backwards, flinging Glissa into the air. She twisted and managed to let her shoulder absorb most of the blow. Glissa came up standing a few paces away from Vektro, but her shoulder felt disjointed and she had no weapon. She saw Vektro's eyes flash red and he held his hand apart, summoning forth another gout of burning magic.

"I still won't kill you," he snarled through a wicked grin. "But I *will* hurt you!"

The fire sputtered and died as a silver blur collided with the big human. The leonin followed through with a wicked kick to the side of Vektro's head, and finished by removing his own pteron-bone helmet and knocking the Vulshok back one more time as the human tried to raise his head.

Glissa grinned at the Kha, who jerked the dazed Alderok Vektro to his feet and quickly bound the big human's hands behind his back. "Raksha," she said, "you might want to take his gauntlets, too, just in case." Surveying the scene, she grinned and added, "And thanks."

Every goblin lay unconscious or otherwise incapacitated by

injury. It appeared the leonin had gone out of their way not to kill the goblins, which Glissa thought wise. Whatever Dwugget was up to, he could still be a potential ally. And she wasn't sure this Alderok Vektro was really in league with the old goblin priest anyway.

The other five leonin—all females, Glissa now saw, which made sense if they were all skyhunters—bound the goblins and saw to serious injuries on both sides that needed immediate attention. Glissa heard Lyese whisper an old healing spell their mother had used to fix small knicks and cuts since they were both little, and was surprised to see that she was using the magic on the Kha. Raksha, meanwhile, yanked hard on the Vulshok prisoner's wrists. The big human emitted a surprisingly high-pitched yelp.

"Thank you, Lyese," Raksha said. "What do you think, Glissa? Are these our goblins? This one's bigger than I expected."

"That human calls himself a Vulshok," Glissa replied, rubbing her wrists to get blood flowing through them again. "Says his name's Alderok Vektro. He's going to take us to see Dwugget. Aren't you, Vektro?"

Alderok Vektro's eyes flashed with hatred, but he was unable to free himself from the Kha's iron grip. "The Prophet will have you skinned alive! Your pelts will line his trophy hall! I shall feast upon your roasted eye . . . AAAAAAIIIIIEEEEE!"

"Quiet, human!" the Golden Cub snarled, twisting the man's wrists. "We shall tear out your throat if you do not cease at once!"

"Wait," Glissa said, shaking off a leonin who was trying to set her injured shoulder in a sling. The hulking human's eyes had glazed over, and his skin was rapidly growing pale. "I think he's passing—"

Vektro went limp.

"—out," Glissa finished.

The elf girl looked incredulously at Raksha Golden Cub. The Kha wore the same light silver plate as the skyhunters, though his bore a golden icon of the yellow sun, or moon, depending on where the viewer came from. He carried no sword, though Glissa did note that all six leonin wore the same long, curved knives hanging from their belts. Like the others, the Kha had a small supply pack strapped firmly to his back so as not to hinder motion in a fight. Tied to Raksha's pack was a larger bag holding something gourd-shaped. The leonin were barefoot, which didn't surprise Glissa. If she had weapons like that at the ends of her toes, she wouldn't wear shoes either.

Glissa accepted her sword from one of the leonin without taking her disbelieving eyes off of Alderok Vektro, and slid the Viridian blade back into place on her belt. "What happened to him? Is he still alive?"

Raksha held the human higher and sniffed him gingerly. His nose wrinkled.

"No. If he'd expired, the human would smell a great deal worse than he already does. He smells like a goblin," the Kha explained. "He may have had a low pain threshold." Raksha let the big human drop unceremoniously to the ground, and picked up the Vulshok's gauntlets. "Or maybe he wasn't as tough as he looked without these." The Kha passed the gauntlets to one of the female commandos, who tucked them into her own pack.

"We'll get back to him," Glissa said. "What kept you?"

"An old friend of yours stopped by," Raksha said, the growl replaced by a brief flash of teeth that Glissa hoped was a smile. It was always hard to tell with a leonin.

The Kha swung the larger pack off his shoulder and tossed it to Glissa. She thought she heard a sound like a muffled yelp. "That's not a gourd," Glissa said unnecessarily, holding the pack out as far from her nose as possible. Whatever was in there, it smelled terrible.

"Open it carefully. He might bite," Raksha said.

"Thanks for the warning," Glissa said, and flipped the pack open.

"Long time, no see," said Geth's head.

CHAPTER 13

TALKING DEAD

Glissa slammed the bag shut again, to the muffled surprise of Geth's cursing cranium.

"What is this, Raksha?" Glissa demanded.

"I'm a 'who.' And I can hear you, you know!" Geth's head shouted. Glissa dropped the bag on the ground, which elicited a yelp.

"This was sitting on a platter in the center of my dining table when I returned to my tent this morning," Raksha said, slipping into informality. "It said it had an offer from Yert."

The head in the bag cackled like a lunatic when the Kha said the name, but Glissa ignored it.

"*Yert?*" Glissa said. "Yert—Yert's dead."

"Death is relative in the Dross," the bag said.

"What's a Yert?" Lyese asked.

"Someone I thought was long gone." Glissa leaned down and flipped the bag back open. "All right, Geth. I'm sure you've got a wonderful tale about why your head's sitting there in a bag, but I don't care. Just talk. What's Yert got to do with this? You told me you killed him. And if you aren't honest with me, I *will* step on you. Hard."

"No need for threats, my dear, old friend," Geth's head simpered. "Here to talk, yes I am. Yes, indeed. Yert says talk, I talk. We talk. All of us ta—"

Glissa pointedly raised her boot.

"So, yes, talking. Yert—oh, he's one to watch. Yes indeed," the Geth's face took on a dark scowl. "An up-and-comer, that one. Should have watched him, eh? Should have made sure . . ." The head blinked and took on a more placid expression Glissa didn't buy for a minute. "But I digress. Been doing that a lot lately. I think my brain's getting a touch of the rot. Yert, he sends a message."

"How is this dead man sending me a message, and why? What did you *really* do to him?" Glissa said.

In reply, Geth's eyes rolled back into his head, leaving empty, blood-red sockets. When the head spoke again, it sounded very different. These tones were much more controlled, a great deal more menacing, over a hundred times as cold as ice, and disturbingly familiar.

"Glissa," Geth's head said with what the elf girl barely recognized as Yert's voice. The sound no longer carried tremors of fear and weakness. This voice was strong, clear, and cold. "And Raksha Golden Cub, I believe? And . . . how lovely. A new girl. Perfect. I would say it is an honor to meet my noble enemy at last, dear Kha, but I do not wish to start out with lies. Plenty of time for lies later."

Glissa saw Raksha bristle, but the leonin remained silent.

"Get to the point, Yert," Glissa snapped. "That *is* you, right? Nice way to repay a kindness. I won't make the same mistake twice."

"It is only because of the kindness you showed me that I am speaking with you now." Yert's voice slithered. "But you are distracting me, Glissa. You are very good at that, you know."

"You talk to much," Glissa replied. She brandished her sword and leveled the tip at one of Geth's red eyes. "Are you using those eye sockets, too?"

"You're no fun anymore, you know that?" the head replied. "All right, no more small talk. I have your mage, the Neurok. She is alive, for now. But her life is in your hands, Glissa."

"Bruenna?" Lyese gasped. "Glissa, we've got to—"

"Yes, Glissa, you've got to! It's tragic!" Yert squealed in a juvenile falsetto. "Time to start rending the garments and wailing at the moons!" The head cackled, for a moment sounding much more like its original owner. "So tell me, who's the sharpshooter? Do I detect a family resemblance?"

"What do you want, Yert?" Glissa demanded.

"Isn't it obvious? I want you, Glissa. Come to me, of your own free will, and I shall release the mage."

Glissa swallowed, and tried hard to sound blasé as she replied, "The Neurok knew what she was getting into. You're crazier than I thought if you think that's any kind of offer. How do I even know she's alive?"

"Glissa, don't even think about it," she heard Bruenna's voice say through Geth's cracked lips. Geth's expression contorted into a crude approximation of Bruenna, a mask of equal parts anger, fear, and grim determination. "He's going to kill me any—"

"I think that's enough," Yert's voice said, and Geth's face broke into a wicked smile. "There, that's all the proof you get. However, I am willing to sweeten the deal. I shall call off my nim. We shall stay within the Mephidross. Kha, I will end all attacks agains the leonin. All I ask in return is the elf girl. Really, it's not as if you need two, is it?"

Raksha spat. "You're a fool if you think the Kha would so easily betray a friend." But something about his expression made Glissa think he might not be as sure as he sounded.

Geth's head somehow lolled over sideways to make empty eye socket contact with the Kha. "Really? Don't even want to think about it, eh? That doesn't sound like a great leader of the noble leonin people, and so on and so on." The head sighed, a sound that came out as more a wet wheeze. "Glissa seems to think this is all up to her. But what do the rest of you say? Your Kha is ready to give up peace for a single elf."

The elf realized she was surrounded by six war-weary soldiers, soldiers who had been fighting the same terrible enemy for a very long time and had seen far too many friends die at the hands of the nim. Soldiers who had just risked their lives on a distant mountain to help Glissa yet again while their fellows defended the den home.

"Raksha . . ." she said warily, glad she already had her sword drawn. Doing so now would have looked far too aggressive, but the weight in her palm helped her to steady her voice. The Kha looked deeply into Glissa's eyes, as if searching for the answer to his dilemma. If he was, it didn't take him more than a few seconds to find it.

"Leonin do not negotiate with nim," the Kha growled. He cast a steely glare at the female warriors. "Nor do we offer up the lives of friends in acts of abject cowardice. Try again, creature."

"You're killing Bruenna as we speak," the head replied. "Well, you're killing parts of her. If you're foolish enough to try and deceive me, you'll force me to expand my efforts. Internal organs are even more fun to play with. Tasty, too."

Suddenly, the head shot into the air and swiveled to face Glissa, hovering just out of sword reach. "This is not a negotiation, this is the offer," Yert's voice snarled. "Take it or leave it."

Glissa seethed. Slobad was still missing, and the answers to finding him—and learning why Vektro and the goblins had attacked her—were up that mountain. Even now, Memnarch might be torturing Slobad to death. But if she didn't do something immediately, Bruenna would surely die.

Something in her gut told her the Guardian wanted her goblin friend alive. Since Memnarch had not issued any demands, it seemed increasingly unlikely that the reason was to simply ransom the goblin for Glissa's spark. As easily as that, her decision was made. It was not a logical decision; it was visceral, but her instincts told her it was right.

"All right, Yert. You win," the elf girl said. "Release Bruenna, and stop fighting the leonin, and I'll . . . ugh . . . come to you."

Raksha and Lyese both opened their mouths to object, and Glissa silenced them both with a glare.

"Don't be ridiculous," the head replied. "You have heard the offer. I expect to see you within a day. If not, the mage dies. Then, and only then, I will call off my nim." With that, Geth's eyes rolled back into place, gazing up at Glissa.

"Wait, you've got to be reasonable—" Glissa said and picked up the grisly transmitter by both ears.

"I miss anything?" Geth's head asked.

"Geth?" Glissa snapped. "Let me talk to Yert."

"Sorry, he's really going to be tied up for the rest of the day," Geth replied, "Or maybe it was other people getting tied up, and he's merely preoccupied. Such a busy fellow, my old pal—"

Glissa dropped Geth's head into the pack without warning and shut the bag. She called the others into a huddle, hopefully out of earshot.

"You cannot—" Raksha began with a whisper.

"I can and I am," Glissa replied in kind.

"You would have to fight your way through the nim. Alone. That is madness," Raksha said.

"What about Slobad?" Lyese asked.

A familiar sinking feeling set in. "He's just going to have to hold on," Glissa sighed. "Memnarch wants him alive for some reason, I'm sure of it."

"Perhaps the Kha could speak with this Dwugget alone," Raksha replied. "We are somewhat experienced in these matters."

"This isn't at all the behavior of the Dwugget I know," Glissa said. "He may not be in a negotiating mood. When Vektro comes too, he can lead you there. Or one of the other goblins. How will I find you after I get Bruenna?"

"Return to Taj Nar. If the mage can signal us, we shall find *you*," Raksha rumbled. "We see now a simple retrenching will not be enough. We need a new battle plan."

"I knew it!" Lyese whispered excitedly. "Raksha and I can talk to the goblins, Glissa, while—"

"No. No, no, no," Glissa said, and added, "No." She scowled when she saw the set of Lyese's jaw. "And don't argue."

Lyese simply stared incredulously at her sister, and Glissa thought of the many, many times over the years she'd been forced to lie to her mother about her whereabouts. One didn't become the greatest hunter in the Tangle by getting in every night by sundown and studying with troll scholars and elf academics. Raksha coughed unconvincingly.

"Think, Glissa. Say you're Dwugget."

"You don't even know Dwugget," Glissa snapped.

"Not my point," Lyese replied. "Say you're Dwugget, and you see these guys." She jerked a thumb at the commandos, who looked up curiously. "You're going to call out the goblin guard and maybe something even worse than that meathead Vektro. Now say you see the Kha and his consort—"

Glissa's eyes narrowed, and Raksha's muzzled dropped open.

"—Or, the Kha and a dignitary from the Tel Jilad Chosen," Lyese deftly continued. "From a distance he might even think I'm you."

"She has a point," Raksha ventured. "Her presence should help us avoid another confrontation. But we should go alone, in case more patrols or 'meatheads' are about." Glissa noted Lyese began to blush dark green. "My warriors shall serve you as they would me, Glissa. They will see you to Bruenna, and help you free her from this Yert."

"Flare," Glissa muttered. "All right, but if anything happens to her, Raksha . . ."

The Kha merely cocked his head to one side and arched an ear. "Your sister shall return alive."

"I'm holding you to that, your Kha-ness," Glissa said. "Thank you. Lyese." She stepped forward gingerly swept her sister into a hug that sent pain down her injured arm, but Glissa ignored it. She leaned in to Lyese's ear and whispered so only her sister could hear—she hoped. "And behave yourself. Don't trust anyone, except maybe Raksha—I really think he's a good man, but I thought Dwugget was too. Remember, a ruler is always going to have his own priorities. And that might not include marrying the Viridian princess, so get that look out of your eye."

Glissa stepped back and held her sister at arm's length. Lyese nodded solemnly, but soon couldn't hold back a lopsided grin. The younger elf blushed a deeper green.

"The most important thing is to find out if they know anything about Slobad. An alliance is important, but if we can't figure out why Memnarch was willing to send so many levelers after Slobad, that all might be beside the point." Raksha nodded his agreement as Glissa continued. "If you can't get to the Prophet, try to find someone else who might know something. But if you do get a chance to talk to Dwugget," Glissa said, "tell him what happened down below, in the interior—what I told you. Both of you fill in the story for him. He probably knows more about the big picture than you think. Tell him about Slobad. If he really is following Krark, he should help you. If not, we're going to have to fight Memnarch without the goblins' help."

Raksha looked a little ruffled at suddenly being on the receiving end of the orders but nodded in agreement. "We shall," he said.

"I just hope we don't have to fight too many of the goblins," said Lyese, rubbing her sore wrists. "They don't fight fair."

"Neither should you," Glissa said. "You should fight to survive."

Raksha arched the wiry whiskers on his brow at this dishonorable notion, but said nothing.

"Take care of yourself, big sister," Lyese said. "Go save Bruenna, and we'll meet you back at Taj Nar."

"Yes you will. I'm not about to become the bride of Yert," Glissa said.

Raksha reached under his breastplate and pulled out a small gemstone pendant hanging from a chain. The stone glowed a faint yellow in the dim light. Without ceremony, the Kha pulled it over his head and offered it to Glissa. "Take this," he said. "It will protect you from the necrogen mists. They can become toxic over several days' exposure. Hopefully you won't be in there that long." He shrugged and added, "You might also say it's lucky."

"Thanks. Now to see if I can get there in time," Glissa said, placing a hand to her temple. "There's got to be a way to cover the distance. Where are your pterons?"

"Safely out of the fight. They are more a hindrance than a help in such close quarters, and frankly Taj Nar can't afford to lose even one. That said, you shall take my personal mount," Raksha rumbled as he waved the nearest skyhunter over. "This is Lieutenant Ellasha. Lieutenant, we are placing you under the command of Glissa, Chosen One and Champion of the Tangle. Do you understand?"

Glissa groaned inwardly. Her supposed status as "Chosen One" was, as far as she was concerned, still in dispute. "Chased

One" was more like it. Raksha's lieutenant didn't seem to find her title that impressive. Ellasha let her lip curl just enough to reveal the tips of her fangs before military demeanor took over and she nodded curtly. "Yes, my Kha." The leonin lieutenant flipped Raksha a crisp salute and returned to securing the goblin prisoners.

Glissa saw that the leonin had left a few of the goblins' weapons lying about—neither team was going to be able to take a number of angry goblin prisoners along, but leaving them tied securely without some way to eventually escape was tantamount to murder.

Yet there was still the problem of what to do with Alderok Vektro, who presented a much greater danger than the goblin guards, but from whom Raksha and Lyese would need directions. The Vulshok's head had started lolling lazily, and he might soon come to. Maybe his power was in the gauntlets, maybe not, but Glissa didn't think it was a chance they should take.

Raksha finally settled on keeping the human's arms tied behind his back, and gagged his mouth with strips of the Vulshok's robes. They were stopgap solutions, the Kha admitted, but should keep Vektro from trying any magical tricks on the journey into the mountains. The gag could be removed briefly to get directions out of the priest, and Raksha promised the human a swift death if he attempted to run. Vektro nodded, in no position to argue. And it might have been her imagination, but Glissa could have sworn that Vektro now looked a little smaller and less muscular without his gauntlets. Perhaps they were simple strength-enhancing artifacts.

With a final farewell and one more assurance from Lyese that she would be careful, the leonin and the young elf set off, their Vulshok prisoner stumbling ahead of them.

Lieutenant Ellasha turned from watching them go to address Glissa. "Your orders, Chosen One?"

The elf girl thought the leonin's effort to disguise her disdain was admirable, if not quite successful.

"We're taking the pterons for a ride into the swamp. Can you lead me to them?" Glissa asked. "And call me Glissa. Please."

"Of course," Ellasha replied. "Glissa, the pterons will have us within the Mephidross before the next sun clears the horizon."

CHAPTER 14

DROSSBOUND

"Weerm geddim clohmz nowm," Geth's head shouted through the leather pack on Glissa's back. The grisly thing hadn't stopped babbling since she'd taken to the air on the back of the silver pteron. Despite her efforts to shut the noise out she realized glumly that she was beginning to understand what Geth's muffled ravings whether she wanted to or not.

"I know," Glissa said, "I can feel it getting closer." She grimaced, and added, "And shut up, will you? You're going to attract carrion birds."

The elf girl loosely gripped the reins. Contrary to Ellasha's warning, the pteron hadn't tried to run her through, but had actually landed at her feet to allow her to mount as soon as she approached. She wasn't sure if it was the same one she'd ridden before, but the pteron hadn't tried to kill her, which was good enough.

Glissa and the skyhunters had built up quite a bit of speed by the time the blackened edge of the Mephidross broke over the horizon. She squinted against the dusty wind that flattened her thick cables of hair flat against her head. The elf adjusted her goggles to ensure they fit snugly around her eyes. Now would not be a good time for blurred vision.

Elassha pulled ahead and to Glissa's left, waving them to follow and take the pterons lower. She wished once again they'd thought to figure out a way to speak to each other up here. Glissa wanted to ask the leonin lieutenant if he had spotted something, or if this was simply the standard procedure for airborne leonin commandos approaching dangerous territory from the air. The leonin could communicate with hand signals, but Glissa could only understand a few simple commands. Fortunately, a slight nudge of the harness sent her pteron instinctively plunging down after the others. They leveled off only twenty feet or so over the razor plains.

The blackened edges of the Mephidross grew until they covered the horizon. Glissa didn't see any activity, nim or leonin, which seemed odd. The razor grass below was dotted with low verdigris shrubs and short stubby trees. She looked off to her left, where the flora grow steadily in size until it ran into the distant Tangle. They had already reached the far side of the Dross, and the battle between Yert's forces and Raksha's people was too far away to see.

It didn't make any sense. If there was an opening into the Glimmervoid, even if it meant taking the long way around to Taj Nar, why hadn't the "master of the nim" sent expeditionary forces through this corridor? For that matter, why had the Tangle always been spared the depredations of the nim? The more she thought about it, the stranger it seemed.

Perhaps he just didn't have enough troops, Glissa finally decided. But something about it continued to bother her.

She leaned forward and urged the pteron after the others. The formation drew out into a long column as the pteron riders broke through the corroded tree line and entered the Mephidross.

Glissa had flown over the Dross before, but that had been one of Bruenna's spells. Navigating a silver reptilian with a ten-foot wingspan through the thick, decaying vegetation and around the blackened chimney towers that belched necrogen gas was something else entirely. Fortunately, the pteron had a mind of its own and dodged the spiky foliage. Mostly.

After half an hour, the group broke into a small clearing in the swamp where the muck was deep enough to prevent even the hardy trees and plants of the Mephidross from gaining a grip. Ellasha wheeled and circled, then floated gently to a landing on a wide, dead copper log half eaten away by the corrosive swamp. The log tipped precariously, but the pteron kept its footing by stepping from side to side. Soon they had all landed in a loose circle on other chunks of solid detritus that broke the surface of the deep pools of brackish oil.

Ellasha signaled three of the skyhunters to take up perimeter positions. The warriors bounded off their mounts into the trees, forming a protective triangle around the group.

The two other leonin had been introduced as Ellasha's direct subordinates. Darlosh was the one with the black tips on her ears, while Tahk was recognizeable by silver streaks in her golden fur.

"Something isn't right," Ellasha whispered.

"Where are the nim?" Glissa asked.

"That's what I mean," the skyhunter replied. "They should be all over this place, if their numbers are as great as we think they are. Someone should have seen us by now."

"Lieutenant, I did spot something on the way in," Tahk said. "I had thought they were just creatures of the Dross, but now I am not so sure. They looked too . . . new. Too silver."

"You should have brought this to my attention immediately," Ellasha snapped.

"Easy," Glissa said. She turned to the chastised warrior. "Where did you see them?"

"About half a mile behind us, clinging to one of those necrogen smokestacks," Tahk said, momentarily relieved. "Two of them, like four-legged spiders, but together they would have outweighed a djeeruk."

"Flare!" Glissa said. "No need to go back and check—I saw them too. Or felt them then saw them. They—they were watching me. Ever seen anything like them in the Dross?" Tahk shook her head.

"They do not sound like nim," Ellasha said.

Glissa grimaced. "I agree. They must be Memnarch's spies."

She didn't want to risk alienating the leonin with information that made her certain. The feeling she'd had when she sensed the small constructs was the same tingle that alerted her whenever the levelers had drawn near.

"Do you believe Memnarch will attack us here?" Ellasha asked.

"Maybe," Glissa said. "I don't know. But I'm pretty sure between the seven of us we can handle a couple of metal bugs. I've taken on bigger ones, and I'm still here."

"Agreed," said Ellasha. "Right now we should focus on the immediate task of finding the human."

"Her name is Bruenna," Glissa said. "And she's a friend of mine. We're not just going to find her. We're getting her out of here."

"Of course," Ellasha agreed. "But first things first."

Glissa nodded apologetically. "Sorry. Just anxious to get this done. I've got another friend in trouble, too."

"Mid mit meverm moccurm moo mamy mum moo matt moo mould mask meem?" Geth's head shouted from inside the leather pack. Ellasha's hand shot to her long knife, but Glissa raised a finger to stop her from doing anything rash. She slung the pack around and flipped the top open.

"Ask you? You expect me to believe you would guide us? I think your head's been off your shoulders too long," Glissa said.

"Don't underestimate the power of hate," Geth's head said matter-of-factly. "You think I hate you? Well, yes, I do. Of course I do. Before you came along, everything was perfect. And you really, really messed up my vampire. But there are degrees of hate. And as much as I'd like to flay you all alive with your own long knives, that's nothing compared to what I want to see happen to that usurper."

"'Usurper?'" Glissa asked. "You told me Yert was in charge now. You seemed happy about that. And you still haven't told me how any of that happened."

"I'll get to it," the head snapped. "I don't like to talk about it. I told you the facts as they are now. Come on, I need *some* secrets. You don't get over being the supreme power of darkness overnight, you know."

"You mean we can trust you because we have a mutual enemy," Ellasha interrupted in an attempt to cut through Geth's convoluted explanation. She turned to Glissa. "Is a mutual enemy enough when it admits it isn't telling us the whole truth?"

The elf girl cast her eyes around the misty darkness that loomed in every direction, here and there interrupted by a flash of moving shadow or the splash of something vile slipping into the muck. She flipped the bag shut again and leaned in close to the leonin, speaking in a whisper. "It might *have* to be enough. I thought once I got in here, something might look familiar. But I've never approached this place from here. I think," she sighed, "we're lost."

Ellasha flashed teeth and growled softly, "I was lost the minute we entered. I was trusting my mount."

"Great. Some rescue team we are." Glissa grinned. She opened the bag and addressed Geth's head. "Okay, you and I are going to take point. If you try anything—lead us into an ambush, shout out at the wrong time, or bite my neck—and you're just another dead head sinking into the swamp. Understand?"

"Crystal clear," Geth said. "But something's gotta be in it for me, eh? How about when this is all over you help me find my body. Make a man of me again."

"What?" Glissa said with an involuntary shudder. "Not a chance. You'll guide us to the Vault, or you're dead. It's that simple."

"Wrong, elf girl," Geth's head replied. "I'm dead already. Well preserved, yes, but dead. So that's no threat, and we all walk out of the Vault together, or no one does."

"How do I know you won't just take control of the nim yourself?" Glissa asked. "Continue the war?"

"You don't," the head said, "And that's a pretty good guess. If the world saving doesn't work out, I think you've got a future in prophesying. But yeah, that's the deal. You're one of those honorable types whether you want to be or not, so I'm willing to take your sworn oath as a guarantee. You're not going to get a better deal than that. But I want a body after I help you. Scrap's sake, it doesn't even have to be mine. I'd even take a leonin if you happened upon one later. And then, when I've got my body and you've got your future, I never want to see you again."

"Likewise," Glissa agreed. She turned to Ellasha. "Call the sentries back in. We're heading out."

"I cannot agree to this," Ellasha snarled. "He as much as admitted he will attack us at the first opportunity!"

"She's got you there," Geth's head agreed.

"Shut up, Geth," Glissa said. "Ellasha, we'll deal with that when the time comes. Until then, we don't have a choice."

"She's got a point," Geth's head added, prompting a slap from Glissa.

"Very well," Ellasha agreed. "But as soon as that thing puts us in danger, I'm putting it down. Permanently."

"Way ahead of you, lieutenant," Glissa said, and made a grimace of distaste as she pulled Geth's head clear of the pack and rested the morbid thing on the pommel of her saddle, where it balanced without much help from her.

"Lead on, Geth," Glissa said.

* * * * *

The trip through the Dross to the site of the Vault of Whispers had taken an uneventful half hour when Glissa spotted the first sign of trouble. Her pteron actually gave her the first indication that something was up ahead, and she squinted into the greenish mist to see what had caused the reptile to buck suddenly.

There. Several shapes like large, man-sized beetles scuttled through the dense foliage. Glissa waved to the others to slow their approach, and placed a hand over Geth's mouth, the signal that told him the elf girl would gladly let him drop this instant if he didn't keep quiet.

The nim hadn't given any indication it had seen them. Fighting the urge to retch at the fetid smell, she lifted Geth's ear to her mouth and whispered, "Are they going back to Yert? Or is this the trap?"

"That's just a patrol," Geth whispered. "Most of his soldiers are on the front lines. I'd say that's why you haven't seen any until now. Lucky you. Those fellows look to be headed back to the Vault, if you ask me."

"We can follow them," Glissa said.

"And they say I'm the one with all the brains," Geth's head cackled. "Just be sure you get in before the last of them. Those doors don't dawdle."

"Then I'll just make sure the last one never makes it through the door," Glissa said.

Glissa stuck Geth back onto the pommel and waved Ellasha, Tahk, and Darlosh into whispering range. Half of the day Yert had given them was gone, and it was time to finalize the plan.

Ellasha argued for complete stealth, slipping in with the nim and staying in the shadows. But while Glissa had no doubt the skyhunter commandos had the agility and skill to pull off such a task, as did the elf girl herself, she still didn't trust Geth. It would be ridiculously easy for the severed head to alert the nim they'd be hiding from. No, they'd best approach stealthily, then surprise the nim and take them out while the doors to the Vault—whatever was left of it after Glissa's last visit—were still open. That seemed to satisfy everyone's concerns, though it would not be easy.

They had to set the pterons loose for now, Ellasha insisted. She could always call them back later, and if they kept flying they might overtake the nim. The team had to proceed on foot from here on out.

After another hour of much slower travel, the lead nim finally halted. Glissa heard an alien chittering noise—was that what nim language sounded like?—and saw the wide trunk of the blackened, rust-covered swamp tree in front of the nim split open. An archway big enough for two nim to enter side-by-side took shape, glowing with the light of necrogen lamps mounted on the inner walls of a long tunnel.

"All right," she whispered, and the leonin turned to her as one. "Let's go in hard and fast, but don't take any stupid chances. The important thing is getting through that door. Remember, go for the necrogen tubes. It won't kill them right away, but they won't last long without that green stuff pumping into them."

"We know their vulnerabilities. We have been fighting nim since before you were born," Ellasha said.

"I doubt it," Glissa said, stuffing Geth unceremoniously

into the pack. "Everyone ready?" she whispered she drew her sword.

Six muzzles nodded in unison, and six silver longblades flashed in the night.

"Go," Glissa said.

The elf girl reached the nim first, charging in with a wide sweep of her blade that met the hideous creature's neck just above its armored carapace, slicing neatly through and out the other side. The remaining nim whirled with supernatural speed Glissa had learned to respect and emitted a cacophony of chittering shrieks. Green necrogen tubes glowed as the nim entered the fray, reflexively attacking their attackers. It seemed like odd behavior for the nim, who would follow whatever order they had last been given until they were dead, or received new directives. Apparently, these had been given the order to patrol and retaliate.

Green necrogen glinted on the silver blade of her Glissa's sword. She wheeled in the tight enclosure near the entrance to the Vault and hacked off another nim head, spraying green necrogen and black ichor onto the tunnel walls.

Ellasha slipped ahead of Glissa and nearly bisected another nim with her silver longknife. The broken nim toppled out of the entrance and slid into the muck, still twitching.

Glissa continued her charge, catching the next nim down the line. Or trying to, anyway. Her blade came down hard on the iron carapace of the scuttling monster and bounced off with a painful clang that made her entire arm numb. The nim, swung around with a massive claw that caught Glissa full in the chest, knocking her back through the doors and into the swamp. The next thing she knew, she was tumbling head over heels through the green mist. She landed head first with an oily splash in the viscous mud.

Something brushed her leg and Glissa scrambled to her feet before whatever it was could take a bite. She still had her sword in her hand somehow, and lashed out at the nearest nim with a cruel uppercut that slit the insectoid nim open like a fish. Greenish-black gore poured out of its open abdominal cavity before the shift in weight sent the nim tumbling onto its heavy back.

Glissa quickly took stock. The leonin were in trouble, and this surprise attack was in danger of turning into a debacle. El-lash, Darlosh, and Tahk were still moving, but the other three skyhunters were being driven steadily back into the Dross. One of the leonin sliced through a necrogen tube with a clawed kick, sending green liquid spouting into the air. The nim attached to the tube swung its vicious arms wildly, and one clean swipe to the leonin's torso cut the female clean in two. Bright red blood mixed with bilious necrogen as the two foes collapsed into the oily mud.

"No!" Glissa screamed and clambered through the swamp to help her remaining allies. A nim came at her from the side, and she whirled with a low cut that should have taken the creature's legs off at the knees. Instead, the nim raised an iron claw and effortlessly blocked the strike, then backhanded her across the face. Glissa staggered, the world spinning crazily around her as she struggled to keep her sword and her balance at the same time. She bumped hard into Ellasha, who steadied the elf with one hand without looking.

The two remaining leonin warriors dispatched two more nim simultaneously with wicked slashes of their longknives, but were almost immediately felled under the blows of heavy nim claws. Within seconds, the two were dead, reduced to wet sacks of broken bone.

Glissa saw Tahk and Darlosh, keeping the other nim busy at the Vault entrance, making sure the door didn't swing shut unexpectedly. And now there were four. Glissa spared a glance at Ellasha. The skyhunter commander nodded in return.

"Charge!" Glissa shouted.

Elf and leonin launched themselves at the undead horrors with all their remaining strength. Glissa found herself facing the same creature that had nearly taken off her head a few seconds earlier. Not the most innovative tactician, the nim again took a swing with one huge claw. The elf girl was ready this time and ducked while bringing her blade down hard on the soft tissue of at the arm's joint, severing the limb. Before the nim could bring down its other claw, Glissa twirled the blade wide and jammed it upward into the nim's torso, gratified by the scrape of metal on metal as the blade emerged from the zombie's iron shell.

Glissa jerked the blade free and rolled to escape the creature's collapsing corpse, colliding violently with the armored legs of another zombie that had been trying to take her unawares. The nim tumbled forward as the elf girl bowled through its legs. Before the heavy, clumsy monster could regain its footing, Glissa had driven her blade through the back of its head.

Glissa turned to the leonin in time to watch in horror as one of the nim grasped Darlosh's leg in one lobster claw and swung the commando violently into Tahk, who had been coming in for a strike from the opposite side. Darlosh's sword impaled Tahk through the soft tissue under her chin and emerged at the top of her head, killing her instantly. A second nim grasped Darlosh, still dazed but alive, by the other leg.

With a sickening series of loud snaps, Darlosh was ripped apart like a wishbone. Her torn corpse showered scarlet gore and leonine guts across the swamp.

Glissa looked furtively at Ellasha, who let loose an agonized roar that shook the trees and made the elf girl's teeth rattle. The leonin went mad, cutting into the remaining nim like a whirl-wind. Glissa, fighting her rising gorge, charged in to help.

Leonin and elf worked as one unit, slicing, tearing, kicking and clawing through the ghouls that had slaughtered their friends. The nim fought as fiercely as before, but now Glissa and Ellasha were driven by something primal, and the zombies didn't stand a chance. After half of minute of furious fighting, Glissa stabbed the last nim standing through the gut, and kicked the body to-ward Ellasha, who finished it off with one sweep of her longknife through the green tubes attached to the vile monster's neck.

The sudden silence was made no less eerie by the green glow that suffused the mist as the dying nim spat necrogen smoke use-lessly into the air. Glissa and Ellasha were covered head to toe in Dross muck and a foul mix of leonin and nim innards. Glissa staggered to the leonin and placed one hand on her shoulder. "Ellasha—"

"Do not say anything. They made their peace with the gods long ago, as all soldiers do. They died warriors, and we should be so lucky," the grim leonin responded. She stooped and said a short, soft prayer over Darlosh's and Tahk's ruined bodies, which were closest to her, then slipped something from each dead warrior's belt. She turned and handed Glissa Tahk's longknife, which the elf girl accepted tentatively. Ellasha slipped Darlosh's into her own belt.

"My sisters have gone to fight at the side of Great Dakan forever," she said with a hint of ceremony. "I now claim the right of revenge."

"That makes two of us," Glissa said. "But their deaths were in vain if we don't get Bruenna out of here."

Ellasha nodded solemnly. "I can see why my Kha is fond of you, elf. You think like a leonin. There is a legend of an elf that fought at Great Dakan's side, did you know that?"

"Uh, no," Glissa said.

"His name is lost to history, but legends called him the Maneless One. He was a warrior of great skill, and ultimately gave his life saving the greatest of all leonin. You have the blood of the Maneless One in you, girl. I can smell it as surely as I can smell my own cubs. You honored them with your actions. Now don't dishonor them with pointless mewling."

Without another word, Ellasha turned on one foot and stalked toward the entrance to Yert's lair. A stunned Glissa followed, sick to her stomach.

CHAPTER 15

NOBODY'S VAULT BUT MINE

Glissa tapped Ellasha on the shoulder and jerked her head toward a shadowed alcove they had just passed.

"What is it?" the leonin whispered.

Glissa didn't say anything, but swung the heavy pack off of her shoulder and held it up meaningfully, looking from the bag and down the tunnel ahead. When the leonin just stared at her blankly, she decided to risk a few words. "This place. Too empty. It's suspicious. Want to consult the head."

"Good point," Ellasha replied softly. "I expected light resistance on the way in, but I would have thought that once we got here it would be crawling with nim. Maybe this is just a little-used passage," she added with a shrug. "I shall stand watch in the tunnel. Let me know what you learn." The skyhunter took a couple of steps and leaned cautiously against the corner of the alcove, well hidden from anyone who might come down the hall but with a clear line of sight in either direction. Her ears cocked forward, scanning for the heavy, clanking footsteps of nim warriors.

Glissa could easily see why Raksha had trusted Ellasha as second-in-command on this mission. She certainly fought with a ferocity and dexterity Glissa had never seen, but the skyhunter's composure was nothing short of heroic.

The elf girl flipped the pack open with one hand and clamped the other over Geth's mouth. She raised a claw to her lips, and was satisfied when the severed head did not sound any kind of alarm, when she uncovered his mouth. Geth's head crinkled his leathery brow and whispered, "What now?"

"Don't talk unless you're answering me," Glissa whispered. "Where are they?"

"Who? Your kitty cats? Beats me. They were all alive when I went in the bag. What did you do to them?"

Glissa silenced Geth with a glare. "The nim. The last time I was here, the place was crawling with them."

"Yeah, funny, isn't it?" Geth said evasively. "Strange to be in the needlebug nest and not find any needlebugs, eh?"

"Geth, I'm going to step on you."

"Okay, okay," Geth hissed more loudly than he needed to. "Fine, no fun for Geth, just stick Geth in the bag. . . ." Glissa's eyes narrowed, and he hurriedly added, "All right, all right. Your leonin was on the nose. Yert's sent almost all of the nim forces to the front lines. He thinks this is the perfect time, with the Golden Scrub away and his cousin in charge. The peace offer was nothing more than nim-waste."

"Really," Glissa said. "You're sure it's not to lure us into a sense of complacency before springing the trap?"

"You know, you didn't used to be so paranoid," Geth said. "I miss that innocent little elf girl who begged me to spare Yert's life. That sure worked out well, didn't it?"

"Answer the question," Glissa said, struggling to keep her anger in check.

"Honestly? You might be right. I wouldn't put anything past Yert these days," Geth's face took on an uncharacteristically thoughtful cast. "But you know, that's what I would have done. You're a fool if you *don't* expect that."

"Right," Glissa muttered. "Great. Anything else?"

"Yes," Geth said. "Duck."

It took Geth's warning a half-second to sink in, and if she'd waited any longer her own skull would have joined his on the floor. A nim claw slammed the rusted tunnel wall with a clang and a shower of blue sparks. Glissa dropped Geth's head and let it roll into the corner, then spun in a crouch, drawing her sword and readying her weary muscles for another fight.

The nim loomed over her, blocking her from the hall and El-lasha, wherever the leonin was. Since she hadn't warned her, she feared the worst for the skyhunter.

Glissa tried the same move that had worked before. With a yell, she jabbed upward with her sword, hoping to impale the nim through its relatively soft underbelly. The creature had taken her by surprise, however, and her strike was off. The hulking zombie caught the blade easily in one crustacean claw and wrenched it from her grip, then grabbed her roughly by the arm in another claw and jerked her to her feet. So much for her good shoulder.

The nim lumbered around slowly until it faced four more of its hulking, beetle-like kin. A pair of large, gray, ghoulish-looking humans that looked like mountains of necrotic muscle held El-lasha firmly between them, one holding a massive knotted hand over her muzzle. There was something about these humans that didn't seem quite right to Glissa. She had seen animated corpses and things like the nim that were a result of the necrogen's effect on those same zombies. She'd seen the towering monsters that Yert had once been tasked with controlling, the reapers. However, she'd never seen humans that looked both dead *and* alive. There was something familiar about the feral look in their eyes, but she couldn't put her claw tip on it.

Whatever they were, Glissa was fed up.

"Well?" Glissa shouted. "Is this how you welcome invited

guests, Yert? Because I have to say, I like Geth's approach better. At least he didn't play games!"

"A game, is it?" a cold voice called down the corridor. "I assure you, Glissa, this is very much the real thing."

At that, the two large gray humans holding Ellasha stepped aside and Glissa got her first look at Yert since leaving the young keeper to Geth's not-so-tender mercies. The elf girl hardly recognized him.

The young human's pale skin had become the same sickly gray as his henchmen. He appeared taller, as well, perhaps an optical illusion created by the majestic black robes that hung from his wiry frame like folded insect wings. As Yert raised his hands to pull back his hood, Glissa saw the tips of two black spikes, like dewclaws, on the underside of Yert's wrists.

"Geth?" Glissa called back toward the alcove. "Let me guess. You fed Yert to your vampire, didn't you?"

"Seemed like a good idea at the time," Geth's head called from the shadows. "I blame you, you know. If you hadn't crippled—"

"That thing still speaks? I guess I should not be surprised," Yert said. "Mercy will be your downfall, Glissa."

Yert sent a fist across Glissa's already battered jaw. "You overestimate your importance to me," Yert said. "Memnarch may want you alive, but I would just as soon open you up and feast upon your innards. I've learned elves have a tangy taste you just don't get in humans. I think it's those special spices you grow in the Tangle."

Glissa opened her mouth to retort, and as fast as lightning, Yert's right palm was pressed against her cheek. She froze. The black spike tip was less than an inch from her jugular. "For now, just a taste," he hissed.

She felt a pinch like a needlebug sting as Yert's feeding spike pierced her neck. Within seconds the loss of blood began to make her dizzy, and she already sensed red unconsciousness flooding her vision. If she didn't do something to stop him, she would be drained and dead within a minute. Nonetheless, she didn't dare try to wriggle free. Yert could tear her throat apart with the spike.

"Help," Glissa gasped.

She'd never felt more pathetic, she thought, as she grew more and more delirious. The mightiest hunter in the Tangle has walked into a snare hidden in plain sight. She should have known that Yert's sudden reappearance was too strange, and that there had to be something else to it. She should have remembered the vampire. And what vampires could do to the living, if they really wanted to.

Yert suddenly screamed and jerked the spike free. Glissa felt warm liquid running freely down the side of her neck. The blackness would take her in seconds. Already everything was growing hazy. She felt a hand press over the wound and heard a voice—Yert?—muttering a few words in some bizarre, guttural tongue big on glottal stops. The flow of blood stopped, and Glissa's vision cleared almost instantly. She spun free of the vampire's grip and stepped back cautiously.

Yert held one palm into his forehead, and straightened with great effort. "Yes," he said to the air, "I won't do it again. Please, make it stop."

Something was hurting Yert badly, something that Glissa couldn't see—but that mystery would have to wait. The other hand was still extended, covered in red blood. *Her* blood. And she took that sort of thing personally. Before she could think better of it, she slammed a fist into Yert's face, sending him stumbling back into the wall.

"Seize her, but do not kill!" he cried, still clutching his head. "The Guardian commands it!"

That explained his sudden headache, Glissa guessed.

Ellasha took advantage of her captor's distraction to bring her legs up and kick off the nearest wall, sending the gray brutes slamming into ironstone with a crunch of snapping ribs. As the pair hit the tunnel floor, Glissa noted twin sets of black spikes on the ends of their wrists. These two weren't human, either. Yert had been busy. If this kept up, humans were going to become extinct.

"Run!" she shouted to Ellasha. "Still have to find Bruenna. I'll catch up." The leonin commando leader nodded and headed down the tunnel at top speed, narrowly evading the grasping claws of the looming nim.

Glissa feinted right, causing a nim to stumble against the pair of vampires before they could recover from Ellasha's blow, then dashed back to the alcove. She scooped up Geth's head, which shouted "Hey!" as she stuffed it into the pack, then set off after the leonin as fast as her legs would carry her. As she passed the last slow-moving nim, she snatched her sword from the zombie's claws.

The tunnel behind her exploded with clanging footsteps as the nim gave chase. Glissa could make out Ellasha up ahead through the pervasive necrogen, and hoped she could keep pace with the fleet-footed feline. As if reading her mind, Ellasha looked back and paused, bouncing on impatient feet.

"Thanks for waiting," Glissa said breathlessly as she joined the leonin. Together they set off at a dead run into the heart of the Mephidross. "You're one . . . fast cat."

"Not . . . a cat," Ellasha said, "and you run . . . like a pixie."

"Elf," Glissa replied.

"Mush moh moo moh, mish mimsn't my maulf," Geth added.

"I actually believe it's *not* your fault, Geth," Glissa said.

"Now you're going to prove it by getting us to Bruenna and out again."

"My mate moo."

"I hate you too," Glissa said.

"The tunnel forks ahead," Ellasha said, stopping short. "Ask it which way to go."

"Might," the head said from inside the pack.

"Right?" Ellasha asked.

"Right," Glissa said.

They set off down the tunnel Geth had indicated, followed by an army of nim and three very angry vampires, one of which was beginning to wonder if an alliance with Memnarch was really such a good idea.

CHAPTER 16

TIME OUT

Glissa and Ellasha barreled along the tunnel, each one stumbling now and again as the strange, flickering necrogen light caused a weird vertigo that made it appear the floor was moving. But by staying alert, they were able to keep each other mostly upright. Geth's head could not have been enjoying the ride.

The elf came to an abrupt halt when Ellasha's open hand slapped her in the chest. The path ended abruptly a few feet ahead, where the tunnel opened into an enormous cavern. Glissa peeked over the edge and could not see the bottom, nor did she see a telltale pinprick of light indicating that this was an entrance to a lacuna.

This hole was just a hole. A very, very deep hole.

Dozens of footsteps tromped noisily down the path behind them, and Glissa was sure she heard Yert barking orders. She swung the pack under her shoulder without unslinging it and flipped the cover open.

"Geth!" Glissa hissed. "Small problem. Your route's not exactly . . . there." She yanked Geth's head from the pack and dangled him over the edge by one leathery ear. The head yelped. "See?" Glissa added.

"Yes, yes, yes, putmedownputmedownputmedown," Geth gasped.

The elf girl continued to dangle Geth's head as the grisly thing squealed, looking over her shoulder down the tunnel. Beetle-like shapes loomed in the green light. The nim would be here any second. Ellasha drew her longknives and stood squarely between Glissa and the oncoming nim troop. "Find us a way out of this," the skyhunter snarled.

Glissa pulled Geth back from the edge and looked him squarely in his glassy, clouded eyes. "Talk. How do we get over this chasm?"

"Don't know," the head gasped. "This path used to be solid, I swear! Probably happened in that cave-in you caused."

"You're kidding," Ellasha growled.

"It's the truth," the head said. "She collapsed half the Vault."

"Flare!" Glissa snapped and stuffed the head back into the pack, which she swung back to her shoulder. Too bad Bruenna was on the other side of the chasm—a little of the mage's flight magic would have solved everything. "Ellasha, I don't suppose you brought along a pair of wings. . . ."

The leonin turned to bark a reply then stopped, one ear cocked sideways in a manner that Glissa had learned displayed uncertainty or suspicion. "I can't believe I didn't think of that," the leonin growled.

Ellasha sheathed her knives in one fluid motion and met the first nim with a solid kick to the chest. "Open my pack," the leonin shouted as the nim collided with the one behind it and both tumbled onto their backs. One of the vampires—not Yert—came at Ellasha from the side. The leonin met it with a fist then gripped the creature's wrist and brought its forearm down hard across her knee. The bone snapped clean.

Glissa scrambled up behind the leonin and hacked wildly at another nim that was creeping in from Ellasha's blind spot. She severed its arm and necrogen tube on her third strike, a lucky hit. The nim went down, but the rest still plodded inexorably onward. Yert's apparent absence disturbed her. She was sure she'd heard him only moments ago. She wondered idly if vampires could become invisible.

In the clear for a moment, she flipped the latch on Ellasha's pack and looked inside.

"The wide pocket in the back," she growled. "Hurry."

Glissa spotted the pocket easily and reached inside. She pulled out what looked like a folded sheet of silver linen.

"What's this?" Glissa asked, baffled, as the pair of them backed closer and closer to the deadly drop.

"Just put them on," Ellasha said as she jabbed her longknives into two nim at once, pushing them back into the clacking mob, "They're for emergencies, so they'll only carry one person. Well, maybe one and a head. Cross the straps over your chest. Do it now!"

"Okay!" Glissa yelled, and slipped two thin cables over her shoulders. The silvery linen rested against her shoulder blades, above Geth's head. Preoccupied, Glissa didn't get her sword raised in time to block another set of nim claws, but the late parry caused her to strike the nim's soft, exposed joints, which worked just as well. She moved shoulder to shoulder with the skyhunter, and risked a look back over her shoulder. More nim were milling about the opposite side of the deep pit as well. Several spread their black beetle-wings and launched themselves lazily across the chasm "Now what?" Glissa shouted as the noise of clacking nim feet and buzzing wings became almost unbearable.

"Your friend!" Ellasha shouted over the din between slashes of her longknives. "She's important? She'll help the Kha save our people and beat these monsters?"

"Of course!" Glissa replied. "But shouldn't we be worried about—"

"Then make sure the loremasters hear of the leonin who died

today," Ellasha said, and shoved Glissa out into open space. As she plummeted into the dark, she heard the leonin skyhunter roar, a sound that drowned out the nim above and was followed by a furious clanging of steel longknives on iron claws.

The elf girl fell at least twenty feet before the silver linen on her back unfolded of its own accord into a set of four thin wings. The wings began to buzz like those of the nim, and Glissa felt descent slow, cease, and slowly reverse. How would she stop?

Glissa stopped.

And to go up? With the thought, the wings responded to her urgent need, gaining speed quickly. It wasn't unlike Bruenna's flight magic.

She emerged between two hovering nim that slowly turned inward to face her, claws clicking menacingly. Glissa willed the wings to carry her higher, which would buy her a few precious seconds to spot Ellasha.

The skyhunter was some thirty feet back from the chasm, awash in a sea of nim, and fighting with utter ferocity. The skyhunter was a gold and silver blur, leaping and twirling through the black mass of zombies with longknives blazing. Green ichor and necrogen steam sprayed in the air.

The leonin briefly made eye contact with Glissa. "GO!" Ellasha shouted.

Glissa's sword arm began to tremble with rage and frustration. The flying nim below were almost close enough strike. Ellasha was buying her time, and the chance to save Bruenna, and the brave skyhunter was going to die in the process. Glissa might be able to save the leonin if she dove into the fray herself, but even then there were only two of them. Yert's supply of nim seemed limitless. They would both eventually be overwhelmed.

"I'll tell the loremasters," she whispered. She turned and

willed the wings to take her onward to Bruenna. Bruenna, who could still be saved.

Glissa gritted her teeth, fighting back fresh tears. If Ellasha's sacrifice was going to mean anything, she couldn't lose it now. She wanted nothing more than to lay into the nim with every last ounce of her strength. Her anger demanded it, but she couldn't waste the time.

Fortunately, Glissa found it was relatively easy to keep clear of the nim's strikes, though she had a few close calls at points where the tunnel narrowed. Flying nim were a problem, too, but they were so clumsy in the air that she had little trouble avoiding them. But every nim turned and followed her.

The elf girl still had no idea what she was going to do when she found Bruenna, or even how she was going to get her out. But one problem at a time. They had to find the Neurok first. Glissa had been forced to remove Geth's head from her pack and carry it along so he could guide her, which would be a liability as soon as she landed and had to turn and face the mob behind her. She would have gladly tossed the undead thing aside, but she still needed Geth to get them out, too. Still, if he didn't lead her to Bruenna soon she might pitch him anyway. He smelled even worse than the nim, and she was beginning to wonder if Geth really knew where he was going.

"Wait, turn, turn!" the head shouted. "Back there, the branching passage!"

Glissa whirled and followed Geth's direction. This offshoot was much narrower, but there were no nim, and dim light was cast by the occasional necrogen lamp.

"This way isn't used much," Geth said, as if reading her mind. "It's the back way."

"Not bad, Geth," Glissa said. "It'll also keep the nim from attacking us all at once. So why don't I trust you?"

"Beats me," Geth replied. "But trust that I want my body back, and I don't see any other way to do it but help you. Now slow down, eh? We're almost there."

The tunnel ahead glowed brighter green, and appeared to open into a larger room. Glissa willed the wings to slow down, and she took a moment to turn Geth's head so it was facing backward. "Nim?"

"I hear them, but can't see them yet," Geth said. "Could you turn me back around now?"

Glissa obliged, peering into the green glow ahead. She could make out a single shape in the mist-filled room, something like a statue on a pedestal. She stopped short and turned Geth to face her.

"Time for you to get back into your pack," Glissa said. "I can't fight with you in my hand."

"See, you know you love me," Geth cackled.

"I despise you, but you're going to get me back out of here," Glissa said. "Before I put you away, can you tell me anything else about that room?"

"Sure. It's a room. There are prisoners. Looks misty. What do you want? I've been severed from my body for weeks," Geth said. At Glissa's scowl, he added, "Okay, there are cells lining the wall, five of them. Probably two guards."

"Probably?"

"That's what I would have posted. Can't speak for Yert. Will you get it through your head I'm not in charge here?" Geth's head smirked. "And that thing in the middle is the torture platform."

"Lovely," Glissa said.

"You're not kidding," Geth replied. "It's amazing. I got it from a vedalken slavemaster who told me he used it for 'motivation through pain' on *all* his stock. It looks like a simple table, but I had it enchanted to transform into eighteen different configurations. And of course it changes size to fit the occupant. That slavemaster knows his—"

Glissa stuffed the head into the pack. "Quiet," she said, squinting into the green light. The pedestal must be the torture table, which made her think that was probably no statue. She couldn't make out anyone else in the room. No nim, no vampires, no Yert, nothing.

It was an obvious trap. But Glissa had to walk into it.

No, not walk into it. *Fly* into it. That was at least one advantage. Still, she decided a cautious approach might be warranted. The nim were some distance back down the narrow tunnel, her ears told her. She could afford to move deliberately this time instead of charging head first—her usual opening tactic, and one that of late had been meeting with mixed results.

Yet as Glissa closed the distance and she could see more clearly into the mist-filled, brightly lit green room, she became even more confused. She saw two cell doors open and facing her, empty. The torture table did indeed appear to be nothing more than a table. But the statue was no statue. It was a person.

Bruenna stood atop the table, wrapped up to her nose in corroded iron cable that held her suspended like an insect in an arachnid's web. Hollow tubes were jammed here and there through the cable into Bruenna's abdomen and back, with one appearing connected to the base of her skull. At first Glissa thought that the tubes were pumping necrogen into the Neurok, but as she drew nearer she saw the tubes were glowing with soft blue light.

The mage's eyes goggled when she saw Glissa, and the elf girl could detect the faintest shaking of her friend's head.

Glissa entered the room, keeping one eye on Bruenna and using the other to scan the torture chamber. It was smaller than she'd expected, but then torture could be a very private matter.

All of the cells were empty, as were most of the shackles hung on the walls. A few of those still held the skeletons of luckless prisoners.

If this was Yert's idea of a trap, it wasn't a very good one. She threw stealth aside and zipped over to Bruenna, descending to stand on the table in front of the hapless mage.

"I'm going to get you out of here," Glissa said. "Can you hear me?"

Bruenna gave the faintest of nods, and winced.

"I have to unhook you from these tubes. Can I do that without hurting you?" Glissa asked.

Bruenna began to shake her head again, wincing with each tiny movement, but refusing to stop.

"At least I can get you out of these cables. Let's see . . ." Glissa said, searching for a loose end she could use to unravel Bruenna's iron cocoon. Nothing. Whoever had wrapped Bruenna in this painful-looking cable had been thorough. "All right, if I can't unravel it, I can cut it."

Glissa's sword flashed, and the two cables holding the mage upright snapped. The elf girl caught Bruenna as she fell forward, and she saw that the cable was beginning to loosen on its own. It was all one piece—that was why she couldn't find a loose thread.

Gently, Glissa began to unwrap the Neurok mage. The nim were getting closer, but with luck she wouldn't be here when they arrived. Bruenna gasped as Glissa pulled the thick cable away from her mouth.

"No!" Bruenna cried as soon as she'd drawn breath. Suddenly the mage disappeared in a flash of blinding azure light, forcing Glissa to—

CHAPTER 17

INTERMISSION

—raise her arms to protect her eyes from the glare. She tumbled backward and landed hard on her back, and something jabbed her painfully in the lower back. A yelp told her that she'd also landed on Geth, who let out a long stream of muffled invective aimed at her parentage. "Shut up, Geth," she mumbled.

Glissa blinked against the glare that filled the air above her and hadn't gone away. She couldn't see a thing, in fact, not the rest of the room, not the torture table . . .

She did see razor grass. Lots and lots of razor grass, disappearing into infinity wherever she looked. Glissa was in the Glimmervoid. But how? She rolled over onto her belly, then pushed off the ground—

"Ow!" Glissa yelped, and jerked back, rolling into a crouch. She turned her hands palm upward and blinked, trying to focus in the sweltering glare. Her hands were green with blood welling from several fresh, thin cuts. "So it's real," she muttered. "How in the name of every last god in the Tangle did I get here?"

"First things first," Geth said from the pack on her back, which must have flapped open. "Who's attached to those boots?"

Glissa turned around, shielding her eyes against the bright sky. She followed the black boots until they met unfamiliar metallic blue armor, and on up to a familiar face.

"Glissa," Bruenna said warmly, a soft rasp in her voice as she broke into a grin. The mage offered her a hand up, and Glissa got a good look at her friend in the bright light of the moons. All five were over the horizon, which explained the heat and glare, with the yellow, sun-like moon (or moon-like sun, if you were a leonin) directly overhead. There was a strange symmetry to the moons. The last time she'd looked the green one was the only one in the sky.

Bruenna's voice and the weird blue armor weren't the only things that had suddenly changed. The mage's face was drawn and angular, more than a little careworn. A jagged white scar emerged from the collar of Bruenna's armor and disappeared behind her left ear. As Glissa released the human's hand she noticed Bruenna wore something that looked like a gauntlet, but with three too many fingers and an extra thumb.

The mage noticed Glissa staring at her hands and raised the bizarre gauntlet, twiddling the digits, and shrugged. "Took it off a vedalken patrol. The vedalken won't be needing it anymore. Besides, they owed me a hand."

"What?" Glissa managed. "Vedalken? Bruenna, what happened to you? Why did you say—how did you—some kind of teleportation spell, right?"

"Plenty has happened to me," Bruenna replied, furtively casting a glance over her shoulder. Glissa, still half-blinded by the bright moons, tried to make out what she was looking at, but saw only what looked like a distant, blurry, dark-colored wall. "But now isn't the time. The nim will be on patrol today." Bruenna raised two fingers to her lips and emitted a series of short whistles and clicks that reminded Glissa of several different avian species native to the Tangle.

In response to Bruenna's call, a pair of long necks rose cautiously over the grass, several paces away. The zauks bobbed their heads from side to side for a second then stood, smoothly rising from a sitting position with a peculiarly clumsy avian grace. The pair of flightless birds, both unsaddled, trotted over to the mage and her perplexed companion. One began to poke its beak at Geth's pack.

"Hey! Shoo! Not food!" Geth squealed. Glissa gently nudged the zauk away and closed the pack tight. "Mank moo," the head said.

"Bruenna, take your time. I mean, nim? We're in the middle of the 'void, in broad daylight. We'd see them coming a mile away. *What's going on?"* Glissa asked, still squinting at that black wall. No, not a wall.

The Mephidross. They were at the swamp's edge, or close, anyway. Glissa couldn't understand why the mage had transported her here. Taj Nar or anywhere else, except a few choice locations in the Dross or the interior, would have been better. Until she got an explanation, though, she decided to keep her mouth shut. Complaining about the exact location of her rescue seemed petty.

"What are the last things you remember?" Bruenna asked and cupped her hands into a stirrup, helping the baffled elf girl clamber onto the patient zauk's bare back. Glissa took the reins the Neurok woman handed her and patted the zauk's neck softly. The bird cooed and flicked its glittering silver headcrest.

"But you were just there."

"Humor me."

"Well, the last thing I—ow, sorry, there, fella—the last thing I remember, you shouted 'No,' then everything went white," Glissa said. "In the Vault. I was trying to free you. Then I was here, getting poked by razor grass."

"Do you remember Ellasha?" Bruenna asked.

"Of course," Glissa said, "She—she died so that I could get to you. She held back the nim, while I—wait, you never met Ellasha."

"You're mistaken," the human replied, pulling herself onto

her mount with practiced ease. "Ellasha eventually fought her way through the tunnels and found me. Was able to free me, since the trap had already been sprung. But she *was* killed in our escape. Noble Ellasha died five years ago today."

Glissa reined her zauk to a halt.

"Five *what* ago today?"

* * * * *

The moons beat down even hotter, if that was possible, as the pair of zauks dashed on lithesome feet across the razor plains, their scaly silver legs easily deflecting the slashing grass blades. Glissa scanned the dark line of the Mephidross. "Shouldn't we be riding away from that?" Glissa asked.

"Easier said than done," Bruenna said sadly. "The Dross is . . . bigger than you remember. It has been a long five years."

"Think you can fill me in on the way back to Taj Nar?" Glissa said. "Where's my sister? Tell me she's alive."

"She is fine," Bruenna said. "As fine as can be expected. There is much to tell, and some of it will be easier to show you. But I shall explain what I can."

"Thanks," Glissa said. "Let's start with how I missed the last five years."

"As you no doubt suspect, I was the bait in a trap set for you," Bruenna said. "Yert used vedalken magic to carve a temporal sigil into the floor. The sigil triggered a spell that was powered by . . . by me." Bruenna shuddered.

"Those tubes."

"Yes," Bruenna continued. "They were drawing magical energy from me into the table, which made the sigil work. Time stopped for you and Geth, and for the rest of us . . ." the mage shrugged.

"Life went on," Glissa concluded. "Flare! So Yert and Memnarch *were* in cahoots. I *thought* that was who that vampire bastard was talking to. But where have I been this whole time? Just standing on that table? Was I even, you know, *here*? Nothing feels quite right."

"Not surprising," Bruenna sighed. "Nothing is. I told you how Ellasha was killed getting me out of the tunnels under the Dross. As soon as I was out, I headed for the leonin base camp. They weren't where I left them—Yshkar had the army on the move. They were returning to Taj Nar."

"Yes, I remember," Glissa said. "Raksha changed his mind after we fought Dwugget's goblins. He decided to return to the city after all. So Raksha and Lyese must have made it back all right."

"Indeed, and their mission was quite successful, as it turned—"

A silver-blue energy bolt the color of Bruenna's armor materialized out of nowhere and slammed into the neck of Bruenna's zauk. The bird managed half a squawk of pained surprise before it exploded in a flash of feathers, slag, and burning avian flesh. Bruenna was blasted into the air by the shock wave, describing a lazy arc that ended when she collided with the razor grass. Hopefully her armor had protected Bruenna from the blades, because Glissa couldn't help the human right now.

The elf girl's zauk was terrified. Glissa struggled to calm the panicked bird, which wouldn't stop squawking and trying to bolt, while scanning the sky for the source of the energy blast.

"Flare," Glissa muttered as her suspicions were confirmed. "Aerophins." At least a dozen of them, in fact. They appeared much bigger and better armed than the ones Glissa had taken out in the Tangle a few days—no, years—ago. The fiendish flying constructs bristling with blades and small, sharp claws, and each carried a ring of black cylinders mounted on the front of their glassy, globular heads.

The cylinders on the nose of the nearest 'phin crackled with blue sparks, giving the elf girl just enough warning to jerk the reins and dodge another bolt of magical energy. The shot from the 'phin's nose-cylinders slammed into the grasslands, tearing up chunks of metal and sending a deadly hail of grass blades flying in all directions. Glissa held up her arms to protect her face, gritting her teeth as the jagged razors cut into her metallic flesh. These aerophins didn't just look more dangerous, their energy blasts were also a great deal stronger than she'd expected.

Glissa heard her zauk emit a strangled, agonized cry. A dozen grass blades had punctured its neck and breast, and one had neatly skewered the bird's head through the right eye and out the left ear. Before she could dismount, the bird whimpered one last time and collapsed on its side, pinning Glissa's leg beneath its bulk.

The leg didn't feel broken, but she was stuck. The aerophins, more than two dozen of them now, circled like carrion birds.

Glissa hadn't traveled this far—through time, apparently, as well as around the entire plane at least twice—to die alone on the razor fields, pinned beneath a dead bird that suddenly smelled extremely pungent.

The elf girl heard a groan coming from where Bruenna had crashed to the ground. Craning her neck, Glissa could just see the Neurok. Bruenna was still alive, but grass blades had slipped through the joints in her armor at several points and appeared to hold her fast to the ground. The plants glistened red with human blood.

Glissa brought her free leg up to her chest and kicked with all her might against the twitching zauk's back, levering it up just far enough to free her trapped limb, then scooted out of the way before the corpse rolled back to trap her a second time. "Just hold your fire a little longer," she said softly to the circling aerophins.

The elf got back to her feet in time to dodge another blast. This one struck the corpse of Glissa's zauk and nearly vaporized it. Only the neatly cauterized head at the edge of a small, smoldering crater remained.

That was it. Shooting at Glissa and Bruenna was one thing, but going after their zauks was just low. "I said *hold your fire!*" the elf girl shouted, and whipped her arms into the sky.

She felt the spark respond to her coaxing inner call. Every time she reached within to touch the pinpoint of strange magic, it had become easier, but this felt like the entire mana core was channeling through her body. Glissa felt the spark-power surge forward like a kharybdog finally set free of its leash. A warm green glow encased the elf girl's arms, spread wide overhead. Glissa's spine tingled and her hair stood on end.

She brought her hands together with a clap, and a blast of crackling green fire immolated the sky and everything Glissa could see within it, one piece at a time.

The wave of emerald energy collided with the globular head of the lead aerophin, shattered it like a glass bowl, and sent sparks, flaming serum, and metal shards raining into the air. The fire leapfrogged from construct to construct with incrementally greater force and destruction. Glissa felt bitter satisfaction as each one died.

Within thirty seconds, the aerophins were gone. Glissa had annihilated the 'phins, making sure each one disintegrated, so this time there was no need to avoid any descending wreckage. Of course, last time Glissa had tried this trick the aerophins had numbered in the thousands, and this time there had been a little more than a dozen.

The 'phins were gone, but she suspected someone was going to be missing them and soon. And since Glissa was more or less a stranger in her own world at the moment, she needed Bruenna.

The human's skin had gone from soft azure to purple—Bruenna's mount had taken the brunt of the blast, but there had been energy to spare. In fact, the Neurok woman was still smoldering. Thousands of tiny red spots dotted her face and arms where bits of metal had pierced the skin. The fallen mage wasn't moving.

Glissa placed an ear to Bruenna's breast, and sighed with relief when she heard a faint heartbeat. "What do you know," Glissa grinned as the mage's eyes fluttered open. "You humans are tougher than I thought. Don't talk, I'm going to do what I can, but this first part is going to hurt. I have to get you free of this grass." Without another word, she grabbed Bruenna by her armored shoulders and pulled the mage into a sitting position, eliciting a cry of pain from the injured woman.

Still flush with the energy of the spark, Glissa easily reached out to the distant Tangle and touched the magic of the forest. It felt a little peculiar, wilder and harder to tame than before, but with a little effort, the elf girl was able to work a few healing incantations and bring Bruenna back from the brink, if not anywhere near perfect health. She was no leonin healer, but she knew plenty of quick fixes for small wounds, and she drew on all of them at once.

The human's eyes blinked against the glare, and Glissa helpfully positioned herself between Bruenna's eyes and the yellow moon. The elf girl held out her hand. Bruenna pulled herself up with Glissa's help, and leaned heavily on the elf girl's shoulder. Glissa scanned the horizon, and saw a few glittering specks of silver pass in front of the blue moon. More hunters from Memnarch, from the look of them. "Can you walk?" she asked Bruenna, and pointed at the distant flyers.

The mage squinted at the aerophins. "They're coming from Lumengrid. We're too close to the sea. I should never have taken us this way."

"Your magic," Glissa said. "Can you disappear us out of here?"

Bruenna closed her eyes for a moment. "I don't think so," she whispered. "Retrieving you from the interior took a lot out of me. Memnarch didn't want to let you go. The safeguards around you were very strong."

"But I wasn't in the interior. I thought I was in the—" Glissa began then switched course. "Okay, tell me about it later. What about flight magic? With my leg and your—well, everything, we don't stand a chance of outrunning more of those things. And I don't know if I can pull off that trick again soon."

"I think I can get us airborne, with a little boost," Bruenna said. She reached out and took Glissa's hands. The metal of the mage's artificial appendage was unnaturally cold.

"A boost?" Glissa asked. "What, from me?" The idea of sharing magic with another wasn't unknown among the Viridians. But Glissa had begun to think of herself as a focusing point, a conduit for the energy of the Tangle. She didn't even know if she *could* share it with Bruenna, who was after all human. But Glissa could try.

"Yes," Bruenna said, closing her eyes. "Just concentrate, as if you're summoning the power for an ordinary, everyday enchantment. Don't try too hard, just let it happen."

Glissa closed her eyes and called the Tangle energy, which didn't fight back this time. The elf felt the power move through her and into Bruenna through their physical connection, then it washed back over Glissa in a cool wave that felt at once alien and familiar—a blend of quicksilver and Tangle, two magical auras merging into something greater than the sum of their parts.

Bruenna flung her head back and pushed away from Glissa, her body glowing blue-white. Glissa herself no longer felt drained, and when she looked down at her body she saw it was giving on a faint green glow of its own.

The mage clapped her hands together and then swung them wide. Glissa once again felt the soles of her feet leave the ground and grinned.

"Time to go. Follow me," Bruenna said, immediately taking to the air. As Glissa launched into the sky behind her, the mage called over her shoulder, "And do *not* go near Taj Nar, even if we get separated."

"Why not?" Glissa asked. She glanced back over her shoulder. The aerophins were receding, but she didn't think that meant they'd given up. She and Bruenna were simply flying more quickly than they'd been walking. Still, it gave them a head start and offered the elf a moment to collect her bearings and catch her breath. Flying was more relaxing than it looked, when you weren't fighting for your life at the same time.

As they rose higher and more of the landscape opened up below her, Glissa noted something strange—here and there, the plains were dotted with thin, silver spires. These enormous needles rose eighty, maybe a hundred feet in the air.

"Bruenna, what are those things?" she asked as they flew past.

"No one's sure," Bruenna confessed. "They appear overnight, and we stopped investigating them after a while. They're completely inert, as near as I can tell. Possibly some kind of mutated strain of razor grass."

"You don't sound like you believe that," Glissa said.

"No, I don't," Bruenna said. "I think there is only one logical explanation."

"Memnarch?" Glissa asked.

"That's what I fear," Bruenna said. "But whatever they are, for now they're only a hazard to low-flying elves. Watch for them when we get closer to home. We're going to need to drop our altitude soon."

"Where *are* we going?"

"Taj Nar hasn't been safe for many cycles," Bruenna said without further explanation. "We're headed to Krark-Home. It's—"

"In the Oxidda Mountains?" Glissa remarked. "Underground? Somewhere near a big furnace, and a hole in the ground the size of that red moon?"

"Er, yes," Bruenna said. "I'm sorry, Glissa. You have been gone so long, I've forgotten what you know and what you don't. It took so long to even find you."

"But you didn't give up," Glissa said. "Thank you, Bruenna."

"You're quite welcome, and forgive me if I repeat what you know. Trust me, things will be much clearer once we get to the mountains."

Already Glissa could see the angular peaks of the Oxidda range coming over the horizon ahead. She was glad to have something else to focus on.

"I am not a leader," Bruenna continued, "Not anymore. My people are long gone. I have not seen another Neurok in years. I have to assume they're dead, or worse. Now I just do what I can for the Kha and her highness. So far, we've kept the nim from taking the mountains, but how long I can't say. Yert's had five years to spread the Dross, and the larger it gets, the greater his power to coordinate the nim grows. As if that wasn't bad enough, there's also Malil and the vedalken."

"I saw vedalken in the interior, when we went down the lacuna hunting for Memnarch."

"I believe they returned to Lumengrid after Memnarch had his way with them. He reshaped them into killing machines, Glissa," Bruenna said. "They lead the construct beasts in endless attacks against our defensive positions, and they're chipping away at us faster than the nim. Some of them have taken to patrolling alone, too."

"Why not turn the nim and the vedalken against each other?" Glissa asked, but feared she knew the answer.

"Lumengrid and the Guardian apparently have maintained some kind of truce with Yert," Bruenna replied. "There's a loose border running between the Dross and the sea, but it's remained stable for the last few years. And there's something else that suggests an alliance—the vedalken and nim often attack us on two fronts simultaneously. That's happened too many times to be a coincidence. And of course, there's the temporal sigil. That's vedalken magic. Yert couldn't have done it alone. As for why Yert has yet to spread the Dross to cover the plains, let alone the Tangle, that's still a mystery. I believe Memnarch is holding Yert back for some reason. I just haven't figured out why yet."

"Yert's a fool," Geth's head interrupted. "Just look at that swamp! The necrogen! If *I* had access to that kind of power—"

"But you don't, so if you don't want me to stick you on the top of one of those spires, you'll butt out," Glissa snapped. "I'm almost afraid to ask," she continued, turning back to Bruenna, "But do we have a plan? Did you just miss me?"

"We all thought you were lost after months passed without word," Bruenna said. "It took me years to identify the sigil that had frozen you, and you were taken almost immediately. After what we had seen that day, I had to assume the worst—that Memnarch had you, or you were dead. And there was no way to get back into the interior to find you, with the war."

CHAPTER 18

KRARK-HOME

"I've lost them," Glissa said, scanning the sky behind them. "Looks like they gave up."

"Very likely," Bruenna agreed. "Such a small force wouldn't last long against Krark-Home."

They followed a familiar path into the foothills from the plains that led to the long, narrow canyon where Alderok Vektro had ambushed Glissa days before—from her perspective. It had not changed much, except for the occasional silver needle spire. There was more tree growth, but not much else.

She couldn't say the same for Taj Nar. They had purposefully avoided flying too close to the fallen leonin city, and even from miles away it had been easy for Glissa to see why. The gleaming silver and white parapets of the city walls looked as if they had been melted by some great heat, and from a distance resembled grasping claws clutching at the distant moons. What was left of the city interior was little more than a burned-out shell of mangled leonin architecture. The palace was entirely gone, reduced to a mountain of rubble in the center of it all. Curiously, one of the odd needle spires punctured the rubble to pierce the sky above.

The mystery of the spires played in the back of her mind. They reminded her of something, and she couldn't quite pin down what.

Instead of dwelling on the needle towers, which Bruenna had already said she knew little about, the elf girl asked the mage why Yert had not pushed the Dross forward to swallow the ruins of Taj Nar as well. Bruenna admitted she wasn't sure. For some reason the mage was tight-lipped about the fall of Taj Nar or the details of how she found Glissa. Too much to go into, the mage told her. Later, when they got to Krark-Home.

"We need to drop down into that draw up ahead," Bruenna said. "Helps keep the spy eyes from finding the exact entrance we're using today."

"Right," Glissa said and followed the mage as she swooped between the steep iron walls lining the canyon trail. Bruenna pointed to a few specific greenish shrubs clinging to the sides of the walls. Glissa examined one more closely and saw a goblin in mottled green armor perched within the leaves, holding a short-bow trained on the Bruenna.

"Get down!" Glissa shouted and launched herself forward to push Bruenna out of harm's way. The pair nearly crashed into a needle spire that appeared abruptly in front of them as they rounded the bend to avoid the goblin's shot, but Glissa dodged the smooth silver surface at the last second.

"Are you crazy?" Bruenna shouted.

"Goblins," Glissa gasped and reached for her sword.

"Those are the guards," Bruenna replied as they floated slowly up the canyon, the urgency to reach the base momentarily forgotten. "I told you, the defenses keep us safe for now. And the guards are part of the defenses."

"But they were getting ready to attack," Glissa said. "This is where Vektro ambushed us—"

"I didn't know you had a problem with goblins," Bruenna replied.

That stung. Suddenly Glissa recalled where she had been

going when she was originally diverted to rescue the Neurok mage. "Slobad," she whispered. "Five years . . . is he—?"

"I'm sorry," Bruenna said. "Glissa, after we lost you, entering the interior to save one lone goblin—even Slobad—was deemed far too dangerous. You haven't seen these beasts Memnarch has unleashed on us, Glissa. And from the few scouting missions that have been able to get down there, we know the interior is crawling with even more of them. He's got an army just waiting to replace every construct that falls on the surface with three more."

"So Slobad . . . he'd dead," Glissa said simply. She didn't voice the thought, but a part of her *hoped* he was dead. The alternative—five years of endless torture as the poor goblin waited for a rescue that could never come—was too horrific to consider.

* * * * *

Slobad hummed to himself as he worked. His primary awareness currently occupied millions of tiny, insect-sized constructs. The scuttling brickbugs were each no bigger than a fly, but had no wings and crawled over one another in a thick, tangled pile. From a distance, Slobad knew (since he could also look at the scene through the eyes of any one of a billion other artifact constructs on the surface) the pile of brickbugs looked like a writhing silver blob. With surprising speed, that blob began to narrow at the top to a point, which slowly rose out of the central silver mass, like a plant yearning for the light. But this was no plant. Thousands of brickbugs effortlessly piled up, one on top of the other, as the mass took on the distinctive unnatural shape of a long, straight, silver needle spire.

With a thought, Slobad ordered all the brickbugs in the writhing silver needle to lock their tiny claws together simultaneously.

He sent a surge of serum energy along the great skeleton of the web, of which the needle spire was about to become a part. The effect was not particularly dazzling: The spire shimmered for a moment then became completely smooth and solid. The brick-bugs were still there, but the Guardian's artisan had fused their exoskeletons into a solid, near-impervious material that was over forty percent stronger than darksteel.

The web was nearly complete. Soon the master would emerge from hibernation and take his place on the ascension platform, and Slobad would be rewarded.

Rewarded? Slobad's a happy slave. A machine. He's gonna change your oil, huh? Or were you gonna just walk out on your own two—oh yeah, never mind.

Slobad ignored the voice. He'd gotten quite good at ignoring things over the last few years. Pain, for one. A part of his mind, a clinical subdivision now permanently connected to a nearby myr, knew that his body was practically useless. His arms and legs had long since been removed to prevent fatal infection—something he had been forced to handle himself with his memnoid builder constructs and no anasthetic, thank you very much—and his sagging grey skin hung over a distended, malnourished belly and jutting ribs. His head looked like a skull covered in melted rust. His deformed jaw, repeatedly battered by Malil whenever the metal man felt the urge, hung open and rested at a twisted angle on his sunken chest.

A dozen pink crystals pressed against his skin, sending thin, steady streams of serum energy into his withered form and his still-vibrant brain—the only part of Slobad that had not become a mockery of its former self in the last five years. Fortunately for Slobad, he didn't need food or water anymore. He now subsisted entirely on a dwindling supply of serum. He had a sneaking suspicion that Malil had been dipping into it lately, but he had yet to catch one of the metal men, even with the myr linked to his mind. Whatever the case, the serum would keep him going until the last strut was fitted into the web, and then it would run out. The great structure now spread from the rebuilt Panopticon to fill much of the open space in the interior, and lacked only a few key connections.

Once those were in place Slobad would rest, at long last.

Die, you mean, the voice sneered inside his head. It sneered a lot lately. He pulled his attention away from the pipefitter constructs and let his subconscious take over their basic operations, which didn't require his full attention. Instead he focused inward on something he'd almost forgotten about.

A bitter, black little ball of *self.* The goblin he used to be, before the Guardian made Slobad his creature. *You know where this leads. Been ignoring me too long.*

No, Slobad thought, done what I must. The master—

Listen to yourself, huh? Sound like elf. Or vedalken. Or nim. The master, the master. You do not serve the master! Slobad's old self raged. *You are Slobad. You are no servant. You not remember, huh? He did this to you. Crab-legs. You got worms in the noggin. Little worms that spread your mind all over the world. Worms stringing you up to those memnoids, and myr, and who knows what else? Memnarch turned you into a toolbox. And turned your brain to mush, huh?*

I don't know, Slobad confessed, and he felt unfamiliar painful twinges on either side of his temple.

Trust me, the goblin's old self said, *It's true. But I waited, huh? Waited for things to get close to the end. Hid myself in that big, messy, spread-out mind of yours. I knew she'd escape before the end.*

Escape? Slobad asked. Who?

Glissa, his old voice responded. *This thing Crab-legs has got you building—it's gonna kill her. And you. But killing* you *might not be so bad, huh?*

Glissa? Slobad's splintered mind asked. Who that?

* * * * *

Glissa, as it had turned out, overshot the entrance to Krark-Home when she charged off in a rage. After a confusing, unnecessary chase, Bruenna dragged her back to the hidden door.

"Mother," Bruenna said, placing her hand against a typical oxidized iron outcropping that looked a little too typical. At Bruenna's touch and the spoken password, the rock had shimmered and disappeared, revealing a long tunnel carved from solid copper ore lit by erratically spaced goblin flame tubes that sparked and crackled in their sconces. They had landed at the threshold and walked from there. Bruenna informed her that Krark-Home was protected by several magical dampening auras for security, and Glissa didn't question her. She'd had no doubt the mage knew what she was talking about.

Geth's head had been mercifully quiet. Probably for his own protection. Glissa kept telling herself she had a good reason to keep the thing with her, and indeed maybe he would be useful. And besides, the Geth was the only other being that had been stuck outside of time along with her. It was a weird bond, but Glissa wasn't ready to sever it yet. Part of her was still having trouble trusting that this was all real, and Geth's head was a grisly reality check. She'd found a few old rags lying about and stuffed them over the zombie head to smother the odor a bit, and so far no one seemed to notice it. Either that, or none of the goblin guards they passed were willing to tell her she smelled like a corpse.

Now, the elf girl was going to learn if the long journey had been worth it. She wasn't sure what to expect from Dwugget. Bruenna had been extremely evasive about who else she could expect to see in the closed chamber before her. Glissa wondered if she wouldn't have been better off just heading for the Tangle. She imagined what five years of growth around the lacuna would have done to the place. The hunting would be fantastic.

"Glissa," Bruenna said, indicating the pack holding Geth's head. "Are you sure you want to bring that?"

Glissa nodded. "He's with me for now."

"Up to you. You're the Chosen One," Bruenna said. "Ready? We're on."

"Will you stop calling me the—" A metallic scraping that ended in a loud click interrupted Glissa, and the heavy clockwork lock on the double doors slid open. The elf girl straightened and shrugged her shoulders in an attempt to make the pack on her back a little less conspicuous. With a rush of equalizing air pressure, the bronze doors swung inward, away from them, with a clang that rang like a gong.

"Presenting Glissa of the Tangle," bellowed a goblin crier, his voice sending tinny echoes resounding throughout the throne room. "And the Lady Bruenna," the crier added, almost as an afterthought.

Glissa stood in the archway of a huge cavern. The rusty red walls were coated with centuries of smoke residue from burning flame tubes. Dozens, maybe hundreds of the tubes lined the jagged walls, and smoke from the flames rushed up a wide central shaft that opened overhead. Glissa couldn't see the end, but the smoke was going somewhere. Cool air also rush in from both sides through vents carved into the walls at floor level.

She wasn't sure what the cavern had once been, but it was now rearranged into a throne room. A path hewn from the rough copper floor ran straight out ahead of her, watched on the right side by a line of twelve armored goblins carrying spears and shields. Along the left were an equal number of leonin warriors in glittering gold and silver plate. The leonin warriors, all males, clutched battle-scythes and stared straight ahead, chins slightly raised, matching the rigid attention stance of their goblin counterparts. The path ended in a short set of wide stairs leading up to a platform that looked like a small mountain of iron ore the the top sliced neatly off.

Atop the platform sat three ornately carved thrones. The largest, in the center, was plated in gold and held an alert but relaxed leonin male Glissa immediately recognized. A short male goblin was seated to the leonin's right, and on his left, once again wearing the engraved slagwurm armor of the Tel-Jilad, was an elf. And elf with one eye but a face that was like looking at a mirror. So that's why Bruenna had mentioned her sister and refused to go into details. If she hadn't seen it herself, Glissa wouldn't have believed it. She clenched her jaw to keep it from dropping open.

"Yshkar? Dwugget . . ." she gulped and forced herself to finish. "Lyese." When none of the three responded immediately, Glissa followed Bruenna's lead and bowed deeply.

"So, what's new?" Glissa asked. "I mean, besides everything."

CHAPTER 19

BRIEF HISTORY

Lyese rose from her throne—her sister was sitting on a *throne*—and walked with unusual dignity and grace down the hewn steps. The elf girl didn't say a word, but when she reached Glissa, she stopped and stared long and hard into her older sister's eyes. Glissa returned the stare, but after a moment she arched an eyebrow and asked, "Looking for something?"

Lyese straightened and called up to the platform, "It is Glissa." She returned to the older girl and swept her into a hug. Glissa held her sister tightly, tears suddenly welling in her eyes. "Lyese," she said, "I'm so sorry. Sorry I've been gone. I was trapped."

"I know," Lyese said, smiling through tears. "We had given up all hope, but then Bruenna found a way to get through—Glissa, you're alive!"

"So why are you—"

"I'm the Khanha!"

"What's a Khaha?"

"Khan*ha*. I'm married to—"

"You're *married?*"

"Yes, I'm the—"

"Khanha. You said that. You mean you're married to—"

"The Kha," Yshkar rumbled, striding purposefully down the steps. "We welcome you to our . . . temporary home. You have come at an opportune time, Glissa of the Tangle."

"Hold on a minute," Glissa said, poking a finger into Yshkar's chest, stopping the surprised leonin in his tracks. "Lyese, you *married Raksha?*"

"Er, no," Lyese said, and her eyes fell to the floor. "Raksha is—Glissa, Raksha is gone. Yshkar and I . . ." Her sister shrugged.

Glissa was floored. Lyese had displayed a crush on Raksha Golden Cub, but Yshkar? It was unexpected, to say the least. "Raksha's dead? Bruenna, why didn't you tell me?"

"We asked her to bring you here without delay," Yshkar said. "Once you'd been detected, we could do nothing else."

"Explaining about Raksha would have just slowed us down," Bruenna explained sadly. "It is not a tale I enjoy relating. Truthfully, he may not be dead, but he is no longer with us."

"Yes, but all say Glissa should know everything, huh?" Dwugget growled, hopping down from his own throne to join the impromptu discussion.

"Thanks, Dwugget," Glissa said the wizened little goblin. "I think. Hey, why did your men attack me last—uh, decade?"

"You full of questions, huh? Just like the rest of us," the old cleric said, nodding sagely. "But there is much to tell, from many angles, and much arguing, that always fun. And we have some time, huh? All talk over dinner. Then, action." He winked. "All friends now, huh?"

"If you say so," Glissa sighed. She didn't know what to make of Dwugget's presence, but he had helped her long ago, when her life had first gone crazy. And Slobad had trusted him. Still, the old goblin seemed filled with tension under his jolly demeanor, shifting on his feet a little too much. She would have to keep an eye on him.

Her belly rumbled. The goblin's mention of food reminded

she couldn't remember the last time she'd eaten, but knew it was at least five year ago. "All friends now." Glissa nodded. "So let's eat."

* * * * *

The meal was set out like a feast, though compared even to the meals that Glissa's mother had prepared for special occasions, the pickings were sparse. The leonin royal family—of which Glissa guessed she was now a part—had obviously fallen on hard times, to say the least. Still, no food had tasted so good in quite a while.

"All right," Glissa began without ceremony, "I'll tell you what I know, or what I've been able to figure out. You fill in the rest, and we'll go from there." She arched an eyebrow when she saw her sister, Dwugget, Yshkar, and Bruenna exchange furtive looks. "We're *all* going to level with each other," she added.

Before she could continue, a goblin guard scuttled into the room and whispered something in Dwugget's ear. The goblin rose politely with the gingerness of the aged. "Excuse, my friends," the old goblin said. "A theological dispute has broken out." Without another word, the goblin followed the goblin out of the dining room.

"Theological dispute?" Glissa asked.

With a wave, Yshkar dismissed the remaining goblin guards, who scuttled after Dwugget. The Kha nodded to Bruenna, who continued.

"When the green sun rose into the sky five years ago, the goblin tribes very nearly degenerated into complete anarchy," Bruenna explained. "The event confirmed many prophecies that the shamanic leaders had long held to be heresies, and hundreds of goblins had been exiled or executed for espousing them."

"The Cult of Krark," Glissa said. "Heretics."

"But the only surviving group of heretics out there, thanks to you," Lyese said. "The goblins didn't *want* to destroy their own society. Nor could they follow the old leadership. Dwugget saw an opportunity, and when he marched right into the shamans' tunnels and started preaching to the tribes about Krark and his journey, about Mother's Heart—well, the goblins lapped it up." Her sister shrugged. "They made him the new shaman. Renamed the mountain Krark. But it wasn't easy for Dwugget to maintain order at first. He'd be the first to tell you he worked with some shady characters to keep the goblins in line back then. Once Raksha and I managed to get in to see him, Dwugget was more than happy to talk about an alliance. For one thing, it let him get rid of thugs like Alderok Vektro."

"Vektro is dead?" Glissa asked.

"Once the alliance was sealed," Lyese said, any of the Vulshok mercenaries that Dwugget knew had been abusive or murderous to goblins ended up breaking ore in the mines. And now, Dwugget personally intercedes whenever theological arguments break out."

"Why?"

"Have you ever seen a goblin theological dispute?" Lyese asked.

"Right," Glissa said. From what Slobad had told her, such disputes were usually considered finished when one side was roasting in the Great Furnace.

Glissa wanted to ask again how her sister had ended up the wife of a leonin monarch, but she decided to wait until the two could talk privately. She catalogued everything else she knew for them, and finally, showed them Geth's head after servants cleared the table of food.

Yshkar's reaction was violent and immediate. "Abomination!" the leonion cried and drew a longknife.

"No, wait!" Glissa shouted. She held her arms protectively over Geth's head. "He's on our side. I know it stinks, but . . ."

"My Kha," Lysese purred, placing a hand on her husband's sword arm, "Please."

The leonin growled, but relented at the elf's touch. Keeping one eye on Glissa's grisly companion, he replaced the blade and returned to his seat but still stared daggers at Geth's head.

It wasn't until then that Glissa noticed she'd readily protected Geth. She chalked it up to the fact that she was still convinced the necromancer's head would prove useful somehow. And it wasn't as if he took up much space, or ate anything. He hadn't even talked for days. In fact . . .

Glissa flipped open the lid to make sure the smelly thing hadn't finally expired. "You all right?" she asked.

"Don't start that," Geth's head replied. Glissa shut the flap and set the bag next to her chair. Good thing they had finished eating. Opening Geth's bag was always an olfactory adventure.

"Now what no one's told me, but I'm starting to guess," Glissa told them all, "is that you've learned something new. You thought I was dead, then you didn't." She locked eyes with Bruenna. "*Tell* me you've learned something. Tell me anything."

"What would you like to know first?" Bruenna asked.

"What happened to Raksha?" Glissa said.

The dining room fell silent except for the clink of silverware on silver plates. Finally, Yshkar sighed. "Very well. We had hoped we could cover this later, but you have the right to know."

"And Glissa, it's important you know it's not your fault," Lyese added.

"How *could* it be my fault?" Glissa asked. "I've been frozen or something."

"Our cousin, the noblest, most honorable Kha since the days Great Dakan walked the plains, disappeared three years ago," Yshkar said.

"Impossible," Glissa said.

"It's true," Bruenna said.

"He saw the end coming, I think," Lyese said, "and decided he would rather all of us die than lose the den home. Glissa, *Raksha* destroyed Taj Nar. If I hadn't caught him in the act, we all would have perished."

"*Raksha* destroyed Taj Nar? That's insane!" Glissa said, slamming her goblet to the table. "How? Why?"

"I told you why," Lyese said sharply. "I found him planting some kind of explosive—"

"It was called a mana bomb," Bruenna broke in. "Apparently Raksha had gotten one from the vedalken. The vedalken created them, but never had reason to use them. Just one can wipe out several acres. Fortunately, Taj Nar itself protected most of us from the brunt of the blast, though at a terrible cost."

"Afterward, Raksha blamed me," Lyese said. "If it weren't for Yshkar, he might have killed me."

"Our cousin was raving, a madman," Yshkar said. "But we could not execute him. Not even after what he had done. No Kha, no matter how insane, can be allowed to face death anywhere but on his feet. Yet we could not allow him back onto the field to face an honorable end, either."

"For one thing, there was no battlefield," Lyese added. "It was all we could do to get the survivors up here, to Krark-Home."

"Exile was the only solution," Yshkar said. "He was given a longknife, a zauk, and cast out in the dead of night."

"That's it?" Glissa said. "Do you know where he went?" Something about this was rubbing her the wrong way.

"A few of our scouts reported seeing a leonin on zaukback

headed into the Tangle the night he disappeared," Yshkar replied bitterly. "That alone should tell you his fate. We should have sent someone to record his death, according to ancient law, but no scouts could be spared, of course. He was mad, but in the end he did the honorable thing. The creatures of the Tangle are fierce, our wife tells us."

"And naturally, you were next in line," Glissa said.

"The men—all of us, after the fall of the home den—needed a leader. A *sane* leader. If Raksha is not dead, he might as well be. He is beyond redemption for his act."

"Sounds to me like there's plenty of blame to go around," Glissa said. "All right, I'll accept that Raksha's out of the picture. I'll even accept that you're the Queen—"

"Khanha," Lyese interrupted.

"Khanha," Glissa said. "And I'll accept Taj Nar's gone. But how did you find me? What—well, what have *I* been doing all this time?"

"A year ago," Bruenna said, steering back to the subject, "I figured out a way to work around the vedalken's dampening fields. They communicate telepathically, now, entirely. It's tied to the serum."

"I figured," Glissa said. "Yert reeked of serum, too."

"Really?" Bruenna asked, genuinely surprised. "You must have gotten close."

"Too close," Glissa agreed.

"How's the neck?"

"Sore."

"Sorry. Anyway, the vedalken are saturated in serum," Bruenna said. "When Memnarch changed them, made them more ferocious, I think their serum production *and* intake increased exponentially. You haven't seen it yet, Glissa, but when the suns go down, there are hardly any stars left in the sky."

"But the stars—they're blinkmoths," Glissa said.

"The vedalken are using them up. Yert too, I guess. Whatever the reason, they can communicate over any distance now at the speed of thought. Their attacks of late have been flawlessly executed. And if Yert reeked of serum five years ago . . ." Bruenna stood and turned to Yshkar, who Glissa still had trouble thinking of as the Kha. "That confirms it, Yshkar. The nim and Memnarch's vedalken armies are attacking at the same time in a coordinated effort."

"Indeed," The Kha growled.

Bruenna turned back to Glissa. "I brought up vedalken telepathy because I found that an enterprising mage with a grudge and a scrying crystal can sometimes hear their thoughts as plain as day." The mage grinned. "It's not pleasant, and Dakan knows I can't understand more than a quarter of it—but I did find a way through the teleportation shield that seals off Lumengrid when one of the vedalken became trapped outside, in the Tangle, I think. He had to have the shield opened to get back in. They're not very creative. It was pretty pedestrian magic once I took a good look at it."

"You broke into Lumengrid?" Glissa asked.

"Teleported in, but to do it I did have to break through some auras," Bruenna said. "That was how I eventually confirmed you were still alive. The vedalken are fanatical about keeping records and archives, and I popped into their central library. My father used to work there as a servant." Bruenna her mug of oily leonin pseudonush and refilled it in one fluid movement. "Even now that the vedalken don't speak, they still write everything down. It's compulsive. There were records of everything—troop dispatch orders, complete lists of every last artifact beast in Memnarch's army, maps of secret tunnels into the interior . . ."

"Tell me you took one of those maps," Glissa interrupted.

"Yes," Bruenna said, "And orders about moving a precious cargo from the Dross to the interior."

"Me?" Glissa asked.

"You," Bruenna said. "So, to make a short story long, I figured out when they were moving you, and made sure I was in a position to pull you out as soon as there was an opening. It wasn't easy, but you know the rest."

"And at last we arrive at the point," Yshkar replied.

"Patience, my Kha," Bruenna said. "Glissa, we could spend all night filling you in on everything. It's been a long five years. But what's important is what you've learned. The Mephidross has grown, and Yert now controls over half the surface. The nim and the vedalken and worse surround us. I've figured out how to break into the vedalken's line of communications. And I found something in the 'grid that might show us a chance to turn our fortunes around."

Bruenna rose and plucked a roll of wide foil parchment from a pouch on her belt and spread it on the table in front of Glissa, pinning down the corners with goblets and cups. "We know that Yert's surging strength has something to do with Memnarch, his part in your abduction. I've found something. It's a talisman that might also be a weapon, if you can get your hands on it."

"A weapon against what?" Glissa asked. The leathery parchment bore a painstakingly colored and labeled coalstone sketch. The sketch depicted a simple round design with angular shapes sliced from the edges, making the shape resemble an asymmetrical sawblade. A pentagon was etched into the center of the object, and at each point on the shape a differently colored gemstone had been mounted.

"I've seen that pattern before," Glissa said. "On Kaldra."

"This might be even older. According to this, it may actually be as old as the Guardian himself," Bruenna said. "It gives the possessor power over the mindless and soulless," Bruenna said. "It's called the Miracore, and Yert's got it."

The mage held her hand about eight inches apart. "It's about so wide in either direction. And heavy. According to this document, it's forged from some alloy I've never even seen. Even Dwugget said he'd never heard of it, and none of the goblin blacksmiths think it's even real. But I saw it. I saw it around his neck when I escaped five years ago."

"So it 'controls the soulless.' How? What does that mean, exactly?" Glissa said.

Bruenna launched into a long technical explanation of the talisman, much of which went sailing over Glissa's head. But the gist of it was that this Miracore could channel the wearer's will-power and force anything without a sentient mind—such as the simpler animals, zombies like the nim, or constructs—to do his bidding. Its origins were unclear, though the angular, geometric vedalken script confirmed the talisman's antiquity.

Geth's head volunteered that *he* hadn't need any such talisman to get the nim to do what *he* wanted.

"That's actually a good point," Lyese interrupted. "What the head said."

"Yert was and still is an amateur," Geth continued from his bag after prodding the flap open with his temple. "He'd be nothing without that Miracore. Now me, *I'm* a wizard. The greatest necromancer this plane has ever known."

"Was a wizard," Glissa corrected. "Don't get any ideas, or I'm giving you to Yshkar." The elf girl returned to Bruenna. "So I get this Miracore away from Yert and the nim lose their controller."

"And then most of the forces allied against us become easy pickings for our troops," Yshkar said. "With this talisman in our possession, we could control the nim ourselves and seize the silver beasts from the vedalkens' grasp."

"With luck, we won't have to," Bruenna said. "There's something more. It was in a separate record. When I located you, I was also able to track down Memnarch. It was dumb luck. I didn't expect to find anything, but I had the time, so . . ."

"What did you find?" Glissa asked.

"Five years," Bruenna said. "Five years, and no one has seen him. His armies spread over the surface, but Memnarch himself? Nowhere. I found out why."

"Bruenna, Glissa is tired. She should rest before we get into this," Lyese said.

"No, my Khanha. I must disagree," Bruenna said. "I looked into the serum transfer records. I found that most of the supply was being diverted to one place. The Panopticon. I dug around a bit more and found out that the serum was for Memnarch. He's hibernating. Burning away some kind of 'taint.' "

"Taint?" Glissa said. "He's making himself sane?"

"It's a contaminant," Bruenna said. "He was being consumed by flesh. He's using half the serum the vedalken can produce to rid himself of it. Memnarch is converting himself back into pure metal."

"Why?"

"He believes it will allow him to ascend," Breunna said. "But he made a mistake."

"If he's metal, I might be able to hurt him," Glissa said. "Maybe—maybe kill him."

"Exactly," Bruenna said. "But there is a catch."

"Of course there is," Glissa said.

"I retrieved you from the interior early," Bruenna said. "There are five days until Memnarch will emerge."

"Perfect," Glissa said. "I can take him out while he sleeps."

"Glissa, you cannot touch him until the cleansing process is complete," Bruenna said. "Like you, he is outside of time in the

Panopticon. Inside some kind of machine. But when he emerges, he will be a different being. One you can destroy. On the fifth day, the suns will rise as one, and you have to be in the Panopticon."

"You will take an honor guard of my finest troops," Yshkar said.

"No. No commandos, no skyhunters, no honor guard," Glissa said. "I've got four days. When I do this, I do it alone, with no one to slow me down. Give me supplies, and I'll take a pteron if you've got one to spare. If not, Bruenna, I'll need transportation."

"Are you sure?" Lyese asked. "We just found you, Glissa."

"And when this is all over, I'll find you again," Glissa said. "First, I have to find Yert, and quickly. Bruenna, maybe teleportation magic—"

A huge rumbling suddenly shook the cave and sent goblets tumbling and chairs toppling. A breathless leonin guard bolted into the dining room and momentarily grabbed the table to keep his balance, something the elf girl had never seen a leonin do before. Glissa struggled to keep her own footing, scooped up Geth's head and slung it over her shoulder, then drew her sword. A weapon might not stop this sudden a quake, but it made her feel more secure.

The harried leonin soldier headed straight for Yshkar and shouted over the thunderous din. "My Kha! The nim have breached the southeast perimeter! They've brought—my Kha, the nim have vampires among them!"

"To arms!" Yshkar bellowed, clutching a small amulet that was apparently enchanted to send his voice rumbling through the tunnels and over the roar of the ongoing quake. "The enemy has entered Krark-Home!"

"Sounds like Yert's coming to you!" Geth's head shouted, only audible to Glissa because of his proximity to her ears. She suspected the head was right.

Not one of them noticed the myr creature clinging to the high ceiling, concealed by shadows and its own chameleonic metal skin. As the elf girl continued to speak animatedly to the mage, the myr's master decided he had learned enough. The small, agile creature scuttled into a ventilation shaft and disappeared.

CHAPTER 20

THE INSIDER

Glissa was amazed at the coordination and cooperation on display between leonin and goblin soldiers as they scrambled this way and that, setting up defensive positions. The rumbling had subsided, through she suspected it might start up again at any minute. Yshkar barked orders, keeping a level head amidst the organized chaos. Lyese, Glissa observed, was strapping on a sword belt.

The elf girl examined her own ancient sword in the orange firelight. There still wasn't a nick or scratch anywhere on it. Elven weapons were made to last.

"Bruenna," Glissa said, "None of this is going to work if I don't get to Yert."

"And the guard said 'vampires,' I know," Bruenna replied, fumbling with one of the pouches on her belt. "He's here. I can sense him."

Glissa closed her eyes, attempting to reach out to the energies of the Tangle. "I can too," the elf girl said with surprise. "He's like a void. And something else. Constructs. They're making my spine tingle."

Bruenna nodded in agreement. "Focus on Yert. The Mira-core should lead you right to him." The Neurok mage produced chain strung with a trio of different colored gemstones, and placed it in the elf girl's hand. The mage explained that each one was infused with a specific magic and keyed to Glissa's voice—Bruenna had prepared them that morning. The green one would transport her instantly to any location she named three times while holding the stone to her lips. Using the same method, the red one would return Glissa to Krark-Home, and the blue one would give her the ability to fly for a short time. Alone among the three stones, the blue flight gem could be used as often as Glissa wished, Bruenna explained with a hint of pride. Glissa thanked her, wrapped the chain around her forearm like a bracelet, and tucked the valuable stones up the long sleeve of her silver leonin tunic.

"I need to stay and defend Krark-Home, or this may all be over before it begins," Bruenna added. "And you must leave for the interior as soon as you retrieve the Miracore. You *must* retrieve the Miracore. I shall help you with Yert as much as I can, but then you must go. Use the stones."

"Oh, I'll get the Miracore," Glissa said, still gazing at her sword. "If I have to take Yert's head off to do it." She placed a hand on Bruenna's shoulder and looked over at Lyese, who was still preoccupied with weapons and armor. "Afterward . . . tell her I'll be back soon. No time for a long good-bye." Glissa didn't add that she wouldn't be able to make herself leave, despite the dire circumstances, if her sister was fighting for her life at the same time. Yshkar had already joined the battle, and Lyese would not be able to avoid it.

"I shall. But now, we go," Bruenna said quietly. "Remember, Yert is the goal. Until you have the Miracore, only fight whatever's blocking your way." Bruenna turned and headed out one of the dining room's many exits. Sparing one last glance at her sister, so changed in such a short period of time, Glissa followed without a word.

Lyese looked up with her one good eye just in time to see the older elf girl's booted foot disappear around a bend in the passage, and she set off after them.

* * * * *

The goblin tunnels that honeycombed the Oxidda Mountains were a complicated network of twists, turns, intersections, and more than one path to nowhere. Cavernous ventilation chimneys appeared at odd intervals, and a few deep pits opened here and there along the way. Unlike the chasm Glissa had crossed while hunting Yert five years before, these pits ended in bubbling orange smelting pools, part of the ongoing volcanic process that continually reshaped the Oxidda range. The goblins had learned to harness that power. But held deep respect for it. The tunnels led to several secret entrances and exits—which were not always the same thing, Glissa had learned—and the main entrance was moved by magic every few days just to be safe.

The nim seemed be in every tunnel at once.

It didn't take long for Glissa and Bruenna to meet the first wave of invaders. The elf girl had hoped they might catch up with Yshkar, but the Kha and his men had apparently taken another tunnel. Glissa felt the empty void of Yert's presence, and the tingling hum of what could only be the Miracore, was in this direction.

The hulking, black shapes of nim warriors filled the tunnel ahead of them. "I'd say they're blocking our way," Glissa said.

"Indeed," Bruenna agreed. The mage closed her eyes momentarily, and moved her hands in a simple pattern. A wall of quicksilver materialized before the pair, blocking the nim—and the rest of the tunnel—from view.

"How are we supposed to—" Glissa began.

Bruenna raised one finger to her blue lips and flung her other hand forward as if hurling a stone. The quicksilver wall shimmered and a shivering, circular dent appeared in the center. As Glissa watched, the dent folded in on itself and then opened inward, forming a long, glowing silver tunnel just large enough for a crouching human and elf to fit through single file. The long cylinder ended perhaps a hundred feet ahead.

"This will get us past this first group," Bruenna said softly, sweat appearing on her brow as the quicksilver solidified. Finally, she exhaled, and urged Glissa forward.

Glissa expected the magical metal to be slippery, but her boots found solid surface. She bounded down the tunnel, her sword held in front of her. Bruenna followed close behind. Glissa looked back over her shoulder and saw that the entrance was closing behind them as she ran, preventing unwelcome pursuit.

At the exit ahead, Glissa saw a pair of pale humanoid shapes standing crouched, ready to pounce. "Vampires," the elf girl cried over her shoulder, pointing. She heard Bruenna mutter the beginnings of another spell as the vicious creatures stepped into the quicksilver tunnel. They looked even more ghastly than usual in the eerie magical light.

"Just keep running," Bruenna said. "Get past them, they're in for a surprise."

Glissa raised her sword in both hands as if she was going to bring it down on the head of the lead vampire, which she was sickened to see had the lithe form and distinctive face of an elf. The vampire fell for the bluff and charged at her low to take advantage of what it perceived to be an opening. Instead of following through with her swing, she slapped her other hand onto the chain wrapped around her swordarm. "Fly, fly, fly!" Glissa shouted then jumped into the air. She was relieved when she didn't come back down, and soared on over the diving creature's head.

"Right behind you," she heard Bruenna shout, "Keep going!"

As she shot from the end of the magical tunnel with Bruenna hot on her heels, Glissa slowed and looked back. The quicksilver wall shimmered, the surface perfectly smooth. The vampires were nowhere to be seen.

"Nice trick," Glissa told Bruenna as the mage caught up.

"It should hold them long enough for us to get away," Bruenna agreed.

Together, they bobbed and weaved through a surprised group of nim and goblins engaged in a life-or-death struggle. Glissa wished she could stop to help the defenders, but Bruenna was right. Yert was all that mattered. In the end, getting her hands on the Miracore would save a lot more people than one more sword in the fray.

"We're getting close," Bruenna said. "I can't believe he's made it this far into Krark-Home."

The pair veered off at a three-way intersection where leonin and goblins were knocking an unending wave of nim into the smelting pools below. Bruenna steered them up a rising path that Glissa noticed was more brightly lit than the rest. It was also strangely empty.

"I don't like this," Bruenna said. "I know where this tunnel leads."

"Where?" Glissa asked, ducking to avoid a hanging copper stalactite.

"The nurseries."

The higher up the tunnel they went, the closer Yert felt. Glissa no longer needed to concentrate to feel the vampire necromancer.

The tunnel ended just ahead. They had yet to encounter anyone in this passage, friend or foe. Bruenna and Glissa slowed and pulled up short, hovering just in front of a set of double-doors that the elf girl would have to duck to get through. Bruenna shook the door latch, but it wouldn't budge.

"I've got an idea," Glissa said. "Stand back." She floated back a few feet and reached out to the Tangle energies, calling on the strength of the forest. She felt a surge of physical power and felt her armor and tunic tighten around her muscles. Glissa felt strong enough to take the top off of the mountain with her bare hands.

Bruenna, impressed, floated aside. Glissa clenched her fists and flew straight at the door, fists held in front of her, a living projectile. Halfway there, she heard Geth scream.

The elf girl's gloved fists connected dead center and shattered the crystalline locking mechanism, sending the small iron door flying inward with a tremendous crash. She plowed headlong into a stunned vampire. Glissa's fists drove straight through the creature's torso like a hot knife through lead. She kept going, willing herself onward, and ripped the vampire in two. Greenish-black gore blinded the elf girl momentarily.

When this was over, she was going to bathe in hot oil for a week.

"Stop!" a familiar, slithering voice bellowed. Glissa whirled in midair to face the voice and wiped foul, stringy goop from her eyes.

Yert stood in the center of the room, flanked by a quartet of vampires. He stood over a pair of leonin corpses in bloodstained white robes. Tiny figures—human children, goblin kids, and leonin cubs—were huddled in terrified clusters around the wall. Nim warriors blocked every exit except the one Glissa had just forcefully opened.

In one raised hand Yert clutched a crying leonin cub, in the other an even smaller goblin infant that wailed and kicked its tiny, flapping feet. Yert smiled and showed two rows of razor sharp teeth, and locked his blood-red eyes with the Glissa's. As she watched, frozen, he licked his lips with a forked, leathery tongue.

Glissa raised her open hands wide and descended until her feet touched the ground. "All right, Yert. You've got me. Again. Put the children down."

"The children are quite safe at the moment," Yert replied. "I can't say the same for the nursemaids."

Glissa felt the chain wrapped around her wrist slide down her arm, and it gave her a terrible idea.

"You will come with me, of your own will," Yert continued. "You showed me mercy, once. It was foolish of you, but I still feel ever so slightly in your debt. You helped make me the man I am today. And you *did* share that lovely repast with me." Glissa felt a twinge where the wound in her neck was still not quite healed. Her heart leapt. With Yert's arms spread wide, his robes parted and revealed a sliver of the Miracore on his chest, glowing a faint greenish-blue. So close . . .

"And so I swear," Yert hissed. "These children and infants will not be harmed, if you come with me. Besides, I've discovered I have a bit of a sweet tooth. And you can't enjoy your sweets all at once."

Glissa nodded, but was doing her best to make eye contact with Bruenna, who finally caught her look. Glissa gave an imperceptible nod that Bruenna returned faintly. The entire exchange took a little over a second, and Yert didn't seem to notice.

"I guess that's the best offer I'm going to get," Glissa said, casually lowering her arms and edging her left hand closer to her right. "But what are you going to do to me?" she asked, trying to inject fear into her voice, which wasn't difficult.

As Glissa spoke, she rubbed her right wrist with her left hand as if trying to get her circulation going, but instead working her fingertips slowly up her arm to the gemstones. "Now hold on, Yert," she almost drawled, "How do I know you won't *Bruenna catch the kids YERTYERTYERT!*"

As the last "Yert" left her lips, she gulped a deep breath of air. The nursery, Yert, the vampires, and everything else flickered out of existence for a millisecond. When she reappeared, she was inside Yert's body. And Yert's insides suddenly had no place to go.

Corroded bone, brackish blood, wiry muscles, fetid tissue, and withered organs exploded violently through Yert's ruptured skin and robes in every direction, tearing his body into tiny chunks of flesh, metal, and blackened bone. The elf girl punched upward, sending what remained of Yert's head flying, then thrust her upturned hands out to catch the Miracore before it could hit the ground. She blinked foulness from her eyes for the second time in as many minutes and found herself in the center of the room. A quartet of very surprised vampires, horrified children, and Bruenna, who held a blood-spattered but still healthy pair of infants in her arms, stood gaping. Everything was covered in stinking bits of Yert.

Glissa didn't give the other vampires time to recover. She swung the Miracore like a bludgeon, collapsing the skull of the nearest bloodsucking fiend, which stumbled over backward and collapsed. The traumatized children scattered and bolted for cover. Glissa shifted her grip and grabbed hold of the heavy chain strung through the artifact and whirled the Miracore overhead like a flail on a very short handle. The chain decapitated the remaining vampires in one clean sweep, and three lanky headless corpses flopped, twitching, to the nursery floor.

"Bet he didn't see *that* coming," Bruenna said, wiping Yert from her eyes and face.

"Bruenna, *I* didn't see that coming," Glissa said. "But it worked." The elf girl gently set down the heavy artifact. She still had work to do. Her sword appeared in her hand, and she stepped forward to face the nim that blocked the other exits but saw they were motionless and silent.

"Meyr mill mooing mum mey—"

Glissa reached back for Geth's pack, but it wasn't there. She looked over to where she had been standing before teleporting herself inside Yert and saw it rolling lazily back and forth. She ran over to the mumbling bag as Bruenna tried to calm the children and herd them away from the nim and back to safety.

"They're still doing the last thing they were told," Geth's head said. "Look at them, the beauties."

"Bruenna," Glissa said, lifting the heavy Miracore aloft. "Do you know how to activate this thing? Can we order them to leave?"

"I hope so," Bruenna said. She took the heavy, asymmetrical disk of the Miracore and held it in two hands, and closed her eyes. As the seconds dragged into minutes, Glissa started to wonder if this was really safe. This was god-like power, and Bruenna was only human.

Finally, the mage blinked. She looked as if she had just walked a hundred miles. "It's done," Bruenna said, her voice a croak. As she spoke, the nim blocking the exits calmly turned and scuttled away down the tunnel, claws hanging at their sides.

The mage handed the Miracore back to Glissa, who slipped the heavy chain over her head. The artifact was awkward and would make swordplay difficult, but she didn't have much choice. She scooped up Geth's bag and slung it onto her back, and placed a hand on Bruenna's shoulder.

"I have to go," Glissa said. "Tell them about the nim. It might be enough. Get the children out of here."

The mountain shook again, causing the children to scream in unison again, and almost knocked Glissa off her feet. She stumbled backward into a pair of waiting arms. As the tremor subsided, the elf girl turned to see who had caught her.

"You weren't going to say goodbye?" Lyese asked.

"Lyese, what are you doing here?" Glissa demanded.

"Catching you," her sister replied. "And checking on the children. But it appears you've saved them already. Big sister, always looking out for me." Something about the way Lyese said "big sister" didn't sound right, but Glissa didn't dwell on it.

"My Khana, Yert is dead," Bruenna said. "We have a chance to turn the tide, but Glissa must go."

"I know," Lyese replied and wrapped Glissa in a tight embrace. "There. Now you can go. Come back as soon as you can."

"I will, Lyese," Glissa said. "Now get these kids someplace safe. Good luck. Both of you."

"And you," Bruenna said. "But none of us should rely solely on luck."

CHAPTER 21

OLD FRIENDS

Glissa shot from the side of the mountain like a goblin flame-rocket into the sky. As much time as she'd spent in the air since that night the levelers attacked her home, she still relished the freedom of unfettered flight. It was her only option for reaching Memnarch in time now—Bruenna had warned her the teleportation gemstone was a one-use-only spell, and the elf girl had used it up when she killed Yert. But since they'd found the vampire necromancer so quickly, she still had plenty of time to reach her goal. She wore the Miracore tucked securely under her jerkin.

The flying elf cast her eyes down on the carnage that littered the battlefield. The mountains, flanked on one side by the shrunken Glimmervoid and on the other by the greatly enlarged Mephidross, were surrounded by chaos. Tiny black nim poured out of the mountain like needlebugs, following the orders Bruenna had given them through the Miracore. The nim collided with even smaller goblin and leonin warriors, who cut into the passive zombies with abandon. Great silver beasts chewed through the defenders, but so far the lines were holding—although they were starting to bend at some points. Glissa silently wished them luck.

The elf girl rolled and let her course gradually rise. She couldn't afford to be delayed by aerophins or vedalken flyers. From this vantage point she could make out thousands of the construct beasts of every size and horrible shape. They hacked and slashed through goblin, leonin, and nim, leaving bloody body parts littering the field behind them. The giant, globe-headed vedalken that moved among them were unmistakeable even from Glissa's vantage point. They were no longer holding back, and dozens of vedalken had entered the fray. Others rode hovering flyers, divebombing the defenders of Kark-Home and slicing into goblin, human, and leonin with well-placed bolts of blue energy.

No two constructs looked the same, and many looked big enough to swallow a goblin regiment whole. But those were insects compared to what the defenders had informally dubbed "quake-beasts." Three of them clung to the sides of Krark-Home. The huge constructs had ovoid bodies with no discernible head, supported by over a dozen radial segmented limbs. The quake-beasts' claws tore large chunks of raw iron from the side of the mountain as larger grasping legs dug deep into the ore, which gave them the appearance of enormous leechbugs on a mile-high vorrac. At each tapered end of the ovoid a pair of pitted silver hammers pounded the mountain mercilessly, sending tremors into the tunnels below.

An even louder explosion drowned out the din, and Glissa saw a ball of orange flame heading straight for her. She couldn't tell where it had come from, and didn't have time to look. The elf girl got out of the way just in time as a massive hunk of molten iron shot past. She turned to follow its trajectory.

The projectile reached its zenith then dropped back down toward the mountain. It struck one of the quake-beasts in the middle of its ovoid body, and both exploded in a conflagration that made Glissa shield her eyes even at that distance. The shock wave from the blast immolated nearby trees and knocked combatants onto the ground.

"What *was* that?" Glissa wondered aloud. She scanned the mountain, trying to spot the source of the huge hunk of molten iron. Had the quakes triggered a volcanic explosion, or had someone been trying to hit her?

Another blast erupted from the mountain, and this time Glissa made sure to backtrack the projectile's path. The ball of flaming metal had emerged from perfectly round, bowl-shaped cylinder mounted on the side of a cliff, and pointing straight up. This second shot wasn't as accurate as the first, and slammed into the mountain several hundred feet from the nearest quakebeast and started a small wildfire. She spotted tiny goblin warriors climbing around the side of the cylinder. Glissa wasn't surprised that the Krark had built such a massive weapon. Slobad would have loved it.

Slobad. Distracted by the battle, she'd forgotten her immediate task. She forced her eyes forward and accelerated as much as her will would allow toward the Tangle. Glissa intended to enter the interior through the newest lacuna, Yshkar's recommendations be damned.

Another explosion sent a wave of heat washing over Glissa, and she involuntarily glanced down to see what had happened.

One of the quake beasts had stopped pounding on the mountainside and had the bright idea to instead attack the massive goblin cannon. The attack had knocked the weapon's barrel at an odd angle and it had fired against the side of Krark-Home itself.

"All right," Glissa said through clenched teeth. "One more delay, and that's it."

The elf girl's nerves almost hummed in the proximity of so many artifact creatures. Glissa didn't know the limits of her destructive power, or if what she had in mind would exhaust it before the final battle, when she might need it most. At the moment, she didn't care. She wheeled in the sky and reached out to touch the Tangle energies. The familiar buzz crackled on her outstretched arms, and she envisioned green fire forcing the massive quake-beasts apart at the seams.

Two rays of blazing jade shot from her clasped hands and struck each gigantic construct squarely in the center of its ovoid body. Glissa willed the power to keep flowing, and the energy obliged, leaping from one quake-beast to another and back again. Finally, they erupted with a pair of successive mushroom explosions that rocked the mountain and sent a visible shock wave of smoke and debris over the battlefield.

The elf girl smelled smoke and realized it was coming from her own body, but she felt no pain. She checked on the Miracore, still tucked safely in her jerkin. The talisman was unharmed—in fact, it was cool to the touch. Glissa was drained and the Tangle energies already felt distant, but it had been worth the effort.

She nearly collided with a tall, familiar humanoid figure covered in mottled silver that rose to block her path. Malil stood astride a larger version of the typical vedalken flyer that bristled with the same iron tubes she'd seen mounted on the noses of aerophins.

"Hello, elf girl," Malil said. "Having fun?"

"Flare!" Glissa muttered, drawing her sword. She hoped that flight spell wouldn't give out any time soon.

"No need for that," Malil replied. "I'm not here to fight."

"Then why are you here? I'm busy," Glissa said.

"I just need this," Malil said, and before Glissa could react, he kicked the flyer into gear and zipped behind her, hooked one finger through the heavy chain supporting the Miracore, and lifted it over her head. Without another word, Malil spun the flyer in mid-air and zoomed off in the direction of the Tangle.

"Flare!" Glissa cursed.

* * * * *

"Stupid, stupid, *stupid!*" Glissa muttered. No matter how fast she pushed her borrowed flight power, she couldn't gain on Malil.

The elf girl had dropped her guard, thinking she had the whole sky to herself.

Stupid.

Glissa poured on as much speed as she could, but the tiny silver shape of Malil's flyer remained as distant as ever. He had been following the ragged line of the Oxidda range for half an hour, and now the Tangle loomed—wild, powerful, and calling to Glissa's soul like an old friend. An old friend that had undergone a growth spurt in her five-year absence.

The Tangle had not spread, like the Dross, but the diffusion of magic five years ago had led to an explosion of plant life. The oldest trees now rose like sentinels above the canopy, joined in their vigil by several of the omnipresent silver spires that seemed to be everywhere on the surface of Mirrodin.

Malil made a wide turn as he passed a circular break in the forest canopy—a venue into the thick foliage that could only be the lacuna. The metal man was heading straight back to his master with the prize. If Memnarch were to come into possession of the Miracore, what could she do? Though willing to try, Glissa didn't really think she could take the Guardian in a straight fight, even if he weren't protected by all the other bizarre constructs she'd seen before. The ones he was obviously still creating at a breakneck pace. Malil looped once and dove straight down into the hole in the side of the world. Glissa followed, closing the distance for the first time since the chase began.

The lacuna was tangled with vines and roots all around the edges, but still provided ample room to maneuver as long as

Glissa stayed clear of the sides. Malil, however, stuck close to lacuna walls, diving around and through the snarl of vegetation. Glissa gained a little more. Why was Malil allowing himself to slow down?

Something flashed far away down the long tunnel, something silver that was out of place in the midst of the vibrant vegetation. As soon as she saw the glint of metal it disappeared.

She must have imagined it. The only silver thing in the lacuna was Malil, and if she didn't do something soon he was going to get away.

As Malil passed by the spot where Glissa thought she had seen a flash, the foliage exploded. A long-haired figure in tattered black clothing vaulted off the side of the lacuna and caught the metal man in a flying tackle. The blow knocked Malil cleanly from the flyer, which spun out of control, rudderless, and exploded against the inner wall far below. Both figures tumbled into open space, and slowly Malil and Glissa's mysterious ally dropped downward. The metal man kicked and flailed, but his attacker clutched him around the waist, refusing to let go. Within seconds, she'd caught up to the pair and was able to get a good look at the man in black.

The man in black wasn't a man at all. He was leonin.

Raksha Golden Cub flashed Glissa a toothy smile. "You're here! You're alive!" The leonin let out a long laugh that bordered on maniacal, and added, "I don't know how much longer I can hold onto this creature! Do something!"

Malil screamed as Glissa raised her sword, but couldn't get his feet or fists to connect with anything. In one smooth stroke, the elf girl brought her blade down on the metal man's neck and out the other side. Arterial spray fanned into the air, but subsided within seconds as Malil bled out. Strange, when she'd tried that five years ago, the wound had healed instantly in a swirl of quicksilver. Flesh had almost consumed the metal man. Glissa slipped the Miracore from Malil's headless shoulders, then Raksha released the body and gave it a shove. The mottled silver corpse crashed into the spiky vegetation that lined the lacuna, where it hung suspended by thorns and vines.

The elf girl slipped the Miracore over her head then grabbed the leonin under the armpits and gradually slowed their descent. Shifting Raksha in her arms to make sure she wouldn't drop him, Glissa floated over to the side of the lacuna and felt the odd sideways turn of gravity. She set the leonin down gently amongst the vines and moss. At that exact moment, her flight spell finally gave out.

Glissa fell sideways and flopped onto the greenery next to Raksha, drawing breath and happy to be alive, happier still that she'd found her friend again—and at such an opportune time. The elf girl had grown accustomed to the constant pull of exhaustion, and the opportunity to just lie there was too much to resist. The relief at regaining the Miracore was palpable. Malil's sudden theft of the talisman had almost looked like the end. Just a few minutes of rest wouldn't hurt.

Finally, Glissa broke the silence. "So . . . you're alive, then?"

Raksha snorted, and burst into that same odd laughter she'd heard before. Apparently, three years in the Tangle had wrought changes in the Golden Cub, both physical and mental. Had the others been right? Had he really gone mad?

The physical changes in the former Kha shocked her. Raksha's black vorrac-leather tunic and trousers were ragged and ripped. A leonin longknife, the hilt worn smooth from use, was tucked sheathless into a knotted cablevine he wore around his waist. Little of his silver armor remained, but he still wore a chest plate carved with deep gouges, one battered pauldron on his left shoulder, and dented iron bracers that were caked with rust. Despite the conditions of his garments, Raksha appeared to have stayed in relatively good shape, if a little underfed. That much was obvious from the way he'd tackled Malil.

"Yes, I live. Your eyes are sharp as ever," Raksha said, his voice a little rougher than Glissa remembered. The elf girl noted the former Kha had also dropped any pretense of his old formal speech pattern. "You came. You finally . . ." He propped himself up on one elbow and stared at her as if he expected she might dissolve into smoke. The bright golden fur on his chin was flecked with white and silver, and his wiry whiskers were shorn clean on the right side. Three pale, ragged scars ran diagonally from the center of his forehead and down across his eye socket to his left cheek, though his sharp eyes were both intact. His mane had become as wild as Glissa's own tangled cable hair, but more nappy, snarled with twigs and sticks.

Raksha sniffed the air and flashed the tips of his teeth. "What is that smell?" He followed his nose to Glissa, and peeked over her shoulder.

"Hi there," Geth's head said from inside the open pack, and winked.

"You brought the *head?*" Raksha growled in disbelief. "How did it even—"

"He might be useful," Glissa replied. "Besides, I'm still figuring out what to do with him. Every time I think about throwing him away, something stops me."

"Who's throwing what?" Geth asked.

"Let's just keep our enemies upwind," Raksha said, and flipped the bag shut.

"Heym, my muz talkim!"

"Shut up, Geth. Raksha, they told me you'd gone crazy. That you destroyed Taj Nar."

Raksha snorted with disgust. "Lies," he said. "You wound

my honor by even asking me, but I admit I am not surprised. But think, old friend. If I were truly mad, why would I save you?"

He had a point. The entire story about Raksha's attempted sabotage hadn't felt right to her. Nor did it strike her as right to doubt Lyese's word, but the leonin standing before her did not look like a maniac, let alone ready to destroy his own home den in a suicidal bid for honor. Her instincts told her to trust him for now. Besides, Glissa didn't have much choice. She did not want to fight Raksha, even if everything she'd been told was true.

"Raksha, there's something else," Glissa said. "In a few days, Memnarch will be vulnerable. This—" she raised the Miracore— "is the weapon that can kill him. I'm the only one who can do it, but I can't try it for another three days."

"Yes, I know," Raksha said.

"You what? How long have you been here, Raksha? Yshkar told me you were most likely dead," Glissa said. "He certainly seemed to hope you were, I'm sorry to say."

Raksha's grin drooped into a scowl, and he flashed his canines as a low growl that sounded distinctly unfriendly rumbled deep in his throat. "Do not speak that name," he snarled. "He's as dead to me as I am to him."

Glissa suddenly felt very exposed, here in the dark lacuna with a possibly dangerous madman. She cast a quick glance at the knife on Raksha's waist, but it was not quick enough to escape feline eyes.

"You injure me," he said. "Glissa, I am not going to attack you. Nor did I do anything that you were told. We were both manipulated, but now we have the chance to set things right. My cousin was a faithless man, and I fear my throne was more important to him than victory over our enemies. He has been duped. And Bruenna, too, I fear."

" 'Dupe' seems a little strong," Glissa said. "Yshkar seems to have the military situation well in hand. He married my sister, you know that? An elf and a leonin. She always liked you, you know. But she seems happy now, even if I didn't expect that kind of life for her."

"Your sister . . ." Raksha said, and grimaced. "Glissa, your sister is dead. The thing that wed my cousin an imposter."

CHAPTER 22

TRIAGE

Bruenna's back itched, but she couldn't reach it. She hated wearing leonin armor, but she hated being cut open more, so she endured the discomfort. The battle had lasted two days, and now four of the suns were already down. The fifth dawn was not far off now. Bruenna hoped the suffering below would prove worth it. If Glissa wasn't successful, there might not be anyone left on the surface to save.

Her zauk trotted cautiously onto the smoldering battlefield at the head of a group of twelve mounted leonin warriors in battle regalia. Bruenna's own armor had been damaged beyond repair the day before, when Krark-Home's last charbelcher had gone up under an aerophin suicide run. The 'belcher had tipped over sideways, causing its molten ammunition to ignite, but not launch. Within seconds, the overheated weapon exploded, taking the aerophins, several levelers, dozens of nim, and far too many Krark-Home defenders with it. Only her sturdy old Neurok battle armor had saved Bruenna.

Now the mage wore a borrowed suit of segmented silver plate that was once worn by Rishan, the seer Ushanti's long-dead daughter and at one time Raksha Golden Cub's intended. Lyese had insisted the mage put it on before heading out onto the field, and Yshkar had concurred. The armor was certainly strong and would no doubt protect her from harm as well as the old suit, but it didn't fit quite right across the hips. Nor, she groused, did it easily allow one to reach the middle of one's back. The mage awkwardly slid the sword on her belt a little forward so it would stop slapping against the side of the bird, which brought a stop to its frequent squawks of complaint.

Bruenna chided herself for worrying about her own discomfort in the midst of an ongoing battle. The carnage the riders passed through was devastating and made her stomach roil. Corpses and pieces of corpses lay everywhere, interspersed with the writhing wounded who couldn't leave the field under their own power—hapless souls who were already dead, but hadn't realized it yet. Twisted chunks of metal and debris from the shattered vedalken quake-beasts and broken charbelchers lay amongst dead zauks, horribly mangled pteron corpses with their delicate wings crumpled and broken, and piles of stinking nim bodies that in their stillness looked more than ever like dead insects. An amber haze hung low over the scene— a noxious fog of blood, smoke, necrogen mist, and steam that spewed from ruined constructs.

The artifact armies had finally been beaten back into retreat with determination, courage, and hundreds of spent lives. Yshkar was already boasting of this "great victory." Bruenna found the Kha's boasting ill-advised, but the leonin had told her that the troops needed a victory, no matter what the cost, to keep going.

The other half of the royal couple was not on the field. Khanha Lyese had not been seen by anyone since returning from the battlefield the night before and entering her quarters. The mage wondered if Glissa's departure was the reason for her retreat. It was strange, though, not to see the Tall Queen leading the defenders. Bruenna had never known Lyese to shirk a fight, and in fact the elf seemed to enjoy it a little too much. Maybe humans could never really understand the behavior of elves.

Bruenna reached the closest fallen defender and reined the zauk to a halt. She half-dismounted, half-fell from the side of the bird, thrown off balance by the new armor, but managed to land on two feet. She dropped to one knee next to a goblin soldier whose legs were gone. The Krark-Home defender was pinned to the ground by what had once been a part of a charbelcher. He moaned pitiably and reached up to Bruenna.

This was why she was here. With so many dead, dying, and wounded, there weren't enough healers to go around. Bruenna had offered to do whatever she could, and the healers had told her they were happy for the help.

The mage took the goblin's hand in her remaining real one and held it tight. "I'm here to help you," she whispered. "Don't try to speak. You're hurt." She locked eyes with his, and Bruenna saw that the goblin knew he was more than hurt.

The mage's clockwork hand opened a pouch on her belt and removed one tiny vial of precious serum. Bruenna had medicines and salves from the leonin healers for the ones she could save, but the best she could do for this patient was ease his suffering before the end. The serum was not anaesthetic, but it would definitely take the sting out of death. Her eyes still locked with the dying goblin's, Bruenna heard two thuds as Commander Jethrar dismounted from his own zauk and stepped up next to her, sword drawn. The dying goblin's eyes widened in terror, and he began to shriek.

"Get back!" Bruenna snapped backhanding the leonin in the gut. "You're terrifying him."

"But we are allies," Jethrar said. "Goblin, you have no need to fear me."

"The alliance had been around for only a few years. Until that time your people kept his as pets. Now, back off, *commander*," Bruenna said, staring the leonin down. "This man is terrified, and at the moment his needs are a lot more important to me than yours."

"But I thought— I thought we were on triage duty. He deserves a warrior's death," said the commander, raising the tip of his blade.

"He's already gotten it," Bruenna hissed. "Now please, get back on your zauk and watch my back, as you were ordered."

Jethrar snapped to attention and did as she commanded. Bruenna had no rank in the leonin army, but she had plenty of unofficial authority.

The mage raised the tiny, almost needle-thin vial of serum so the goblin could see it. "This will make the pain go away. May your soul find rest, defender of Krark-Home." Bruenna tipped the open vial to the fallen soldier's cracked lips, and he swallowed the serum with a wince.

The goblin's eyes glowed a faint silvery blue, and he visibly relaxed, drawing faint, shallow breaths. Bruenna held his small hand for maybe half a minute, keeping eye contact, until the goblin finally exhaled heavily.

The mage sighed and rose, wondering what she had been thinking coming out here. She was no healer. Death, she had seen, and up close. Her entire village, all her people, were gone. But that had been . . . detached. There had been nothing she could do for her fellow Neurok. The deaths of her people had been violent, but they had been quick.

This war was different, and Bruenna hated it even more. She slumped a bit in the saddle and guided her zauk to the next injured soldier, a skyhuntress who looked like she had been thrown from her mount at a great height. The emergency wing pack every skyhunter wore lay in tatters at the fallen leonin's side, shredded and burned by aerophin energy blasts. The skyhunter was wheezing hard, and Bruenna didn't dare move her. Most of the leonin's bones had shattered, and broke through her skin at several points. A pool of blood spread in a halo around her body. Another one who wouldn't make it.

The leonin looked up, pleading, and Bruenna pulled another tiny vial from her pouch. She'd never have enough serum to help them all, but the mage was determined that what she had left would go to good use. Bruenna tipped the vial into the female's mouth. Bruenna waited with her as she had with the goblin, until the leonin breathed her last.

A zauk, not her own, squawked a warning call. Bruenna scanned the horizon and immediately saw what had frightened the big bird. A growing cloud of silver and black arose from the direction of the Mephidross. Only the yellow sun still hung in the sky, but the cloud—no, swarm, she corrected herself—passed in front of it and clearly showed the tiny outlines of thousands of winged creatures.

Bruenna's growing despair suddenly flared into anger and hatred for their relentless attackers. Even warring ogres allowed the other side to retrieve the dead. True, they ate them, but still. The mage struggled to her feet in the heavy plate.

"Jethrar, do you see that?" Bruenna asked. With a heave she hauled herself into the saddle and drew her sword.

The commander squinted against the setting sun and his eyes widened. "How many of those things does Memnarch have?"

"Too many, my friend. Far too many. I think the Kha may have boasted too soon," Bruenna said. When she saw that Jethrar and the other leonin continued to gawk at the approaching flock of deadly constructs, she shouted, "One of you get back to Krark-Home and warn them this isn't over yet!"

Jethrar, jolted from shock, nodded to a lieutenant. The leonin warrior kicked his zauk in the flanks, bolting back to the last bastion of living surface dwellers.

The commander wheeled his mount around in a circle, scanning the area. "Take heed, men," he said. "The skyhunters' ranks are depleted, so we may not expect help from that quarter. The rest of the troops have fallen back to defend Krark-Home. Until Lieutenant Zelosh returns with reinforcements, we're on our own. I know this was supposed to be triage duty, but we just became the vanguard."

Bruenna shielded her eyes from the glare of the dimming sun and checked on the progress of the new wave of attackers. She could already make out familiar shapes among the aerophins and other, stranger flying constructs. Beetle shapes.

"Nim," Bruenna whispered.

"What?" Jethrar asked, and looked in the direction Bruenna pointed.

"Those aren't just aerophins," the mage said. "I'm not sure why, but there are nim flying with them."

"But Yert is dead," Jethrar said.

"I know," Bruenna said. "I know." She mentally ran over the fight with Yert, and her use of the Miracore. Had she done this somehow, in an arrogant attempt to control the nim without truly understanding the nature of the ancient talisman? Had she served only to put the nim under Memnarch's power?

Bruenna shivered.

CHAPTER 23

OGRE AND UNDER

"Let me go. We've got to warn them!" Glissa yanked herself free of Raksha's grip and began to march back up the lacuna.

"I already told them," Raksha snarled, bounding after her. "They didn't believe me. Yshkar convinced them I was mad, and Lyese—the imposter Lyese—let them believe it." He caught up with the fleet-footed elf girl easily, and spun her around by the shoulders. "Glissa, listen to me," the leonin said, looking her in the eye. "Every instinct I have is telling me to do exactly what you're doing. My heart cries out to join my people in battle. The leonin have been manipulated and tricked, thousands have died needlessly. I know all that, but still I am asking you to hear me out. After that, you can return to the surface, or meet your destiny in the interior. But know that *I* will go after Memnarch by myself if I must."

"Raksha," Glissa said, "what really happened at Taj Nar? What happened to Ly—to my sister?"

"The imposter has been there for five years," Raksha said. "I will tell you, but not here."

"Then where?"

"Somewhere safer," Raksha said. "Mirrodin can't afford to lose the Chosen One to an accidental fall or a rogue kharybdog."

"All right, somewhere safer. Lead the way."

The leonin guided her back up the lacuna to the surface.

Strange, Glissa thought, that the open Tangle felt claustrophobic compared to the lacuna. Raksha led her a few hundred yards down a narrow game path to an ancient Tangle tree stump that had weathered and split with age, a slim crevice just wide enough for Raksha to slip through sideways. Glissa followed, more relieved than she let on to finally have found someone she truly trusted in this strange future.

The crevice opened into a small cave formed by the ancient root structure of the long-dead tree. The warm orange glow of a single coalstone lamp lit Raksha's den, glittering on the worn silver bedroll that lay in the corner next to a pair of chairs assembled from scraps of tanglewood and wire vines. A battered iron pot hung over a fire that had been extinguished for some time. Raksha bade Glissa sit on one of the homemade seats and sparked the coalstone to life. It burned without smoke, bringing the contents of the pot to a rapid boil. The leonin poured two cups of a syrupy brew and gave one to Glissa. The elf girl tentatively sipped the hot drink, and found it was pleasantly sweet and immediately calmed her nerves. Raksha paced the small room, not meeting the elf girl's eyes.

"Raksha, this is safe enough. You say you didn't destroy Taj Nar, and that Lyese is a phony?" Glissa said. "Convince me."

The leonin stopped pacing for a moment, inhaled deeply, and let out a long, sighing growl. "Your sister. The trouble began about an hour after we parted ways and you left for the Mephidross."

* * * * *

Kha Raksha Golden Cub and the Tel-Jilad warrior Lyese of Viridia marched up the winding moutain path, following a bound and defeated Alderok Vektro, who stumbled drunkenly ahead. The leonin split his attention between the prisoner and the iron walls of the narrow draw. The walls rose higher the farther up the path they went, and could easily conceal another goblin ambush, or worse.

Raksha did not like the mountains in the first place, but the claustrophobic confines of this narrow mountain trail made him downright jumpy.

Fortunately, he found it helped his nerves to shove Alderok Vektro every once in a while, and the Vulshok priest seemed glad to give Raksha frequent opportunities to do so. Vektro would stop walking without warning, and often cocked his head as if listening for something. Not surprisingly, the Vulshok refused to tell Raksha what he was listening for no matter how the leonin tried to coerce him. The Kha knew many, many ways to coerce people, including a few he really didn't want to use in front of the elf girl. Yet Alderok Vektro had said very little even when they removed his gag, and would give them only the sparest of directions.

As it turned out, Glissa's insistence that Lyese accompany him had proved fortuitous. The young elf had proven a serviceable tracker, and assured the Kha that they were following fresh goblin footprints.

Raksha and Lyese had been separated from Glissa for a little over two hours when Vektro stopped in his staggering tracks yet again. Without warning, the Vulshok collapsed in a heap on the rusty iron path.

"This had better not be a trick, Vektro," the leonin growled. Lyese and Raksha crouched over the fallen human, and with an effort they rolled the big man onto his back.

Alderok Vektro's glassy eyes stared up at the sky. His mouth was wrenched open in a grinning rictus, and his tongue lolled out, swollen and dry. Bright red blood trickled from the human's nose, ears, and mouth.

"Correct us if we are wrong," Raksha said, "but this human appears to be dead."

Lyese patted Vektro's lifeless form, and Raksha did likewise. There wasn't a mark on the dead priest that they couldn't account for, and certainly no arrows or other projectiles had struck him.

"Raksha, I think he just...died," Lyese finally admitted.

"Do humans do that often?" the Kha asked. "Perhaps because of the stress of capture?" It wasn't that far-fetched. In his youth, he'd spent many a season capturing live animals to be slaughtered for royal feasts. For special occasions, the leonin would forgo typical prey animals for more dangerous game. But he'd learned that many of the strongest natural predators went catatonic when locked in a cage, unable to hunt, run, or roam their territory.

"Humans aren't *that* different, as far as I know," Lyese replied. "Not this different. But sometimes people just die."

"They certainly do, but the timing is suspicious in the extreme. It must be foul play," Raksha whispered. "Keep your voice down." He scanned the high walls of the draw again, but could spot no movement. The shadows in the craggy ironstone cliffs could be hiding almost anything, even from his sharp feline eyes.

"What should we do?" Lyese asked. "Head back? Or should we try to find this Dwugget on our own? Vektro wasn't a very good guide, anyway. I think I can follow these tracks to—"

A thunderous crash erupted from high above, cutting the elf girl short. The pair stood and craned their necks upward at the sound. "What was that?" Raksha asked and drew his longknife, Vektro suddenly forgotten.

His answer came in the form of a gigantic humanoid figure that leaped from the walls above and crashed onto the narrow trail several yards ahead. The ogre's feet, each one half as big as the leonin monarch, fractured the path beneath and knocked Raksha and Lyese onto their backs. The hulking monster was the color of rusted ironstone and stood almost twenty feet high, wearing a loincloth made of dried goblin skins tied crudely together. Wiry, tangled hair covered the creature's head and arms but couldn't hide a complex network of scars. The ogre drew a deep breath with a rush of wind, then its toothy mouth split open to release a deafening roar that forced Raksha and Lyese to cover their ears.

With a slow, deliberate movement, the misshapen creature reached out with a simian arm and wrenched a tree stump from the ground. As easily as Raksha might pick up a sword, the ogre raised the stump overhead like a club.

"Raksha," Lyese said as they helped each other stand, "I think maybe we should get back to Taj Nar. Right now."

"Perhaps a new plan is called for," he agreed.

Raksha grabbed the elf girl by the arm and began to back away from the ogre. Sudden movements might have made the creature charge. Instead of pursuing them, it slammed the tree stump club into Alderok Vektro's corpse and flattened the dead Vulshok to a pulp with one strike. The ogre raised its heavy head to glare at them, and there was little doubt about the target of its next strike. Raksha's instincts finally overcame his resolve, and the pair broke into a dead run back down the path.

They shouldn't have bothered. The gigantic ogre caught up to them with only three steps. It tossed the stump club aside and easily scooped each of them up in a massive hamfist. The ogre was displaying remarkable restraint, Raksha noted as he wriggled in vain to break free. It could have squeezed him into jelly if it wanted to, but the monster exerted only enough pressure to keep them restrained.

The ogre held Lyese up to its scarred, pitted face and sniffed her gingerly. The elf girl screamed, twisting in the creature's grip. Then the ogre did the very last thing Raksha would have expected. The gaping maw it wore for a mouth broke into a wide smile, and it burst into mad, thundering laughter.

"Raksha, what's it doing?" Lyese shouted.

"How should we know?" the leonin bellowed.

He hadn't expected an answer—ogres weren't known for their eloquence—but the monster spoke. Its voice was a deep rumble that sounded like crumbling ironstone grating on copper ore, with something else—a quality at once familiar and chilling—running underneath.

"Quiet," the ogre said, and knocked Raksha's head against the elf girl's. Everything went black.

* * * * *

"Now hold on," Glissa interrupted. "You said Lyese was dead."

"Who's telling this story?" Raksha said.

"All right then, I'm listening," Glissa sighed. "None of this is remotely like the story I got at Krark-Home."

"It was within Krark-Home that I awoke," Raksha said. "It was very different then."

* * * * *

"Raksha," Lyese said. "Raaaaksha."

The Kha felt something scratching at the top of his head and realized it was a set of elven claws. He opened his eyes and saw the elf girl courched over him, her hand atop his head and—

"Are you scratching our *ears?*" the leonin demanded as he brushed the elf girl's hand away.

"I was trying to wake you up," Lyese replied. "You've been out for a while. We're safe now."

"Yes, safe, huh?" a gravelly voice broke in, and Raksha blinked to take in his surroundings. He was inside a large underground room with walls cut from the same ironstone they had been hiking through for most of the day. They had to be inside the mountain.

A tiny, wrinkled goblin in rust-red priest's robes very similar in cut and design to what Vektro had worn stood next to a smoldering brazier near the center of the room. Rickety copper shelves lined one wall, filled with bottles, beakers, tubes, and several thick, weathered books that looked very old. A heavy iron door hung in an ill-fitting frame on the opposite wall. He could see no one else in the room. He smelled the tang of incense and the unmistakeable odor of goblin, but only a lingering trace of ogre. The creature was nowhere to be seen.

The leonin sat up and growled. His longknife was still tucked securely in his belt, and he was not bound or restrained in any way, so he decided to take a diplomatic approach.

"Dwugget, we presume?" Raksha asked. "Where are we?"

"Yes, that's me, huh?" the old goblin said. "Dwugget of the Krark." He looked distinctly uncomfortable, but gave the leonin a quick, nervous bow. Nervous, no doubt, because of the goblin's proximity to a fully conscious leonin warrior.

"Raksha," Lyese said, interjecting herself between the two, "They're going to help. We've been talking."

"*You* have been talking?" Raksha snarled. "On what authority do you, an elf, negotiate for the leonin people?"

Lyese looked like she'd been slapped. "On the authority that I was the only one awake? That I was the one that woke up and surprised that ogre with a knife to the palm that made it drop us? Maybe the authority granted to me by dragging your unconscious carcass all the way to this cave and finding the goblins, who were able to chase off the ogre, which chased me *all the way up this damned mountain?*"

"Please, no fighting, huh?" Dwugget interrupted before Raksha could respond. "All friends now. Kha, we talk, you and Dwugget, huh? Give you all the details?"

The leonin composed himself and returned to the elf girl, his ear pointed forward in embarrassment. "We apologize, Lyese," Raksha said. "We are grateful to be alive, and thank you for opening the negotiations." He bowed deeply, which he did only rarely, and returned to the goblin, who shifted from foot to foot. Raksha supposed he would be nervous too, in Dwugget's place. "Dwugget, your people attacked us. Is that how you negotiate?"

"Mistake, huh?" Dwugget said. "Have to defend my people."

Raksha appraised the little creature before him. The leonin had been raised to think of goblins as inferior beings. Even Slobad, though a friend, had really been little more than a slave. But he could understand *this* goblin. He was a leader, like Raksha. Of course he had sent guards to meet them. What would the leonin have done if he had encountered a gang of well-armed goblins trying to enter Taj Nar?

"Dwugget of the Krark," Raksha said, "is there a place we three negotiators may go to work out the details?"

Dwugget led Raksha and Lyese to a door the leonin had not noticed before. They followed the goblin through a short tunnel lit with flame-tubes. "We go eat, and talk, huh?" Dwugget said. "Food and negotiation."

The meal, as it turned out, took longer than the negotiations themselves. Raksha had been out for almost a day and a half, and he was impressed to see how well Lyese had done in the interim. The Krark would prove to be valuable allies, now that the initial confusion was cleared up. He had seen them fight, and knew the goblins were fiercer than he'd once believed.

They spent one more night in Krark-Home. Dwugget threw a

banquet in their honor, which included as entertainment his own account of the tale of Krark, the legendary goblin hero who long ago discovered the world was hollow—a tale that had originally spurred Glissa to seek out Memnarch in the core. Raksha was struck by the story's similarity, at points, to the myths and legends surrounding Great Dakan, his own leonin ancestor and the first to unite the leonin under a single Kha.

The next day, they set off down the path from Krark-Home for Taj Nar, accompanied by forty of Dwugget's finest fighters. More would come later. This force was no more than a token, but would serve to convince the leonin army that the goblins would honor their commitment.

Raksha didn't know it at the time, but Lyese was already dead.

CHAPTER 24

TUMBLING DOWN

"Already dead?" Glissa snapped. "It doesn't sound like it."

"I did not learn what really happened until much later," Raksha said. "I told you it was confusing."

"So when did you figure it out?" Glissa said.

"Two years after the treaty was signed," Raksha said. "The day Taj Nar fell."

Now they were getting somewhere. "Bruenna refused to talk about that," the elf girl said. "But what does it have to do with Lyese?"

"She had become attached to Yshkar," Raksha said. "Or so I thought. I had little time to give her, and thought she was doing all she could to fit in. Lyese asked to join the forces on the ground, and I could not deny her the right of combat. She'd already spent a year helping me co-ordinate with the goblins as an ambassador, which kept her clear of the fighting for the most part. I'd hoped it would be what you wanted. I still harbored hope that you lived, though no one had heard from you for so long. Bruenna had not given up hope, and spent much time trying to figure out a way into the Lumengrid. She thought there might be knowledge there that could free you."

"There was," Glissa said.

"Once Lyese took the field, it took only a few weeks for Yshkar to promote her," Raksha said. "She proved to be an amazing fighter. Yshkar and Lyese soon became inseparable off the field as well. I encouraged this, again in what I thought were your sister's best interests. I could not watch over her all the time, the responsibility of the Kha did not allow it."

"Makes sense," Glissa said. "You gave her the best protector you could. Your own blood."

"Yes, and I had to focus on the ultimate defense of Taj Nar, but my inattention ultimately led to the loss of the home den," Raksha said. "The war had been raging relentlessly. Yshkar—perhaps under the influence of the false Lyese, perhaps through his own bullheadedness—made a grave tactical error that cost us the last outpost den in the 'void. I ordered him to pull all of our forces back home. He initially resisted, and cost us more men. When he finally called the retreat, the nim followed hot on his heels, and closed in on all sides."

"What about the Krark?" Glissa asked.

"The Krark were under siege themselves. They spared us what fighters they could," Raksha said. "Dwugget and I assigned them to protect the supply lines running between Taj Nar and Krark-Home. As it turned out, that's the only reason the leonin survived at all."

"The mana bomb," Glissa said. "There was really a mana bomb, right?"

"Yes, though I certainly did not set it. There is no honor in such a death, despite the imposter's convoluted explanations. Yshkar refused to hear my words. Taj Nar could have easily resisted a siege, under the plan we'd formulated," Raksha said. "But not the enemy within."

* * * * *

The Kha held a long-range spotting scope to one eye and looked out over the roiling mass of nim. Even with the magically augmented lens, Raksha could not see where the nim ended and the horizon began. Silver aerophins circled in formation, almost too distant to make out against the golden sun. The constructs looked like scavengers waiting for carrion. The levelers had not been seen, and the scouts he'd sent to track them had not returned.

With a frustrated growl, he closed up the telescoping eyesight and hooked it onto his belt. Raksha didn't need the scope to see that the nim would breach the wall soon. It was inevitable. The sheer volume of nim corpses was forming a natural ramp, and every one that died brought the grisly mounds of stinking corpses and chittering vanguard attackers that much closer to the top.

Raksha heard a reptilian screech, and tossed a wave at the skyhunter that flashed by. The skyhunters were always in the air now, beating back the attempts of clumsy flying nim. The slow-moving undead were no match for the pteron riders in a dogfight, but the tactic was successfully keeping the leonin flyers tied up. Had they been able to spare skyhunters to attack the nim on the ground . . .

They could not, so that was a futile train of thought. Raksha crouched and leaped from the lookout tower to the worn path atop the wall and landed silently next to his cousin. The top of the wall was a flurry of leonin warriors and a few goblin soldiers scrambling to ready the siege defenses.

"What did you see, my Kha?" Yshkar asked. "How long before they're over the wall?"

"At the rate they're piling up, we have no more than a few hours," Raksha sighed. "We had to see it for ourselves. The scouts are right. There really is no end to them."

"What of the construct armies?" Yshkar asked. "Why have we not seen them?"

"Aerophins circle on the horizon," Raksha replied. "The levelers—"

Raksha was cut short by a crash of thunder that shook the wall beneath his feet. He grabbed the edge to steady himself, and caught Yshkar's arm before his cousin tumbled onto the nim below. The two of them pulled themselves over the lip of the wall to see where the explosion had come from.

Thick black smoke stung his disbelieving eyes. Three gargantuan six-legged silver constructs had emerged from beneath the infinite carpet of nim that covered the Glimmervoid all around them. Each construct's central body consisted of a huge globular power source that glowed an eerie blue through the haze. Their "heads" were massive cylinders, one of which was belching a misty blue fog.

Yshkar gasped, military formality lost in shock. "What in the name of Dakan are those?"

"Something new," Raksha snarled. "It appears that only one has fired. We must expect another volley."

"My Kha, you should let me take command of the defenses and get to the throne room."

"Don't be ridiculous, Yshkar," Raksha said. "You've been listening to that elf girl too much. Our place is here with you. If we are to die we shall do it as the Kha, and our enemies shall regret the day they—"

Another cannon-construct fired at that moment, sending a house-sized ball of blazing blue energy into the wall below them. Before Raksha could react, a whole section of Taj Nar crumbled beneath his feet and gave way.

"My Kha!" Yshkar bellowed.

Raksha plummeted into the pit that had just opened beneath him.

The Kha barely heard his cousin. He dropped through floor after floor as an entire section of Taj Nar gave way, but fortunately he collided with several outcroppings on the way down that slowed his fall. Raksha landed with a crack of broken armor on a rough metal floor, and after a few seconds managed to scramble to cover beneath a stable block of rubble that had once formed part of the lookout tower upon which he'd recently stood.

The cave in continued for almost a minute, forcing Raksha to cover his ears as several tons of metal crashed down all around him. Only the overhanging block he'd chosen as cover kept the leonin from being crushed as the rain of debris poured in.

Raksha wiped iron dust from his eyes and took stock. He'd fallen all the way to a basement sublevel, which until recently served as the royal army but had been converted to temporary barracks only a week before. The main wall still stood, down here at least, and he could see sky far above. Light streamed into the dusty air above through two large holes that had been blasted through its side, but otherwise the main exterior wall had held almost all the way to top. The interior of Taj Nar was less well protected, and too many supports had been destroyed to hold up the weight where Raksha had been standing. He was extremely lucky.

Damnably lucky, for he feared he was about to see the end of his people. If Taj Nar fell, where else could they go? Krark-Home?

Raksha crawled out from his refuge and searched vainly for some path through the wreckage, a way to get out of this hole. As the haze cleared, the outlines of over a dozen leonin bodies littered the ground all around him, and he offered a bitter prayer for the dead.

From the corner of his eye, the leonin spotted movement in the rubble.

"Raksha!" Lyese called. "My leg's pinned. Can you help me?"

"Don't move!" he shouted. "We're on our way!" Maybe he hadn't been able to save Glissa from Memnarch. Maybe this really was the end of Taj Nar. But as long as he lived, so would Glissa's sister—he owed his lost friend that much. With as much caution as Raksha could spare, he navigated the maze of debris and death to the elf girl's side.

Lyese's leg was stuck beneath a rectangular chunk of inner wall and tangled in a mess of support cables. The elf girl sat upright, her back pressed up against a round hunk of debris that looked like something that might have been left over from the old armory. Her face bore a few minor cuts, but Lyese appeared more or less unharmed. Raksha dropped to one knee to get a closer look at her leg.

"It does not appear broken. Are you bleeding?" Raksha asked.

"I don't think so," the elf girl gasped. "I think it's . . . ow . . . I think it's just stuck. If you could pull on it—gently—I think I might be able to wriggle free."

"Of course," Raksha said. He dropped onto his belly, draping himself uncomfortably across the elf girl's body, and reached in to take hold of Lyese's leg. "Let us know when you're ready, and we will pull together."

"Ready," Lyese said, and brought the knee of her free leg up into Raksha's belly.

He gasped as the air left his lungs and his ribs cracked. The leonin brought himself up to all fours with an agonizing effort and fought back his gorge.

"What in the name of—?" Raksha coughed.

Lyese easily slipped her leg free of the cabling and leaped to her feet. She followed with a sharp-toed boot to Raksha's gut. He spat up silvery red blood and flopped onto his side, clutching his belly, and was unable to avoid yet another kick that caught him behind the ear. The sky above spun lazily, and the leonin fought the urge to pass out.

"Raksha, Raksha, Raksha . . ." Lyese said, driving a boot into his side with each repitition. "You're not supposed to be here. You were supposed to die up there, with Yshkar. You really should have done that."

"What are you talking about?" Raksha croaked. "What are you doing?"

"My job, your Kha-ness," Lyese replied. Keeping one eye on the leonin, she backed over to the metal ball she'd been leaning against when she was "trapped" and crouched over the strange object, which Raksha could now see bore ancient carvings that looked vedalken. Two blue crystals mounted on top of the artifact began to glow and a low hum struck the leonin's sensitive ears. "Sorry you had to find me," the elf added. "You're not going to be as easy to cow as that fool Dwugget, or as easy to seduce as your idiot cousin. And you know what that means, my Kha. I get to kill you *personally*."

"Lyese, why?" Raksha whispered. "Glissa would—"

Lyese laughed, a cold, tinny sound unlike anything Raksha had ever heard. When next she spoke, her voice changed. The tones of the young elf girl he knew were underlaid with a low, masculine baritone that filled the air all around the leonin's head.

"Who are you?" Raksha whispered.

"Ah, he figured it out," the Lyese-thing sneered, and gave him another kick. "You should have gone along with the Vulshok, cat-man. You'd still have your elf girl, and your precious palace would still be in one piece. Of course, *you* would still be dead, but what is the life of a Kha compared to those of his subjects?" The false Lyese tapped out a pattern on the glowing artifact and stood, apparently satisfied.

"Release the girl," Raksha coughed. "Or I will kill you who-ever you look like."

"Idiot. Leonin, the girl is right here. She's terrified, let me tell you. I'm going to enjoy consuming her mind when I move on."

"Move on?" Raksha asked.

"Tell me, did I squeeze you too hard, my Kha?" the elf said as she brought her fists together. "You can't imagine how tricky it is to use only enough strength when you're an ogre."

"Ogre?" Raksha managed. He was already recovering, but tried to hide it. If Lyese got close enough, he might be able to surprise her.

"Gave you too much credit, I see," Lyese said. "I'll make it easier for you. Here's a riddle. What do a Vulshok priest, an ogre, and an elf girl have in common?"

"Sounds like a bad goblin joke," Raksha said.

"You are the opposite of fun," Lyese said. "Vektro, at your service." The elf strolled around the glowing artifact, which now hummed louder than before. When she reached the leonin, she took a deep bow with exaggerated flourish.

"Alderok Vektro?" Raksha said. "Alderok Vektro is dead."

"Just Vektro, if you please," the thing that wore Lyese's body said. Vektro brought elf girl's visage mere inches from Raksha's and added, "The human Alderok is nothing but a smear on the path now."

Raksha brough a gauntleted fist crashing into the imposter's borrowed face, knocking Vektro backward. The Kha rolled forward onto his feet and spun into a crouch, faced the imposter, and roared. "I am Raksha Golden Cub, Kha of Taj Nar. I have no need of your services."

The imposter screamed and charged the leonin Kha. Raksha had lost his sword, but no leonin was ever defenseless as long as he had his claws. He blocked Vektro's first punch with his palm and drove a fist into the imposter's gut. Vektro doubled over with a cough, and the leonin followed through with a knee to the face that knocked the imposter backward, stunned.

"Whatever you are, Vektro, it's good to see you can take a beating no matter what you look like," Raksha snarled. "Now get out of that body before we rip its head off. We really don't want to do that."

"No deal, Kha," the imposter coughed. "I've been waiting a long, long time for a body all my own, and now that I've got it I'm not leaving. The master says this one is mine to keep. And I intend to."

Raksha launched himself into a forward roll and tackled Vektro around the legs, bringing the ersatz elf to the hard metal floor of the old armory with a crash. He followed with a fist to the jaw and pinned Vektro's head back with one elbow as he threw himself across the elf girl's stolen body. "That device," Raksha said. He nodded to the glowing ball of humming silver. "It is a weapon?"

Vektro smiled, and looked pointedly over Raksha's shoulder. All traces of the strange Vektro-voice gone, Lyese screamed. "Yshkar! He's gone mad! That artifact is going to destroy Taj Nar. We've got to get out!"

Raksha didn't see Yshkar's blow coming until it was too late. He was thrown back and struck his head hard enough to make the world spin. Yshkar crouched over him and placed a hand against Raksha's forehead, then muttered a standard spell used by the leonin on those rare occasions it paid to take live prisoners in war. Raksha's muscles went slack, and without ceremony Yshkar slung the Kha over his shoulder. Raksha would be paralyzed below the neck for hours.

"What is that?" Yshkar said, jabbing a claw at the whining silver globe.

"It's a mana bomb, and he said it's going to go off any minute," Lyese said. "Yshkar, he's betrayed us all. You have to leave him, or we won't have time to save the rest of your people." She leaned in closer and whispered loud enough for Raksha to hear, "*Our* people."

"Most have already evacuated. I gave the order after that last blast," Yshkar said.

"Good," Raksha mumbled deliriously.

Lyese was already heading toward the cable ladder Yshkar had used to get down to the basement level. Within seconds the elf girl—and the being that controlled her—scrambled up the ladder and away from the glowing, whining bomb.

"Damn," Yshkar growled, and followed. "Raksha, I will see you dead for this. But not today." He followed Lyese up the ladder, and within minutes Yshkar and the elf girl were well clear of Taj Nar.

Yshkar dropped Raksha to the ground without ceremony and propped the paralyzed leonin against a pile of leonin bodies that reeked of blood and rot. "Yshkar," the Kha croaked. "She is not—"

Before Raksha could finish, Taj Nar disappeared in a blinding flash of blue and white. A half second later, the deafening thunder of the mana bomb explosion reached his ears and blasted the world into silence. Unable even to shield his eyes, Raksha was forced to watch as his home, his kingdom, and the future of his people were laid low under a rapidly expanding cloud of destruction.

* * * * *

"You saw it go up," Glissa said. Something tickled her cheek, and her hand came away covered with tears she hadn't noticed until now.

"I couldn't look away," Raksha said. "Though my soul very nearly died that day."

"I think I can figure out what happened next from what they

told me," Glissa interrupted. "Vektro accused you, and all Yshkar could see was you trying to kill the woman he loved. It sounds like she would have killed everyone if you hadn't stopped her."

"It was Yshkar's evacuation order that saved everyone," Raksha said. "My discovery only saved the imposter."

"But what *was* Vektro? How can I get Lyese back?" Glissa's eyes flashed with fury. "You told me she was dead, but this is worse. A lot worse. She's still in there, Raksha. I know it."

"It doesn't matter," Raksha said with a sigh. The leonin placed a firm paw on her shoulder. "He will not leave her until she is mortally wounded. We would have to kill her to save her."

"I can't accept that," Glissa said. "We have to figure out what he is, and how to get him out. I want my sister back, Raksha."

"Glissa, she's dead. She has to be," Raksha replied.

She stood to look the leonin eye to eye and jabbed a finger in his chest. "Why?" Glissa demanded.

"Because we have a chance to stop what's coming now," Raksha said. "If you choose to confront Vektro, you will fail to strike Memnarch when the time comes. That is why she must be dead. If there is a way to force Vektro out, we will do it. But you cannot concern yourself with her now. It's one life, one life that might not even exist."

Glissa knew the leonin was right. There was nothing she could do but fail if she tried to save Lyese now. "All right, damn you," she said. "I'll set Lyese—I'll set her aside. But why even carry on this war? Lyese—Vektro—is a monarch. It doesn't make any sense. She could have simply ended the conflict and let the nim in years ago. Why the bomb?"

"The war serves Memnarch's ends," Raksha said. "I do think I was meant to die in the bomb blast, but luck conspired to let me find it, and Lyese—and Vektro's treachery before it was too late. Vektro only accused me as a last resort. I owe my life to Yshkar, despite what has come since. With Taj Nar destroyed, the nim and leveler armies could have moved on to Krark-Home, and maybe that was the original plan." He stopped pacing, and placed a hand on Glissa's shoulder.

"How did you learn all this hiding out in the Tangle?" Glissa asked, still unconvinced.

"Do you remember the name Ghonthas?" Raksha asked.

"Who?" Glissa said.

"She was a Sylvok. One of Vektro's vessels," Raksha said. "She knew you."

"I don't know any—wait," Glissa said. "There was a Sylvok judge at my trial. In Viridia."

"That was Vektro, inhabiting Ghonthas," Raksha said. "The imposter was, at the time, trying to ensure the Viridians didn't execute you, which would have spoiled Memnarch's plans. When you escaped, Vektro was forced to leave the Slyvok."

"And showed up on the mountain with a pack of goblins," Glissa said.

Raksha nodded. "A few months after I'd entered the tangle, I encountered Ghonthas while tracking a vorrac. The human had been wounded by a pack of kharybdogs, but she recognized me. She remembered everything Vektro knew, including the length of Memnarch's hibernation, the Miracore, and the part you were bound to play. And you've confirmed everything she told me. That cannot be a coincidence."

"What made you believe her?" Glissa asked. "A dying human wandering in the woods?"

"She knew things," Raksha said. "Things about you. The story you told at the trial did not fall on deaf ears." He flicked his ears in leonin embarrassment. "And perhaps I believed her because my heart wanted it to be true. It gave me hope."

"Well, it's a start," Glissa said.

CHAPTER 25

DAWN'S EARLY LIGHT

Glissa awoke to the sound of Raksha putting on another kettle of homebrew. He offered the elf girl a simple meal of fruit and jerky, which they ate in silence. Neither spoke as they filled their packs with a two-day supply of food. Even Geth remained quiet.

"The journey down the lacuna will take the rest of the day," Raksha said when they had finished packing, breaking the spell of silence and anxiety. "That will give us the night to reach Memnarch. Will that gemstone of yours work for me too?"

"I think so," Glissa said. "Bruenna said it had an infinite charge." She pushed back her tunic sleeve and held the blue stone up for him to see. "Here, try it. Just put a finger on it, then say 'Fly, fly, fly.' "

"Clever," the leonin rumbled. "I really must speak thusly?"

"It's simple," Glissa replied. "Easy to remember. Stop stalling, your Kha-ship."

Raksha placed a fingertip on the gem. "Fly, fly . . . fly."

The leonin floated a few inches off the ground, as if blown by a gentle breeze. "Amazing!" he said and cautiously floated about the room. "Forget what I said, we can get to the interior in about an hour."

"We should still be on the move," Glissa said. "I'd rather have a chance to peek around the corner before we walk in. Ghonthas didn't say *that* would ruin everything, did he?"

Raksha did an experimental loop, and a stalactite nearly took his head off. "What?"

"I said we should get moving, and you should be careful," Glissa said. She hung the Miracore around her neck and tucked it under the leather jerkin, then slung Geth onto her back, eliciting brand new insults as she cinched up the strap. "Are you ready, Raksha?"

Raksha slowly descended from the high ceiling. "Let's go," he said and patted his belt to make sure his longknife was still there.

Glissa placed a clawtip on the blue stone and said, "Fly, fly, fly." Together, they floated out of the cave.

* * * * *

The second major attack against Krark-Home came just as the suns went down on the fourth day and the battlefield fell into blackness. The few scattered stars in the sky provided little light to fight by, but Bruenna had been impressed with how quickly Yshkar scrambled to troops. Jethrar's unit had joined six other detatchments of leonin warriors and half again as many goblins. The goblins seemed excited about something and were talking animatedly, but she didn't have time to ask them why.

Fortunately, their enemies glowed in the dark. Finding them wouldn't be a problem. Seeing her environment and her allies would present a greater challenge. She'd been saving her strength for more aggressive magic, but at the moment they needed light more than energy bolts. Bruenna whispered a few arcane words and described a symbolic pattern in the air, calling up a silvery blue aurora that materialized in the night sky.

As if cued by the light, a dozen aerophins broke in one direction, while a pack of eyeless, bat-winged nim shriekers dove in the opposite. Bruenna's well-trained zauk squawked in challenge and stood its ground as a pair of shriekers dropped on her from above. She thrust her sword into the sky and twin spheres of crackling blue-white energy flew from the blade, each one homing in on a shrieker and encasing it in writhing worms of electricity before they plummeted, smoldering, to the ground. She kicked the zauk's flanks and charged into the fray.

Bruenna didn't have time to cast a spell before the next attack came: twin streams of silver fire that slammed into the ground behind her and threw up shards of hot iron that struck her zauk's haunches. The bird bolted.

Rather than attempt to regain control of the terrified animal, the mage released the reins, wished the bird luck, and quickly conjured another flight spell, rising from the zauk's back just before it disappeared beyond the edge of the blue aura that covered the field.

Bruenna felt back in her element, but it wasn't hers alone. She wove through the swarming constructs and nim, striking with her sword where she could and sent more bolts of deadly magic singing through the air.

The Neurok mage heard explosions below and saw a trio of aerophins flying in a tight formation, scattering the forward defensive lines with energy bolts. As the goblins and leonin ran for cover, they ran into the waiting claws of a line of nim lashers, where they were easy pickings.

Bruenna summoned another energy bolt and wondered how much longer Krark-Home could possibly hold out.

* * * * *

"That's not good," Glissa whispered.

"No, definitely not," Raksha agreed.

They had reached the end of the lacuna without further incident, and pulled up short as agreed. They had crawled the last few yards on hands and knees, and now sat crouched at the lip of the exit.

Glissa had forgotten how dazzling the blazing mana core was after the long, dark descent through the lacuna. And now, the light was reflected from a thousand different silver surfaces that comprised…something. Glissa truly had no idea what she was looking at. Just that it was huge, as big as the interior itself.

The rebuilt Panopticon was still in place. The massive round disk with the hole in the center sat directly below them, attached to the towering structure at roughly midpoint. But other than that, Glissa didn't recognize anything.

The crystalline mycosynth towers were gone, leaving most of the interior surface smooth except for scattered shrubbery. In their place, millions, maybe billions of silver needles—the mirror images of those that littered the surface—pointed from the interior surface directly at the core. Five enormous buttress-like structures, each as big around as all of Taj Nar and also a gleaming silver, were mounted to the inside of Mirrodin like gigantic parodies of the needles. They ended not far from the core, where they held the most amazing part of the bizarre structure in place: a skeletal spheroid made up entirely of interlocking pentagonal rings. The mesh completely encased the core.

Glissa cast her gaze back down to the ground, and saw that it was still crawling with billions of small, scuttling constructs. Amongst them walked, crawled and flew much larger construct-beasts, all heavily armed but so far seemingly unaware of her and Raksha's presence.

That was about to change. Four columns of marching steel centipedes were scuttling right for them, undulating over their kin like quicksilver ribbons. It seemed that Raksha's prediction about Viridia's fate was coming true all too soon.

They ducked back into the lacuna, out of sight. "We need a plan, fast," Glissa whispered.

"Doesn't change anything," Raksha said.

"There's an army about to march in here!" Glissa almost shouted.

"No one sends an army against two people," Raksha said. "Those are reinforcements or scouts. Trust me, they will ignore us."

"How can you be sure?"

"They could not have missed us," Raksha said. "They didn't react or accelerate their pace. Just get out of the way and wait."

The elf girl scowled, but Raksha was right.

The first of the centipedes appeared at the lip of the lacuna, flowed over the edge and undulated inside. The line of constructs was close enough to reach out and touch, yet as Raksha had predicted, they completely ignored the elf and the leonin. The lacuna rang with thousands of tinny metal footsteps.

* * * * *

Bruenna whirled in mid-air, catching a trio of shriekers with a series of rapidfire spells. A cloud of shrapnel materialized in the nims' flight path, launched into the shriekers, and tore their abdomens out. Fetid guts spilled out and poured down on the ground, followed a few seconds later by the nim themselves.

She shot a salute to a skyhunter who soared by overhead. Fewer than two dozen of the female warriors remained, but they were holding their own against the swarms. Four times as many trained, riderless pterons engaged the attackers in vicious dogfights, but these proved easier pickings for 'phin energy bolts and shrieker claws.

Bruenna felt a surge of magic disrupt the flow of mana directly beneath her and jinked to one side just in time to avoid a fireball. The sphere slammed into a wolfpack of heavily armed aerophins she hadn't heard approaching. Dwugget waved from below.

"Thanks," Bruenna mouthed.

Bruenna scanned the horizon, seeking the telltale glow of aerophin power sources and felt suddenly dizzy, terrified, and exhilarated all at once. Victory suddenly seemed possible again. On the horizon, five soft halos of diffuse pre-dawn glow played at the edges of night. The colors matched the stones mounted on the Miracore.

"I hope you're paying attention down there, Glissa," Bruenna whispered, and drove her sword through the torso of a buzzing aerophin, which sparked and spit black smoke before it plummeted from the sky. "It's almost showtime."

* * * * *

"Raksha, it's almost dawn," Glissa said.

"How do you know?" Raksha asked.

Glissa considered. "I'm not sure how," she said, "But I am sure I'm right. I can feel the moons moving. Rolling into place." The elf girl patted her breastplate and added, "I feel it in here. I think it's the spark."

The steel centipedes had given way to a wave of spider-like constructs covered in blue and purple crystalline eyes, followed by a detachment of leonin-sized scorpionoids with blast-cylinder stingers. Now they endured the indignity of hiding as thousands of silver frog-things with wide, toothy mouths and long hooks at the end of their forelimbs hopped past. None of the constructs had paid the pair any heed. Memnarch had to know Glissa was coming. Why hadn't he sent even a scout? She'd expected a brutal fight. Being ignored when she knew she was expected was much worse. It meant Memnarch no longer thought her a threat.

Glissa was about to make sure he remembered how much of a threat she could be. She held out her wrist, the blue stone facing up. "It's time," the elf girl said. "I have to get to that platform. He's up there."

"A sound judgment," Raksha replied. He placed a finger alongside the blue stone, and Glissa did the same.

As they emerged from the lacuna, a cacophony of clattering feet, clicking pincers, and strange, mechanical chittering broke out all around them, joined by a chorus of whining cries.

"They're awake, Glissa," Geth's head said.

"Careful what you wish for," she muttered and placed a hand on her sword hilt. The cries of a million tinny voices reverberated through the interior of Mirrodin, and soon it sounded as if every last construct—with the exception of the strange automatons—was sounding the alarm, chirping and singing like frog mites on a cold night. So much for being ignored. But despite the noise, not one of the constructs made an aggressive move. "Raksha," she asked over the din, "does this seem a little too easy?"

"Glissa!" Raksha shouted and slammed into her with his shoulder as a silver flash streaked past, missing them both by inches.

CHAPTER 26

BORROWED TIME

For the first time in living memory, humans, leonin, goblins, and elves saw the suns of Mirrodin rise at exactly the same time. Each of the five spheres glowed more brightly than Bruenna had ever seen, and five distinct colors light streamed into the sky from all directions. They blended into a blinding white glare over the Krark-Home battlefield.

The Neurok mage had never been so exhausted. She'd just gone to the well too many times, and her system refused to take it anymore. The quicksilver energy that powered Bruenna's magic felt very far away, and she had been forced to the ground. She wanted to sleep for a week, but drew her sword anyway and joined the retreating ground troops on the mountain.

The last skyhunter had fallen, and with Bruenna's power sapped the air was enemy territory. Wolfpacks of aerophins and a wide variety of the fierce-looking asymmetrical winged construct beasts—each as large as as a five aerophins put together—blasted the ground behind the defenders. Shriekers swooped and divebombed at odd intervals as the lumbering nim drove the leonin and goblin inexorably back.

Bruenna shielded her eyes as four goblin fighters were vaporized right next to her, peppering her forearms with shards of hot iron and molten blood. She stumbled blindly sideways and by sheer luck avoided a small avalanche of ironstone rubble the constructs' shots had knocked loose from the cliffs above.

Bruenna raised her sword to deflect a swinging nim claw and jumped back, slamming into something armored that snarled. She swung her sword around blindly, but her blade connected with another.

"Careful, mage," Yshkar growled. He lowered his longknife and guided Bruenna's blade tip away from his left eye. "Someone could get hurt."

"Look out!" Bruenna cried, and shoved the Kha aside as an energy bolt blasted the ground nearby and tore a scorched scar up the cliff wall, igniting a few of the scrub trees that still clung to the high reaches. "My Kha, you've got to call a full retreat, or you're not going to have any subjects left tomorrow. We don't have the strength to hold them here. We have to close up Krark-Home and save as many lives as we can."

"Retreat? Tuck our tails, run, and hope Glissa will succeed?" Yshkar roared. "Look around you, Neurok. She has failed. And we will face our death on our—"

The leonin paused in midsentence and stared down at his chest with a look of faint surprise. A thin, blood-coated silver blade emerged from the center of Yshkar's breastplate and glittered in the glare of the five suns. With a sickening slurp, the blade disappeared back into his chest and the leonin dropped dead at the mage's feet.

The lithe figure behind him danced back a step and twirled her bloody blade.

"I can't tell you how long I've wanted to gut that fool," Lyese said.

* * * * *

Glissa followed the silver blur as it skimmed the surface of the interior and swooped back up for another pass. Behind her, Raksha bellowed, "Another one—move!" A second silver shape dove straight between them, missing Glissa but apparently striking a glancing blow at Geth's head, which yelped.

"What are those things?" Glissa shouted over the dull roar of billions of hand-sized metal insects having a collective fit. "They're too fast!"

"I don't—"

A third silver blur appeared, and this time Raksha couldn't dodge in time. "Ooof!" the leonin managed as the flying object carried him away. Glissa didn't get a chance to follow, because the original flyer was on the way back up. She finally got a good look at the silver blur as it rapidly accelerated toward her. At the last second, she launched herself backward and dodged the ascending hovercraft. The elf girl was so surprised when she finally identified the rider that the second caught her a glancing blow on the boot as it swooped up beside its duplicate.

The identity of the first rider had been unmistakable. So had the second. He had a few more pink blotches of flesh marring his perfect silver skin, but the cruel, angular face had been burned into her mind. It was the face of a dead metal man she'd killed herself.

Without waiting for the first two to come at her another time, Glissa gave chase to the third identical copy of Malil, the one that had grabbed Raksha. She glanced back but didn't spot either of the other two attackers.

"They're following, but holding back," Geth's head shouted. "They obviously fear my power!"

"Just keep an eye on them and tell me if they change their tactics," Glissa hollered over one shoulder.

Glissa flirted with the idea of sending a little destructive spark energy into the Malil-clone that had spirited Raksha away, but decided against it. These Malil replicas were partly flesh. The energy only seemed to work against true constructs. Besides, she would probably need it soon. The biggest challenge was still ahead.

"Okay, now one of them is—incoming!" Geth's head shouted. Glissa tucked her chin and dove. The whine of the flyer's energy fields was almost deafening, but thanks to Geth's warning the attack just missed her.

"Geth! Keep that up and I'll get you a body personally!" Glissa shouted.

"How about yours?"

"Don't push me, head."

* * * * *

Bruenna backed away from the Yshkar's fallen body and raised her sword in her good hand. Lyese stepped over the dead leonin and kept her sword tip pointed at the mage's heart.

The mage cast about desperately with her peripheral vision. The ironstone avalanche had cut them off from the main battle. She was on her own. Maybe that was for the best, the mage mused, since she was about to engage the Tall Queen of the leonin. There was no guarantee the defenders of Krark-Home would come to Bruenna's aid.

"Lyese," Bruenna said. "What have you done?"

"What I should have done years ago," the elf said in a strange voice that sounded like two. "I could have led these primitives on my own, but the master thought it served his purposes better to leave that oaf in charge."

"He was a good man," Bruenna said. Then the rest of what Lyese had said sunk in. "Master?"

"You're even slower than Raksha," the elf girl said, her voice still resonating weirdly between Lyese's lilt and something deeper and much darker. "I'm not here to get you up to speed." Without another word, Lyese danced forward, her blade singing. Bruenna parried clumsily, but the elf girl kept coming. The tackle lifted the mage off her feet, and she landed hard on the iron ground. The murderous elf held her pinned with a forearm and two knees then raised her sword as Bruenna struggled just to draw breath. Her sword arm felt numb.

"Why?" Bruenna managed to cough. She closed her eyes, waiting for the blow. "Your sister—"

A wave of heat washed over the mage and she felt the elf's weight lifted. She sat upright and saw Lyese flying backward, a small goblin flamerocket embedded in her chest. The elf girl collided with great force against the avalanche debris, and the projectile held Lyese fast against the ironstone. The elf's eyes flashed red and she dropped her sword, then reached up and grasped the sputtering rocket with both hands, and heaved it aside. The sputtering flamerocket spun out of control and exploded against the cliff wall.

"Back off, huh?" Dwugget growled. He offered Bruenna a hand up and she saw that the goblin held an iron firetube trained on the writhing Khanha.

"Thanks, Dwugget," Bruenna gasped. "How did you know?"

"Always known," Dwugget said sadly. "Since that ogre brought Raksha and Lyese to me, huh? I'm sorry. He said he'd destroy Krark-Home. There's a bomb—"

"No!" The elf—if she was indeed that, which Bruenna was beginning to seriously doubt—roared like an ogre. She climbed like a broken automaton down from the rubble and scooped up her sword. She clutched at the bleeding hole in the center of her chest and coughed up a spray of blood, but remained on her feet. She glared at Bruenna. "This was supposed to be a body that would last, Neurok. Now I'll have to take yours."

Dwugget stepped up to her side and she heard a loud click as he slotted another flamerocket into the tube. "Can outrun a rocket, huh?" the goblin asked.

The thing that had taken control of Lyese seethed, but stayed put. "Dwugget, what's going on?" Bruenna snapped. "What bomb?"

"It doesn't matter now," Dwugget said. "We are lost anyway, huh? That—that's no elf. It's something called Vektro. Thing took her body, she's not in there anymore. It's Memnarch's tool."

"I'm going to gut you too, goblin," the bleeding elf snarled.

"But it's her body, Dwugget!" Bruenna said. "I can't kill Glissa's sister."

"I can," Dwugget said. "I'm already a murderer, many times over, huh?" The goblin raised the firetube and placed his thumb on the lever that would release another rocket into Lyese's body.

Bruenna lunged sideways and knocked the flametube aside, sending the rocket spinning uselessly into the sky.

"Stupid!" Dwugget shouted. He stumbled with the impact and went over onto his side, Bruenna following, and they crashed together in a tangle of robes and limbs. Bruenna got to her knees in time to see Lyese's body convulse violently, then drop like a sack of bones. A blood-red humanoid shape rose from her fallen form, hovered for a moment in the air, then condensed into a glowing ball. Bruenna felt the sphere pulse with mana and energy then accelerate into the ether. It disappeared into the haze of war.

"Lyese," Bruenna gasped and crawled on all fours to the elf girl's side. She pressed an ear to Lyese's chest. "She's alive. Barely."

Dwugget scrambled to her side, and the mage held him back

with her artifact hand. "You've done enough, don't you think?" Bruenna said.

"I had no choice," Dwugget began but fell silent at a look from the mage that threatened to burn through his skull.

The elf's eyes fluttered open as Bruenna tore strips from her robe and pressed them against Lyese's chest wound. "Lyese, can you hear me?" Bruenna said softly, thankful that the nearby fighting had not yet spilled over the rubble.

Lyese stared hard at Bruenna for a moment, then her eyes went wide. "Bruenna," she said softly. "He's gone." The elf girl smiled. "He's gone. The things he did . . . made me do. I'm sorry. I'm so, so sorry." Against Bruenna's protestations, the elf girl sat up.

"Wasn't you," Dwugget said. "He's gone."

"Lyese, you're badly hurt," Bruenna broke in. She fished at her belt for nearly empty medical kit. She pulled out a small, transparent gem and held it over the elf's wound. She whispered a few words in leonin, and the healing stone spread soft golden light over Lyese's chest. The light grew in intensity until it was nearly blinding then faded. When it was gone, the hole in Lyese's armor remained, but the blood had turned black and no longer flowed from her chest. The wound had closed, leaving a star-shaped scar on the exposed green skin.

Bruenna wiped beads of sweat from her forehead and sat back on the ground. "If that didn't do it—"

The elf girl pulled herself to her feet. "Mana bomb...it's in the Great Furnace," Lyese said breathlessly. "I—he—Vektro put it there. It will take out this entire mountain."

Dwugget gasped. "You know where it is? Then we can stop it?"

"No," Lyese said. "There's no time. It's set to go off one hour after the fifth dawn."

Bruenna stood and spun Lyese around by the shoulders. "The

people in Krark-Home are not warriors. You have to get them out of there," the mage said.

"Me?" Lyese said. "But I—"

"You're the Khanha," Bruenna said.

"That was a sham!" Lyese said. "I mean, I remember everything, but it wasn't me doing it. Vektro was in control. I'm not a leader."

"You're the only leader they've got," the mage said. "We'll be with you, but you are the Tall Queen. I know you didn't ask for this, but they need you."

Without waiting for a response, Bruenna reached out to the energies of the Quicksilver Sea and felt the lines of power burn with her desperation. Within seconds the trio was airborne. The familiar flight magic took hold, and the trio floated upward. Lyese's mouth opened in shock when she saw the carnage on the other side of the iron rubble that had shielded them from the battlefield.

"Flare!" Lyese said. "Let's go. We have half an hour."

* * * * *

Glissa could only watch as the elusive Malil-clone disappeared over the edge of the Panopticon disk. The second Malil continued to buzz her as she followed the first and third but hadn't actually done her any harm, yet. They seemed more interested in annoying Glissa, keeping her distracted. It was working. She had the uncomfortable feeling she was being herded again.

Glissa passed the edge of the disk, noting that though it looked thin relative to the five massive support struts holding up that strange mesh sphere, it was at least four times as thick as she was tall. She rose over the surface, scanning for Raksha, but could spot neither the leonin nor his captor.

She cast a quick glance over her shoulder and saw two

identical silver faces peeking over the edge of the disk. They grinned simultaneously and nodded, silently urging her onward. That was one difference between the copies and the original—these Malils seemed to have no affection for their own voices. If they even had voices.

Glissa flew cautiously toward the rebuilt Panopticon, where a bronze access door hung wide open. Next to the door, a flyer hovered a few inches off the ground, riderless. She walked with a calm she didn't feel across the wide platform, reaching up to scratch her neck with her right claw. In the process, she tapped the ever-present pack slung over her shoulder.

"Geth," Glissa whispered. There was no answer, though she could tell by the weight that he was still there. She pulled the strap and shook the bag.

"They're not following," Geth replied. "Just hovering there, smiling. I know creepy smiles, and sister, I could take lessons from those two."

* * * * *

"Go, go, go!" Bruenna shouted. Five years of endless war had prepared the denizens of Krark-Home for the worst, and the mage was impressed with how well the evacuation had gone so far. She charged down the flame-lit tunnel behind a mass of chattering, screaming children and their nurses then glanced back to check on Lyese's progress. The girl who had never wanted to be the Khanha had slipped into the role with ease and now held open a heavy iron door, urging the mass of terrified leonin and goblins onward. Dwugget had gone back down to the Great Furnace over the objections of Lyese and Bruenna to search for any lingering goblin engineers who had not heard the evacuation alarm, but had not yet returned.

Bruenna waded through the crowd and drew up next to Lyese. She would have rather flown, but wanted to conserve her strength. "You're doing it," she said loudly enough for only Lyese to hear.

"I just hope it's in time," Lyese said. "Where's Dwugget? We've only got a few minutes!"

"Coming!" a gravelly voice shouted from the tunnel below. Dwugget led a band of some twenty goblin engineers, their dark green skin blackened with soot and oil. The old goblin stumbled over the uneven floor and rolled to a stop at Bruenna's feet. He had both arms wrapped around a delicately engraved silver ball that leaked hot red light through thousands of tiny slits on its surface.

"Dwugget, is that—?"

"Yup," the goblin said. "Turned out the engineers were looking for it already, huh? They thought it was just debris blocking some vent, but when I told them about the big bomb . . ." He shrugged. "Can tell you more later. What do I do with it?"

"Bruenna, you can do it," Lyese said. "Teleport it out into the middle of the nim."

"I'm exhausted," Bruenna said. "And a mana field that's so compressed—"

The glowing ball began to emit a keening buzz. Dwugget jumped back and collided with the wall of the tunnel. Bruenna and Lyese stepped back, and the mage went over the formulae for such a spell. The mana in the bomb was the problem. It would require more power than one mage could safely channel.

"All right, but I'll need a boost," Bruenna said. "From both of you. Give me your hands."

Dwugget nodded and placed his hand in hers. "Disappearing magic not my specialty, huh? But fire, Dwugget knows. You worry about moving it, Dwugget'll make sure it not blow up in our faces."

Lyese took another step back from the bomb. "Bruenna, I'm not a mage. I don't have Glissa's . . . whatever that is."

"You will do fine, my Khanha," Bruenna said. "Just give me your hand."

Bruenna gripped the elf's hand and closed her eyes. She felt anger, fear, exhilaration, and crushing guilt. That would be Dwugget. The power that she drew through the goblin was fierce and destructive, like the explosive artifact on the ground. Bruenna then sought out Lyese, who was wracked with uncertainty, but also righteous determination. There was also great hatred there. The elf girl's five years imprisoned in her own mind had not been pleasant ones.

Wild Tangle magic surged into Bruenna, who felt her feet leave the floor as the power lifted her physically from the ground. Equations and formulae raced through her mind as a rapidfire Neurok incantation flew from her lips. The mana bomb's persistent red glow disappeared within a quicksilver cocoon that faded into existence around the ovoid shape. The bomb screamed, and Bruenna felt a warm trickle of blood run down her right earlobe. As the power reached a fever pitch, she threw her fists forward. A translucent wave washed over the artifact and knocked the three of them off their feet.

The quicksilver encasing the bomb imploded with a sound like shattered glass as the object within was pulled forcibly into an invisible conduit that ended miles away. Bruenna visualized the bomb appearing in the center of the enemy armies and was rewarded with an almost simultaneous explosion in the distance. She smiled.

"Good job," Bruenna gasped. "Both of you."

"S'nothin'," Dwugget croaked.

"I . . . you . . . ow," Lyese added, which Bruenna thought summed up the situation nicely.

"What now, huh?" Dwugget said.

Lyese pulled herself to her feet. "Now we get those people back in here. We might have a chance to win this after all. And they're going to need a leader." The elf girl straightened and placed a hand on her sword hilt. "Bruenna, when you think you're ready, can you spare the Khanha a pair of wings?"

CHAPTER 27

THE WEB

Forced to take Geth's word she wasn't being followed, Glissa stepped to the bronze door hanging open on one side of the re-built Panopticon. Glissa entered at the bottom point of a diamond shaped section embedded in the platform.

Dark and empty from outside, the room erupted flooded with light from blue and white glowstones as she stepped into a sort of foyer. A large round door that appeared to swing on a central axis was set in the far wall, and a few small, harmless-looking artifact creatures skittered about on the floor, taking no notice of her entry.

"Okay, the twins have gotten tired of watching," Geth's raspy voice whispered. "I think it's time to go in. Is there a door?"

"Wait, I'm not—"

"Ready?" the head retorted. "Too bad. Come on, they're getting closer!"

Glissa glanced over her shoulder, and saw the pair of Malils approaching on twin hovercraft. She pulled the bronze door shut to buy a little extra time and then pressed against the right side of the circular disk-shaped door, which swiveled on its center and slid ninety degrees inward. She slipped inside and swung the door shut behind her.

She stepped into a much larger round room that was eerily silent and less brightly lit. It appeared to be a storage area, and she had to step over even more of the small arachnoid constructs that littered the floor. More than once she got the strange feeling that their eyes were following her even as they went about whatever they were doing.

A flat round disk sat floating a few inches off the floor in the center of the room. The room had no doors that she could see. Glissa cautiously stepped onto the flate round plate and walked to the center.

The ceiling hissed and slid apart directly overhead. Glissa held her sword out for balance as the disk lurched and floated upward. She placed a hand on the Miracore to make sure it was still secure as rose through the floor of the room above.

This had to be an important control center of some kind. The cavernous room with a domed ceiling that also appeared to be devoid of people. The walls were lined with silver panels inlaid with crystals and gemstones that pulsed with arhythmic light. In the exact center of the room, a huge silver ovoid structure lined with inscriptions, more pulsing gemstones, silver and copper pipes, and giving off just a little steam sat expectantly. The panels displayed moving images of several different locations on Mirrodin, including what looked like the battlefield of Krark-Home. Glissa choked back a cry at the sight of the devastation.

Glissa had not yet seen Memnarch, but she had a good guess where he might be. That giant, ovoid egg was just big enough to hold him and still afford a little breathing room. The half-empty translucent tank of serum that was fused to the side of the machine looked murky, like stagnant oil. But the tank was a dead giveaway. If the Guardian wasn't in there now, he spent a lot of time in the structure.

"Glissa?" Geth hissed over her shoulder. "Turn around, but whatever you do, don't scream."

Glissa turned around, and screamed.

The elf girl could not believe her eyes. Glissa had walked right past him, focused on the images of Krark-Home and the ovoid. But there he was, plain as day, and alive—barely. She could only tell because the limbless, sallow form hanging in the barbaric-looking rack was drawing shallow, erratic breaths.

Slobad.

The elf girl had no idea how to get her friend out of this, or if he could even survive if she did. Pink crystals, focal points for serum energy, were embedded in his skin and all over the top of his withered, bald head. His skin had gone the same dingy gray as the clouded serum in the tanks before her.

"Slobad," she whispered and tentatively reached out to touch the goblin's sunken cheek. His eyes were open, and appeared milky and unfocused. Perhaps even blind. But his ears, and his nose, appeared intact.

Sombody tapped Glissa on the shoulder, and she whirled.

No one was there.

Another tap, this time on the other shoulder.

"Glissa?" Geth's head said, "There's something on your shoulder."

"Gyah!" Glissa yelped, and flailed blindly. She connected with a hard metal object and knocked it away.

One of the numerous little arachnoid constructs clattered to the ground on its back, legs kicking. Glissa picked up the small construct with both hands, careful to keep out of reach of its diminutive legs. It resembled, she realized, a tiny version of Memnarch She turned it over a few times in her hands, but didn't see anything on it that looked like a weapon, so she set it back down on the floor.

Glissa had expected the tiny construct to flee, but it simply stared at her with a single gemstone eye.

"Shoo," Glissa said, glancing nervously at the ovoid as it

vented a hiss of blue steam. The construct followed her to the ovoid and tapped her on the boot, then began tapping its tiny feet against the floor in an odd rhythm.

"What?" Glissa asked. "What do you want? Geth, what does it want?"

"I don't know. Do you hear hovercraft?"

The miniature Memnarch lifted one thin leg and pointed at Slobad. Then it slowly pointed to itself.

Twice.

"Um," Glissa stalled, not sure she wanted to believe what her eyes told her. She got down on all fours and whispered, "Slobad? Is that you?"

"Are you dense?" Geth's head said. "Of course it is. Even I can see that. Look at your friend, there. He's getting a constant stream of serum. He's hooked into this whole . . . machine . . . hmmm."

"What?" Glissa asked.

"This big diamond building is connected to the disk, right?" Geth replied. "And the disk is connected to those struts, which are connected to…everything else."

"You're not making sense," Glissa hissed over her shoulder.

"No, the—those buttresses and supports . . . those big needles, and the Panoppi-whatzit, everything," Geth said, sounding oddly excited. "They're all part of one machine. And we're standing— okay, *you're* standing—right in the middle of it."

"You're saying Memnarch made some kind of . . . giant artifact . . . out of the *world?"*

"Couldn't be him," Geth said. "He's de-fleshing himself. Had to be the goblin."

The four-legged bug began to hop and click.

"Slobad did this? I don't—that's crazy," Glissa managed.

"He's telling you the truth, elf," an arrogant, tinny voice that

Glissa knew well called from above. Glissa looked up into a smaller round door now open above her.

She was looking into the face of Raksha Golden Cub, his face twisted in pain. She heard a thud, and the leonin dropped like a sack of gelfruit at Glissa's feet.

"Raksha!" Glissa cried.

"He's alive, for another few minutes," Malil's voice said again, drawing Glissa's attention away from the unconscious leonin. Looking down imperiously through the small opening was Malil. Or rather, the Malil who had left his flyer parked outside. The metal man's eyes flashed red with hate, and maybe something else.

Something familiar. Something that reminded her of a Vulshok priest she'd fought long ago in the Krark foothills.

"Your sister sends her regards," Vektro said with Malil's voice. "I had to leave her, I'm afraid. She just wasn't holding up under the pressure. Or that rocket she took in the chest."

Without warning, the metal man took one step forward and dropped through the hole. He landed with a resounding clang on the floor directly in front of Glissa. He threw a gleaming silver boot into Raksha's side, lifting the unconscious leonin bodily in the air and slamming him against the wall. The Kha sank to the floor in a heap and didn't move.

Vektro lashed out and seized Glissa by the upper arms, then squeezed with superhuman pressure. Glissa let out a strangled cry as she felt bones snap, and her sword clattered to the floor.

Glissa looked around her feet for the Slobad-bug, but it had disappeared. Vektro shook her violently, snapping her head back. The body the thing had taken was definitely one of the oldest Malils, assuming one could judge their individual ages by the size and number of flesh spots mottling each body. Not quite as old as the one she had beheaded in the lacuna, but getting there.

Glissa wondered dizzily as her head collided with a wall whether Vektro could possess a being of pure metal. As the chamber spun madly about her head, she felt herself lifted as easily as a rag doll. Vektro carried her to another vicious-looking piece of torture equipment on the wall opposite Slobad, shoved Glissa roughly into the rack, and strapped her in with blurred, magically augmented movements. When he was finished the elf was unable to do much more than wiggle her fingers and toes, which were already starting to feel numb.

Vektro yanked Geth's pack from her shoulder and kicked it across the floor, then slipped the Miracore from her neck and held it aloft in Malil's mottled hand. The hand betrayed an nervous tremble as he slowly lifted the chain over his head and—

A loud hiss and a cloud of blue-white steam erupted from the base of the ovoid in the center of the room. Vektro jumped and almost dropped the Miracore, but caught it before it slipped away.

"Watch yourself, Vektro," Glissa said. "Daddy doesn't like sharing his toys."

The imposter backhanded Glissa across the jaw, and her head struck solid darksteel. Vektro/Malil stepped to the ovoid, dropped to one knee and bowed, holding the Miracore above his head like a shield.

A thin, glowing blue line appeared in the center of the ovoid, and grew wider as clamps released, atmospheric pressure found equilibrium, and whining gears slowly pulled the apparatus open like an overripe fruit. A looming shadow appeared in the steam and fog, took on definition, shape, and finally identy.

Memnarch's skin shone like quicksilver. Glissa could not see any of the flesh that had once mottled this Guardian's skin as it had Malil's. Memnarch radiated power from the glowing serum tanks that he carried on his back to the insectoid legs that held up his massive metal bulk.

The Guardian stepped confidently from the hibernation chamber and into the light. "Karn," he thundered, "I am restored. Pure. The flesh is cleansed." The crab-like metal man looked down at his servant. "Malil . . . no, my Creator, it is not Malil."

"Master—" Vektro began.

"Vektro was to remain on the surface, yes!" Memnarch said. "It should not be here. But that is unimportant." The Guardian snatched the Miracore from the false Malil's hands and held it up to the light. Vektro remained, his head down.

"Master," Vektro repeated, "the surface battle is all but over. The fools could not have reached my explosive, and it is only a matter of time before—"

Without removing his eyes from the Miracore, the Guardian swept a gleaming silver hand through Vektro/Malil's torso, neatly slicing him in half. There was no explosion of gore, but a thin mist of glowing red energy seeped into a cloud. The plasma swirled as if trying to gain cohesion.

"It was useful, Karn," Memnarch said wistfully, "but ultimately a failed idea. A creation of a tainted mind." He waved a hand, and the glowing red energy that was Vektro blew away like smoke before the wind. Memnarch waved again, and a swarm of the small four-legged construct bugs scuttled into the room and covered Malil's corpse. Bright blue beams of energy shot from their gemstone eyes and reduced the remains to nothingness. The bugs scuttled back to their corners, and one of them tapped Glissa deliberately on the toe as it passed.

The elf girl's stomach did gymnastics. Slobad was alive, apparently controlling those little machines somehow, but what kind of life was this? Was Glissa going to find herself nothing more than a mind connected to a machine, only able to communicate via bug-talk?

"I'm sorry, Slobad," Glissa said softly.

With a smooth flourish, the Guardian lifted the Miracore's chain over his head and let the asymmetrical disk dangle on his chest. On the Guardian, the talisman looked miniscule.

"Rest, Karn," Memnarch said with a cheerfulness that made Glissa wonder if that tone was just the beginning of the torture. "Rest and recuperation was what we needed. A good long rest to cleanse the soul. Good for the spark, too. It has kept the spark safe. It returned, as we knew it would. Now, in this pure body, I shall surely be worthy, Karn."

"Nice," Glissa said. "Very shiny."

"The spark thinks it needs a tongue to be of use to me, my Creator," the Guardian said. "Perhaps I shall remove it." The bulky silver creature crab-walked to a silver panel and tapped out a pattern on colored gemstones. The entire Panopticon, including the rack that held Glissa in place, began to vibrate with a deep hum. She felt her guts lurch as the diamond-shaped structure started to slide toward the center of the great platform outside, taking them all with it. After a few minutes, a loud clang sounded as an enormous latch somewhere below snapped into place. If Glissa didn't miss her guess, they were now sitting directly over the large hole cut into the center of the platform. There was nothing between her and the simmering mana core but this structure, which suddenly felt much less solid.

"It is genius," Memnarch said. "You see my new form, and the mycosynth spires are gone. The time of flesh has passed." He gazed out a tinted crystal window at the enormous struts and spikes that comprised the world-sized machine Memnarch—or someone—had built into the interior.

"I know what it thinks," the Guardian said. "It thinks I built this great machine. But it cannot understand how, if I have been sleeping for five years. It thinks five years is a long time." He laughed, a cold, mechanical sound. "Of course, the goblin built it, as you advised me. And I took the time to rejuvenate myself. To cleanse the spore. The goblin did very good work, don't you think?"

Even if Glissa had thought Memnarch was speaking to her—and apparently he wasn't—she wouldn't have answered. What the Guardian said had just sunk in. Glissa stared at poor Slobad, a hunk of sentient meat connected to nothing but serum and the tiny artifact creatures. In thrall to the Guardian.

"Yes, wonderful work, built to specifications but with a few special idiosyncratic touches that shows it was goblin-made," Memnarch said. "My very own Ascension Web."

CHAPTER 28

SPARKS FLY

"Can it feel the power gathering above? In the caged mana core below?" Memnarch asked. "Does the spark it has stolen tell it the time is near? Does the spark cry out, ready to feed my ascension?"

Glissa *could* feel the power gathering. She strained against her bonds and said, "I can't feel anything—all my blood's stuck down in my boots. Think you could loosen this thing a little?"

"How could you choose such an unworthy vessel, Karn?" Memnarch called to the sky. There was no answer that Glissa could hear. Memnarch nodded as if listening to a good joke, then burst into laughter. "Ah, of course," the Guardian chuckled.

"Uh, what did . . . er, Karn say?" Glissa asked.

"Yes, all vessels shatter eventually, my Creator," Memnarch said, ignoring her. "Mere storage."

Glissa's skin was beginning to tingle. The alignment of the suns—moons—was so close she could taste it, and from the way Memnarch was raving he could tell, too. In desperation, Glissa tried to call on the destructive spark-magic. But something was cutting her off completely from the power. She hoped that didn't mean the Tangle was already gone.

Light poured in from above as the Guardian slapped another gemstone, and the top half of the diamond-shaped structure split open like a budding flower. What had been the ceiling folded flat against the exterior, and Glissa stared up into a reflection of the dazzling mana ball, occulted by the black shadow cast by the core of Memnarch's Ascension Web.

Memnarch slipped a pair of slim silver disks into his palm and scuttled over to Glissa. Without preamble, he slapped one disk to her forehead, where it stuck. He slipped the other one into a thin slit on the top of the Miracore. Then he busied himself with examining the flat panels that lined the walls, occasionally muttering, "Yes, yes," or "Not long now, my Creator."

The elf girl bit back a cry as a sharp pain jabbed into the side of her neck. She strained her eyes and saw one of the construct bugs had mounted her shoulder and extended a thin silver needle into a spot just below her ear.

Glissa, a familiar voice sounded inside her head, giving her a start.

"Slo—" she caught herself. *Slobad?*

What is left of Slobad. Glissa must listen. Must know what will happen. Maybe can stop. Huh.

Why didn't you say something before?

Couldn't. When crab-legs woke up, I could. Crazy magic. Huh. Did you see the needles?

Needles? An image of the strange spires that dotted the surface flashed unbidden in her mind.

Those needles. Seen them. Huh.

Yes. What are they?

They're part of web. I made them from littler constructs. They're filled with serum. All the serum left in the world, huh?

Glissa examined the huge struts again that supported the mesh ball that caged the mana core. *The serum absorbs magic, doesn't it?*

Yes. The needles will take from suns and send it to the lacunae. The soul traps—

Soul traps?

Had metal man collect them all. All in those needles closest to lacuna. Those ones are hollow. He needs souls to charge serum. When suns line up over each lacuna, crab-legs sends all that hypercharged energy into the core. Then second wave destroys core, wipes out last soul traps, and takes your spark.

Soul traps? Glissa repeated. She didn't hear Slobad's mental response, if he sent one, because she suddenly received the most powerful flare she'd ever experienced. She stood in a clearing in the strange forest that she had seen long ago. Several other elves, their bodies made of soft flesh, surrounded her. She felt without knowing how that they had come here to hide. She also knew somehow that these elves were the last of their kind on this strange plane.

Suddenly the elf closest to her disappeared in a flash, and within seconds the others popped out of existence one by one. Finally, a bright white light swallowed Glissa whole and the flare world vanished.

Crazy streaks of color flooded her vision next. Flashes and streams of energy streaked past at impossible speed. She could not feel her own body, only the sensation of constant acceleration, faster, faster. The silver globe of Mirrodin appeared in the center of the light show and grew rapidly, and filled her vision entirely. This was a Mirrodin free of life, covered in odd geometric shapes. Unable to slow herself, she rapidly approached the surface then veered off toward a snarled mass of silver that she realized was the Tangle—only this ancient forest did not yet contain a hint of green. Disembodied Glissa skimmed low along the smooth silver forest floor then collided with a small boxy shape surrounded by leafless vines.

She felt herself enter the shape, or maybe it absorbed her. Then, in another blinding white flash, Glissa was standing next to the small box, panting and out of breath. She looked down at her hands and saw the familiar green skin covered in metallic plates. She shook her head and felt cords of tangled cable hair whip at her ears. Glissa heard voices, and cautiously set off in their direction through the weird silver Tangle, the small box forgotten.

As abruptly as it had begun, the flare ended, and she blinked. She was still bound into the rack within the Panopticon.

Soul traps, the voice in her head said.

That's how he brought us here, Glissa thought. Memnarch was still scuttling about the Panopticon.

Originally. But now he's gonna use them.

But why kill so many people? If he needed their souls?

There was no response.

Slobad?

They not dead.

What? There are thousands *of dead.*

Nope, the voice rang in her skull. *Bodies fallen. Don't work. But the souls can't go anywhere. It's—*

Ghastly. What will happen when he drains the traps?

That, not sure. Wasn't important to construction. Maybe everyone goes home. Maybe all die.

Can't you do anything?

Can't yet. Working on—

The voice ceased, and the elf girl felt a twinge of discomfort as the needle retracted from her neck. Memnarch had finally stopped fussing with his controls and crystal panels and now clacked his way over to Glissa.

"It thinks Memnarch a fool," the Guardian said. "Thinks I cannot hear. I shall have the spark, the power, and a new, pure world to shape. Before, I was as a child, playing with his father's sword but grasping the wrong end through sheer ignorance, Karn.

I allowed the flesh on this world out of hubris, thinking I could change it. Now we shall start over, you and I, as equals."

The air was humming like a swarm of wasps. At first, Glissa thought it was the energy continuing to build, but it sounded more like actual wasps, big ones.

Or beetles.

A monstrous, rusty iron blur dropped through the open roof of the diamond structure and slammed into the side of the Guardian's head. The blow didn't topple Memnarch—he was far too stable—but surprised him enough to make him momentarily forget the elf girl. Before he could locate the first attacker, another large black shape smashed into his back, shattering one of the bulbous serum tanks he wore and sending glass and silver-blue fluid spraying about the chamber. Memnarch screamed in fury.

With that, the nim attacked en masse. They poured from the black lacuna in a great swarm, descending on the Guardian again and again, refusing to give him a chance to recover.

"Psst!"

Glissa looked to her left. Raksha was crouched in a shadowed alcove, holding Geth's head by the ears so the necromancer's eyes could stay on the nim. Glissa's eyes widened and a silly grin spread across her face.

"Told you I was the best damned necromancer on this plane," Geth hissed with glee. "Body or no body. Just took me a while to get them to listen."

"Enough!" Memnarch screamed from the center of a dizzying black whirlwind. Memnarch's shout had magic behind it, and a translucent blue sphere formed around his body. Several nim bounced off the force field and were sent flying off in every direction. The blue sphere expanded outward, washing over Glissa, Slobad, and the hidden Raksha without any effect. Geth's head, however, was torn from the leonin's grasp by the

expanding anti-necrotic shockwave and flew high in a lazy arc. Glissa lost sight of Geth almost immediately, unable to turn her head.

The effect of the wave on the flying nim was even more devastating. Geth's head had bounced off the waved like a ball, but every nim that collided with the sphere disintegrated into a gaseous green cloud. By the time the sphere had reached the interior to dissipate harmlessly against the silver surface, the nim were gone.

Simultaneously, the leather straps holding her in place went slack and dropped to the floor. Glissa felt a sudden surge of power as the restraining magic released her, and she stepped out of the rack on unsteady legs, not really sure what had just happened.

"No!" Memnarch bellowed and crab-ran to Glissa once more.

"NOW YOU PLAY FAIR, HUH?"

The voice emanated from millions and millions of tiny, insignificant builder constructs.

Memnarch skidded to a stop just in front of Glissa, staring at the silver sky above him. With a quick glance at Raksha, who nodded, Glissa launched herself at the Miracore as the leonin dove into one of the Guardian's spindly legs.

The Guardian howled with rage as all around them his plan did its best to come to fruition without him. The air was thick with the odor of ozone and a vibration that Glissa could feel in her bones more that she could hear. The elf girl grabbed hold of the Miracore and yanked down with all her might, but the chain was too strong, and didn't give. Glissa felt warm blood flowing into her hands as the edges of the talisman sliced into her skin, but she refused to release the Miracore.

At the same time, Raksha collided with Memnarch's leg,

which buckled and folded under his body. The combination of suddenly losing one corner of his support and the violent downward pull Glissa exerted on the Miracore was too much to take. Memnarch toppled over and fell sideways onto the lift disk that had carried the elf girl into the chamber in the first place. The round metal plate dropped under the Guardian's weight. As power continued to pour into the web with nowhere to go, Memnarch roared from below as the disk reached the floor of the foyer level. Glissa heard a series of clacks and clangs as he opened the doorway heading out.

The elf let out a battle cry and jumped feet first into the hole, Raksha landing with a clang and a little more grace beside her. They tumbled out onto the occultation disk and scrambled after the Guardian onto the surface into the humming air above the mana core.

Magic surged and made her bones hum. Glissa could barely hear herself think. But she didn't need to think to get her hands on the Miracore. Glissa and Raksha charged toward Memnarch, side by side. To the millions of watching gemstone eyes that encircled the Ascension Web, they looked like suicidal insects attacking a hungry vorrac.

Memnarch continued to scream and rage, his fury no longer expressable in words. The last-minute breakdown in his plan seemed to have driven the Guardian completely mad. Glissa wasn't listening anyway. She was stretching her mind out to the Tangle.

"Raksha, stay back," she said as they barreled toward the Guardian.

"Not a chance," he replied.

"Sorry, someone's got to get back to the surface and tell them what's happened," Glissa said. "You're the only one who can do it now." Before the leonin realized what was happening,

Glissa spun and landed a solid punch on the leonin's muzzle. He dropped in mid run and rolled to a stop, unconscious. Glissa, still running, whirled and continued headlong into Memnarch, who had his fists in the air, imploring the wild energy all around the interior to enter his body.

"You want the spark?" Glissa yelled. *"Then you can have it!"*

The elf girl vaulted into the air from a dead run, her skin tingling with suppressed spark energy and Tangle magic, and finally released the destructive power into Memnarch's face. His new metal body writhed under the emerald fire, and the Guardian clawed the air, screeching in agony. Still channeling the destructive energy, Glissa slammed into the Guardian's chest and dug her claws into his silver skin, which melted under her touch.

Menarch brought up an insectoid leg and swiped at Glissa, who had to release her grip to dodge the blow. She lost her her concentration, and swore as she felt the destructive energy fizzle out. Somehow Memnarch still stood.

The two combatants circled each other warily. Memnarch moved slowly and smoldered, his shiny new form blackened and scorched, but the blast of destruction had only weakened him. The remaining serum tank on his back started to glow and pulse, and he turned to close on Glissa. The elf girl tried to get around him, but she was too near to the edge of the occultation disk.

Memnarch raised his humanoid hands, which began to glow as the Guardian summoned his own destructive spell. This was Glissa's chance. When the Guardian shouted his incantation, she ducked under his raised arms, seized the Miracore in slippery, bloody hands, and jerked it free, breaking the chain from which it hung. She dove under Memnarch's torso and through his arachnoid legs, emerging on the other side, and onto her feet in one smooth gymnastic motion. Dizzy, she turned back to face her foe.

Memnarch lumbered around to face her, their positions suddenly reversed. Using every ounce of will she had left, Glissa drew in the power of the Tangle above and felt the spark energy reignite. She raised the Miracore in both hands and slammed it flat against Memnarch's chest, pouring green destruction through the ancient artifact and into the Guardian, who now had no flesh to resist her power.

Memnarch screamed anew. The Guardian, his spell forgotten, stumbled back . . . back. Glissa pressed forward, pain beginning to blossom in her forearms as the Miracore melted into the Guardian's silver skin. The artifact fused with Memnarch's metal body in the blazing heat.

Glissa still had the Miracore firmly in her grasp when Memnarch's two rear legs slipped from the edge of the disk. Memnarch didn't stop screaming until the entangled enemies passed through one of the wide openings in the mesh sphere and plunged headlong into the mana core.

* * * * *

Though his mouth hadn't spoken a word in years, Slobad screamed when Glissa and her nemesis fell into the mana core. He saw Glissa die from a thousand different angles and points of view, each one causing him to scream anew.

The only friend he'd ever had. . . .

But Slobad didn't have time to scream any more. The intricately planned Ascension Web was still operating as designed, despite the deaths of the two beings that were supposed to be on the receiving end. Slobad watched from his bug constructs' eyes as the web sent more and more magical energy into the mana core, which started to glow brighter and brighter until even his remote crystal eyes couldn't stand the glare.

As the mana core reached its limit—something no being on Mirrodin had the power to change, even Memnarch—the energy boomeranged back into the web and immediately exceeded the carrying capacity of even a plane-sized artifact. Purified, amplified, and devastating, the wash of power was like nothing Slobad had ever felt before, even in the last five years of being connected to the machine.

The magic surged into the goblin's withered, limbless body through his connection to the rack. Slobad suspected he screamed again, but if he did he couldn't hear it. Millions of tiny pinpricks of pain stabbed his mind from the inside as the energy of all the soul traps on Mirrodin forced its way in.

* * * * *

Raksha Golden Cub, back broken, legs useless, pulled himself through the small narrow door at the base of the diamond structre in his best attempt to escape the blistering heat of the core. He flopped onto his back in the small room, neither knowing nor caring that his bare feet still protruded from the entrance.

The energy struck the occultation disk like a tidal wave, but the leonin, protected by darksteel, easily survived the initial blast.

The victory was short lived. Rolling on to collide with the reflective silver surface of the interior, the wave shattered a small, square, glowing object, one of thousands within the needle spires that lined the lacunae above.

Raksha Golden Cub was dead before he hit the floor.

* * * * *

In a narrow draw lined with craggy ironstone walls, a wizened old goblin prophet stood between a pair of lumbering megathreshers and a few hundred of the last free people on Mirrodin. Even Vektro's bomb had not ended the attack, and things looked grim once more. Dwugget had both hands raised, palms out, and they started to glow red. His guilt over his complicity long forgotten, if not forgiven, the goblin was determined to save those he still could.

"Hochocha!" Dwugget cried, and twin spheroids of devastation launched from each hand. The fireball clusters engulfed the mighty constructs in flame, and after a few seconds the fire was no longer magical as the creatures' delicate innards ignited. Black, oily smoke roiled into the sky.

Dwugget spun around to see who was still with him. He'd been fighting so long, he didn't even know if the Khanha or Bruenna were alive. They'd left so long ago, and if the battle had reached this far, he suspected they were already dead.

Three seconds later, so was Dwugget. It was a small blessing that the long-suffering goblin didn't see that the people he had tried to save, leonin and goblin, young and old, dropped dead at the same time. Krark-Home went from refuge to graveyard in a heartbeat.

* * * * *

"Lyese, I'm hit," Bruenna said. An aerophin blast had finally scored. She whipped out an arm and blasted the flying artifact, one of the last stragglers on the field. It spiraled out of control and collided with a pile of dead nim, which burst into green flame. Bruenna listed in her saddle and nearly fell off. She placed a palm against her ribs and they came away wet and red. Blood poured from a hole in the mage's side.

The elf girl jumped from her zauk and helped the mage dismount. Bruenna felt a wave of nausea as she saw claret running down Lyese's forearms. She slumped into the elf girl, who gently lowered the human to the ground. "Bruenna, what can I do?"

"My belt," Bruenna said. "There's a vial. Just pop the top and—"

Lyese's eyes opened wide and she threw her head back. She flopped back onto the ground as Bruenna spasmed once, coughed, and fell still.

CHAPTER 29

ACCIDENTS HAPPEN

Slobad felt fluid running from his ears, and hoped it wasn't his brains. Despite his pathetic condition and the dark, suicidal thoughts his hidden self had entertained over the last few years, the goblin's self-preservation instinct was very much intact. He gritted his remaining teeth and fought the urge to pass out as his hollow body bounced and jerked in the rack, muscles spasmodically twitching as a plane's worth of mana and souls entered him, surrounded him, consumed him, and vice versa. Slobad's body glowed with a dim white light, grew more luminous by the millisecond, and was soon almost as bright as the mana core itself.

With one last rolling boom of thunder, it was over.

Slobad gulped deep, sweet breaths of ozone-charged air. He blinked, and squinted against the unbearably bright core.

Actually, it wasn't *that* bright. He opened his eyes a little more and stared directly into the mana core, which the book of Krark promised would burn your eyes to cinders and cause your feet to turn into hooves. He'd never understood that last part, but the first part had always made sense.

Only it didn't hurt to look at it. Not even a little.

The goblin unbuckled the leather straps that had held him in the rack and stepped down from the device for the first time in five years. He searched, but didn't see Glissa anywhere. Or

Memnarch. He scratched the top of his head and tried to rember the last place he had seen—

He was scratching his head. With his finger. Which was attached to his hand, leading naturally to an arm. Slobad's eyes kept going down his body, which ended, as they once had, in a pair of short legs with wide, bare feet.

Slobad wiggled his toes and was gratified to see the toes wiggle back. Yes, those were his feet.

Magic. He'd taken the brunt of the power backlash, and somehow it had made his fondest wish come true. His body was restored.

But had that really been his fondest wish? If his wishes had come true, why wasn't Glissa here?

"Why is she still dead?" a baritone voice asked. "She is not the only one, I am afraid."

"Yeah, why?" Slobad pleaded. "I've got arms, and legs. Memnarch's gone. But Glissa, well it's just no—" The goblins froze and turned to face whoever had just spoken.

A gleaming golem, his shimmering body rippling like liquid quicksilver, leaped with catlike grace from atop Memnarch's scorched hibernation chamber and landed without a sound beside Slobad.

"Hello," the golem said amiably. The quicksilver giant extended a hand large enough to scoop Slobad up and have room for two more goblins, and Slobad cautiously extended his own. The golem gently placed his other gargantuan mitt over the goblin's hand. "I am Karn," the golem said.

"Karn?" Slobad said. "You mean he was—there's a—but Menarch was—"

"He was many things," Karn said sadly. "An explorer, a scholar, a visionary, and at one time a friend."

"Too bad he went nuts, huh?" Slobad said as sympathetically

as he could manage. "But I guess maybe he wasn't *that* crazy, if you're really here. If you actually exist. Why couldn't I see you before?"

"I was not here," Karn said. "But Memnarch thought I was. He is a being a great power, power that I foolishly allowed him to shape on his own. His certainty—perhaps faith is a better word—was so strong, that the specter of his false Karn kept me from manifesting on this plane. He was no planeswalker, nor was he meant to be, despite his ambition. But his faith was stronger than I could ever have imagined." The golem planeswalker sighed. "In my desire to create one like me, I gave him far too much power. A great . . . mistake. One of many."

"Waitaminit—you made him, right?" Slobad growled. "You—this is all your fault!"

"Yes and no," Karn admitted. "I created this world, and named it Argentum. I transformed the Mirari into Memnarch long ago, and left him to his own devices."

"Mirwhoeee?

"Mirari, it is—was—will be—an artifact of great power," Karn said. "It was also intelligent. Sentient. I charged the Mirari with collecting information on the planes of the multiverse, and when it finally returned to me, it provided me with knowledge that would have taken millennia to learn on my own. I believed the Mirari had earned the right to walk and experience the world as a living being. And I wanted—offspring isn't the right word . . ."

"Kids?" Slobad offered.

"One like me, but not me," Karn replied. "Something to go on when I am gone."

"But you're a big-time planeswalker, right?" Slobad asked. "Don't you live forever?"

"It seems like it," Karn said. "But please, I have already

gotten too far from the point. We have much to discuss, Slobad. You will need a mentor."

"Well thanks, really," Slobad said. "But I just want to find my friend. You're a planeswalker, can't you do it?"

"Planeswalkers are not gods, Slobad," Karn said. "Do you feel like a god?"

"Me? Why, I—" What Karn had said about a mentor finally worked its way to the front of Slobad's brain. *"Me?"*

Karn smiled, and reminded Slobad of his old friend Bosh. "Yes, you," the golem laughed. "The power had to go somewhere. Memnarch had an amazing machine here. It worked as intended, truly amazing. Living souls are not channeled lightly."

"Hey, I know about those, huh?" Slobad said. "Had a long time to look around while your not-offspring was sleeping in that big egg. That's how Memnarch got people from other planets—no, wait, planes? Dimensions?"

"All of those are appropriate. The mana backlash wiped the traps out. My Argentum is an empty place again. The surface is littered with the dead."

"So if all the soul traps are gone, why am I alive?" Slobad aksed.

"Simple," Karn said. "The spark chose you."

"It chose me? You said the spark hit me because I was strapped to that rack!" Slobad shouted, his temper starting to flare. "I didn't even want it, huh?"

"And yet you have it," Karn said. "And you now have a choice. I did what I could to protect the people of Mirrodin. Though I could not return physically as long as Memnarch lived, I could send messages. Energy. Parts of myself."

"What you talking about?" Slobad asked.

"The spark," Karn said. "It gave me a tentative link to Glissa that allowed me to circumvent Memnarch's interference. I sent the flares to Glissa, to show her the world she came from. All I could do was try to guide her. I am afraid that I failed again." The quicksilver golem bowed his head.

"Everybody dead?" Slobad whispered. He looked up at the concave surface of the interior, which looked smooth as a mirror. "Everybody? But—you've got to do something! And if you won't, I will! Slobad the planeswalker, huh? Okay, so . . ." Slobad closed his eyes and held his hands in front of his face in a crude approximation of Bruenna's spellcasting moves. "I summon Glissa!"

He opened his eyes and was still looking at Karn, whose face was grim.

"True reanimation is difficult, Slobad. Even I cannot return the dead to life, not in a way that recreates the original person. There are simply too many variables."

"You just told me I'm a g—a planeswalker," Slobad said. "What *can* I do? I don't want to walk the monkeyverse or whatever! Just want my friend back, huh? I want everyone to be alive. I want it the way it was. Even if I have to go back to living in a cave by myself. There's got to be something I can do. I'll, I'll give the souls back. Everyone better, huh?"

Karn was quiet for some time. When he spoke again, his voice was tinged with disappointment. "There is a way, perhaps. If you act soon. The souls of millions are in your veins, so to speak. They are still individuals entities, but soon they will merge into your larger self, the planeswalker Slobad. But what you ask . . . I feel for the dead as you do, goblin. Perhaps more, in a way you were all my children, even more than Memnarch. But you must realize what it will cost you."

"My life?"

"Worse. The spark," Karn said. "The spark blossoming within you is still new. It wants to return to where it came from. But it couldn't find her, so it went into you and is beginning to take hold.

With every passing minute, you will feel your power growing. And Slobad, to have tasted that power and then . . ."

"Then what?"

"Then lose it," Karn said. "To bring Glissa and the others back, you and she must *both* sacrifice the spark. We have time, Slobad, maybe an hour. In that time, I could show you worlds you've never imagined. Galaxies the size of a thimble, pocket universes, alternate realities, worlds shaped like perfect cubes, planes as flat as a serving dish that ride on the back of giant reptiles. You will understand that there are things greater than a single world, and they will all be open to you."

"All right, all right! So I *won't* see, then no problem, huh?" Slobad said. "How do I get her back, Shinypants?"

Karn smiled. "What you do, none has done before. You remind me of someone I once admired very much, in another life."

"Goblin?"

"No," Karn said, "A human. My . . . captain. Yes, that's the word. She, too, would never hesitate to sacrifice for her friends. I had not thought I would meet her like again for several lifetimes."

"You have to stick around, meet Glissa, huh?" Slobad said, clapping the golem on the elbow. "I mean, we'll still be able to see you, right?"

"If it works, I shall will myself to be seen," Karn said. "In a way."

"Well, now we're talking, huh?" Slobad grinned. "So what do I do first?"

"Well, first, I'll need to take back your arms and legs," Karn said and reached for Slobad's hand. The goblin leaped backward and was rather surprised to see that he stood on the air, thirty feet up. Karn looked up at the goggle-eyed goblin and laughed, a warm, gentle sound that was nothing like the raving howl of Memnarch.

"See?" Karn said. "The spark is in you. You just used it. You are still using it without thinking."

"Get me down!"

"Get yourself down," Karn said, and walked out onto the occultation disk toward the crackling mana core. The geodesic mesh had been vaporized. The five mighty struts that had supported it now ending in charred slag that still glowed a faint orange.

"Sure," Slobad muttered, "then you'll tear my arms off, huh?"

"No, that was a joke," Karn said without turning around, "and a trick. To show you a sliver of what you can do. I know you say you don't want the power, but no one should give up such a thing without a taste." He raised one hand a jabbed a finger in Slobad's direction. "Are you going to stay up there all day?"

"Um," Slobad said, and closed his eyes. He pictured himself standing on the disk next to Karn.

He opened his eyes and *was* standing on the disk next to Karn. "Neat!" Slobad exclaimed. "Uh, but not mine to use, huh?"

"Oh, it is, if you choose the power instead of Glissa and the others," Karn said. "Once you do this, there is no going back. Souls that died will finally die, and those that still lived will return to their original plane. You will remember this dimly if at all but will know for the rest of your life that you gave away something wonderful. Have you decided?"

Slobad took a deep breath then exhaled long and hard. "Yes. Tell me how to get her back."

Deep in the heart of a metal world, an elf and a goblin wandered through a chattering swarm of tiny builder artifacts that chirped at them with friendly whistles. The larger combat constructs had fallen silent, their power sources gone dark, their clawed feet and deadly blades frozen in mid-strike. The Panopticon was completely gone. Not even the heavy support struts still stood. The mana core seemed just a little smaller than before, and no longer quite as bright. The ball of energy gave off soft warmth that filled the interior.

For the first time since she could remember, the Glissa didn't have a care in the world. Just a wicked headache.

"How did you do it?" Glissa asked.

"Do what?" replied Slobad.

"I remember charging Memnarch, and he started to go over. I was still holding on—"

"Oh, *that*," Slobad said. "It was pretty funny, huh? Memnarch starts going over backward, you lose grip and smack head on platform. Memnarch drops into that big ball," he added. "Then the big boom-wave hits, and after a few minutes of that Slobad blacked out. Woke up not far from here. You were there, too. Asleep. You been out for days."

"So we won," Glissa said. "But if I was out for days . . . where is everyone? Surely they would have sent someone looking for us if the attacks have stopped."

"Slobad thought that too, huh? Went and checked it out," the goblin said. He produced the chain of charms Bruenna had given the elf girl and placed it in her palm. "You keep that, huh? This goblin's been in the air enough for a hundred lifetimes."

Glissa took wrapped the chain around her forearm and buried the urge to scream. If they'd won the battle against Memnarch, only to lose the war . . . "What did you see? Are they—are they dead?"

"They're not anything," the goblin said. "They're gone. All the nim are dead, huh? And none of the constructs work, except these little guys." The goblin let a small Memnarch-like artifact scuttle up one arm and down the other. "Slobad has theory."

"Really?"

"Slobad can have theories! It's just—the soul traps. Can't explain exactly how I know, but when Slobad was hooked to that machine, felt a—a mana backlash. And the traps are gone, too, huh? Had a few days to look."

" 'Mana backlash'?" Glissa said, covering a smirk. "You were in that rack for too long." She leaned down and kissed the goblin on the forehead. "And I'm glad you got your arms and legs back. You looked *terrible*."

"Well, yeah, magic. Crazy stuff," the goblin continued, waving at the exhilaratingly close mana ball that still crackled with energy overhead. "Woke up, and there they were. Never know what magic's gonna do, huh?"

"Wait," Glissa said, "If the soul traps are all gone, why are we—"

"Get back, vermin! I'll kill you! I'll kill you all! Back!"

"Flare," Glissa said. She drew her sword and took off in the direction of the voice. Slobad followed with exaggerated care over the carpet of scuttlers.

"Close that—get out of—ow! I'm going to tear you apart!"

"With your teeth?" Glissa asked. Geth's head sat next to a perfect silver sphere the size of the elf girl's fist in a large silver chest lines with a soft purple material. The leathery gray skin that clung to Geth's skull looked fresher somehow, the black eyes a little less withered. He didn't even stink that badly. "Geth, why are you still here? Slobad, why's he still here?"

"Glissa!" the head exclaimed. "Get these things away from me! I was taking a nap, then one of these insects figured out how to unlatch my lid, and—"

"Why is he here at all if the soul traps are all gone?" Glissa asked no one in particular. "Why are *we* still here, Slobad?"

"That, I can answer," Geth said. "Someone gave me a message. But first, you've got a promise to keep."

"What you talking about, head?" Slobad said.

"I said someone gave me a message to give to the two of you. But I've done enough work for free. Glissa owes me a body. No body, no information."

"No deal!" Slobad snarled, glad to have found someone he could finally kick around.

"Wait, Slobad," Glissa said. "Geth, there's no one else here. Not even bodies." She picked up one of the scuttling mini-Memnarchs, which buzzed with irritation and kicked at the air with four small legs. "Just these."

Slobad took the scuttler from Glissa and held it close to his face, whispering. He nodded a few times as it hooted a response. Finally the goblin placed the scuttler back on the ground, and it stood next to the open chest. "Okay, head," Slobad said. "This little guy agrees to be your body. Good enough?"

Geth considered, clicking what was left of his tongue against the latticework remains of his cheek. "It'll do what I say?" he asked.

"For now. After a while, it'll do what you *think*," the goblin said.

"Slobad, you can do that?" Glissa asked.

"Yeah, I . . . I can," Slobad said, somewhat surprised. "I can talk to them, too. And this one's volunteered, so I'm okay with it, huh?" The goblin sidled up to the elf girl and whispered, "I think they're a little scared of you, so this one wants to do this so you won't fry his buddies. Won't believe me when I tell 'em you won't. Try not to step on any, huh?"

"I don't think I could if I wanted too," Glissa said quietly. "It's gone, Slobad. The spark. I can't feel it." It was true, she realized. She tried to reach the energy, but it had left her. She felt relieved and abandoned at the same time.

"I'll take it!" Geth interrupted. "I can always work my way up. Look at Memnarch."

"Good," Glissa said, glad to think about something else. "Now talk."

"Not until—"

"Geth, he'll do it. But talk. Now. Or I put that ball through your skull and out the other side. What is that, anyway?"

"Okay, okay," Geth said. "Who else am I going to tell? There was a golem. Said to make sure you got the ball."

"Bosh?" Slobad gasped. "Bosh is alive?"

"Don't be stupid," Geth said. "This golem was big and quicksilver, as you well know. Like he was melting and frozen at the same time. Friendly fellow. Said that you two were supposed to hold onto that ball for him, and he'd come back. You're supposed to wait for him, if you want. And one more thing. Two, really. Lift me up."

"No," Glissa said. "Slobad, is that true? Do you remember a golem?"

"Maybe," Slobad said and scratched his head. "Sounds familiar, but . . ." He shrugged. "Sorry."

"Lift. Me. Up," Geth said. "It's part of the message. This box has a false bottom."

"And a false top, if you ask me," Slobad muttered, but Glissa did as Geth asked. She set the head wet-end down atop the patiently waiting memnite. Geth fit atop the tiny construct like a gelfruit on a juicing tool. She lifted the soft lining of the chest and found two small, glowing rectangular objects that felt warm to the touch.

"Slobad, these are *our* soul traps," Glissa whispered. "Can you feel it?"

"Yeah," Slobad said. "Kinda like hearing yourself talking in another room."

"So the golem—hey, you know, this doesn't look to bad on me—so the golem said that Memnarch had kept those in a safe place. They were protected when everything went off," Geth said.

"So why you still here?" Slobad said. "There's only two traps here, where's yours?"

"I've been dead for years," Geth said. "No soul to trap."

"Do you know what this means?" Glissa said. "We can go back. Back to the world Memnarch took us from. If we break these."

"The golem said that was your choice," the head continued. "Break these and disappear, or wait for him."

"Sounds like a trap," Glissa said.

Slobad leaned over and scooped up the silver ball. He looked at it for a long moment, then tucked it into his satchel. Then he slowly closed the lid on the chest. "Think we should wait. Slobad's spent his whole life hiding from the world. We know everybody's safe, huh? Now there's no need for Slobad to hide from anything. And something . . .Slobad don't know why, but he want to trust that golem." The goblin leaned down to pat a scuttling artifact. "Besides, don't want to leave all these little guys alone with Geth, huh?"

Glissa stared at the box. She could leave this world, return to a home she'd never known. Or she could stay with her friend and explore Mirrodin as she'd never been able to before. Maybe, someday, she'd get some answers. "You sure there's not anything you want to tell me?" she said. "You're acting stranger than usual."

"Course not," Slobad said. "Just a weird feeling. Slobad just glad to have legs and arms and eyes, huh? Want to use them a bit."

Glissa took a long look at the mana core, and then took Slobad's hand in hers. The carpet of scuttlers parted, forming a long path that led to the entrance of the green lacuna. "You know, we never did come up with a name for that new moon," she said. "I think I like 'Lyese.' "

"Good name, huh?" Slobad said.

"Wait, where are you going?" Geth shouted. "Goblin, I'm not hooked up yet! Construct, I order you to follow them! Move, you stupid thing. Move!"

"He should learn to ask more nicely," Slobad said. "They don't like to be shouted at."

"He'll figure it out," Glissa replied, "but let's get to the surface before he does."

* * * * *

Bruenna smiled as the leonin zauk riders come over the rise and descended down the path into the seaside village of Lume. The large flightless birds looked out of place this far from the grasslands, and she noted a few of the younger-looking leonin riders gaped at the dazzling blue sea beyond the settlement. She wondered if what she'd heard about cats and water applied to cat-people as well.

The goblins had also agreed to send envoys, and she expected Dwugget would arrive before long. The signing ceremony was mostly a formality, but it would be the first time the leaders of the elves, goblins, leonin, and humans had assembled in one place. The treaty had taken her months to hammer out with the other leaders, but her earlier experiences with the elves had proven quite valuable. The alliance would see an end to thousands of years of pointless conflicts. The humans and elves had shown the other peoples that it was possible. Still, she was glad Yulyn had honored her wish that he go hunting this morning. Bruenna would rather greet the leonin without the old elf there—he was a good and honorable man, but could be abrasive at times.

"Lyese," she said, calling her apprentice from the study. The elf girl staggered out under a pile of bound leather books, which she half-dropped, half-set on the heavy wooden table in the center of the conference hall.

"They're almost here," Bruenna said.

"They're magnificent," Lyese gasped.

"Keep your awe in check," Bruenna said, smiling. "We don't want to scare them away."

The leonin riders reined their mounts to a halt, and the leader slid easily from the saddle. He removed his silver helmet and shook free a flowing mane that was a little darker than his golden fur.

"Kha Raksha Golden Cub," Bruenna said as she walked out under the golden sun and met the leonin with a deep bow, "on behalf of my people, the humans of Lume, and our allies, the elves of Jilad, I welcome you."

"The honor is mine, Lady Bruenna," Raksha said. "We are pleased to finally meet you."

FORGOTTEN REALMS

R.A. SALVATORE'S
WAR OF THE SPIDER QUEEN

THE EPIC SAGA OF THE DARK ELVES CONTINUES.

New in hardcover!

EXTINCTION
Book IV
Lisa Smedman

For even a small group of drow, trust is the rarest commodity of all. When the expedition prepares for a return to the Abyss, what little trust there is crumbles under a rival goddess's hand.

January 2004

ANNIHILATION
Book V
Philip Athans

Old alliances have been broken, and new bonds have been formed. While some finally embark for the Abyss itself, others stay behind to serve a new mistress—a goddess with plans of her own.

July 2004

RESURRECTION
Book VI

The Spider Queen has been asleep for a long time, leaving the Underdark to suffer war and ruin. But if she finally returns, will things get better... or worse?

April 2005

The New York Times best-seller now in paperback!

CONDEMNATION
Book III
Richard Baker

The search for answers to Lolth's silence uncovers only more complex questions, allowing doubt and frustration to test the boundaries of already tenuous relationships. Sensing the holes in the armor of Menzoberranzan, a new, dangerous threat steps in to test the resolve of the Jewel of the Underdark, and finds it lacking.

May 2004

Now in paperback!
DISSOLUTION, BOOK I
INSURRECTION, BOOK II

CHECK OUT THESE NEW TITLES FROM THE AUTHORS OF R.A. SALVATORE'S WAR OF THE SPIDER QUEEN SERIES!

VENOM'S TASTE
House of Serpents, Book I
Lisa Smedman

The New York Times Best-selling author of *Extinction*.
Serpents. Poison. Psionics. And the occasional evil death cult. Business as usual in the Vilhon Reach. Lisa Smedman breathes life into the treacherous yuan-ti race.

THE RAGE
The Year of Rogue Dragons, Book I
Richard Lee Byers

Every once in a while the dragons go mad. Without warning they darken the skies of Faerûn and kill and kill and kill. Richard Lee Byers, the new master of dragons, takes wing.

FORSAKEN HOUSE
The Last Mythal, Book I
Richard Baker

The New York Times Best-selling author of *Condemnation*.
The Retreat is at an end, and the elves of Faerûn find themselves at a turning point. In one direction lies peace and stagnation, in the other: war and destiny. *New York Times* best-selling author Richard Baker shows the elves their future.

August 2004

THE RUBY GUARDIAN
Scions of Arrabar, Book II
Thomas M. Reid

Life and death both come at a price in the mercenary city-states of the Vilhon Reach. Vambran thought he knew the cost of both, but he still has a lot to learn. Thomas M. Reid makes humans the most dangerous monsters in Faerûn.

November 2004

THE SAPPHIRE CRESCENT
Scions of Arrabar, Book I
Available Now

From *New York Times*
Best-Selling Author
R.A. SALVATORE

In taverns, around campfires, and in the loftiest council chambers of Faerûn, people whisper the tales of a lone dark elf who stumbled out of the merciless Underdark to the no less unforgiving wilderness of the World Above and carved a life for himself, then lived a legend...

The Legend of Drizzt

For the first time in deluxe hardcover editions, all three volumes of the Dark Elf Trilogy take their rightful place at the beginning of one of the greatest fantasy epics of all time. Each title contains striking new cover art and portions of an all-new author interview, with the questions posed by none other than the readers themselves.

HOMELAND

Being born in Menzoberranzan means a hard life surrounded by evil.

March 2004

EXILE

But the only thing worse is being driven from the city with hunters on your trail.

June 2004

SOJOURN

Unless you can find your way out, never to return.

December 2004

The Minotaur Wars

Richard A. Knaak

A new trilogy featuring the minotaur race that
continues the story from the *New York Times*
best-selling War of Souls trilogy!

Now available in paperback!
NIGHT OF BLOOD
Volume One

As the War of Souls spreads, a terrible, bloody
coup led by the ambitious General Hotak and
his wife, the High Priestess Nephera, overtakes
the minotaur empire. With legions of soldiers
and the unearthly magic of the Forerunners
at his command, the new emperor turns
his sights towards Ansalon. But not all his
enemies lie dead...

February 2004

New in hardcover!
TIDES OF BLOOD
Volume Two

Making a bold pact with the ogres, and with the
assurances of the mysterious warrior-woman
Mina sweetly ringing in his ears, the minotaur
emperor Hotak decides to invade Ansalon. But
betrayal comes from the least expected quarters,
and an escaped slave called Faros, the last of
the blood of the lawful emperor, stirs up a fresh,
vengeance-driven rebellion.

April 2004